ACCLAIM FOR REBECCA ST. JAMES AND NANCY RUE

Sarah's Choice

"A thought-provoking and stirring story of painful choices and their ramifications. For any woman who has had to make a difficult decision, this book, cowritten by Grammy Award–winning St. James and Christy Award–winning Rue, will provide inspiration, hope, and solace to battered souls."

—*Library Journal*

"The realities of being single and pregnant are not sugarcoated in *Sarah's Choice*. The protagonist's struggle to do the right thing reinforces that her decision is not one to be taken lightly. The writing style is conversational, making it easy to engage in the novel. This story provides a bit of encouragement and hope to those facing a difficult decision."

—*Romantic Times*, FOUR STARS

"Written with deep compassion, gentle humor, and incredible insight, this story takes Sarah through a maze of turbulent emotions on a journey that ultimately leads back to a God she had turned her back on when her father died. An excellent book for a woman facing an unplanned pregnancy, this book is also an inspired guide for friends and family to model helpful responses to a young woman's dilemma."

—*CBA Retailers + Resources*

"Welcome to Sarah's world! And right now, it's not an easy place to be. With poignant insight and passion, Rebecca St. James and Nancy Rue have birthed a story that immediately draws you in, and, before letting you go, will touch the deepest levels of your heart."

—Robert Whitlow, BESTSELLING
AUTHOR OF *The Confession*

"Rebecca St. James and Nancy Rue have crafted a beautiful and moving story about how an unexpected difficulty can truly be a blessing in disguise. Anyone reading will not only be entertained, but also inspired as *Sarah's Choice* reveals that no matter the circumstances, God does work everything for our good. Having traveled the country to speak to thousands of young people, I think this book is especially timely for the challenges many of us are facing. I am sure this book will touch many hearts!"

—LILA ROSE, PRESIDENT OF LIVE ACTION,
A MEDIA-BASED NONPROFIT DEDICATED TO
BUILDING A CULTURE OF LIFE

The Merciful Scar

"Grammy and Dove Award–winning St. James (*Wait for Me: Rediscovering the Joy of Purity in Romance*) and Christy Award winner Rue (*The Reluctant Prophet*) tackle a tough topic with sensitivity and forthrightness in an intense novel about self-injury, self-esteem, and the numerous shades of love. Highly recommended, with crossover appeal for New Adult readers."

—*LIBRARY JOURNAL*, STARRED REVIEW

"St. James and Rue show their amazing teamwork by focusing on an issue that could be a little unsettling for some readers: cutting. The authors paint a very realistic picture of a bright young woman's non-suicidal self-injury habits with a smooth and relatable writing style that's certain to pull the audience in."

—*ROMANTIC TIMES*, 4-STAR REVIEW

ONE
LAST
THING

Also by Rebecca St. James and Nancy Rue

The Merciful Scar
Sarah's Choice

Also by Rebecca St. James

What Is He Thinking??
Pure
Wait for Me
Sister Freaks
SHE
Loved
40 Days with God

Also by Nancy Rue

The Reluctant Prophet series
The Reluctant Prophet
Unexpected Dismounts
Too Far to Say Enough

The Sullivan Crisp series
Healing Stones
Healing Waters
Healing Sands

Tristan's Gap
Antonia's Choice
Pascal's Wager

Mean Girl Makeover series
So Not Okay

ONE

LAST

THING

A NOVEL

REBECCA ST. JAMES
AND NANCY RUE

THOMAS NELSON
Since 1798

NASHVILLE   MEXICO CITY   RIO DE JANEIRO

*For Marijean Rue, who moved out
of the pain and into herself.*

Published in Nashville, Tennessee, by Thomas Nelson. Thomas Nelson is a
registered trademark of HarperCollins Christian Publishing, Inc.

Authors are represented by the literary agency of Alive Communications, Inc.,
7680 Goddard Street, Suite 200, Colorado Springs, CO 80920,
www.alivecommunications.com.

Thomas Nelson titles may be purchased in bulk for educational, business, fund-
raising, or sales promotional use. For information, please e-mail SpecialMarkets@
ThomasNelson.com.

Scripture quotations are from the KING JAMES VERSION of the Bible and from
The Message by Eugene H. Peterson. © 1993, 1994, 1995, 1996, 2000. Used by
permission of NavPress Publishing Group. All rights reserved.

Publisher's Note: This novel is a work of fiction. Names, characters, places, and
incidents are either products of the author's imagination or used fictitiously.
All characters are fictional, and any similarity to people living or dead is purely
coincidental.

Library of Congress Cataloging-in-Publication Data

Rue, Nancy N.
  One last thing / Nancy Rue, Rebecca St. James.
    pages ; cm
  Summary: "Tara had always imagined her happily ever after. But her fiancé's secrets
are changing this story into one she doesn't even recognize. Tara Faulkner and Seth
Grissom grew up next door to each other in Savannah's historic district. Their parents
are best friends. They finish each other's sentences all the time. Their fairytale
wedding is a foregone conclusion...until Tara discovers another side to Seth three
weeks before the wedding. Reality has crashed in on Tara's fairytale--but hope will
lead her to a future she couldn't have planned for herself"-- Provided by publisher.
  ISBN 978-1-4016-8927-8 (softcover)
  1. Fiancé--Fiction. 2. Fiancé--Fiction. 3. Life change events--Fiction. I. St.
James, Rebecca. II. Title.
  PS3568.U3595O54 2015
  813'.54--dc23
                                        2014037554

Printed in the United States of America

15 16 17 18 19 20 RRD 6 5 4 3 2 1

O N E

What happened to Seth and me changed everything. Everything. And yet it began with a completely innocuous question: *Where are we going to put the couch?*

As a romantic I wish it had started with Seth coming to me and looking into my eyes and saying how he needed to share something with me, something deeply personal and disturbing, so I could help him, walk beside him, stand behind him. You know—be every preposition a woman can be to her man. If I'd found out that way, the whole thing might have unfolded differently. More like a bolt of silk.

Instead it reeled off slowly and painfully like a spool of barbed wire.

We were standing in the empty living room of our townhouse, Seth and I. Actually it was still technically Seth's townhouse for twenty-one more days. As soon as we could get to the bank after we exchanged *I dos, then* it would be ours.

Ours was at that point among my favorite words—right up there with *scathing* and *translucent* and *feckless*. You don't earn a master's degree in literary criticism without befriending your vocabulary. The simple word *ours* breathed from me like Jane Austen prose.

1

As I said, we were standing there, both of us in our bare feet on the heart-of-pine floor. Seth had the tape measure. I had the dimensions for the couch we'd ordered written on a slip of good stock parchment paper with *Tara Grissom* printed in burgundy at the top in Lucida typeface. Even though I was still Tara Faulkner, a whole set of matching notepads, sticky notes, note cards, envelopes, and shopping lists had arrived from GrandMary two weeks before, so I could get used to seeing my new name. Little did my grandmother know I'd been writing it on notebooks, textbook covers, and just about any other surface I could put a pen to since I was fifteen years old. But I digress.

"It'll fit," Seth said.

"I know it'll fit," I said. "But will it look right? I mean with the end tables and the coffee table and two chairs? I was going more for casual elegance—not doctor's office waiting room."

Seth put his hands on hips no wider than a snake's and smiled until the almost-dimples almost appeared just above his dark beard. "You have absolutely no sense of spatial relations whatsoever, do you, Tar?"

"I don't even know what that is."

"Okay . . ." Seth went to the wall we'd just measured seven times and stretched out against it on the floor. On the *floor* in a starched white Oxford shirt and pressed jeans.

"What are you *doing*?" I said.

"I'm six-two. How long is that couch again?"

"If I have no spatial relationships—"

"Relations."

"Then you have no memory. It's eighty-six inches including the arms."

Seth stretched his over his head. "I'm the couch."

He was nothing like a couch. Six-pack abs. Cut pecs. Ripped everything that was supposed to be ripped. Seth was the exact opposite of a couch.

"Picture an end table at my head and one at my feet."

I dove for him and planted what we in the South call my fanny on his belly and lounged. "Cute," I said, "but not very comfortable."

He rolled out from under me and came up on one elbow, dark eyes twinkling. If I were critiquing a piece that had *his eyes twinkled* in it, I'd comment about cliché. But his actually did. They were right up there with the proverbial little star we all wonder about in song as toddlers. He gave one of my long curls a signature tug and twirled it around his finger.

"We'll figure it out when they deliver it," he said. "What else are they bringing besides the living room furniture?" Another tug. "Or do I even want to know?"

My turn to twinkle, although my eyes—blue—tend to ponder rather than sparkle. Or so I was told by a street artist on the Parisian Left Bank when I was thirteen. I've hung on to that description ever since.

"Bookcases and a desk and a big ol' comfy chair," I said.

"For?"

"The study?"

Seth eased his fingers into an entire hunk of my mop. "What study?"

"Mine?"

"Did we decide on that?"

I poked at a dimple. "Like I said, you have no memory. Or maybe it's just selective."

"Uh-huh." Seth gave me a quick kiss and vaulted to his feet. A long-fingered hand reached down for me, but I batted it away and untangled myself.

He headed for the kitchen. "What did you bring me?"

"That was a total non sequitur," I said.

Feet padding on the still-rugless hardwood, I trailed him between the french doors and through the vacant, large-windowed dining room and tried to get to the Tupperware container on the kitchen island before he did, but he slid it off the granite countertop and put it behind him in one smooth move.

I took a second to savor that countertop: vanilla cream with flecks of gold and chocolate and cranberry. Seth's mother said it wasn't practical. Mine said it was a dream. What mattered was that it picked up the brass in the pot hanger over my head where the All-Clad sauté and saucepans were going to hang.

"Cookies," Seth said. He peeled up a corner of the lid and sniffed. "Madeline make these?"

"I am so insulted right now. No, my mother did not make these. I did. They're *dulce de leche.*"

Seth grinned. "Sounds more like a cocktail."

"I can always take them home," I said. "Kellen'll eat them."

But Seth already had half of one in his mouth. His eyes closed as he chewed and a soft moan furred from his throat. Seth always had the right response. He didn't even have to mean it and it still worked.

"You having one?" he said. An oatmeal-colored crumb escaped and rested on his lower lip. Lucky crumb.

"Uh, no," I said. "My last fitting's tomorrow and I have to be able to zip that dress. You're going to want milk with that."

"The dress?"

I opened the refrigerator. "Don't you have any real milk?" I'm seeing Almond Silk . . . Rice Dream . . . organic soy. "You obviously just made a Brighter Day run."

"Cow's milk is for baby cows," he said, mouth still stuffed.

"So . . . isn't soy milk for baby beans? Sproutlets? How do they get milk out of a bean anyway?"

I closed the fridge and turned to Seth. He was biting into cookie number two.

"You're eating another one?" I pressed my hand to my chest, feigning shock. "Look out, now, darlin'—you won't fit into that tux."

Seth's mouth stilled in mid-bite. The air in the kitchen went abruptly testy.

"What does *that* mean?" he said.

I laughed. He didn't. There wasn't a twinkle within a Savannah city block.

"I was joking," I said.

"Were you?"

"For the love of the land, Seth, you could probably eat the whole dozen and still not gain an ounce." I wrinkled my nose at him. "Not that you couldn't stand to."

Seth's eyes deadened as if someone had pulled the plug on them, and he pushed the container away. It bounced nervously against the umber Southern Pottery jar that held a bouquet of virgin wooden spoons. He spread his hands and looked down at his waspish waist. "Is this a problem?"

"What? Your body?" I could feel my eyebrows intersecting over my nose. "You're kidding, right?"

"Are *you*?"

"I said I was."

It was getting weird. As in, this kind of stupid bickering never happened between us and I had no idea what to do with it. I just stood there staring at him in the sudden silence. The only sound was the rain splatting against the window behind me.

It wasn't quiet in my head. My brain started about six questions: *Is he . . . did I . . . was it just me . . . ?*

I finally came out with, "What just happened?"

I still expected a soft grin, a shrug of those shoulders, a reach for the hair I was piling on top of my head with one clueless hand. I got none of that.

"Nothing. Forget it," he said, and snapped the lid onto the container.

That was a glimmer of the Seth I knew. It was every guy I *ever* knew, including my father, my brother, Kellen, and the last thirteen-year-old boy I saw standing sullen-faced with his mother in the checkout line at Publix. Every guy who tells himself, *You just said something stupid. Shut up. Shut down. Wait for the Coax.*

I was good at the Coax.

"Darlin', have you ever heard me complain about your body?" I put my arms around his neck and looked up the eight inches between us.

He turned his face away, but I kissed the side of the beard that browned his chin like it had been painted on by Rembrandt. I punctuated each word with another kiss, making my way to his mouth: "You. Are. A. Crazy. Person."

His lips hesitated at first, but that was the game, right? I persisted—one, two, three—and he was kissing me back.

It was the five thousand and third time I wondered how we were keeping our vow not to sleep together until we were married. Three years is a long, long time when the man is tender, unselfish . . . and hot.

Seth's arms tightened around me and he lifted me off my feet. I kicked one foot up the way Doris Day always did in the Rock Hudson movies—couldn't help myself—and nuzzled next to his ear.

"Tell me again why we're waiting twenty-one days?"

He let me go. I staggered against the dishwasher and it swooshed within, and Seth seemed to snap back from wherever he'd gone.

"You turned it on with your fanny," he said, sounding too forced for talk of fannies and cookies and waistlines. He also made a far bigger deal than he had to out of pushing buttons, opening the door, closing it again.

What. On. Earth?

We were back in unmarked territory, and I didn't know which way to go. "Okay," I said finally. "Let's review: we'll feel better if we wait."

"We'll *be* better if we wait," he said to the control panel.

I wrapped my arms around myself. "Does that mean we can't even kiss? I'm feeling like a piranha at the moment. No, pariah. What the heck am I trying to say?"

I tried to laugh again. He didn't again.

"I just don't want us to start something we shouldn't finish." As Seth turned to me, his voice took on a tone even too paternal for my father. "Come on, Tar, we've talked this to death."

"Are you *scolding* me?" I said. "What am I, five?"

My own voice did a thing it never did with Seth—hadn't done with anyone since middle school when I tried to flirt with an eighth-grader and came off like a mosquito.

Seth's face was impatient. "No, I'm not scolding you. I'm just hitting replay."

"Really?" I said. "Because I feel like I'm being reprimanded for wanting you."

"You're not," he said. With a martyred sigh. It was the sigh that wouldn't let me leave it alone.

"Correcting, then," I said. "Rebuking? Remonstrating?"

He opened his mouth but I held up both hands. Time to end this stupidness. "Never mind. I need to go. Can we just forget we had this conversation?"

"I'm good with that." Soft places appeared around Seth's eyes. "You know this is about respecting you."

Respecting. Not lecturing?

I didn't say it. His sudden attempt to lighten up was glaring in my face.

"You meeting the Bridesmaids?" he said.

"Just like every Sunday afternoon," I said.

He followed me through the dining room and then the living room, where I grabbed my purse from the mantel and shoved my feet into a pair of black ballet flats.

"What minutia are y'all down to at this point? Who's gonna wear what color on which fingernails?" He reached for a curl but I shook him off.

"It's like a thing now," I said. "See you tomorrow?"

I pecked his cheek and turned to go toward the foyer, but he wrapped his fingers lightly around my wrist. "Not later?"

I put my face close to his. "Aren't you afraid we'll start something we shouldn't finish?"

Another peck and I was gone. I'd just extinguished the twinkle again.

T W O

It always seemed ridiculous to drive in the Savannah historic district when everything was so close to everything else. I could have walked to the Distillery on Montgomery in fifteen minutes. But I'd arrived at our townhouse on Jones earlier with a carload of everything I'd even glanced at on my last trip to Pottery Barn with my mother, and which she'd insisted I had to have if I were going to be even slightly content as a new bride, so I was saddled with her Beamer SUV.

Still, as I wended my way around Pulaski and Orleans Squares—two of the twenty-two charming spaces that gridded Savannah—I wished I'd left the car and walked. Even with the rain slanting down in sheets, I could have sorted things through more easily. I knew the predictable nineteenth-century rowhouses with their Georgia grey bricks and the clapboard homes with their high stoops would whisper . . . *You're making life more complicated than it is . . . Come in . . . Have a sweet tea.* Driving, I had to pay too much attention to what I couldn't see between slaps of the windshield wipers.

By the time I pulled into the parking lot at the Distillery, all I had in my head was how the scene between Seth and me *should* have played out.

ME: (*presses hand to chest, pretending astonishment*) You're eating another one? Look out, now, darlin'—you won't fit into that tux.

SETH: I know, right? (*selects another cookie*) It was only a matter of time after I put the ring on your finger that I would let myself go.

ME: Well, give me one, then.

TARA reaches for a cookie. SETH redirects her hand around his neck and kisses her tenderly. FADE TO BLACK

It needed editing. Even *I* wasn't quite that sappy. It should definitely take a more Austen-esque tone. But what *did* go down wasn't any closer to reality, at least as we knew it. Again, Seth could do "Never mind—forget it—I'm going to pout" with the best of the male population. But testy? Scolding? Holier than freakin' thou? That right there—that was a first.

The rain was pounding by then and the wind wailed so wild I ditched the idea of using the umbrella and bolted from the car and splashed across the parking lot. A total of fifteen seconds and my feet were squishing in my flats and my hair stuck in tangled hunks to my face. Give it fifteen *minutes* and it would be frizzed out so far I wouldn't be able to pass through an antebellum doorway. I stood inside to drip and regroup.

When the Distillery wasn't being touted as "Savannah's Only Craft Beer Bar," it was advertised as "A Prohibition-Style Pub." The Bridesmaids and I met there because it was close to the SCAD bookstore where Lexi worked on Sundays and because it had the best alligator tail in Georgia, beer-battered and fried Southern-swamp style, with a honey jalapeño remoulade. That wasn't on my prenuptial diet, but the first time we came here after the wedding, I was *so* ordering it.

The other reason was the ambience. The building went up in

1904, which is new by Savannah standards, but the folks who turned it into a local watering hole in 2008 had done a fabulous job of making the cement floor and the brick walls and the steel posts work with remoulades and ganache and caramelized onions. Lexi, Jacqueline, Alyssa, and I were retro-and-remoulade kinda gals.

That Sunday, just a few days after Thanksgiving, lit garlands festooned the bar and the railings on the stairs I climbed to get to the Bridesmaids. I knew they'd be up there at our usual round table in the corner, the one that rocked and had to be shimmed with several folded napkins so Jacqueline didn't lose her mind. Stuff like that drove her right up the crazy tree.

Seth was right. We'd planned all the bridesmaidsy details of my wedding over the last six months, right there in that corner every Sunday afternoon. We'd discussed and debated and decided everything from the pros and cons of false eyelashes to whether they should go down the aisle in descending or ascending order of height. I had drawn the line at them wearing matching lipstick. But the four of us got so used to meeting, we just kept showing up. Once Lexi asked if we'd still be doing it after Seth and I were married. The responses were, simultaneously:

JACQUELINE: Well, yeah. Why not?

ALYSSA: Only if Seth lets her out of bed long enough.

What does *that* tell you about their personalities?

As I headed for them, Vic, the ponytailed server who even had freckles on his lips, called out, "What are ya drinkin', Tara?"

"Coffee," I told him. "With cream. No, hold the cream. Skim milk. Okay, maybe two percent."

"This isn't Starbucks, sweet cheeks. All we got is half-and-half."

I nodded and moved on to the corner. I heard him tell a table of Guinness drinkers, "Dude, I'll be glad when she finally gets married."

I was halfway out of my trench jacket when I got to the table.

Alyssa stood up to reach across for a hug and stopped when her hand slithered down my arm.

"Geesh!" she said. "You look like a shampooed poodle."

"Nice." That came from Lexi, who politely pretended I wasn't dripping on her like said dog.

Jacqueline blinked very bright brown eyes as I hung the jacket on the back of my chair and sat.

"You're the only person I know who wears a pink trench," she said.

Alyssa shook her head. Precisely blonde shoulder-length hair dared not fall into her eyes. "Leave her alone. She looks amazing."

"I didn't say she wasn't amazing. She's just . . . pink."

I glanced almost unseeing at the table and barely registered their already half-empty glasses and the hummus plate that had apparently only recently arrived because the pita points were still steaming. My *head* was still teeming with the scene I'd just walked out of.

Lexi gave my hand a squeeze. "You okay?"

"Clearly not." Alyssa brought her very round, very blue eyes down into slits. "Something's wrong. What's wrong?"

"Cripes, give her a chance to answer." Jacqueline squinted at me too. "Yeah, you do look vexed."

Alyssa raised a pair of tailored eyebrows at her. "You did not just use the word *vexed*."

I was fine with her and Jacqueline getting into a discussion of J's lexicon because I wasn't ready to discuss what was now defined in my mind as the Seth Scene. I snatched up a menu, stuck it in front of my face, and said, "What's everybody having?"

Twelve years of friendship—nearly half of our twenty-five years of life—hadn't been wasted on them. Alyssa grabbed the menu and tossed it aside. Jacqueline leaned into the table, arms folded over her appetizer plate, and Lexi rested her wide, soft, creamy face on her hand, smushing her short honey-brown hair into her cheek. I wasn't getting off without at least a vague explanation—if not a detail-by-detail account of my last two hours. That must be what comes from going through middle school and high school together and landing back in the arms of your hometown after the obligatory I-want-to-see-something-of-the-world-besides-this-place foray into the larger world.

"Someone tried to mug you," Alyssa said. "Right? No."

"No," I said. "Seth and I just had a . . . discussion."

"Discussion." Jacqueline tucked the sides of her fudgy-brown bob behind her ears. One strand got caught in a gold hoop and hung there. "No, see, a discussion doesn't leave you looking like you just got knocked sideways."

"He hit you?" Alyssa said.

I was aware that the Guinness drinkers had stopped talking, foam unwiped on their lips.

"No!" I said and waited for them to go back to their pilsners. "We were just talking and it got weird and I left."

Jacqueline edged closer to the table. "Weird how?"

"Maybe it's none of our business," Lexi said.

Alyssa waved her off. "Of course it is. Isn't it?"

"It's no big . . . I mean, the thing is . . . I'm just—"

Jacqueline waved both palms. "Stop. Just stop, and then start from the beginning."

"If you want to," Lexi said.

"She wants to," Alyssa said. "You do, right?"

I told the story and tried to go with the slant that I was only doing it so they'd get off me. Truthfully, I did want to talk it out, and although I could have predicted their responses, there would be something comfortable about hearing them.

Alyssa, I knew, would say some outrageous thing. She was always the most out-there friend I had. Beautiful in that sexy-but-not-slutty way, she was the kind who made the girls in high school think she was trampy because all her friends were guys and all of them wanted to date her. She definitely played them but they knew it. I was basically the only girl who was friends with her back in our Veritas Academy days, and that was probably because I wasn't a threat to her in the boy competition. As in, I didn't even enter. She made me laugh and at times made me go, "ALYssa!" especially when she was describing her escapades as a concierge at the Mansion Hotel. I suspected she did it on purpose, just to get me to show some shock-and-disapproval. Because her parents never did.

Jacqueline, on the other hand, would come up with a practical solution for me. Though cute as a bug or a button or any of those other things often referred to as adorable but in actuality are not, she was far from cutesy. She was the smartest of the four of us and had gone straight from grad school at Auburn to a job in PR at the Savannah Tourism Bureau and could out-Google the Internet. She had an in-your-face style that would have been a downer if it wasn't for the thousand-watt smile that flashed on just when you were thinking, *Get OFF me.*

As for Lexi, she probably wouldn't give me any advice at all, which was why I considered her my best friend. She had been a "scholarshipper" at Veritas and couldn't afford to get anything lower than a B. In fact, she couldn't afford much of anything, but her not being in our socioeconomic class—i.e., a few pegs lower than Bill and Melinda Gates—made no difference to me.

I was spot-on about their responses.

"You have to go back over there right now and fix this," Alyssa said.

"How?" I said.

"Seduce him."

"What?" Jacqueline said.

"I'm totally serious. He *says* he wants to wait until your wedding night, but this whole testy thing? He's just sexually frustrated—"

"I am so not going to do that!" I said.

"Did you miss the part where he was practically shaking his finger at her?" Jacqueline said. "You should go with the other issue."

"There's another issue?" Alyssa said.

"The deal with him not fitting into the tux. Take him a dessert. Take him one of the double-chocolate, deep-fried moon pies."

"He got mad when she teased him about a second cookie," Alyssa said. "He's not gonna eat caramel sauce."

Jacqueline rolled her eyes. "That's the point. It shows him that she thinks his body is awesome no matter what he eats." She turned to me, tucking her hair anew. One strand was still wrapped around an earring. "You attacked his manhood. The boy pumps iron like he's going out for the Falcons."

"How do you know?" Alyssa said.

"We work out at the same gym. I'm not saying he's vain, but he does like to keep himself in shape."

Alyssa wiggled her eyebrows. "Yes, he certainly does. Which brings me back to *my* suggestion—"

"Y'all come on." Two red blotches had formed at the tops of Lexi's creamy cheeks. "Tara's not doing either one of those things."

"What have *you* got then?" Alyssa said.

"I got nothin'. I think it's just pre-wedding jitters." Lexi shrugged. "Guys get freaked out too. They don't cry because you can't get daisies in December, but they have to show their stuff somehow."

"She could have a point," Jacqueline said to me. "You have been like the total opposite of Bridezilla this whole time, but something could just hit you wrong and you could get snappy."

"Nothing ever hits Tara wrong." Alyssa pointed a manicured finger at me as if she were making an accusation. "You're like the poster child for patience. If I didn't love you so much, I'd hate that about you."

I suddenly noticed that Vic must have brought my coffee, and I cupped my hands around the lukewarm mug. "I wasn't all that patient tonight. He tried to make up with me and I just left."

"All the more reason to get over there now and make it up with *him*," Alyssa said. "You don't even have to try to seduce him—"

"Thank you," I said drily.

"I agree with Lyss," Jacqueline said. "Put your little pink coat on and go back to the townhouse."

"But put your hair up first," Alyssa said. "You've got that whole Irish girl 'fro thing goin' on right now."

I laughed and got up and hugged them each in turn. Then I pulled on my jacket as I trotted down the stairs and dodged the puddles toward the car.

But I didn't put my hair up. Seth liked it down, where he could tug on my curls.

The rain had stopped when I got to the townhouse and went up the sideways front steps. They were the nineteenth-century owners' way of avoiding taxes on front yards. As in, there were none. I stood on the small square-pillared porch the rowhouses were known for and got myself into this-is-our-home mode again.

I really did love everything about it. The traditional front door painted red, ostensibly to ward off evil spirits. The dolphin downspouts found only in Savannah. The windows long as the doors with the shutters we would close when a storm threatened.

My favorite part, however, was the memory of Seth surprising me with the keys in May, the day I graduated from Duke. We both got tangled up in my master's mantle and my hair and the unending promise of our life together. And why shouldn't we?

We'd been in love for three years. Much longer than that for me alone.

Our families loved and supported us and each other and had since before I was even born.

On Thanksgiving Day, when we went around the table while Dad was carving the turkey, telling what we were thankful for as fast as we could so the mashed potatoes wouldn't get cold—because according to my brother, Kellen, there is nothing on this earth worse than cold mashed potatoes drowning a slow death under congealed gravy—Seth nonchalantly said he was thankful that he had just been promoted to CFO of Great Commission Ministries. Which meant I could focus on my doctorate without having to work.

We were going to seal it all with a wedding that rivaled the British royals'. My father pretended to wince every time my mother and Seth's mother and I regaled him with another layer of plans—a coach and two, a reception at the Harper Fowlkes House, a five-piece orchestra for the dinner followed by a jazz quartet for the dancing—but with tears in his eyes the day Seth and I were engaged, Dad had whispered, "Have your fairy tale wedding, sugar. Have everything you've ever dreamed of. This is a good man."

So why was I turning one ridiculous discussion into the Lincoln-Douglas debates? I could wait twenty-one days and have the happily-ever-after honeymoon night to go with the Cinderella wedding. Seth's motivation was admittedly more biblical than mine, but that was a gift, too, right? Son of a pastor—the pastor I grew up with—spiritual head of the household and all that. Granted, I probably wasn't as godly as he was, but I was trying to get there. I'd have more time to devote to that after the wedding. The last time I tried to read the Bible—the story of Jesus turning the water into wine—I found myself thinking if those people had hired the right caterer they never would have run out of cabernet in the first place. Yeah, it was a little hard to focus at that point, but Seth and I had plans to make quiet time a regular part of our life together.

Right now the only thing in my head was the impending scene. I previewed it as I let myself in and peeled off my soggy shoes in the marble-floored foyer and soundlessly closed the red door behind me.

SETH: Tar! You surprised me!

ME: That was my plan. I hope it's a nice surprise.

SETH: The best. Come here.

SETH takes TARA into his arms and sighs into her hair.

ME: Sorry I was snitty.

SETH: I was the snitty one.

ME: Love me?

SETH pulls TARA out to look into her eyes.

SETH: You can ask me that as many times as you want, but just know this: You never *have* to ask. It will always be true.

ME: Do you want a cookie?

SETH: No. I want you.

ME: Twenty-one more days.

SETH: I'm counting the minutes.

It didn't quite achieve *Pride and Prejudice* status, but I was getting closer.

I wriggled out of my jacket and tossed it with my purse on the one piece of furniture we had downstairs, the Frances Herrera console I'd fallen in love with at a home show in Atlanta, the fourteenth item my mother had deemed "a wedding present from your father and me." I shook out my hair a little, imagined a long finger twirling a curl, and only then noticed that the place was strangely quiet.

I knew Seth was there because his Audi was parked at the curb and he wasn't the walker I was, especially in the rain. He also wasn't one to sit around in a soundless house. There was always music or the TV or a YouTube video. Grey noise, he called it. When I'd checked my cell phone in the car, it was only five o'clock. No way he was taking a nap. I was the napper. If he was sleepy during the day he got on the treadmill.

I listened. I didn't hear that either.

These were the times when my love affair with film did not serve me well. As I crept through the long dining room and into the kitchen, every man-shot-execution-style-in-his-home movie I'd ever seen suddenly vied for a viewing. I flipped through all of them in my mind and literally shook myself out. This was absurd. He was probably at his computer. He'd mentioned upping his megabits per second or some other Internet speed thing, a goal he worked at as hard as he worked at his abs. That's where he was: so engrossed he didn't even hear me come in the house.

Internally swearing never to watch another girlfriend-discovers-the-body thriller, I grinned to myself as I went through the other set of french doors to the stairs and began my tiptoe ascent up the wide wooden steps. The computer was in the master bedroom—he'd promised to relocate it before I moved in—and that's where I headed. I could barely stifle a giggle. Seth was harder to surprise than Leroy Jethro Gibbs. The Bridesmaids were right: if I pulled it off, this was going to be good.

When I reached the bedroom door I fluffed out my still-damp hair and held my breath. That was when I heard it. A low, droning moan like that furry-soft sound he'd made over the *dulce de leche* . . . only thicker. And almost desperate.

It was a sound that made me wrench the knob and shove the door open.

What I saw inside became a montage.

Of Seth jerking up from the desk chair in a spasmodic reach for a Kleenex box . . .

Of the box tumbling toward the floor and Seth snatching it from the air and pressing it against himself . . .

Of the computer screen exposed and filled with a thick mane of dark female hair that flipped back and revealed the head of the man she had been leaning over—and her own rolling, sweating, naked body.

Seth turned and fumbled with the keys and it was gone. The screen went blank and all I could see was Seth's face coming toward me.

Or was it Seth? I had never seen that look of doggish shame. This was some stranger who came at me with his arms straining forward. Some person I didn't know saying, "Tar, it's not what you think!"

Perhaps if he had uttered anything else but those lying words used by every man caught in an act of infidelity in every B-grade movie ever made, I might have reacted differently.

Or not.

No matter what he'd told me, I would still have been caught in an unwinding spool.

Porn. He was watching porn. And not just watching it—

"Tar, please," Seth said. He reached for my hair.

Rage ripped into the horror and I slapped his hand away. Slapped it as hard as I could and recoiled backwards from the room and into the hall, where a few moments before I'd stood with my ear to the door thinking he was eating my cookies.

Seth moved with me but my straight-arming brought him up short. "You have to listen to me," he said. "It doesn't mean anything."

"Stop! Just stop!"

He didn't. I was screaming as I stumbled down the stairs, but he didn't stop saying it over and over—"It doesn't mean anything!"—as he tore after me.

I didn't stop either screaming or running. I didn't stop until I was at the front door with my pink trench coat and my purse. I didn't stop until he said it one more time, with tears clogging his voice.

"Tara, it doesn't mean anything."

Slowly I turned and stared at him. "No, Seth," I said. "It means everything."

T H R E E

I didn't sleep.

I went straight to my room, grateful that at least my parents were out, and I stood in the shower until my skin pruned and the water went tepid, and then I spelunked my way under the covers. But I didn't sleep. Not until nearly dawn, and even then I was aware of lying just beneath the thin slumber line that could break through to awful wakefulness if I moved or blinked or breathed.

I finally gave up when nausea brought me groaning from beneath the comforter that didn't comfort me because nothing could, not even the thought I'd had every morning for the last 345 days: *How many more days until I marry Seth?*

Only twenty until the church packed with loved ones and roses—and the five-course dinner for two hundred—and the custom-designed gown that ran my father into five figures. Twenty more days until the dream that had become a nightmare in one horrific glance at a computer screen. One sickening look at Seth's face.

I couldn't go there again. I'd already spent the entire night in that place and had come out with nothing but what I was sure were eyes swollen almost shut.

I heaved the covers back and avoided the mirror over the dresser as I made my way to the window seat. I hadn't even bothered to close the shutters when I'd torn off my clothes and hidden in the bed, so the dawn-light seeped in unhindered. I grabbed the corner of a throw and pulled it out from under my wet coat on the chair and wrapped it around me like an old lady's shawl. I did feel old.

My fourth-floor bedroom overlooked Forsyth Park, an expanse too long to be classed with the cozier squares the town was known for. A Savannah early morning mist hovered, fine as romance. All I could see were the outlines of the live oaks and the Spanish moss hanging like grey wedding veils. And all I could think was—

What. Am I going to do?

During the night all I'd been able to conjure up was the scene on the computer screen and the look of Seth and the meaningless protests coming from his mouth. All I could do through the darkest hours was throb with the hurt and the horror and the disbelief.

But now, with the lights winked on at Seth's parents' house kitty-corner from ours on Whitaker Street, all I had in my mind was what lay at stake beyond that. Beyond how it felt to discover something horrific you didn't know about the love of your life twenty days before you were supposed to marry him.

Obscene amounts of money had been spent on the wedding. My parents never talked about a number, but I knew how much things like sit-down dinners prepared by food network–worthy chefs cost.

Out-of-town relatives with nonrefundable plane tickets and hotel reservations had planned their Christmases around it. Fritzie had rearranged her whole work schedule to come. GrandMary had already sent her grandmother-of-the-bride dress ahead so she wouldn't have to carry it on the plane.

GrandMary. I shifted miserably on the window seat. In a little over a week she would be sleeping right across the hall in the bed she and Granddaddy had always shared, the one Kellen and I used to crawl into when they visited from Williamsburg and snuggle with her wonderful smells while Granddaddy sat in an armchair by the fireplace and crackled his dry comments like the flames themselves.

They were the reason I knew Seth was the One. When something amused them, something that couldn't be acknowledged out loud, they used to nudge each other; it meant, "We'll laugh about this later." The first time Seth did that to me, I knew. I was fifteen. He was twenty. He thought of me as Kellen's annoying little sister. But he nudged me when *his* little sister, Evelyn, said "hanga burger" for hamburger and I knew. I really thought I knew.

Now what would GrandMary be showing up for? A wedding as false as reality TV? She would see through that. She was Virginia aristocracy and Tidewater class, and she saw through everything that wasn't what it should be. Or would she come to find me broken and fooled in a way she never would have been?

A figure emerged from the mist below, and for an awful moment I thought it was Seth, but it was Kellen, leaning around a bend in Forsyth Park on his run. He was shorter and slighter than Seth, and he'd recently shaved his head because even at thirty his hairline was receding according to the Faulkner male tradition. But it was still easy to mistake him for Seth and Seth for him.

They had been inseparable since they were five years old and we'd moved into this house on Gaston Street, diagonal from the seven-bedroom Victorian Seth's mother, Randi, had inherited from her grandparents, just as my father had inherited ours from mine. Some of my first memories were of Kellen and Seth going off to school with their matching Spider-Man backpacks and lunch boxes while I stood wailing and left behind in the doorway.

Kellen and Seth tearing around the park on their five-speeds as I tried valiantly to keep up on my pink tricycle.

Kellen and Seth coming back from crabbing with Dad or playing tennis with Granddaddy, visibly more grown-up than when they left.

Kellen and Seth.

I let my forehead crash into my knees. Even I couldn't envision telling my brother his best friend gave me the righteous purity speech an hour before he turned on a porn site and . . . *participated* in it. With that the avalanche cracked and broke and roared over me.

Seth's father. The head of one of the largest churches in Savannah. A spokesman for the faith in his books. A face of Christianity in the South.

Seth's mother, like my father, a highly visible community figure, both of them with careers that balanced on their images of integrity and values.

Seth himself, an executive officer in one of the most respected Christian ministry organizations in the nation. A ministry that was all about living with purity in an impure world.

Bring all of that down? Or pretend that, like Seth said, it didn't mean anything?

I dug my fingers into the throw pillow by my foot and hurled it across the room. And then another one. And then another until the window seat was naked and all I had left to throw were the words that spurted out between my teeth. Words I'd never said before and won't now. They were the only words that could give voice to the rage.

The nonprofane ones were these: *Look what you've done, Seth. All I'll see when I walk down the aisle is that woman. But what if I cancel the wedding? Everybody will want to know why, these people who love us. If I out you, everyone suffers. Look what you've done!*

I closed the plantation shutters so the Savannah below wouldn't wake up to see me clawing at my own back and sobbing.

When the tears ran out I needed coffee. I knew Daddy always left for work at sunup and Mama never emerged from the master suite until she could answer a question with something more than a grunt, so I thought I'd have the kitchen to myself. I wasn't expecting Kellen to be there with his head in the refrigerator.

It was a long kitchen—you'd be hard put to throw a lemon from one end to the other unless you played for the Braves—and I could easily have made it out of there without him seeing that I had everything but a decision scrawled all over my face. But I couldn't avoid everybody until I did know what to do. Time to do my Julia Roberts imitation. I put on a big-toothed grin.

"Don't you have food at your place?" I said. I buried my own face in the mug cabinet.

"I'm out of protein powder," Kellen said.

"I don't think Mom keeps it in the refrigerator."

I couldn't even make up my mind which mug to use. I yanked out one with *Duke University* emblazoned on it and turned to see Kellen dumping an armload of orange juice, frozen berries, and yogurt on the counter next to the blender.

"None of that looks like protein powder," I said.

Kellen's blue-like-mine eyes crinkled at their corners. "I figured why come all the way down here, get the powder, go back up to my place, make the smoothie, and then come all the way back to return it?"

I stuck my mug under the coffeemaker and pushed the button. "*All* the way down?" I shouted over the bean-grinding. "It's like seventeen steps from your front door to our back one."

"I'm conserving energy."

"I just saw you run five miles."

"Different kind of energy."

Kellen turned his back to me and commenced with the scientific concocting of a smoothie. It was another chance to escape, but I didn't want to be alone with my head anymore. As wrenching as it was not to cry out, "Do you know what *happened*?" I could still draw on his big brother safety just by standing on the other side of the kitchen island from him. I always could.

I had and still have no qualms about admitting that I idolized my brother probably from the first moment he leaned his five-year-old self over my bassinet and, according to family legend, said, "She doesn't do much, does she?" followed by a cock of his head and the pronouncement, "Babies look like old people."

But it wasn't long after that, I was told, when he took on the big brother role with all the valor and nobility of Lancelot. My conscious experience bore that out. At age two and a half, I was about to toddle down from the gazebo one summer evening when a moth the size of a bat flew right into my face and sent me shrieking back up. Seth, at seven, took my hand and led me down, one maddening step at a time, all the while assuring me: "I will protect you. I will always protect you."

I counted on that. Although in truth there wasn't much to be protected *from*, seeing how we led a life more sheltered than the Obama girls. I don't think I ever heard a swear word until I was in seventh grade. I repeated it to Kellen, who was a senior, and he made me do two things. One, promise never to let it cross my lips again. And, two, tell him who said it to me so he could take him out.

I felt adrift when Kellen went away to college at eighteen, and the first thing he always asked me when he came home on breaks was whether any guys were hitting on me. When we went to Paris as a family the summer I was thirteen, he was more concerned about the size of my swimsuit than our parents were. I always thought it was a good thing I decided not to date in high school because no guy would have stood a chance of surviving. I didn't have to worry about that with Seth.

I realized my cup was full and the steam was already dissipating. As I made a halfhearted search for the cream, I had a flash of Kellen trying to take Seth out. I'd always thought of my brother as larger than life, but he was only a head taller than me and at least twenty muscular pounds lighter than Seth.

Besides, it was too late for Kellen to protect me. I gave up on the cream and moved to the window in the breakfast nook.

The mist had cleared and a bright, flawless-blue day was showing off out there. It was one of the three hundred days a year that the sun shines in Savannah, and it mocked me.

"Knock, knock!"

"Who's there?" Kellen said automatically, although the voice was as familiar to us as the figure that strode into the kitchen from the courtyard door and took it over by sheer presence. "Hey, Tara, it's your mother-in-law."

I sank into the padded bench at the breakfast table and tried not to drop my mug. On my best day, Randi Grissom could send me into a spin like a centrifuge, and today did not qualify as my best day. I turned to Kellen to telegraph *Don't leave me* with my eyes, but he was already in the nook, tilted against the snack bar with his smoothie in his hand. He wasn't going anywhere. Kellen loved to strip Randi bare until everybody in the room knew it but her.

Randi headed straight for the coffeemaker with her Italian leather messenger bag still slung over her shoulder. She had straight, dark, collar-length hair that she made even straighter with a flat iron and highlighted in blonde. I knew she paid more to have it done that way than Vic made in a week at the Distillery, but in my opinion it didn't really work. Although she could've been as bald as Kellen right then and I wouldn't have cared. I just wanted her gone before I actually had to try to fake it to those eyes.

Randi's eyes were small and dark and snappish and intelligent. I'd never seen her in court, but I could only imagine the holes they could drill into someone she was cross-examining. My godfather, the district attorney, said she was a formidable opponent, which was why

I had tried to stay on her good side long before she became my future mother-in-law.

"Help yourself to coffee, Randi," Kellen said, eyes on me.

"I shouldn't," she said. And then strode possessively around the island and set her mug on the table. "I've already had three cups. I've been on the go for hours." She glanced at Kellen, said, "How's it going?" and then didn't wait for an answer.

Kellen smirked at me.

Randi took my left hand in hers as if she owned it. "Let me see that ring. You're taking good care of it, I see."

"Hey, Randi," Kellen said. "How much would you say that rock's worth?"

"It was my grandmother's."

"No kidding? Have you ever had it appraised?"

Randi held the two-carat diamond, my hand still attached to it, up to the sunlight, the way she had just about every time she'd seen me since the day Seth proposed.

"Of course I've had it appraised," she said, squinting. If I'd somehow defied the laws of geology and scratched it, I was toast.

"And?"

"I don't give out that kind of information."

"C'mon, Randi, you know you want to."

"Do I? And that would be because . . ."

"Because you want to establish the fact that the Grissoms are better off than the Faulkners."

"I think we established that a long time ago," Randi said.

Kellen took a long drag from his smoothie, eyes popping at me. Boom.

Randi looked as if she'd just been jostled by someone in a crowd and wondered if she'd been pickpocketed. I would have enjoyed it if my mind hadn't been screaming: *Don't say anything,*

Tara. Don't even open your mouth or she will reach down your throat and drag it out.

She finally let go of my hand and took a sip of her coffee and gave it an almost approving nod.

"I hope we're serving this blend at the reception," she said. "Speaking of which, that's why I came by."

"Mmm?" I said.

"I talked to Dillon Saturday—"

"Who's Dillon?" Kellen said.

"The chef at the Harper Fowlkes," she said, just as she would if Kellen had inquired who Brad Pitt was. "We—the partners—had a dinner there last night for all the potential junior partners and their significant others. I'm sure they had no idea we were auditioning their spouses."

"None whatsoever," Kellen said.

"And Dillon did up a bourguignon that we *have* to have as the beef entrée at the reception."

If I could have trusted myself, I would have told her the menu had already been set in the stone of my father's credit card. But did it matter? Did it even matter?

"Just mention it to your mother." Randi glanced at the Geneva wall clock. "I need to go. More lawyers per capita in this town than any other city in the United States and I still can't keep up with my own caseload."

"It's because of the open cup law," Kellen said.

Randi paused on her way to the door and said, "What?"

"The open cup law. You know, where people are allowed to walk around town with uncovered cups of alcoholic beverages—"

"I know what the open *container* law is, but what does that have to do with my caseload?"

"Clients that get drunk and disorderly down at the—"

Randi winced and headed for the courtyard door again. "I don't even touch those cases."

"Don't blame you. You could get head lice."

"Tara, talk to your mother and get back to me. Kellen, always a pleasure."

Kellen at least waited until we could see her striding across the lawn to the Victorian-home-turned-law-office next door before he spewed a laugh and a portion of his smoothie.

"You're shameless," I said.

"She didn't give you a chance to say a single word that whole time." Kellen drained his glass and then looked at me, eyes sober. "But it's not like you to let her get away with that."

He was going to ask me what was wrong, and if he did I was going to tell him. So I made a large production out of looking up at the clock and said, "Aren't you late for work? I know your boss. He'll have your job."

There was enough truth in that for Kellen to leave his glass in the sink and take off for his apartment over the carriage house. Daddy didn't cut him any slack at the Faulkner Corporation. The bloodline and an MBA at the number one–ranked Booth School of Business earned Kellen about as many perks as the receptionist got.

As soon as his footsteps faded up the carriage house steps, I let my head fall into my hands. I'd only had to keep up the façade for two people and I was already circling the drain. All I wanted to do was crawl back into bed.

I got only as far as the first curve in the staircase when my cell played a jazz piano ostinato. Seth's ring.

My other hand sliding on the wide cherry rail, I continued up the stairs and let the piano riff twice more before I pressed the phone to my ear. Seth started talking before I could even say hello. Or good-bye.

"Tar, don't hang up. Please. Just listen."

I didn't know what there was to say, so I said nothing. He took that for listening.

"I want to come over," he said.

"No."

"I have to talk to you!"

"Not here."

"Where?"

I leaned against the wall on the third-floor landing and stared down the hall to the round-topped window that looked out over my Savannah. My world. Maybe if I went out in it, I would discover I was still the same as I was twelve hours ago. That somehow *we* were the same.

"The park," I said.

He didn't have to ask which one. "By the fountain?" His voice was wobbling its way back from some teetering edge.

Whatever conversation we could possibly have, I couldn't have it in the one place every tourist had to see, even on a Monday.

"The garden," I said.

"Anywhere you want. I can get away at eleven."

I nodded, as if he could see me, and hung up. And then I slid down the wall and sat on the Persian runner and sobbed.

F O U R

By ten thirty the day had warmed into the kind Savannah visitors love to wander around in. The kind that makes them think about living here and slowing down and returning to the simple romantic times that never were. Sixty degrees on December first. A light breeze drying the brick walkways and freeing the leaves to float back onto lawns, where gardeners would whisk them away almost before they touched the grass. A seamless blue sky with only a few puffs of cloud for character. Sunlight dancing down through the live oaks and magnolias and splashing ahead on the broad sidewalks as tourists went strolling.

Only tourists stroll. The rest of us have an agenda beyond, "We have a tour at two, so we ought to think about lunch so we can squeeze in a look inside the Catholic church. They say you shouldn't miss it, even if you aren't Catholic." The rest of us jaywalk our way across town and hurry through the squares, bodies slanted forward because we have stuff to do just like anybody living anyplace else.

Both of those kinds of people filled Forsyth Park when I crossed the street from my front door and neither strolled nor slanted down the broad walkway toward the fountain. I trod. That's what I did. I trod.

Normally I loved walking under the canopy the live oak trees formed overhead with their curved arms and their drapes of Spanish moss. I'd passed through that sun-dappled tunnel in a stroller, on a hot-pink tricycle, doing cartwheels, and running full bore on gangly preadolescent legs. And even when I'd finally gotten self-conscious teenage control of my height and my gawky limbs, I dreamed. Always I dreamed under that leafy roof of possibilities. Normally, that was what I did.

Today wasn't normal.

I didn't look for Seth when I got to the fountain. It was too early still and that was okay. I needed to be there and figure out what was still true.

It was true, wasn't it, that Seth and Kellen and I and even trucu-lent little Evelyn had grown up in this park, at this intersection where our two houses meet? Didn't we all have our heroic falls from the playground equipment? Didn't we all learn to play soccer here, with varying degrees of proficiency? Didn't I watch Seth and Kellen on the basketball court and shriek for Seth every time he swished one in, so he would notice me?

Didn't our mothers play tennis in tans and white shorts on the courts here? Didn't our families play football on this lawn every Thanksgiving afternoon? Didn't we feel like we owned this twenty acres of wonderful? Wasn't this our front yard? Wasn't this where I sat on a bench at age sixteen and pretended to read *Jane Eyre*, when I was really designing a wedding cake that would look like our Parisian fountain?

Yes. Yes. Yes to all of that. This place was our life, Seth's and mine, from the time we were too young to know it. He even pro-posed to me on the steps of the Confederate memorial.

We had actually started out at the fountain, but the wind was blowing that day and the spray was like rain in our faces. I had an idea from the way Seth-who-never-stammered was stammering that he was about to propose. I'd dreamed up every scenario known to Hollywood, and standing there feeling my hair frizz and watching Seth wince and shiver with every drop that pattered his eyes wasn't one of them.

As much as I hate to admit it now, I was almost in tears. Then Seth shook the droplets from his wonderful sticking-out black hair and grabbed my hand and pulled me around the spitting fountain and down the walkway. We stopped at the Confederate memorial, which was surrounded by a fence to, as the sign said, "sustain its culture and longevity." Which meant a pair of high school vandals had gotten in there and painted a mustache on the unknown Confederate's statue and the city gatekeepers decided, after the massive sandblasting effort, that so wasn't happening again.

Seth grinned at the fence and then at me.

"Really?" I said.

He made a stirrup with his hands and I climbed over and waited, giggling, on the other side as he followed. Grabbing my hand again, he led me up the forbidden steps to the statue, and under the severe watch of the soldier who guarded the park, ready to take up arms against invading Yankees, he said the words I'd longed for since I was fifteen: "Tara, will you please, please marry me?"

I had, of course, rehearsed my response, everything from:

TARA: Of course. I've loved you all my life. (From *The Firm*)

To . . .

TARA: What took you so long? (From *The Return of the Jedi*)

But what did I do when the moment came? I nodded dumbly. Didn't say a word. Just bobbed my head up and down until he slipped Grandmother Fiest's ring on my finger.

"I'm sorry I couldn't do this by the fountain," he said. "That's how I always pictured it."

"Don't be sorry," I said. "*Everybody* gets engaged by that fountain."

"Right. We risked incarceration for this."

We laughed. We laughed right into each other's faces until we couldn't find each other's mouth to kiss. Seth chased me to the other side of the monument and took a picture of me stopping against a cabbage palm to gaze at his great-grandmother's diamond.

I twirled the ring around my finger now but I couldn't look at it. All of that was real. The life we'd already had together had been true. I knew Seth. I knew him like I knew every stony paver and iron bench and azalea bush in this park.

Didn't I?

A few shoulder widths away, a middle-aged couple with cell phones pointed at the fountain turned their heads in perfect unison to look at me, identical startled expressions on their faces. I must have made some kind of pathetic noise because they both tilted their heads, both lifted their greying brows, both bit their lips as if they were chewing on what words to say. Both at exactly the same time, like people who have been married longer than they haven't.

I shrugged—a wonderful representation of hospitality in the Hostess City of the South—and moved away from the fountain and toward the garden. Seth would be showing up soon.

The Fragrant Garden—so called because it was planted with scent-producing flowers so the blind can enjoy it—is a favorite spot for Savannah weddings, but I was sure nobody would be getting married on a Monday afternoon. Maybe it wasn't the best choice for the conversation we were about to have, but the reason it was a popular wedding site was the same reason I picked it today: because it was private and had almost no foot traffic. I had no idea what I was going to say, what Seth was going to say, but whatever it was, I didn't want anyone else to hear it.

I hurried now, northwest of the monument toward Whitaker Street, and reached the pathway that led to the garden, another romantic walk lined with azaleas that would bloom in February and the ever-present live oaks that hovered like protective uncles. I leaned against the white cement wall, designed to keep the fragrances in, and let the heat from it warm my back. I hadn't been able to get warm since I left the townhouse last night.

I guess I lied to myself when I thought I had no idea what we were going to say. I'd tried to formulate a dozen scenes after Seth called—

SETH: Tar, please, I need you to listen to me.

TARA: I'm listening.

SETH: (*silence*)

And . . .

SETH: There is nothing I can say to erase what you saw. All I can do is try to explain.

TARA: How do you *explain* having cybersex when you have a fiancée who worships the freakin' ground you walk on, Seth?

SETH: (*silence*)

And . . .

TARA: Make me understand, okay? Make me believe this doesn't change anything.

SETH: (*silence*)

We finished each other's sentences all the time. We started the same conversation at once practically every day. Sometimes we sat not talking and then one of us would say, "I'm still thinking about that thing," and the other one would know what that *thing* was and run with it. But now? I couldn't imagine what could possibly come out of Seth's mouth.

No wonder I couldn't get warm.

I was wearing a robin's egg–blue Old Navy sweater, the kind that shows your jeans through the fabric when you stretch it across your thighs. But it wouldn't have mattered if I'd had on a full-length down coat. The cold was coming from the inside. I hugged the sweater around me anyway and folded my arms in a tight squeeze and watched Seth make his way down the path.

He still looked like Seth. Pressed black slacks and the signature Oxford button-down shirt, grey-striped today, and a leather jacket hanging by one finger over his shoulder. For anybody else his age he would've looked overdressed. The cut of his muscles, though, and the long-legged stride dared anyone to critique his wardrobe.

But he was a different Seth too. As he got closer I saw the sag of his eyes and the drawing in around his mouth. Before he even reached me I could hear his breath coming hard and heavy. A man who bench presses 250 pounds doesn't breathe like a locomotive from walking down a garden path.

He stopped an arm's length from me and switched the jacket to his other shoulder.

"Hey," he said.

"Hey," I said.

"Thanks for meeting me."

I nodded.

He looked around. His profile cut sharply against the white wall. He was a beautiful man.

"So can we sit someplace?"

I slid down the wall until my seat met the ground. He stood staring down at me for as long as it takes to calculate a dry cleaning bill, and then he saved himself by easing onto the grass beside me. He held out his jacket.

"You want to sit on this?"

"No, I'm good."

"You warm enough?"

"Seth, stop." I pressed my thumbs into my temples, fingers spread across my forehead. "Just say what you need to say."

"What do you need to hear?"

"Something that will make me believe you."

He parked his elbow on one raised knee and squeezed the bridge of his nose. It occurred to me that he hadn't looked me in the eyes since he'd arrived. I waited for his gaze to settle somewhere, even if it wasn't on me, but it darted—not aimlessly, but as if the words he wanted were hidden in the grass, the cracks in the wall, the space between my nose and my upper lip.

Finally he let it light on my knees, which I held close to my chest. "I know it has to be disgusting to you," he said. "And I hate that you saw it. And I hate myself because now you can't erase it. Right?"

"Right."

My voice was barely audible, even to me. That seemed to give him a reason to touch my forehead. "You've probably made a whole movie out of it in there, huh?"

"No! Where would I get the material for a movie like that?"

He pulled his hand away and rubbed his mouth.

"Just tell me why," I said. "Just straight-out tell me why. That's what I need to hear."

"I can do that. Yeah, I can do that." He spread his hands. "I watch porn because—"

"Wait. You don't just watch porn. You *do* it."

"What are you saying?"

"Don't *make* me say it! You were part of what that woman was doing."

"No—"

"You were. Having. Sex. With her. I *heard* you, Seth."

His face turned ashen and his hand went back to his mouth. I pressed my back into the wall, hard. I didn't go off on anyone like this. No one. But especially not Seth.

"All right," he said. "I—do—porn because it's a release. Women maybe don't get that." He paused but I didn't move. "And the release is partly sexual. You and I have waited a long time and that builds up."

"You are so not going to tell me it's physically dangerous for a guy to go without having sex."

"No. I'm not." The almost-dimples were hairline fractures in his face. "It's the pressure, Tar—the wedding, the job, the house." He glanced at my lips again and then took his eyes away. "Waiting for you. For us."

"*That*, what I saw, is a substitute for *us*?"

"No. It's nothing like us. I tried to tell you that last night. It doesn't mean anything. It's just what I said: it's a release. You're a woman—you don't—"

"And what about after we're married?"

Finally Seth looked at me. A sheen of sweat covered his forehead, and his dark eyes begged. That was what he didn't want me to see. The pleading. Seth Grissom did not plead.

"Everything is going to be different after we're married," he said. "I'll have you. We'll have us. I won't need . . . that."

"Are you going to quit your job?" someone who sounded like me said.

"*What?*"

"Is the job pressure going to go away because we're married?"

For the first time his eyes flickered with something besides desperation. It was gone too quickly for me to name it. "No," he said, "but I won't have all the other stuff on top of it. And I'll have you." His voice thickened. "Please tell me I'll have you, Tar."

I put my thumbs to my temples again and felt my hair coming loose from the messy bun I'd forced it into. I pulled the tie all the way out and pushed my fingers deep into my curls. Think. I had to think. Now I knew the other reason why Seth couldn't look at me. Who could think, who could even speak with a writhing struggle going on in the eyes of somebody you loved? Loved in spite of everything.

"I don't know how to do this," I said.

"You don't have to do anything," Seth said. "Tar—this is *my* responsibility, okay? I stayed up all night getting rid of everything. I've ordered a whole new hard drive and I took out the old one. I'm done. It's over. You have my word."

I looked up. "Your *word*?"

"Yes. My word. I never lied to you, Tar."

I knew my smile was cold. "You didn't have to. I never said, 'Hey, Seth, just out of curiosity, do you ever look at porn?'"

The bite in my voice seemed to surprise him. It flabbergasted me. I had no control over what was coming out of my mouth, or apparently, over what my body did. I was shuddering the way you do after you throw up.

Seth shook his head. "I don't know what else to say. But I'll keep saying this as many times as you need to hear it: I'm through with porn. I saw what it did to us that fast." He snapped his fingers. The sweat on his hands made it a dull sound. "Do you want me to say it again?"

"No," I said. "Just let me get my head together."

"Take all the time you need."

I didn't need any. Something else spewed from my lips.

"This feels sick to me," I said.

His face whitened again.

"I think you should see somebody. Are there counselors for this?"

"Done."

His fingers shook as he reached into his shirt pocket and pulled out an ivory business card, which he handed to me.

"I'm seeing him tonight," he said.

Gavin Johnson, it read. My eyes blurred over the string of letters after the name.

"He's in Brunswick. I found him on the Internet—at work. This morning."

I felt my eyebrows rise. Seth rubbed at the perspiration on his forehead.

"Come on, Tar, you don't walk up to the guys in the break room and say, 'Hey, anybody know a good shrink for a porn habit?'"

"Not funny," I said.

"I wasn't trying to be."

A palling silence fell between us. I could feel him wanting to break it with more promises, more reassurances. More begging. But he let me think and breathe. There was that at least.

"Can I do this?" I said. "Can I get past this?"

"*We* can," Seth said.

"Am I ever going to close my eyes and not see her? And you?"

"I can take that away." Seth's voice was thick again. This time when he touched my cheek I didn't turn from him. I didn't turn toward him, but I didn't turn away.

"Just give me that chance." His hand slid down my arm to my hand, which he pressed between both of his. "Look, I took the rest of the day off so we can talk, or not talk—whatever it takes for you to feel right about us again."

"I can't," I said.

"Tar—please—"

"I have a fitting for my wedding dress," I said.

His face crumpled. And for the next five minutes I held him while he sobbed.

Seth Grissom does not sob.

Calla's Bridal was on the ground floor of an 1800s Greek Revival brick sidewall house just off Calhoun Square. Mama and I—yes, like most Southern girls of genteel breeding, I called my mother Mama— walked to it with her doing an upbeat monologue the entire four blocks up Abercorn Street.

It wasn't that my mother wasn't perceptive. She knew the minute I came down the stairs—re-showered, re-dressed, re-made-up, and re-coiffed—that something wasn't right with me. I knew she knew because the I-will-keep-the-conversation-going-until-she-decides-to-talk-to-me approach kicked in. Usually it worked. Usually I would eventually break in with, "It's okay, Mama. I'm better now, thanks," and she would hug my neck—another piece of Southern breeding— and it would be over. Truth be told, I never had much angst worth talking about, and if I wanted to discuss something personal with somebody . . . I just got over the impulse and moved on.

So as we headed for my final fitting, Mama crooned over subject matter I didn't hear but pretended to. The occasional nod was all she needed.

Let's be clear: I have great respect for my mother. She was the milk-and-cookies-after-school mother none of my friends had, not because theirs were working but because they were off in Tahiti with their husbands or presiding over a charity event or sleeping off the overflow of sherry from said charity event. Mama never had a nanny for us, only Fritzie, the twentysomething-back-then hippie-esque woman who stayed with us when both Mama and Daddy had to travel. Seth's parents used her, too, more often than mine did. I'd heard baby Evelyn call her Mommy, which Randi found hilarious. My mother would have smothered herself in shame.

In spite of the fact that they were somehow friends, Randi Grissom and Madeline Faulkner were direct opposites. My mother wore her hair soft around her face and let a few strands of silver show through the beauty shop strawberry blonde. Her eyes were as round and blue and bubbly as a pair of spas, and her smile always filled her face with what could only be called mirth. Mama saw the good in everything, and if it wasn't there, she became nothing more harsh than pensive until she found a way to cushion it in some kind of hope. For example, surely Osama bin Laden had had a "nasty childhood." What did we know about his "people" (i.e., family of origin) that would explain his behavior? Couldn't somebody take *his* children in now? Daddy always stopped her short of volunteering for such jobs.

Mama and Randi still played tennis once a week, and while Randi had that sinewy, every-morning-at-the-gym thing going on, Mama was just as fit in her more feminine way. Like every other woman brought up in the United States of America, my mother critiqued her hips and thighs, but they provided her with great curves I didn't inherit. I had been dipped first in my father's gene pool, but when it came time to dunk me in Mama's, Kellen had already soaked up all the good stuff. At least I wasn't going bald.

"Tara, honey?"

"Ma'am?" I said. The manners were automatic.

"What should I tell her?"

"Who?"

Instead of answering, Mama laughed, a surprisingly husky sound. People who heard it for the first time often said it wasn't what they were expecting, coming out of such a lady. Mama always responded with, "You're so cute!" and wrinkled her nose and let the lines from perhaps too many tennis tans spread lightly under her eyes like the work of a silkworm.

"You're the only person I know who dreams more when she's awake than she does when she's sleeping," she said.

"Who are you telling what?" I said.

"Never mind. Calla's in there waiting on us."

Calla Albrecht greeted us as we took the two steps down into her posh—there is no other word for it—boutique. My kitten heels sank into the carpet, and I had to let my eyes adjust to the sudden plunge into lighting so dimmed and focused and arranged for ambience that the place was like a page from the American Express magazine.

Calla herself worked hard at a look that fell just short of theatrical. She wore her ash-blonde hair in a perfect wedge I was sure she trimmed daily, and her green eyes were fringed with lashes that comprised only one precise part of a makeup regime I figured took her at least an hour in front of a well-lit mirror. I'd never seen her in anything but a flowing silk, skinny pants, trendy belt ensemble that revealed what she did with the money she made talking brides into loving the dress with the highest price tag and believing they couldn't get married without her services as a wedding coordinator.

But she was the best in town and we knew it. The first day Mama and I sat down with her and I started in on my vision, she stopped me, put a hand on my arm, and said, straight into my eyes, "You've been dreamin' about this since you were a little girl. You want a royal wedding, and I am going to see that you have it." That was the day I decided she could work at pulling off posh as much as she wanted to. She caught my vision. And she hadn't let go of it since.

She kissed me now, of course, and then pretended to wipe her lipstick off my cheek with her thumb even though we both knew she'd never wear a brand that came off *that* easily.

"Look what I've done. Honestly." She took my hand between hers, which were always cool. "Are you *excited*?"

I nodded.

"How many more days? I know you count them." She looked at Mama for corroboration. "She counts them, doesn't she?"

"Twenty," I said.

"Fabulous." Calla was pulling me toward a set of bamboo doors that swung into what she called the ooh-aah area. "If they've done what I told them to do, your gown should fit like it was sculpted right on you—and I'm sure it will because these people are fabulous. I wouldn't have them if they weren't."

No, there would be nothing that wasn't fabulous.

"But just in case we need a little tuck somewhere, I want to check." Calla stopped me outside the next set of doors that separated us from the dressing room. "You look like you've lost weight, sweetie, which is exactly why we're doing this. Have you lost weight?"

Probably ten pounds in the last eighteen hours.

"That always happens to brides those last few weeks," she said to Mama, while at the same time wafting her to the white leather couch. "I think I'll get married again just so I can get rid of these thighs."

Calla had thighs like a praying mantis.

While Calla and Mama discussed the woes of middle-age weight maintenance, I pushed through the dressing room doors and closed my eyes. What was wrong with me? I liked Calla. I loved coming here and letting her spin the fairy tale for me to step into. But today my thoughts sounded like the snarky barbs of a girl on her third maid-of-honor gig with no hope of ever wearing the white gown herself.

"I'll be right in to help you, Tara, sweetie," Calla said through the door. "I'm going to get some sweet tea for your mama." The rest of her words trailed off. Something about Betsy needing to have these things ready when her guests arrived.

Paying guests, that is.

I put my hands over my face. I had to stop this. The wedding was still going to happen. The carriage was still going to take us from the church to the Harper Fowlkes House in a blissful film of confetti and kisses and my six-foot train. We were still going to dance to "At Last" and toast with GrandMary's heirloom silver goblets. None of that had changed. My vision was still as clear.

As far as I had ever seen it.

I sank into the armless white brocade chair and bent over into my lap. Seth and Tara lived happily ever after. That was the ending to the story I'd created.

But what about the beginning? What about being married to Seth? The Seth with the side I didn't know about. The side that could be pushed in by pressure—

"You all right, sweetie?"

I sat up and made a pretense of putting my hair up. If Calla noticed I didn't have a hair tie, she didn't point it out.

"I was just having a moment," I said.

"I never knew a bride that didn't need one. And if that's as intense as it gets before your wedding day, you get the prize for composure. You have been the calmest bride I have ever had, so if you need to have a little meltdown at some point, nobody is going to fault you for that." She tilted up my chin with her cool hand. "You are my favorite bride ever. You tell anybody that and I'll back you up."

She gave me an appropriate laugh and slid open yet another wide door to reveal my gown.

"Here it is," she said in a reverent whisper. "Is it still as fabulous as you remember?"

Fabulous, no. That wasn't my word. Exquisite, that was my mother's. The Dress—that was how my father described it. From the first sketch Calla showed me, I had simply thought of it as Seth-Perfect.

The top was softly shimmering ivory satin, with a sweetheart neckline and off-the-shoulder straps. It was fitted down to a drop waist and ruched to create a wrap effect. The waist was accented with a rhinestone belt and an off-center Cherokee rose positioned above my left hip. From there, it went into a floor-length light organza skirt layered in asymmetrical ruffles.

Still perfect? I couldn't tell. It blurred before my tears like a Cézanne painting.

"Let's get you in it and show Mama," Calla whispered.

It doesn't fit.

That was my thought as I stood before the shining wall of mirrors and watched Calla fix the rose lace veil to my head by its silver tiara. The gown did look, as Calla said, as if it were part of me, but it felt like a plastic costume that snapped onto a Disney princess figure. I shouldn't be wearing it. It belonged to someone else. Some other bride who knew she was doing the right thing.

Take it off, I wanted to cry out to Calla. *I'm not sure—please take it off of me.* Before I scream.

But I didn't scream and I didn't fumble for the zipper. I just breathed and breathed. And then I breathed some more. That was as far as I could get.

"Sweetie, you are divine." Calla stood back and clasped her hands to her negligible chest. "We're only missing one thing."

"Mmm?" I said.

"A smile. Let's see that glow."

A switch to flip would've been a nice touch right then, because I could *not* walk out into the ooh-aah room and stand in front of my mother looking like the stand-in for the real bride. I couldn't do that to her. I had to fake it somehow. Why didn't I ever learn to fake?

When had I ever had to?

"Sorry," I said to Calla. "Are you sure it's—I mean, am I—is it—"

"You are a vision," she said.

I tried on a smile. My reflection gave me something thin and wobbly. I pushed it further, forced a laugh. I looked like Mr. Potato Head.

"Think about that handsome groom," Calla whispered. "And he is gorgeous, I have to say."

No. Do not think about Seth.

It was too late. He was already there. Begging. Sobbing. Pulling himself away from the image of a black-haired woman to turn his guilty eyes on me.

"Okay!" I said.

Calla startled.

"Let's go!" I said. "I'm ready!"

That was more exclamation points than I'd used since the eighth grade, when I peppered my school papers with them. But they gave my face an expectant look, and it was apparently glowy enough for Calla. She pushed the doors open and said, "Here she is, Mama."

I moved through the doorway and stepped up onto the raised circle, a princess about to twirl on a music box. It hadn't felt like this the last time. Standing here felt like magic then. Someone close this box so I don't have to dance.

"Oh, Tara."

I looked at my mother. Her fingers were pressed to her lips and her blue spa-eyes shimmered and I had never seen her look so beautiful. Mama still had the magic, because she didn't know.

"Oh, Tara," she said again. "I don't even have the words. That's saying something, isn't it?" She laughed, even more huskily than usual in the thickness of tears. "How about perfect? Does that do it?"

Calla was enough of a pro not to answer. She let Mama savor the moment. She probably thought I was savoring it, too, and in a way maybe I was, because for the first time since I left Seth at the park, I knew I had to put this dress on again in twenty days. I had to walk down that aisle the way everyone expected me to. I had to believe Seth was going to fix this thing.

I had to, because I couldn't steal that magic from my mother's eyes.

F I V E

In case I haven't mentioned it, I was in the habit of looking at my life as scenes in a feature film.

That started when I was fifteen and Lexi's parents left the four younger kids with her grandmother and took the two of us to see *Finding Neverland*. I liked it. Johnny Depp was handsome and whimsical, and I wanted to be Kate Winslet's character, except when she died of course.

Afterwards the four of us went to the Waffle House way down Abercorn Street, far from my neighborhood, and over hot waffles and hash browns scattered, smothered, covered, chunked, diced, capped, and every other thing you could do to cut-up potatoes, we discussed the movie. I didn't know people did that.

Was it okay that the James Barrie portrayed in the movie probably wasn't identical to the real author of *Peter Pan*?

Why did it make us cry—even Lexi's low-key dad?

Did it make us want to go do something truly authentic?

That night was a turning point because two things happened. One, I began my deep relationship with film, and two, I started to watch my life as if it *were* one.

The six days after my gown fitting and my decision to go ahead with the wedding were like a montage. You know—where a John Williams score plays in the background and scenes meld from one to another without dialogue, showing the passage of time, the development of a relationship, the transforming of a character. Think "Gonna Fly Now" being played while Rocky trains.

My montage for the next six days was scored with Samuel Barber's Adagio for Strings. That wasn't terribly original of me—it's been in a dozen movies, from *Platoon* to *The Scarlet Letter*—but it worked for my series of Scenes of Suspicion. Everything Seth did made me look for the dark side.

When he was late coming over for dinner Tuesday, I wondered what kept him. Was he reloading his computer with the Dark-Maned Vixen? I feigned an attack of food poisoning and left him at the table with my parents.

Wednesday he sent a dozen white roses with a note saying one whole room in the townhouse could be my study and library. Was that a guilt thing?

Thursday night he had to go to Dallas on business. He left me a long letter, describing our honeymoon, outlining a plan for our first year together, predicting our children. I scrutinized the thing for what might be between the lines: *I'm taking my laptop, Tara. I never said I cleaned that off. I'll have a TV in my hotel room. I can order pay-per-view. I can take DVDs you've never heard of. The pressure, Tara, you don't understand the pressure.*

By the time he left Savannah, I'd montaged myself to the brink of a raging meltdown. But my continuing role was to act like none of that was roiling in my head.

Tuesday I had lunch with Alyssa and Jacqueline at the Distillery—Lexi had to work—ostensibly to discuss the schedule for the wedding day: what time we were meeting at the salon for hair and nails, when we were piling into the limo to go to the church to put on our gowns, when we could make our last possible trip to the bathroom. They knew all that. Jacqueline had been taking notes for months. I guessed they just wanted to find out what happened Sunday night.

Alyssa barely waited for us to order our salads before she was leaning across the table, scarf dipping in her iced tea, fingernails tapping on the table.

"So?" she said. "Did you seduce him like I told you to?"

"Lyss, you can't *ask* stuff like that," Jacqueline said.

"You want to know too. You know you do."

"I don't want to know *that*." Jacqueline hooked her bob behind her ear, revealing a tasteful pearl earring. She was in full professional mode. Fifty minutes for lunch doesn't give you long enough to get out of it. "But y'all are okay, right?"

I stuck on the Mr. Potato Head smile. "If you mean is the wedding still on, yes."

"It never got that bad," Alyssa said. "Y'all never fight like *that*."

Her head bobbed like a dashboard dachshund.

"I love how you tell her the way it is when you don't even know," Jacqueline said.

I actually did love it. It kept me from having to answer.

"I had my final fitting," I said.

"Is that dress gorgeous on you?" Alyssa said. "I bet it's gorgeous on you."

"Was Calla there?" Jacqueline said.

"Yes."

"Was she fabulous?"

My guffaw was genuine. "Of course she was."

"Just ask her. She'll tell you." Alyssa spread her fingers. Jazz hands, Lexi called them. "I could not *believe* that day we went in there to try on the bridesmaids' dresses and I asked her if she got me a size two and she goes, 'No. You're a four.' And I go, 'I have never worn a *four* in my life,' and she says, 'Sweetie, it'll be fabulous.'"

Neither Jacqueline nor I reminded her that the four fit her like a second skin. At the time Jacqueline, a decent size six, rolled her eyes completely into her head and Lexi, a size zero, convinced her the dresses ran small.

"What would be fabulous right now would be our food getting here." Jacqueline glanced at her cell phone. "I only have twenty minutes left."

Alyssa went on as if Jacqueline were invisible. "Okay, here's another thing I would hate about you, Tara, if I didn't love you so much."

I knew my face was incredulous.

"You are never going to have to work. In your whole life you're never going to have to give directions to Juliet Gordon Low's birthplace for the five thousandth time or"—she waved a hand in Jacqueline's direction—"try to convince people that Savannah is a *great* place to visit when it's a hundred and *two* degrees outside."

"I'm not just going to sit on my tail," I said.

"Well, right," Jacqueline said. "But you can if you want to. How late did you sleep in this morning?"

My mouth was feeling like the Mojave and I'd long since licked the gloss from my lips. I had gotten up at seven, but I hadn't been asleep since three when images of Seth, alone but not alone in a hotel room, thrashed their way into my dreams.

"I don't want to know," Alyssa said. "Then I'll really want to hate how much I can't hate you."

"That didn't even make any sense," Jacqueline said.

I was overjoyed to see lunch arrive, even though I didn't want to eat it.

One thing struck me as I reviewed that scene for editing on my walk home: neither of them seemed to notice that anything was going on with me. Either I was about to go up for an Oscar, or they didn't look past the words that came out of my mouth.

Somehow both of those options were depressing.

My mother knew I was off, of course, but she still didn't ask me. She just kept sounding like a cheery newscaster on speed. My father, I knew, could be a whole different thing. Fortunately I didn't see him much until Thursday night, when he came in from work just as Mama was warming up plates of chicken cordon bleu left over from the night before. I'd planned to take mine up to my room and maybe in the dead of night go out and bury it in the backyard, but he was so insistent that I join them in the small dining room—as opposed to the formal one—I didn't have the heart to beg off.

That was the thing about Daddy . . . and let me stop there and say that Daddy is what every well-bred Southern girl calls her father. I point that out because my first week as a freshman at Chapel Hill, when I told my roommate I needed to call my daddy, she said, "Daddy? What are you, five?"

"What do you call your father?" I said.

"Eric," she said.

I couldn't even conjure up a scene in a horror movie where I would call my daddy Dennis. She was from California. I decided she didn't know any better.

Back to the thing about Daddy: I loved that man. I was told that when I was a baby, he was the first person I ever reached my arms out to. His name was the first intelligible word I uttered. As a toddler I pitched fits consolable only with massive amounts of graham crackers every time I watched him leave the house.

I eventually stopped having tantrums and got used to the fact that he was always off to work already when I got up and was seldom at the dinner table with Kellen and me. I learned to live for Saturday mornings, because that was when he focused on being a dad. He made pancakes you could use to stuff couch cushions, but I stuffed them in my *mouth* while he asked me about my week. And then I climbed into his lap and waited for whatever plan he had for us for the day. He always had one, and it almost always involved Forsyth Park or Hilton Head or a massive pizza feast after Kellen's and my respective sports games, where he cheered and whistled through his teeth as if either one of us was any good at them.

Saturdays were what I had with Daddy, or at least parts of them when Kellen and I got interested in different things and he divided himself between us with the skill of the executive he was. But the three-week summer vacations were always taken together, the four of us, and no one reveled in a family Christmas the way my father did. He was the one who had suggested a holiday wedding to Seth and me. It would bring the entire clan together, he said. And he literally beamed.

At the moment that thought cast me into a shadow. I still hadn't figured out how I was going to pull this off with GrandMary. She was even more perceptive than my mother and not one to pretend whatever was there wasn't.

Bless my mother for still keeping up her running commentary on anything she could think of. For the first ten minutes we were eating, Daddy barely had a chance to look at me. I did look at him, though.

Dennis Faulkner is what women call an attractive man, because they find themselves, well, attracted to him even though he isn't classically handsome. The way Seth is. I know that because Randi Grissom explained it to me when I was sixteen and our families were vacationing together on Amelia Island. As I watched my father teaching skinny eleven-year-old Evelyn how to body surf, I commented that he looked like Harrison Ford.

"No," she said to me. "He isn't good looking enough. Not technically."

"Yes, he is!" I said.

Randi looked at me over the tops of her sunglasses. "Don't get your bikini in a bunch, Tara. I didn't say he was ugly. What you're seeing is his charisma. It doesn't matter that he's losing his hair and his chin juts out a skosh too far. He has an energy that a lot of men with perfect profiles don't have."

In those days I believed most of what Randi Grissom said. But even now, I still think she was right about that. Daddy has a vitality that takes control of a room without minimizing anyone else in it.

Did *he* ever look at porn?

My fork clattered onto my plate, and both Mama and Daddy jerked their heads toward me.

"You okay, sugar?" Daddy said.

I stared at him, into his Faulkner-blue eyes, deep into those eyes. No. No, this man didn't even think—wouldn't even be tempted—what was I even thinking?

I picked up my fork and stabbed the innocent chicken breast as if it were trying to fly off my plate. I was going to wonder about every man I knew now, wasn't I? And every man I met. Or saw at the grocery store picking out his cantaloupe. For the rest of my life.

"Tara?"

"I'm good," I said.

"That got cold, didn't it?" Mama said, nodding at my plate. "Let me warm it up."

"Mama, it's fine," I said. "It's great. Go on with what you were saying."

Daddy shook his head. "Not that your mother isn't fascinating—"

"Thank you, darlin'."

"But I want to know about you." Daddy nudged my arm with his knuckles. "Do you have that house ready for *Southern Living* magazine yet?"

"Almost," I said. "The rest of the furniture's being delivered Monday."

"She's having her own library and study," Mama said.

"All right, and what does Seth get—the man's usual fifteen inches on the couch?"

Mama batted at him with her napkin. "What are you *talkin'* about?"

"You never heard that?" Daddy said, eyes practically doing the cha-cha. "All your average husband needs is fifteen inches in the bed and fifteen inches on the couch and he's happy."

"How about the fifteen inches at the table?" Mama said. "And can I just say that you take up way more than fifteen inches in that bed."

"You know what?" I said. "I think I will warm this up."

"I can do that for you . . ."

With my mother's protests fading away in the dining room, I hit the kitchen, where I poked a few buttons on the empty microwave, dumped my plate into the garbage, and fled up the back stairs to my bedroom.

ℐℓℓ

Seth returned to Savannah late Friday afternoon with barely enough time to shower and change before our dinner reservation.

"I'm taking you to the Mirage," he'd told me when he called from the airport that morning.

"You don't have to court me, Seth." I heard the edge in my voice and I tried to soften it. "I'm still marrying you."

"I'm never going to *stop* courting you," he told me.

What he didn't tell me was what I found out when I went to the townhouse to give him some extra time. I hadn't been there since Sunday night, and I shivered when I crossed the living room. It had never seemed hollow before, even without furniture, and that made me feel even colder.

Seth greeted me at the bottom of the stairs, wearing a black shirt that fit as if his muscles had given him permission to put it on. If his mother had said *he* wasn't technically handsome we would have a serious discussion. Even now.

"Hey, beautiful," he said.

He pulled me into a kiss that was long and lovely, and I let it be both. I melted into him because frankly I was tired of fighting off how much I loved him. He'd dropped a big black cloud in the middle of my vision, but if I walked through it, he would still be there. He still held me and whispered that he loved me and held me some more.

I only pulled back far enough to search his eyes. "Is it really over?" I said. "Are you really done?"

Seth held my face with his hands, fingers tangled in my hair. "I've done everything I promised. I've talked to Gavin Johnson twice this week, and he says I'm golden. But"—he kissed the place between my eyebrows I knew I was pinching in—"I'm going to keep seeing him until the wedding. I want to be clean for you."

I believed him because his eyes weren't lying to me. I believed him because his voice was rich with the tears he was obviously holding back. I believed him because I wanted to.

"We should go," he said. "I want us to get there first."

"First?" I said.

"We're the hosts. We should get there before—"

"Hosts of what?" I wiggled my shoulders. "Do you have a surprise for me?"

Seth kissed my nose and let me go. He reached for his jacket, which hung on the banister. "It's more a surprise for *them*."

"Who?"

"My new staff," he said. "Didn't you bring a jacket? You're always freezing—"

"Your whole staff is going to be there. From GC."

"I want them to meet you. A couple of them you've already met—"

"No," I said. The back of my neck prickled.

Seth stopped ushering me toward the front door. "No—what?"

"No, I can't go to dinner with the people you work with. Not tonight."

Just as they'd been doing in every scene I'd lived through with Seth in the past six days, the words marched out of my mouth before I thought them and with more force than either of us expected. I could tell that from the irritation in Seth's eyes.

"I don't get it," he said.

"I can't sit down at a table full of people and act like everything is okay."

"I thought it *was* okay."

"It's *going* to be okay. I think it is—it *is*—but Seth, you can't expect me to just turn off what I saw and pretend it doesn't make any difference—"

"It *doesn't*!"

"Yes, it *does*!"

Seth let his jacket go against the wall and stabbed his hands onto his hips. "Is it going to be like this from now on? Are you going to throw it in my face every freakin' minute?"

"No, but right now—"

"You said right now Monday. And Tuesday. And every day. When are you going to get over it?"

"Get over it?"

Seth locked his hands behind his head and stared at the floor. I could see him reining himself in. "I'm not expecting you to forget overnight," he said finally. "Maybe you won't be able to forget at all. But I did think you could forgive me."

It was a new thought. Clearly I hadn't gotten that far.

"Do you?" he said.

I had no idea what that would even look like, although I knew it didn't look like this. Me suspecting that every aberration from the plan was because he was using again. Me reframing every sweet gesture as a gift he'd brought back to me from his guilt trip. Me putting off facing the world together just because he'd made a mistake.

Forgiveness didn't look like that.

So I said, "Yes. I forgive you."

He closed his eyes and nodded. "Okay. So can we do this? Please?"

"We can," I said.

I got through the dinner only because my mama and daddy raised me to take my social graces to every occasion and behave appropriately. A lot of people assume that if you come from money you've been cosseted and indulged into bratdom. That didn't happen at the Faulkner house. Kellen and I were brought up to appreciate what we had and never to consider ourselves better than anyone else. Mama was the one who told us what people would assume about us and that we should always surprise them.

That was how I managed the introductions and the toasts and the female foray into the ladies' room between courses. Fortunately all any of the other women seemed interested in was the wedding. I had been talking about it for so long I didn't have to formulate answers. They just came out like the Pledge of Allegiance, while inside I was still fighting a civil war.

"You were awesome," Seth said to me when he walked me home.

The December evening was black-velvet soft and the single white candles set in windows for the holidays winked at us like approving aunts. *Go ahead*, they seemed to say. *Love him.*

"You were, too, darlin'," I said.

He was. While I was acting like the corporate wife my mama raised me to be, I saw that Seth was almost the polished businessman my father was, and I did feel proud. Obviously his staff respected him— laughing at his quips because they were actually funny, tilting forward to listen because he honestly had something intelligent to say, watching him with admiring eyes because he had an authentic aura of confidence they clearly found irresistible. Especially the women.

"That little bookkeeper, what's her name?" I said. "The one that up-talks? All the time?"

He grinned. "You mean Candace?"

"Yeah. She has a crush on you."

Seth stopped under one of the streetlights on Madison Square made to look like a nineteenth-century gaslight. A holiday garland had been wrapped around its black pole and tied at the top with a red faux-velveteen ribbon. He leaned against it and twirled one of my curls around his finger.

"Do *you* have a crush on me?" he said, eyes twinkling.

"Yes," I said.

Because I'd had one for so long, it was automatic. Because if I said it I might truly feel it again. And because I just didn't want to fight anymore.

⚬⚬⚬

We actually didn't fight that weekend. There wasn't much chance because GrandMary arrived, and Saturday and Sunday were all about family. The *whole* family.

Randi and Paul had us at their house for brunch on Saturday morning. Mimosas. Eggs Benedict. Smoked salmon. That afternoon it was tea for us girls—even the always inexplicably disgruntled Evelyn—at the Ballastone Inn with GrandMary presiding as matriarch over the silver tea service. Saturday night Mama brought in John Mark and his people, the group she used for special dinner parties, and we were all at the table until ten p.m., at which point the men retired to Daddy's study and we ladies went over the wedding plans yet again in the adjacent parlor. It was like an episode of *Downton Abbey*.

With so many people adhering to such a tight party schedule, I didn't have to have too many one-on-one conversations with anyone. Including my grandmother. But Saturday night, when we were climbing to the fourth floor to go to bed, she said to me, "Tomorrow morning. Eight a.m. My room. Bring the coffee."

Just when I'd started sleeping again.

_ℳℒ_

I spent half the night in the window seat creating and scrapping scenes.

Take One . . .

GRANDMARY: What's wrong, baby girl?

TARA: I caught Seth having cybersex, GrandMary.

GRANDMARY: I'm appalled. Cancel the wedding at once.

Take Two . . .

TARA: Seth has a sexual issue, GrandMary.

GRANDMARY: Baby girl, what man doesn't have some kind of issue? Marriage is about making a go of it in spite of the issues.

TARA: What does that *mean*?

GRANDMARY: It means put your big-girl panties on, Tara.

Take Three . . .

GRANDMARY: What is it, baby girl?

TARA: I don't know what you mean. I'm fine, GrandMary.

GRANDMARY: I was mistaken then. Let's just enjoy our coffee.

Takes one and two both terrified me. Take three made me laugh. It was the one that had the least chance of happening.

I gave up at seven, and at 7:55 I was in GrandMary's room, tray in hand. The thin china sugar bowl and creamer did a nervous dance as I set it on the round lace-draped table GrandMary had pulled with two Queen Anne chairs in front of the fireplace. It didn't help that one of my ancestral grandmothers was pursing her nineteenth-century prune lips at me from the portrait above.

Someone had started a fire for us, though who GrandMary got to do that at this hour I had no idea and I wasn't asking. When my grandmother has an agenda, you don't bring new business to the meeting.

She was still in silk pajamas, and can I just say that she is the only woman I know who actually wears a bathrobe, though I guess you could hardly call the mauve, tailored silk wrap a robe, and I would never have gone near a bathtub with it. GrandMary dresses better to go to bed than most people do for the ten o'clock service at church.

Her silver-white pixie cut had been fingered into place, and what little makeup she wore had been applied. Now that she was finally showing her seventy-three years, the powder collected in the fragile lines across her forehead and her signature rosebud shade feathered on her lips. As she reached for the daisy-patterned cream pitcher, I noticed faint tan spots on the backs of her porcelain hands that weren't there the last time I saw her, at my graduation in May. She'd always seemed so young compared to other people's grannies, although now that I thought about it, her graceful, careful stepping into age had begun four years ago, right after Grandaddy died without warning from a rare heart infection. I still hadn't gotten over not being able to say good-bye to him. I couldn't begin to fathom what that felt like to her after forty-five years of a Great Romance, as my mother called it.

It was hard to tell where my sudden tears were coming from—missing him, missing them, or being afraid I would never know what they knew.

"What is it, baby girl?" GrandMary said.

I'd gotten that part right, anyway.

"I'm fine, GrandMary. It's probably just—"

"I don't think it's just anything. I think it's a lot of something."

Did I know this woman or what?

I let the tears fall—it was pointless not to—and used the five seconds it took her to tease a clean tissue from her sleeve to clear the waiting sobs out of my throat.

"Did you have any doubts before you married Grandaddy?" I said after I'd blown my nose.

I expected, *None whatsoever.*

Instead she propped one satin-slippered foot on the chair and let her arms fall gracefully around her knee. Matte-finished nails stacked one over the other like small pink shells.

"That depends on what kind of doubts you're talking about. I had doubts about whether I could be a good wife."

"No, you didn't!"

"I certainly did."

She reached for the french press, filled an almost translucent cup, and raised her delicate eyebrows at the sugar bowl. I shook my head. She put in half a teaspoon anyway, and a generous splash of cream, and handed it to me, silver spoon poised on the saucer. There was no use trying to continue the conversation unless I took a sip. It helped.

"I was as protected from the world as this set of china," she said. "I didn't know how to run a household or hostess a dinner party. And I certainly didn't know how to make love to a man."

I spewed coffee all over the tablecloth. She mopped it up with a linen napkin without batting a mascaraed eyelash.

"I didn't. There was no sex education at St. Catherine's School for Girls, and my mother certainly never told me anything. In fact, I don't know how she and my father ever came to produce my brother and me, as much of a prude as she was."

"Okay, GrandMary," I said. "I get it."

"So I take it that isn't the nature of your question. You've been sheltered, too, but in this day and age, I'm sure you—"

"I'm good there. I mean, I know about everything, but we haven't . . . it's fine."

GrandMary's lips twitched. I drained the cup. I definitely hadn't dreamed up *this* scenario.

She poured herself another and stirred thoughtfully. "In terms of any doubt about whether I loved your grandfather, I had none. I fell like a truckload of bricks over William Patrick Kellen, and I don't think I ever picked myself back up. Never wanted to."

I felt like something was falling *on* me.

"But I was one of the fortunate ones," she said. "If he had been a jackal like some of the men my girlfriends married, that wouldn't have been a good position for me to be in. If I had known how it *could* have turned out if he had been a different kind of man, I might have been more careful about how hard I fell. But as I said, I was lucky."

She observed me over the top of the cup, her clear grey eyes never straying from my face. I should just tell her. She was seeing it anyway, wasn't she? The very kind of doubt she was talking about simmering under my skin? Didn't she already know it was there?

"Seth's a good man," I said. "He has his issues, but like you said, every man has them."

"Did I say that?"

I could have bitten off the end of my tongue. Yeah, she'd said that, in my imagination.

"That must have been somebody else," I said. "But it's true, isn't it?"

"Well, there are issues." GrandMary dabbed at her mouth with another napkin. "And there are issues. Leaving his dirty socks beside the bed is one thing. Chasing after other women is another."

"Seth isn't doing that!"

"That was just an example, baby girl."

One designed to do exactly what she'd just done: push my buttons. I took in a long breath.

"I guess every bride gets nervous, right?"

"Yes, but there's nervous over whether anyone is going to show up and there's nervous over whether she's doing the right thing." She set her cup and saucer on the table and rested her hands on her thighs as she leaned toward me. "Let's stop chasing this around, Tara. If you're having second thoughts, now is the time to face them."

"I just don't know if they're really—I mean, Seth says, and I believe him—that—I don't know—he *is* a good man and I can forgive one . . . mistake."

GrandMary didn't say anything for a minute. I mean, a full minute. Which is an eternity when someone is seeing into your soul.

"If you're trying to convince me, there's no need," she said finally. "If you're trying to convince yourself, that's another matter. And if you want to talk about it, it goes no further than that door."

I knew the silence that settled over the room then was only going to be ended by me. My whole being wanted to tell her, because who else wouldn't make some judgment about Seth if they knew? She liked him; she'd always said so, and GrandMary never bothered saying anything positive about someone if she didn't mean it. She just didn't say anything about them at all. Or *to* them, for that matter, and I had watched her the night before, sitting next to him at dinner and quizzing him about his workout regimen as if she knew what crunches and bench presses even were. But she wasn't attached to him. It wouldn't rock her world if she knew this about him. I could tell her.

I might even have opened my mouth to shape the words. I'm not sure now. But I do know that when she stood and picked up the fireplace poker and used it to push back the hanging screen, I saw the shape of her backbone through the cling of her silk robe. Each vertebra was a separate, fragile thing that no longer seemed connected to its neighbors, so that the column didn't bend together. It was a regal kind of stiffness but it betrayed how easily she could break.

Could a woman who spent forty-five years with a man whose only real issue was dirty socks by the bed bear up under what I was about to dump on her? Maybe she could. Probably she could. But I was and always would be Baby Girl to her. I couldn't risk inflicting even a thread of a crack, any more than I had been able to steal the magic from my mother's eyes.

"People are going to show up, aren't they?" I said.

"If they don't they ought to have a darn good reason."

"And dirty socks. I can pick those up."

"Or tell him he'd better do it or he's going to find himself barefoot after you've done the laundry that *did* make its way into the hamper."

"Oh, I can totally do that. So I'm good to go. Here, let me do that."

I took over the poker and made enough sparks to start another fire in the far corner of the room. That seemed like long enough for GrandMary to busy herself with something else. But when I turned around, she was blowing into her third cup of coffee and gazing at me through the steam.

"One of the things I have always loved about you," she said, "is that you can't lie. Now is not the time to start." She motioned me to her and kissed me on the forehead. "Especially to yourself. Now, we'd better both get dressed. I don't think the Reverend Paul Grissom would appreciate us showing up in his sanctuary in our pajamas."

Like I said, GrandMary dressed better going to bed than most people did entering that sanctuary. She looked better and she saw clearer—and I had to get away from her.

I made it to the door before she said, "You always know where to find me, baby girl."

"I do, GrandMary," I said.

SIX

Seth called me at eight o'clock Monday morning to tell me that we were getting married in thirteen days. And to remind me to be at the townhouse before ten because the people were coming to deliver the furniture.

"I'm sorry I can't be there, Tar," he said. "Just promise you won't sit on anything without me."

"Oh, I'm so going to," I said.

We were close to being back to normal, so I'm not sure why I did what I did after we hung up. Maybe it was my conversation with GrandMary. Maybe I just had to be sure.

We'd had rain the night before, which made the air clammy-warm. It was the kind of morning that kept the tourists inside the coffee shops and breakfast places longer, so the roads were almost empty as I made the six-block walk to Jones Street. I waited until I was well on my way before I called Jacqueline, because GrandMary was right about my lying skills; even passing strangers would have known I wasn't telling the truth.

"I need your computer expertise," I told J when she answered.

"'Kay," she said.

"I want to buy Seth luggage for a wedding present and I know he's been looking for some online."

"You're just now ordering it?"

"I was having trouble deciding."

I really was bad at this.

"Anyway, is there a way I can tell what he's been looking at on his computer?"

I felt myself grimace. Could I be any more obvious?

"Sure. You can see his viewing history. Just start to type in the name of the company, and whatever related websites he's been on should show up." I could imagine Jacqueline tucking her hair. "You seriously don't know that?"

"I was in Lit Crit, right? All I ever did was look up articles about dead white men. Computers are not my friend."

"Okay, so, consider me your Internet guru," Jacqueline said. "It's what I do. It's all I do."

She said something about getting herself a life, and I hoped after I ended the call that I'd responded somehow. My mind was already picturing me sitting in front of Seth's computer. My palms were already sweating. I felt like a hacker.

When I got to the townhouse I had a half hour to spare before the delivery people arrived, and as I made my way up the stairs to the second floor I told myself it was only going to take five minutes to be reassured that Seth was telling me the truth—that he was clean. Wasn't that the way drug addicts talked—about being clean and sober?

I squeezed the bedroom doorknob. This was an addiction? Something Seth had to have or he went into withdrawal?

I made a sound that came out as an unbecoming snort. Looking at Seth's viewing history wasn't me checking up on him. It was me stopping myself from creating scenarios that didn't exist.

In June when Seth moved in, we'd bought our cherry sleigh bed and matching dresser and armoire, and I'd carefully placed the white quilted satin bedspread and mounds of pillows and organized Seth's clothes by category and color in the walk-in closet and put every pen and paper clip in a compartment in his desk. Today, the bedroom looked like it had been searched by a team of police investigators. Items of clothing were dropped where he'd evidently taken them off, a damp monogrammed towel lay midway between the bed and the bathroom door, and protein bar wrappers trailed from the night table to the trash can but never quite made it in. Every drawer hung out with T-shirts and running shorts belching from them, and the closet doors yawned open as if they were bored with Seth's refusal to close them. I almost giggled when I spotted not one but two pairs of socks next to the bed. Seth was generally a dead ringer for Mr. Clean, minus the shaved head, but he must've been in a hurry this morning.

The computer was on when I rolled the leather desk chair up to it, which, I decided, accounted for the unmade bed and the half-full mug of cold coffee on the dresser and the sweat pants I had to knock off the arm of the chair. He'd either gotten up early and worked or stayed up too late working.

Or.

I didn't go to Or.

I swished the mouse back and forth on its pad and the screen sprang to life with a picture of me out at Hilton Head, head thrown back, mouth open to let out a laugh and take in the salty air, hair flying everywhere in the wind. Okay . . . he used Mozilla for his Internet . . . I got there and jittered my fingers on the tops of the keys. Jacqueline said to just start typing in the luggage company in the Google line.

What was I really supposed to type in? Porn sites? Naked women? Cybersex?

I pulled my hands from the keyboard and fisted them against my mouth. This was so not me doing this. I didn't poke around in other people's business. I didn't sneak onto my fiancé's computer like a slit-eyed suspicious she-wolf.

I didn't look for pornography.

With my feet I shoved the chair back and rolled until it hit the end of the bed. If I didn't trust Seth now, when was I going to start? What if I didn't find anything on this brand-new CPU today? Would that be enough for me? Or would I be tempted to slip in and follow his tracks every time he left the house?

I shivered and rolled back to the desk to close out of Mozilla and leave the computer the way it was before I came. My hand found the mouse and I moved the cursor. The white arrow hit the tool bar and I found myself staring into something I couldn't name at first. Not until the unseen camera pulled out and gave me a long shot of a bed.

Then it was all flashes—captured hands and pulled hair and enslaved cries. Whether those flashes were in the film for dramatic effect or only existed that way in my mind because my eyes couldn't stay on the cruel images they saw—I still don't know. It didn't matter. I let go of the mouse with a panicked shove and sent it sliding over the edge of the desk.

Kicking against the pine floor I got myself out of the chair and careened against the bed. The room spun so hard I had to grope at the walls to find the doorway. When I did, I ran, half-tumbling down the steps and landing at the bottom in a heap. I was crawling for my shoes in the foyer when the doorbell rang, filling the house with Westminster chimes like a taunt.

The words, "Go away!" croaked out of me.

I went for the door and flung it open. A startled African American man fumbled slightly with his clipboard before he said, "We're here to deliver your—"

"Take it back," I told him. "Just take it back."

He stared at me for fifteen bewildered seconds before he fished in his shirt pocket. "I'm gonna have to call my—"

"I don't want it," I said. "I don't want any of it."

Somehow I managed to get past him and down the steps. Somehow I got myself pointed toward Gaston Street, slipping like a fawn on ice over the wet Belgian block walkways all the way. All I saw was the Spanish moss hanging forlornly from the oaks and the sycamores. All I felt were its tears falling down on me, weeping with me as I made my barefoot way toward home.

When I got to the corner of Gaston and Whitaker, my phone riffed in my right hand. When I had picked it up I had no clue. Clutching my side with my left hand, I slid my right thumb across the screen and slammed it onto my ear.

"It's over, Seth," I said.

"Tar—what is going on? The furniture guy just called me—"

"You lied to me! You didn't stop!"

"What the—"

"I saw it—on your computer! You lied to me! I can't trust you—how can I trust you?"

"Where are you?"

The panic in Seth's voice overrode mine. A car slowed at the corner and the driver peered from a lowering window. I turned my back to it and waited for him to move on.

"I'm almost home," I said.

"I'm coming over."

"No."

"Tara, I have to."

"No! I can't look at you, Seth."

"We have to talk about this."

"And say what? What can we say? There's nothing. You asked me to forgive you and I did and then you just went on and—it was *horrible*, Seth! It wasn't even sex. It was—violence!"

The silence was so dead I thought he'd hung up. Except for the rasping sobs.

"I'm sorry, Tara. I thought I could stop."

"And you can't."

"Not by myself. I need help."

"I thought you *got* help."

This time he didn't even breathe into the silence.

"You lied to me," I whispered.

"I went to Gavin and I thought it took, but last night when I got back to the house and I was alone and it all started crashing in on me—"

"What crashed in on you, Seth? The idea of marrying me?"

"Dear God. Please." I heard a ragged breath. "No, Tar. The *only* thing I want to do is marry you."

He was sobbing again, and I was glad he wasn't there with me because this time I wouldn't have taken him in my arms.

"That's obviously not the only thing you want," I said. "I can't do this, Seth. I'm canceling the wedding."

"No." He muttered something I couldn't hear and then he said, "Please just let me come over."

I stepped off the curb and started toward my house. "No."

"Then don't cancel. Please, not yet. Postpone—can we do that? Until I can get more help?"

"Postpone until when? How am I supposed to know . . . I can't just tell people to . . . What *am* I supposed to tell them?"

If Seth panicked before, I didn't know what to call the shrill cry that came from some dark, forgotten place in him now.

"Don't tell them about this," he said. "Please, Tara, I'm begging you—tell them anything you want. Tell them I'm a jerk. Tell them—"

"I'm not going to lie. You're the one who lies so well—*you* tell them."

He was suddenly quiet.

"You *should* be the one," I said.

"I'm not the one who wants to call it off. I'm the one who wants to try to make this work."

I sank onto the wet slate of my front steps, barely aware of the dampness seeping through my jeans.

"I don't know how to make it work," I said. "And I can't marry you until I know."

He started to cry once more, in soft gasps. "You're not saying never."

"No. I'm not."

"Then if we're going to have a chance at all, Tar, this can't become common knowledge."

"I'm not going to out you," I said. "If that's all you're worried about—"

"It's not. I'm trying to protect you too. Protect us."

I wasn't sure I believed that. I wasn't sure I even believed I was still Tara Faulkner who grew up with Seth Grissom in Forsyth Park. I closed my eyes—and there she was again. That black-haired woman hanging her mane over—

"Tara?"

"I won't tell," I said.

I hung up.

I expected to cry, but I didn't. My mind was clear and cold and I knew what to do next. It was the only thing I knew to do.

The house was quiet as I took the three flights to my room and found a pair of scissors in the bottom of a drawer and went into the bathroom. Grabbing handfuls of curls at a time, I slowly cut off my hair. Methodically. Watching each dark bunch Seth loved tumble onto the floor. Cutting with strong, slow clips until no strand was long enough to twirl around a finger.

When all but a ragged bob was left on my head, I stood amid the cast-off clumps and stared at the person in the mirror. The Tara almost-Grissom who could never again pretend to be a princess. No matter what happened.

⸎

I wasn't lying later when I texted Mama and told her I was feeling horrible and the only thing to do was stay in bed.

Of course she came to my locked door several times, and so did GrandMary. At the first few attempts I told them I was fine. After that I pretended to be asleep.

But there was no sleeping. I didn't even try. I spent the night alternating between staring out at the park from the window seat and sitting in the middle of the bed writing out what I was going to say to my father.

He was the first person I had to talk to. Not just because he was the one who was about to lose serious amounts of cash to florists and chefs and photographers who didn't refund deposits. But because he was the rock in our house. If he stayed solid, Mama would too. If he didn't badger me, Kellen wouldn't either. If he said the world as we knew it wasn't coming to an end, GrandMary . . .

I got hung up there. GrandMary didn't need Daddy to tell her that. She was going to want to hear it all from me, and there was no lying to her. At about three fifteen a.m. it hit me. I could tell the truth, which was: I wasn't sure I was ready to marry Seth. I wasn't sure I could do life with him. And I couldn't walk down that aisle until I was.

Was it a lie not to tell them what all that uncertainty had erupted from?

If it was, it was too late now. I'd made a promise to Seth. Whether I regretted it now or not, I'd promised.

Even before the first pale light sifted through the shutters, I slipped downstairs to catch Daddy. I was fully aware that cowardice made me choose that time. He wouldn't be able to linger long. I could tell him and he would leave for work and when he came home that night he would have it all settled in his mind.

Clearly, I had lost mine.

I didn't even wait for him to turn from the coffeepot. I blurted out "the truth" to his back, and then I closed my eyes so I wouldn't see the first expression on his face—the unguarded, unedited one.

But it was still there when I opened my eyes to a whispered, *"What?"*

I didn't repeat any of it. He'd heard me. His eyebrows were so far up his forehead they almost reached the hairline that was no longer there. I thought his head might twist off, and his lips were still parted. But it was his eyes that made me look away—not because of what was in them, but because of what wasn't. He didn't understand.

And it was the first time ever.

"What have you done to your hair?" he said. "Tara—*what* is happening?"

He didn't wait for an answer but took me by the elbow and escorted me into the breakfast nook. I dropped onto the bench and stared at the holly-bordered place mat.

"Unh-uh," he said. "Look at me."

I did. He parked himself onto the edge of the table and shook his head. "I'm not buying 'I'm not sure I'm ready.' You are always sure—and you've been sure of this since you were sixteen years old."

Fifteen. But I didn't correct him.

"I'm sorry, Daddy," I said. "I know you've spent a lot of money, and I'll work to pay you back."

Where that came from I had no clue. Nor did I have any idea how I could ever make that happen. I hadn't had a job since I shelved books at the library as an undergrad. Random thoughts were pinging like radar, and it was scaring me.

Daddy lowered his head to look me straight in the eyes. "Do you really think that's what I'm concerned about? You think I care about losing money when you are obviously miserable?"

I swallowed.

"Tara, answer me."

"I don't know. I'm just so confused."

He slid into the bench across from me. "Confused we can work with. Let's get Seth over here and we'll all sit down—"

"No!"

Daddy's eyes narrowed. "Then there is more to this than you getting cold feet."

"Do you want me to get married with doubts about whether I should?"

"No, of course not."

I closed my eyes again and tried to find the monologue I'd written. But I'd already said all of that, and my father was feeding me lines I hadn't rehearsed.

"Look," he said, "nobody is going to force you to go through with this if you aren't ready. You postpone, cancel, do whatever you need to do. But—"

"Thank you," I said and extricated myself from the bench. "I'll take care of everything. If people bug you with questions, send them to me. This is my responsibility and I'll handle it."

I leaned over to kiss his wonderful head, and that was when I lost it. Daddy stood up and took me by both shoulders. "Talk to me, sugar," he said.

Everything in me wanted to. He didn't understand because I

hadn't told him everything. If I did he'd get it. He always got it. And then I wouldn't have to carry this around by myself.

Just as with GrandMary, I might have, even though I'd promised Seth I wouldn't, if something hadn't stopped me. This time, it was a figure standing in the kitchen doorway, face a shade paler than pale.

It was my mother, unraveling like a tapestry.

SEVEN

I was right about one thing: Daddy was Gibraltar. He shooed me out and, I assumed, broke the news to Mama and stayed until she stopped coming apart. Meanwhile, I took a shower and faced the mess I'd made of my mop. Curly hair is forgiving, so with a few more snips it looked less like I'd had a close encounter with a weed eater. And more like it belonged to a crazy woman who was cutting off parts of her life.

Even if I hadn't whacked off six inches I still wouldn't have looked like the girl I was two weeks before. No amount of makeup, not the right scarf or pair of gold hoops could restore that. I doubted even Calla Albrecht could have painted me back to the blushing bride.

Calla.

My stomach turned completely over. How was I going to tell her the fairy tale had taken a strange twist?

But it was Mama I had to face first. She deserved to hear this from me. I was headed downstairs to find her when a text message swished onto my phone—from Randi Grissom.

Meet me in my office in ten.

I stared at it while every possible reaction flipped through my mind like a deck of shuffling cards—everything from my early child-hood fear of her slashing me with her tongue to my current and unexpected fury that she would raise a kid who—

Never mind. If I could get through this conversation with her, the rest would be cake. I mean, right?

I didn't bother to text that I was on my way. I just went.

The law office building was so close to our house we could have heard all the business of Spencer, Groate, and Grissom if either of us ever opened the windows and disturbed our climate-controlled environ-ments. I was there in five, and Randi's secretary, whose name I didn't know because her assistants never lasted long enough for me to keep up, just nodded me toward the double mahogany doors.

Randi's office was nothing like her home. Although the inher-ited house on Whitaker Street had state-of-the-art infrastructure, it looked very much the same as it did when her grandmother died and left it to her. It was furnished in nineteenth-century antiques, some from even earlier eras: dark and polished and restrained. I'd thought since I was little that even the dust must be old, that every time Virginia, the housekeeper, feathered it away, it hid somewhere and floated down again just as it had done for a hundred and fifty years. The place was both beautiful and stifling.

Her office, on the other hand, reflected the hard, smart, flinty side of Randi Grissom, Attorney at Law. It was all black and chrome and glass—clean lines and sharp edges. The décor didn't fit the Victorian-era building that housed it. But then, neither did Randi.

In her pencil skirt and cropped jacket she was a total anachro-nism as she rose from the chair behind the glass desk and rounded it to come just within five feet of me. I'd seen enough legal thrillers to know this was the distance between the defense table and the witness stand.

"I don't understand the haircut," she said.

"Did you want to talk to me about something?" I said. That was my substitute for *I don't give a flip whether you understand it or not.*

She pointed to a black leather couch clearly stuffed with cement block and said, "Have a seat."

"No thanks," I said.

"Is this the way you want to play it?" she said.

I didn't even know how to answer that. I wasn't playing anything. Unless trying not to become the cowering suspect was a game.

"Seth says you've postponed the wedding."

"*We* have," I said.

"That isn't what he told me."

"It was mutual," I said. "Based on the circumstances."

"What circumstances?"

"That's between us."

"Really?" Randi's eyes bored into me like drill bits. "Because I don't think Seth knows what those circumstances are. He seems totally confused. Just like the rest of us."

She backed up and leaned against the edge of the desk. Her palms pressed the glass on either side, and she waited.

Was this some kind of courtroom strategy? I was no longer trying not to cringe. I was trying not to pinch her head off.

"Am I on trial here?" I said between my teeth.

"No."

"Then why are you cross-examining me?"

"Tara, I am not—"

"Something happened that made me not sure that getting married is the best thing right now. That's what I'm telling you, and that's *all* I'm telling you."

I was stretched up to my full height, several inches taller than Randi, but she was apparently undaunted. The only thing that moved was her mouth, pronouncing each word with elastic lips as if to be sure the court recorder got it all.

"Have you set a new date?"

"What?" I said. "No."

"So the wedding is postponed indefinitely."

"I guess you could put it that way."

"What other way is there to say it . . . ?"

She all but added, "Miss Faulkner." If she had, I might have smacked her.

Except . . . what right did I have, really? She was as nonplussed as my parents, as stunned as everyone else was going to be. This was Randi Grissom for *I've been knocked off kilter and that is not a place I like to be.*

Who did? I felt myself deflate.

"I'm sorry, Randi," I said. "I know this puts everybody in a bad position, and if there were any other way, believe me, I'd do it."

"The only person whose position I'm worried about is Seth's. He's clearly heartbroken. When did you first start having misgivings?"

"Sunday a week ago," I said. And then wanted to smack my*self*. I could see why she won so many cases. She wheedled.

"Why didn't you say something then?"

"I did," I said. "To Seth."

Again she waited. I stood with my arms at my sides and willed myself not to cross them over my chest in defensive mode. Not that it mattered. Whatever I was accused of, she was already convicting me with her eyes.

Only . . . she wasn't the judge now, was she?

"I'm doing what I have to do," I said. "So if we're done here, I have a lot of people to talk to."

"Wait."

Randi straightened from the desk, momentarily unsettling the broom-straw-straight hair, and held out her hand. I looked at it blankly.

"The ring," she said. "I'll hold on to it until indefinitely is over."

The fingers on my right hand went involuntarily to the diamond.

"You can't have it both ways," she said.

"It's up to Seth to ask for it back," I said.

"I was the one who offered the ring to Seth for you. It has been in my family for generations."

I knew that. I also knew that for the first time since I was born, my place in that family was being questioned.

It's not my fault! I wanted to scream at her.

A rush of resentment pushed through me. I knew this was only the first of the scenes I was going to have to endure because the girl with the black mane had a stronger hold on Seth than I did.

I didn't realize I'd let out a cry until I saw Randi's face change. For an instant she was the Randi Grissom who taught me how to drive a stick shift on the hard sand of Jacksonville Beach and gave me the rules for assessing the intentions of guys before I went off to college. She was the woman who cared about me in the only way she knew and in a flinty way no one else was going to.

It wasn't hard to slide the ring from my finger because my hands were slick with sweat. I tucked it into her palm before the Randi-love left her face.

"I'm sorry," I said. "I really am."

She didn't call my name until I was halfway out the door, but I didn't stop. I was holding back sobs with my naked left hand.

~§~

GrandMary was waiting for me in the parlor, as we called the small sitting room just off the dining room, a leftover from more genteel times. She called to me when I crossed through the kitchen and I knew she'd been listening for me. Which also meant she had a goal for this meeting.

If there was one person who could make me break my promise to Seth, it was GrandMary. I steeled myself and went to her.

She was sitting in a cushioned cane-back chair near the floor-to-ceiling window with the morning sun playing on her hair as if it loved her. She motioned for me to join her in the other chair, and I sank into it and took the teal throw she offered me. It must have been obvious that I was freezing, despite the sun warming the alcove. I might never get warm again.

"Where's Mama?" I said.

"She's seeing people," GrandMary said. "I told her she could cancel things over the phone but she insisted on doing it all in person."

I threw off the blanket and stood up. "She shouldn't be doing that. It's my mess to clean up, not hers."

"Let her do it, baby girl. It's holding her together."

I dropped back into the chair and held the throw in a wad in my lap. "I hate this."

"I hate it *for* you."

"But I followed your advice," I said. "I was having second thoughts and I faced them and I didn't lie to myself."

I expected—or at least hoped—for the nod that would somehow make this okay. I didn't get it. GrandMary folded her hands under her chin and delivered one of those clear-eyed looks that made me want to sort back through my words and figure out which one was wrong.

"There are outright lies," she said, "and there are lies of omission. I think it's what you're leaving out of your explanation that is making you do things like take the shears to yourself."

I wanted to swear.

"Okay, you're right," I said instead. "But I promised Seth I would keep certain things to myself."

"Well, then, you absolutely have to, don't you?"

I blinked.

"If you can't trust each other, what do you have?"

"Absolutely nothing," I said.

If she heard the bitterness in my voice, she didn't comment. She just tilted the pixie head. "What concerns me is that this secret, whatever it is, appears to be eating you up." She leaned toward me, blue-veined hands still neatly folded. "I'm not asking you to share it with me, Tara. In fact, I sense that you shouldn't. But I think you need to tell someone."

"I can't—"

"Hear me out. Someone who doesn't know the family, maybe someone you don't even know yet yourself."

"Like a counselor?"

The resentment was rising again. Why should *I* be the one seeing a shrink when *Seth* was the one with the problem?

"Maybe, maybe not," GrandMary said. "I think whoever it is will come to you when you're ready. In the meantime, I'd be talking to God about this."

I shivered, and her eyebrows rose.

"Is that a problem?" she said.

"No," I said. "It's just hard to imagine taking this—thing—to God."

Not that I'd taken anything to God, probably since I walked unprepared into my Victorian Lit final junior year. For a churchgoing family who was there every time the Reverend Paul Grissom opened the doors, we didn't talk much about God himself. The question *What are you talking to him about today?* didn't come up over dinner.

"This thing that God already knows about?" GrandMary said. "Is that the thing we're talking about?"

She smiled and reached across the small space between us and covered my hand with hers. It was both frail and strong.

"I suspect it's been a while since you two have talked, but don't worry about that. God is patient."

GrandMary straightened and looked at the silver watch dangling daintily on her wrist. "You're supposed to meet your mother for lunch at eleven. The Soho South Café, I think she said?"

Conversation over. I was both relieved and sad. The longing to tell her ached in my chest.

"You're coming with, right?" I said.

She shook her head. "I have to pack."

"You're leaving?"

"Tonight."

"You're not staying for Christmas?"

"I may come back."

She stood up and held out her hand to me. I stood up and took it.

"Your timing was actually good," she said. "Yesterday I discovered something—nothing serious, I'm sure, but something I want to see my own doctors about."

"What's wrong?" I said.

"Probably nothing. This is just a ruling-out process."

She wasn't going to tell me anything more. Her face was set, and her body was already turning toward the door. It occurred to me that GrandMary and I might be alike after all.

"You're going to be all right, baby girl," she said, and then she kissed my forehead. "I think I should stop calling you that. You're not behaving like either a baby or a girl."

"No, don't stop," I said. "It's your name for me."

She smiled again and then she was gone. I stood there for a while, wishing I was that innocent small child again. Wishing I didn't know what I knew now.

The Soho South Café on Liberty Street was a classy, eclectic place that had a sunny bar in front with turquoise-upholstered barstools you could see through the glass front. There were lamps with fluted shades, stucco walls cracked to expose the brick beneath, and in the foyer where I waited for Mama, an ornate old-fashioned chandelier was juxtaposed with contemporary paint-flung-on-the-canvas art. I hadn't been there since it reopened under new management, and I would have dug it completely if I wasn't dreading the conversation I was about to have with my mother. I hadn't planned to do it in a public place, but Mama apparently had. Probably because she wouldn't come undone in front of other people. She just wouldn't.

But the moment she walked through the glass doors, I knew that process had already started. She was polished and impeccably dressed in winter-white slacks and a pale yellow sweater combination, so that wasn't what tipped me off. It was the too-cheerful smile and the pseudo-bouncy step and the high-pitched voice that greeted the hostess, all before she even noticed I was there.

I had never seen my mother resemble a Barbie doll before.

"Mama," I said.

She went into a mini-spasm as she turned around. Her usually poised blue gaze was all over the place.

"I'm getting us a table!" she said.

The two people behind the reservation desk exchanged glances. One of them looked as if someone had just run a fingernail across a Styrofoam cooler.

I linked arms with Mama and nudged her to follow the hostess so she wouldn't wander off to the bar or back out the door.

"We'd love a corner table," I said to the girl.

She led us to one tucked near the window and shielded from the rest of the dining area by a ficus tree. I pulled a gold gilt chair out for Mama and perched unsteadily on the one across from her. I felt like I should be ready to pick up any pieces that fell off of her.

Even as I thought that, she dropped her clutch bag on the floor. Our server retrieved it and gazed at it with enormous, mesmerizing eyes.

"This is lovely," she said to Mama. "And so are you."

Mama's reply—"You're so cute!"—was automatic, but the exchange seemed to calm her somehow, as if she'd finally come upon something normal in a morning of things that weren't as they should be.

Our server introduced herself as Ruth-Starr, described the specials, and floated off to get waters. I opened the menu, the first page of which listed the beverage offerings. I wasn't big on cocktails, but I was tempted by one called Corpse Reviver.

"It all sounds good!" Mama said. "You like tomato bisque, don't you? Should we try that?"

"Mama."

"I've heard the crab cakes are just to die for—ooh, now I have never had a salmon BLT—"

"*Mama.*"

She looked at me over the top of the menu that hid the lower half of her face.

"Can we not pretend we care about the food right now?" I said.

The wounded look in her eyes made me feel like a chump. Of course she was going to try to cheer me up. When Andrea Breneman found out her husband was having an affair, Mama took her shopping in Atlanta. A suddenly widowed college friend she hadn't seen in years got a plane ticket to join her at a spa in Tampa. It was just what she did.

"I'm sorry," I said. "I haven't felt much like eating. Why don't you pick something out for us to share?"

Ruth-Starr reappeared and Mama ordered the asparagus quiche and I tried to regroup. On top of learning that her mother had some kind of something a doctor needed to look at, Mama then had to go out and tell a bunch of vendors that her daughter had for some mysterious reason canceled the wedding that was probably supposed to pay their Christmas expenses. I couldn't expect her to understand what I needed at that point. I didn't even know myself.

When Ruth-Starr had gone off to get our house salads, Mama picked up the black cloth napkin and smoothed it across her lap. She was visibly pulling her scattered self together.

"How did it go with Randi?" she said.

"Mama, first I want to tell you myself what—"

"Daddy told me," she said, hand up. "I won't make you go through it again. Was Randi rude to you?"

I felt my eyes narrow. "Why?"

"Well, she was a little prickly with me—"

"You talked to her?"

Mama nodded. "She came by while you were in the shower. Fortunately your father had already gone, because I think he would have thrown her out. Bodily." She waved her hand. "I understand she's upset, so it didn't bother me . . ."

Now there was a lie. She was refolding the napkin in her lap for the third time.

"But I didn't want her hurting your feelings. This is hard enough for you."

"My feelings were hurt before I even walked in there," I said. "What did she say to you?"

"She just needed to vent."

"Mama."

She shook out the napkin. "She said Seth didn't tell her anything that made any sense, and she was going to get to the bottom of it with you. Did she push you?"

"She tried."

Mama abandoned the table linen and looked sadly at the chrome saltshaker. "Randi is one of my best friends, but when she starts acting like Jack McCoy, I just can hardly stand her."

I laughed for the first time in days. "Are you talking about the guy on *Law and Order?*"

"Isn't that his name?"

"It is." My grin faded. "I hope this doesn't come between you and Randi."

"That'll be up to her. Oh, now that looks wonderful."

Ruth-Starr wafted salads in front of us and offered fresh ground pepper, which gave me a chance to gather my own scattered pieces. Friendships could come loose because of this. My mother wouldn't be the only one unraveling because I'd pulled out the string.

"You don't have to do all the canceling," I said when Ruth-Starr was gone again. "I feel bad that you're dealing with the florists and everybody."

Mama poked at a crouton with her fork. "I don't know what I can say to help you. I know I can't fix it for you. But I can take care of the arrangements. That's what I can do."

She was so close to tears I could feel them in my own throat. I didn't know what to do to help her either. Maybe all you *could* do for an heirloom teacup was make sure you didn't shatter it.

"Try the dressing," she said. "It's lovely."

"Mama . . . I feel so bad . . . I hate for you to have to face your friends—"

"Tara."

Her tone startled me.

"Do not worry about what I'm going to tell my friends. That is the farthest thing from my mind. People will think what they're going to think. We can't do anything about that."

I knew my mouth was hanging open. And yet, why was I

surprised? Madeline Faulkner might be coming apart in a few places, but underneath, she was still pure class.

If that was all she could give me in this, that was enough.

So I tried the dressing and ate some quiche and let my mother think she was cheering me up. That was what I could give *her*.

~*ℓℓ*~

I waited until Thursday, the eleventh, to tell the Bridesmaids. It was the first time I could get all of them together, for one thing, and for another, I needed the space to come up with the possible scenarios, all of which started with:

TARA: I have something to tell you and I just want you to listen until I'm all done.

It went nothing like that. Nothing.

In the first place, the minute I saw all of them gathered at our round table at the Distillery, it hit me that this could be the last time we would get together like this, in this place. I sat down with them and burst into tears.

"Oh my gosh, *Tara*, what's *wrong?*" Lexi said.

"You cut your *hair*!" Alyssa said.

"Where is your *ring?*" Jacqueline said.

The babbling stopped and all eyes went to my left hand, which currently covered my mouth. Alyssa grabbed it and examined it as if the diamond might be hiding in the folds of my knuckles.

"He broke up with you?" she said.

"*We* broke it off," I said. "For now."

"What does that mean?" Jacqueline said.

"It means I—we—have postponed the wedding. Indefinitely."

The stunned silence lasted only seconds. Alyssa's very round blue eyes flattened. "Is this about that fight you had?"

"I can't really tell you what it's about," I said.

That silence was even more stunned. Jacqueline's lips blued as if she were going into shock.

"What do you mean you can't tell us?" she said.

"Maybe we should leave her alone."

They both looked at Lexi as if she'd suggested they drop me off a cliff.

"First of all," Alyssa said, ticking off fingers, "we've been friends since forever. You don't just announce you're canceling your wedding and not at least tell us something. And second of all, I mean, don't we deserve it?"

"Why?" Lexi's usually soft voice cracked like an eggshell. "Tara doesn't owe us an explanation."

"Maybe I do," I said. "I'm leaving every one of you with a floor-length gown you'll probably never wear."

"Until you reschedule." Jacqueline folded her arms. "I'm keeping mine. I can't believe you and Seth are really breaking up for good. You've been together too long. You're too good together."

"Evidently not." Alyssa leaned on the table. "I know you, Tara. You wouldn't call this off if something heinous hadn't happened. So dish. C'mon, we're your friends. We can help you."

"No," I said, "you can't. Well, yeah, you can—by just trusting me on this and not trying to make me explain."

Lexi immediately nodded. Alyssa did not.

"I don't know," she said, face stiff. "This kind of ticks me off. You're obviously hurting. You chopped off your hair. Geez, this is reminding me of, like, Britney Spears when she went off the deep end—"

"I'm not going off the deep end!"

"Then tell us—or you totally will. You look like you're about to explode."

"Lyssa, leave her alone," Lexi said.

Alyssa sat back hard in her chair and stared over our heads. Beside her, Jacqueline pressed her eyelids. I had only seen her cry once before—when she told us she and Oliver had split up.

"This must be like déjà vu for you," I said. "I'm sorry—"

She shook her head and jammed her bob behind her ears. "It isn't that. I just feel like you're shutting us out and I don't understand it. Talk about trust—it doesn't seem like you trust *us*."

"I do trust you." I reached back to pull up the hair that wasn't there. "But I promised Seth I wouldn't talk to anybody about it."

"It's that bad?" Jacqueline said.

I looked at each of them—Alyssa smoldering in anger, Jacqueline tearful with hurt, Lexi brimming over with compassion that had no place to go—and I imagined myself telling them that no matter what Seth said, he wanted porn more than he wanted me. What would their faces tell me then? That they were disgusted? That I was a fool not to have seen it? That I wasn't Tara the Good One anymore?

The realization hurled itself into my face. It wasn't just Seth I was protecting. Why would I? He hadn't protected me. No—it was myself I was shielding. I didn't even know until now that I was suffocating in shame.

"I'm sorry," I said. "I'm sorry for all of this, but I just can't."

Before they could see any more of my humiliation, I left the table and ran down the steps, nearly plowing into Vic on my way.

"You married yet?" he said.

I sobbed all the way to the door.

I was halfway across the parking lot when I heard Lexi calling to me. I only stopped because I couldn't catch my breath. When she reached me my lungs were clawing for air.

"Tara, are you okay?"

I nodded—yet another lie—and let her put her arms around my

waist. Lexi's face only came to my chest, and I let my own face rest in her hair as I cried.

"I'm not going to try to make you tell me," she said. "But I'm here, okay? Even if you just need a place to go and not talk."

"Okay," I said.

I pried myself away and told her good-bye and blindly crossed the parking lot and Montgomery Street. Not talk. That really was all I could do—not talk.

Not to my best friends.

Not to my big brother. Or my parents. Or my grandmother.

GrandMary told me *to* talk—to someone who wouldn't be hurt by what I had to say. Who would that be for a churchgoing girl like me? My pastor? Seth's *father*?

I didn't stop half-running, half-wheezing until I got to Chippewa Square, where I sank onto a bench in front of the statue of James Oglethorpe. Tom Hanks as Forrest Gump sat in that very spot, on a bench created by Hollywood set builders, and talked to anybody who would sit next to him and listen. For me, there was no one.

Anxiety needled through me and came to an uneasy stop in my core. And there it stayed.

E I G H T

Two more things became apparent to me.

One I realized that night when Kellen asked me to come up to the carriage house, just to hang out and watch some TV. I was thinking, *Aw, what a sweet big brother,* until I walked into his living room and found Seth sitting on the edge of the couch between a pile of Kellen's unfolded laundry and a half-empty bag of Doritos. Kellen made a hasty exit to his bedroom and cranked up Dave Matthews and left me alone with my former fiancé, who looked even worse than he'd sounded when we talked on the phone.

That had happened several times a day since Monday. Seth called and said he wanted to meet and talk things over, and I said there was no place to go and nothing to say. Now here he was, eyes underscored with deep, dark half-moons. His whole face was imploring me, and I couldn't turn away.

"Your hair is cute," he said.

I couldn't say the same for his, which was standing up in unkempt spikes like he'd been raking his fingers through it all day. Saying nothing, I fell into Kellen's red corduroy beanbag. Seth slid off the couch and sat cross-legged on the floor facing me. Just behind his head, salsa dripped over the side of a Tupperware bowl.

"I'm sorry about the ring," he said. "I didn't know my mother was going to do that. I wouldn't have asked you for it."

"It's fine," I said. "Randi is going to do what she's going to do."

"I *will* put it back on your finger, Tara." Seth's voice was suddenly steady. "I'll fix this."

"Do you have a plan?" I said. "Are you seeing Gavin Johnson?"

Seth shook his head. "No. He obviously wasn't helping me. When I told him what happened he just said everybody relapses at first."

"So it *is* like an addiction."

"I don't like to think of it that way. It makes me feel like there's no way out, and I know there is."

"So what is it?"

I hated the way my own voice was sounding—prickly and judgy and everything I hated in the way girls down-talked to their boyfriends. But then, what didn't I hate right now, really?

"I've been looking at programs—"

He cut himself off but I knew he'd been about to say online. I let it go.

"There's nothing around here that looks decent. I'd have to go away and I can't do that right now."

"Why?"

"I just started in a new position."

"You were going to take time to go on a honeymoon," I said.

Seth stared at me. "Thanks, Tar. Thanks for making me feel worse than I already do."

"I'm not trying to make you feel worse. I'm just trying to tell you there's no reason for us to have a conversation if it's going to be you saying you want to change and me asking how you're going to do that and you saying you don't know. What's the point?"

I tried to get out of the beanbag, but Seth put the palm of his hand on the front of my shoulder. "I'm afraid to go away," he said.

His mouth trembled enough for me to stay where I was.

"I'm afraid you'll move on while I'm gone. I'm afraid you won't wait for me. I'm afraid you'll stop loving me."

I closed my eyes. "Really, Seth? Really? Do you think I'm that shallow?"

"What?"

"Do you think I could really just go on without you, like nothing ever happened? I have loved you for *ten years*. I *want* you to get out of this thing you're trapped in. I *want* things to be like they were before. But just because *I* want it doesn't mean it's going to happen. *You* have to make it happen."

"You'll wait, then?"

"Yes," I said.

"For as long as it takes?"

"Yes."

Seth let out air as if he'd been holding it in for days. "As long as I know that, I can do this. It could mean being away for two weeks."

"Whatever," I said. "Do it."

"And when I come back, then—"

"Stop," I said. "Just—one thing at a time."

Seth put his arms behind him and leaned on the heels of his hands. "What aren't you saying?"

Why did everyone want to know what I didn't want to say? Like, *How will I know it's gone? What will the signs be that I can trust you? Will I ever be able to get those images out of my head—the ones that shoved my visions for us completely out of the picture?*

"Tar?" Seth said.

I had to say something. Everybody wanted me to say something.

"You go and do this," I said. "And then we'll take it from there."

"That's it? That's all the reassurance I get to take with me?"

"I can't predict the entire future!" I struggled out of the beanbag and stood over him. "I had a vision, Seth, and it got shattered, so excuse me if I can't construct a new one yet. Okay? I love you. I'll wait while you go get help. What more do you want me to do?"

Seth got to his feet but he didn't reach for me. He clenched and unclenched his hands at his sides. "So—a porn addict is all I am to you now."

"*What?*"

"You can't see past that to anything else that I am."

"That's not fair."

"That's what it sounds like to me."

"Then you aren't hearing me," I said. "And that is why it's pointless for us to talk about this anymore."

I was right. Seth had been raking his hands through his hair. He did it now, leaving the spikes at rakish angles that mirrored everything I was feeling.

"I'm sorry, Tar," he said. His chin quivered like a small boy's.

"Me too," I said. "Let's just leave it like that for now, okay?"

He nodded, and I left.

I was glad the night air was bracing, because my face was so hot I was sure it would blister. When I got halfway to the main house, mere steps away, Kellen caught up with me, and I was surprised when he grabbed my arm.

"How do you expect to work this out if you won't even talk to him?" he said.

The light on the walkway was dim, but I could see Kellen's eyes glinting.

I pulled away. "What did he tell you about why we're postponing the wedding?"

"That you aren't sure you're ready to marry him," he said, as if that was the single lamest excuse he'd ever heard.

"That's all he said?"

"Yeah."

"Don't get all up in my face until he tells you the real reason."

"Why don't *you* tell me?"

"Because I promised him I wouldn't. So if you want to yell at somebody, yell at him."

"I'm not yelling!"

"Yes, you are!"

In fact, we both were, in voices raw and shrill and dangerously close to rage. It was the first time ever.

One more thread pulled out of the tapestry. Pretty soon there wasn't going to be anything left of our rich, perfect, former lives at all.

⁓ℓℓ⁓

The other thing that became apparent to me was that I had to find something to do. And that wasn't going to be hanging out with the Bridesmaids. Their texts and voice mails ranged from Alyssa's *R U trapped under something heavy?* to Jacqueline's pleading with me to let her tell me how miserable *she* was being single and how I was making a big mistake. Et cetera. The only one I actually answered was Lexi. *Just give me some time*, I texted her. Her answer: *Sure*. The hurt stung right off the screen, but I couldn't help her. I couldn't even help me.

By Monday I was bordering on hopeless, another first for me, and I had to get out of the house. The day was bright and sunny and cloudless—the complete antithesis to my mood—and I walked aimlessly around the historic district, shivering. Only a slight breeze nipped the air but I was still chilled, just like I'd been for fifteen days. Those were the ones I was counting now—the days since I found out, not the days until I was supposed to marry Seth.

At one point I found myself on East Charlton Street, a block from Flannery O'Connor's birthplace and childhood home. I'd done my master's thesis on Flannery and had spent most of my Christmas and spring breaks in there my last year of grad school doing research with the docent. I wandered down the block and stood in front of the narrow, unpretentious house and for about five seconds considered going in to see if he needed an assistant. I could tell people more than they really wanted to know about her strange little childhood—so different from my classically happy one.

But the house was only open on Saturdays and Sundays for three hours each, and Flannery's story was enough to make you reach for the Prozac. I was close enough to that as it was.

So I moved on down Charlton, and the more I walked, the more bleak I became. I was as melancholy as the Spanish moss, which, I thought randomly, was neither Spanish nor a moss. Maybe nothing was as it seemed.

When the bells in the St. John's Church tower pealed out "O Come, O Come, Emmanuel," I had to get away from them. I hadn't taken GrandMary's advice and gone to God with this whole thing, and it sure didn't seem as if God was coming to me. In any form.

My flight landed me at Bull and Perry, where the corner doors of Piebald Espresso opened to let someone out. Piebald. Like the splotchy black-and-white horses. A metaphor for being composed of incongruous parts.

I went in.

Mercifully, inside, I couldn't hear the bells anymore. I stood there for a minute, trying to decide whether to get a coffee or just hide in a corner. I hadn't been in there before, actually. People talked about it, but I wasn't a hang-out-in-a-coffee-shop kinda gal, even in grad school. I liked a latte as well as the next person, but I'd only indulged when somebody was making a Starbucks run. Maybe there was something too trendy about it. I couldn't even remember my reasons now. That seemed like another lifetime. Somebody else's lifetime.

A glass case displaying teapots and cups and wineglasses divided the Piebald into two parts: one with small tables for two and four, the other with a mishmash of used upholstered couches and armchairs and donated dining room chairs, some of which were too high for the tables. Fans spun on the rustic, open-beamed ceilings. Some of the walls were brick, some stucco in a dark brown, and all boasted the work of local artists, probably SCAD students. But the entire front of the place was made up of large windows that gave it light and brought in the bustle of Bull Street. The place was alive and I wasn't. I decided to stay.

I crossed the wood floor to a ramp bordered with a wrought-iron railing that went up to the counter. I ordered a latte from a girl with the tiniest of gold rings in her nose whose name tag read *Wendy* and found an armchair amid the friendly chaos. Around me people talked as openly as if they were in their own living rooms, chatting across me and then going back to their books and their iPads. On the other side the tables were occupied by business types on laptops, each working alone with coffee and a scone. As I sat there, a steady stream of people came through the corner doors headed for takeout, looking like they had someplace to go and knew how to get there. My anxiety pulsed so hard in my chest I let the latte go unfinished.

A station that announced itself as Christmas Traditions was playing everything from Dean Martin singing "It's a Marshmallow World" to the Boston Pops Orchestra doing "Hark! The Herald Angels Sing." When Neil Diamond started in on "The First Noel," I said out loud, "Isn't he Jewish?"

A guy with a thready goatee and John Lennon glasses looked up at me and said, "Yeah. That's just wrong."

For some reason, I could breathe again. The latte was lukewarm so I decided a tea might go good.

I headed back to the counter, where this time a skinny kid waited on me. He looked to be about twelve and was wearing a vest over a white T-shirt and had a bandana inexplicably tied around the ankle of his left boot. His name tag was on upside down but I thought it said *Zoo-Loo*.

"I'll brew that Earl Grey Creme for ya," he said. And then wandered off into a kitchen that, frankly, looked a little scary to me.

While I waited, I couldn't help noticing the guy who was obviously in charge. He was maybe the owner but at least the manager. Good-looking in a raw, Italian kind of way, he wore a fedora and a name tag that said *Ike*. Even while he was exchanging quips with the customers like a New Yorker who had taken a wrong turn and ended up south of the Mason–Dixon Line, he was apparently not pleased about something because his smile didn't reach his eyes, and judging from the crinkles around them I had the feeling usually it did.

When the girl who waited on me first—Wendy—finished ringing up someone's hummus and pita, Ike leaned his head close to hers. His deep whisper just reached me.

"Jason quit on me," he said.

"The afternoon guy?" Wendy said.

"Yeah. He gave me two days' notice and acted like that was doing me a favor."

"Jerk," Wendy said.

Ike stepped back so the skinny kid could hand me my tea. "You having anything to eat with that?" he said to me. He motioned toward the chalkboard on the wall behind him, which was crowded with offerings in someone's whimsical printing. "We have a nice cheeseboard."

"I'm good," I said.

I paid Zoo-Loo, but I lingered as if I were admiring the pastries. Ike continued his conversation with Wendy.

"I'm gonna have to find somebody to replace him. We're about to hit the height of the Christmas visitor season, and I need more than one barista in the afternoon."

Wendy smiled at me. She had perfect teeth. "Did you find something?"

"Still looking," I said.

She turned back to Ike. "It's not like you don't have an entire folder full of applications."

"I don't have time to go through all of them and do interviews—"

"Excuse me."

They both looked up at me, which indicated that I had indeed spoken. I wasn't sure until then.

"I need a job," I said, "and I'd love to work here."

They looked at each other. Wendy then gazed at me, a long, hard sort of appraisal, shrugged at Ike, and turned to another customer. Ike leaned on the counter.

"Have you ever worked as a barista?" he said.

"No," I said. I didn't add that I had barely worked as *anything*. "I'm a fast learner, though."

Ike adjusted his fedora with one finger. "Ever done any food service?"

"No."

He gave me half a smile. "Ever drink coffee?"

I smiled back. "Oh yeah."

"Have you ever been convicted of a felony?"

"No!"

"Do you have any entanglements?"

"I'm sorry?"

"Child care issues? Transportation problems?"

"No. No kids. I live within walking distance. There's nothing that would keep me from showing up at work whenever you need me."

The words fell sadly between us. Whether that was what made

him hire me—the fact that I clearly had no life and desperately needed one—I couldn't tell.

"Four days a week, five hours a shift," he said. "I'll give you some paperwork to fill out and run a background check. If you don't have a rap sheet or a bad work history, we'll start training you Wednesday."

"You won't regret this," I said.

Ike looked at me curiously from under a ridge of dark brows. "Don't you want to know how much it pays?"

"Sure," I said.

But I really didn't care. I'd just taken the first step away from the vision that was never going to be. And that was what I cared about.

NINE

If I had worked up a scenario for the scene where I told my parents I got a job in a coffee shop, it wouldn't have included my father stopping with a forkful of rib eye halfway to his lips and saying, "You did what?"

"I need something to do," I said. "And I want to make a little money. I can't keep sponging off you and Mama."

"You're not sponging," Mama said. "This was our agreement."

I looked down at the steak I'd carved into bite-size pieces on my plate so it would look like I was eating. "The agreement was that I would live here at home until the wedding. Now that there isn't going to be a wedding . . . yet . . . I have to come up with a new plan."

"So go to grad school like you were originally," Daddy said.

"Seth was going to help me pay for that—"

"You know I'll—"

"No. Daddy."

I breathed in through my nose until it whistled and tried to remember the last time I raised my voice to my father. I came up with never.

"I don't know what's going to happen with Seth," I said, tone more even. "I don't want to get into a program until my life isn't so up in the air."

"That makes sense." Mama glanced at Daddy. "Don't you think?"

"Besides," I said, "I still have to apply and all that. I couldn't get in until summer anyway."

"So just apply," Daddy said. "Put your focus there."

I pressed my fork tines into the baked potato I was also pretending to consume. "Do you have something against me working?"

"No. But in a coffee shop?"

"The Piebald is fun," Mama said. "I've been in there several times. They make a nice mocha. And I love the name. I had to look it up."

"Madeline," Daddy said, without looking at her. "That's not the point."

"What *is* the point?" I tried to laugh. "Are we being a little snobby here, maybe?"

He didn't find that amusing. In fact, he pushed his chair back and tossed his napkin on the table. I expected my mother to pick it up and start folding it. Or maybe I would. This was so not what we did here at our house.

"You just spent two years getting a master's degree at *Duke*, for Pete's sake. I'm sure if you want to work you can get something better than . . . what's this paying? Minimum wage plus tips?"

"To start," I said.

Wrong thing to say, apparently. Daddy's scowl could have put Scrooge to shame.

"You planning on staying on there awhile?"

"What else am I going to do, really? With my degree I can either write a book about somebody's work that hasn't been dissected before, or I can teach college students how to do that—which was my plan, but I need a doctorate to compete."

"Have you tried?"

I stared at him.

"Honey, I don't think she has the energy to try right now," Mama said.

"I can't believe we're even having this conversation," I said. "I'm doing the best I can. That's all I've got. Excuse me."

The china jittered as I, too, pushed back from the table, knocking off the fork that had never made it to my mouth. It sounded like one more shard of my old dreams hitting the floor behind me.

$\sim\!\!\mathcal{S}\!\mathcal{U}\!\mathcal{U}\!\curvearrowright$

I tried not to keep track of the people I couldn't talk to anymore, or as in the case of my brother, who weren't talking to me, but I spent the empty day before I was to start work at the Piebald missing all of them. Walking was the only thing that kept me from actually taking out pen and paper and making a list. I started to, but the notepad I found in my desk had *Tara Grissom* printed across the top in a burgundy font.

Yeah. I went out for a walk.

I was on East Liberty, digging my sunglasses out of my bag, when I literally ran into a girl coming out of the Book Lady with a burlap-and-bead shoulder bag that was almost bigger than she was.

I said, "I am *so* sorry—"

"No worries," she said. "Oh—Tara."

I found myself looking straight into the olive-green eyes of Evelyn Grissom. She stared back at me out of her pale face, what I could see of it between the two lank panels of hair the shade of toast. If I hadn't gone to the hospital when she was born and stood on tiptoe to look at her in her bassinet through the nursery window, I would always have sworn she was adopted. And for more reasons than just that un-Grissom-like coloring that made her look as if she were recovering from a long bout with some mysterious illness.

"Evvy," I said.

"Yeah, huh?"

She hadn't hurled an epithet at me yet, so I took a chance. "Are you still speaking to me?"

"Are you *serious*? Can we *talk*?"

"Sure," I said. "Do you want a coffee?"

She didn't answer because she was already dragging me across Liberty. I let her zigzag us all the way to Madison Square, where she let me go and dropped herself onto the base of the statue where Sergeant William Jasper everlastingly hoists a flag in the 1779 Siege of Savannah. Both of her legs disappeared under the muslin skirt that only stayed on her negligible hips with the help of a bangled belt reminiscent of a belly dancer. She pulled her hair behind her and looked at me again with the green eyes that had fascinated me since she was a baby. She used to stare at all of us until Kellen would say, "Make her stop looking at me like that. She's freaking me out."

"Before you ask me anything," I said, "I can't tell you any more than Seth already has. I'm sorry."

She rolled her eyes. "Seth hasn't told me anything and if he had I wouldn't have believed him. I had to gather what little I do know from listening to my father talking to somebody on the phone."

"Your mom hasn't told you—"

"My mom is who I'm not speaking to. Or at least, as little as possible."

"Should I feel honored that you're speaking to me?" I said.

"Honored. No. You're just the only sane person I know right now."

I laughed out loud. It was a rusty sound.

"Look," Evelyn said, "I don't know what went down between you and my brother and I don't even want to know. Okay, maybe I do, but since nobody's telling . . . All I know is I'm glad it happened. I don't see how you could ever consider marrying him in the first place."

That wasn't exactly news to me. Seth and Evelyn hadn't been close for almost as far back as I could remember. He was ten when she was born, so he wasn't terribly interested in a baby girl—not like Kellen was with me—and he and Kellen were always off being boys. But the outright animosity that had developed between them didn't start until Evelyn was—maybe five? Then it was always as if Seth emitted toxic fumes she didn't want to breathe. That had gone through several stages—from sibling rivalry that bordered on World Wrestling Entertainment to a brick-wall silence that commenced when Seth went off to college and hadn't let up since. When I'd asked her to be a bridesmaid in the wedding, you'd have thought I was requesting one of her kidneys. I took that as a no.

Evelyn rearranged her legs. "I just wanted to say I'm glad you saw the light."

"What light?" I said.

She waited for a woman with a leashed bulldog to pass before she tilted toward me. "He's not the mirror of Christianity everybody thinks he is. I've known it forever, but nobody wants to hear that. Especially from me."

The anxiety stuck out its spines in my chest. "What have you known?"

"That he's a total fraud." She dragged her hair over the front of her shoulder and hung onto it like a rope. "He looks like this perfect evangelical role model on the outside, but he's not. There's another side of him."

"What side?" I was pushing it and I shouldn't be, but I was also starting to panic. If Evelyn knew, *I* had to know or people were going to get hurt. As much as she despised Seth, she'd have no qualms about putting the entire thing on Facebook.

"The seamy side," she said.

"Explain."

"You want details? I don't—he's just not that person. I've lived with him my whole life. I should know."

I closed my eyes and let relief drive the anxiety back into its hole. Evelyn *didn't* know. She sensed something, maybe, but she couldn't name it.

"What?" she said.

I opened my eyes. Her own were in slits the width of hyphens.

"You *do* have the details," she said. "You didn't break off the engagement because *you* had issues. You did it because *he* has them and you know what they are."

"I thought you said you didn't want to know."

"I lied."

Evelyn flipped her hair to the other shoulder and leaned toward me again over the lotus position she'd pretzeled herself into. "He did something to you."

"No, he did not do something to me."

I tried to sound dismissive but her eyes weren't buying it. "He did something you can't live with, though. That's why you're not marrying him."

"Okay." I put up a hand, the one I wanted to use to pull her up by that rope of hair at the moment. "I've said all I'm going to say. Discussion over."

She nodded sagely, as only a twenty-year-old who knows everything can. "You're telling me this is none of my business."

"I don't mean to be rude, Evvy, but yes, it's none of your business."

"Yeah, well, you're wrong. It's my business and it's always been my business. So I'm going to say this."

She stopped as if she were waiting for me to invite her to go on.

"I don't think I can stop you," I said.

"You're protecting him somehow and I think—no, I *know*—you're better than that. You're better than *him*."

Somehow she untangled her legs and hiked the gigantic beaded bag over her shoulder.

"I'll be there for you when this all goes down," she said. "And it *will* go down if I have anything to do with it. Which I will."

The panic I'd been pushing away came all the way up my throat, but by then she was already headed toward Bull Street with everything swinging: hair, bag, skirt, attitude. She would smear her brother in a heartbeat. The only thing preventing her was lack of information, and since she was never going to get close enough to Seth to find out anything, maybe that would be the saving grace.

Still, I pulled my phone out of my bag and contemplated calling Seth to warn him. Poking my fingers on the screen, I left him a text instead. *Evelyn suspects something. Be careful.*

But I was no longer fooling myself. I wasn't just protecting Seth anymore. I was protecting me. And I was so angry that I even had to. I picked up a handful of wet oak leaves and threw them. They fell right back to their original places and plastered themselves on the Belgian block.

~ℓℓ~

I showed up for work the next day before two, as prepared as I could get for something I knew absolutely nothing about. Not even enough to come up with a script.

My hair was pushed away from my face with a red headband, and I had on a relatively new pair of skinny jeans and ballet flats and a tank under my long-sleeved cranberry top to try to cover the fact that my ribs were starting to show under my clothes. I'd even done my nails the night before, which hadn't happened in seventeen days.

To my surprise Wendy was there when I arrived. She actually looked a little surprised, too, and not pleasantly so.

"Ike changed my shift so I could train you," she said.

"I'm sorry," I said.

She pulled in her chin, a finely chiseled feature to match the rest of a face that appeared to have been formed out of fine marble and stained lightly with tea. "Why are you sorry?"

"Because I need training?"

Wendy rolled the deepest shade of violet eyes I'd seen since Elizabeth Taylor in *National Velvet,* and somehow that particular piece of body language looked completely different from when Evelyn did it. Evelyn's eye-roll said, *Are you stupid or what?* Wendy's said, *I'm about to make you feel better.*

"Everybody needs training," she said. "No matter how many shops you've worked in, every one is different so it's almost like starting from scratch."

"Um, I *am* starting from scratch," I said.

She handed me an apron that used to be white at some point and watched me tie it on. "You really are, aren't you?" she said.

"Ike didn't tell you?"

"Tell me . . ."

"That I've never worked as a barista before? Or in food service? At all?"

The eyes rolled again. "No. But he really didn't have to."

"I'm sorry," I said.

"Okay, first of all, stop saying that. He hired you. You're here. Let's get started."

This girl was incredibly hard to read. She was, in fact, like a Faulkner novel, which I'd always found impossible to plod through.

The Sound and the Fury was the only book I'd ever used CliffsNotes for in college or grad school. I had a feeling I was going to need them to understand Wendy.

The first thing I discovered as I followed her to the coffee counter was that I was overdressed. Wendy had on ripped jeans and Nikes and a faded blue T-shirt that said *Life Is Good? Are You Serious?* on the front. Her dark hair, dyed the color of Randi Grissom's mahogany doors, was braided and then tucked into a bun at the crown of her head. There was a lot of it, but it looked like it didn't dare fall down.

I was feeling that way myself.

It didn't really go that badly to start with. I shadowed Wendy for the first hour, and then she stood behind me and to the right while I took orders, attempted to work the register, fixed the noncoffee drinks (she said I wasn't ready for barista training yet), and served the constant food that came out of that scary kitchen. Fortunately I didn't have to go in there. From what I could tell it was small and steamy and things clattered and Ike barked. I was content to stay out front where it was all smiles and coffee.

Then three o'clock hit. Clearly every third resident of Savannah and *every* visitor chose that hour to come in out of the waning sun and have some kind of complicated drink and a food item with five substitutions. They were all some degree of cranky. Blood sugars were low? People were snarky because they still had two more hours to work? Husbands were sick of following their wives into one house museum after another?

I didn't have time to analyze it. Suddenly I was expected to take orders, fill orders, ring up orders, and do it all without asking any questions.

"What goes on a cheeseboard?" I said.

"It's on the list."

"What list?"

"By the thing. That will be twelve-oh-two, sir—pennies are there in the dish—Tara, this gentleman needs his fruit bowl."

Fruit bowl. Where the heck were the fruit bowls? While I was looking around for something to dump strawberries into, Wendy wrenched open the glass case, pulled a plastic container of melon and blueberries off the ice, and plunked it into my hand.

"You just fill the orders I give you," she said. "I'll do everything else until it slows down."

"I'm sorry," I muttered. I couldn't help myself.

Okay, deep breaths. How hard could this be? I had a master's degree for Pete's sake.

"I need a baklava and a blueberry scone!"

Baklava—already in pieces—put it on a plate—scone, blueberry—no, that was raisin—

"Excuse me, honey?"

I looked over the glass case at a woman about GrandMary's age with a salt-and-pepper bob and a pair of hazel eyes that blinked at me from behind round red-rimmed glasses.

"Yes, ma'am?" I said. "They'll take your order over there."

"I already got my order but I was just wonderin' . . ." She held up a plate bearing a sandwich with one bite taken out of it. "Have y'all changed the Brie and pear sandwich?"

I knew I looked exactly like Bambi in the path of a semi. Wendy appeared at my elbow.

"Is there something wrong, Ms. Helen?"

"No. This is delicious. I think it's smoked ham and Swiss, but I did order the Brie and pear. You know how much I love that combination."

"I know you do." Wendy's smile could have lit the place in the event of a power failure. "I think what happened is that they're right next to each other in the case and somebody just grabbed the wrong one. I am so sorry. Let me just get you a Brie and pear."

"Let me!" I grabbed the sandwich that clearly said *Brie and Pear* on the wrapper and plopped it on a plate which I handed over the counter.

"You're going to want that heated up, aren't you, Ms. Helen?" Wendy said.

She took the plate and, without making eye contact with me, headed for the toaster oven.

"I'm sorry," I said to Ms. Helen. "That was my mistake. It's my first day."

"Well, bless your heart," she said. "Don't you worry about it. Now that I know that ham and Swiss is s'good, I might order it next time."

"Still need a blueberry scone!"

"I'll let you get back to work." Ms. Helen lowered her voice to a whisper. "You're doing just fine."

Yeah, well, not according to Wendy. When things slowed down she pulled me behind the loose teas display.

"That lady, Ms. Helen?" she said.

"Yeah?"

"She's a regular."

"She was really nice."

"And she knows everybody. We can't have her going around telling people the service has gone downhill at the Piebald."

"I'm so—"

"Do not say it. Look, you'll get the hang of it, but just be careful, okay? Ike's really strict about customer service."

"Okay," I said.

Her violet eyes drifted to the top of my head. "Go in the bathroom and put yourself back together, why don't you? And you might want to wipe the mustard off of those jeans before you ruin them. How did you get mustard on yourself anyway?"

I had no idea. What I did know as I escaped to the restroom was that even though Wendy and I were probably about the same age, she had at least a decade on me when it came to experience. I'd been to Europe, I'd been to Duke, I'd been to a dinner at the governor's mansion, but I couldn't tell one sandwich from another—and that was what I needed to do in order to keep from losing my mind.

I settled my hair down with some water on my fingers, but I didn't bother with the jeans. Maybe it was time I got a little mustard on me.

~~∂℮~~

My shift wasn't over until seven, but things were winding down after the dinner rush so Ike let me go. I was envisioning a skin-pruning bath in my claw-foot tub as I headed for the door, but halfway there I felt a touch on my arm as if a cat was passing by. I looked up at the long, lean form of the Reverend Paul Grissom.

Seth's father. My pastor.

"Hey, Tara," he said.

Pastor Paul had a voice like honey when you spread it on a warm English muffin. It worked for preaching sermons, placating Randi, and talking various members of his flock off the ledge. But right now, it was among the bottom ten voices I wanted to hear.

"Hey," I said back.

"Can I buy you dinner?"

Buy me dinner? My antennae went up. I loved Paul, always had, but when had he ever invited me for so much as a Coca-Cola? This was a busy man with a huge congregation and a book coming out every other year. Nah, this was an ambush if I ever sensed one.

"I've already eaten," I lied.

"A walk then? It's a nice evening."

I would rather have walked off the wall down at the riverfront, but I was going down the drain by the minute and I didn't have what it took to refuse.

"Sure," I said.

It wasn't until I'd followed him out onto the corner that it occurred to me to ask how he knew where to find me.

"Your mother outed you," he said.

The choice of words was chilling. I hugged my sweater around me and pulled the sleeves down over my hands.

"You cold?" he said.

"I'll warm up when we get going."

I turned toward Bull Street, hoping we would move in the direction of home, but he steered me west on Perry, where the walking crowd had thinned to a trickle of tourists in search of dinner. It was as private as you could get in a public place.

"You know," he said, "sometimes it's hard for me to separate me as your future father-in-law from me as your pastor. Does that make sense?"

He looked down from his six-foot height, down the long, slim nose that gave him a profile that seemed cut from smooth granite. He had dark eyes like Seth and the same dark hair, frosted with grey as if Randi had sent him to her colorist. Unlike my father, he was classic handsome. Also unlike my father, he was one to beat so far around the bush you couldn't remember where you'd started.

I wasn't in the mood for bunny trails.

"You want to talk about Seth and me, but as my pastor, not as Seth's father," I said. "Right?"

"Right." He sounded a little disappointed. He'd probably had a whole homily planned, and under different circumstances I probably would've even enjoyed it. I longed for different circumstances.

"I'm going to tell you what I've told everyone else," I said. "We're not ready to get married."

"Actually I wasn't going to ask you about that." Paul's smile was wistful. "Seth's made it perfectly clear he doesn't want to discuss it with me."

"I know he's hurt and I'm sorry."

Paul curled his fingers around my upper arm at the corner of Perry and Whitaker and let a carriage go by. The hooves of the Percheron clopped on the Belgian stone in rhythm with the driver's soft patter about the Sorrel Weed House. Her two fortyish passengers weren't listening. He was nuzzling her neck while she tugged at the lapel of his tweed jacket and laughed without sound.

Right on cue.

"Seth *is* hurting," Paul said as we crossed Whitaker and turned south on it. He let go of my arm. "But so are you, and you're the one I'm concerned about right now."

I started to say I was fine but decided to save my breath for the fast pace he'd established with his long legs. I knew he wouldn't have believed me anyway, not from the concern carved into his face like the words below the statues in the squares.

"Let's cut to the chase," he said. "Something is going on with you—some anxieties, some doubts—things that go deeper than just not being ready to get married. How am I doing so far?"

He looked down at me again, face fatherly, ready for me to pour out my soul to him. I'd done that once when I was fourteen and convinced that no one understood me. Nobody understood now either, but this time he wasn't going to be the one to help me sort that out.

"It's not that deep, really," I said.

He stopped at the corner of Harris. "You won't join me for coffee and dessert? We can cut right through here and go to the—"

"No. Thank you. I really need to get home."

Paul nodded as if that had been his idea in the first place. "Then let's head that way," he said.

We were still ten blocks from Gaston Street. Plenty of time for him to try to ferret out the issues I didn't have.

"Where are you with God right now?" he said.

"I'm good," I said. Was that blasphemous?

"Okay."

We walked in silence for a block, during which I wanted to cave. He was just doing his job as my pastor. If he had all the information, he would be talking to his son, not me. I couldn't blame him. Not really.

Just after we passed Madison Square he said, "I can understand why you don't want to talk to me about this. I just thought it was worth a shot since we go way back."

"I'm sorry," I said for the eightieth time that day. And I was.

"Don't be. You have to feel comfortable with whoever you talk to, and I want you to talk to someone. I know some great counselors, one of them I think you'd really relate to. She's—"

I stopped so abruptly he took three steps beyond me before he realized I'd done it. I left my attempt to cut him slack back at the corner. "Why do I need a counselor?" I said.

"Because you're confused. Maybe a little depressed."

I dug my fingernails into my palms through the sweater. "We're separating you as Seth's father from you as my pastor?"

He smiled down at me. Come to think of it, he was doing everything down at me. "We're trying," he said.

"Then I'm saying this to you as my pastor: I am not the one with the issues."

"I'm not saying Seth doesn't have his, but Tara, there are always two sides." He shoved his hands into his pockets more roughly than he meant to, I was sure. The softening of his eyes was deliberate. "If you can't work this out together, then at least try to work out your individual stuff separately or you'll never have a chance at a relationship." He pressed his lips together before he finished with, "And that is your pastor talking."

I could have said at least five things that would have made Paul my pastor order an immediate exorcism. He didn't deserve any of them. But since there were no other options, I didn't say anything except—

"Thanks for being concerned. I'll work it out, okay? I'll work it out."

Then I turned and ran, undoubtedly leaving Paul the whoever convinced that I was just as messed up as he thought I was.

T E N

For the next two days I slept and worked and tried to forget that I was supposed to be getting married on Saturday. Seth made that last one hard to do.

Thursday he insisted we go for a drive, and I gave in on the condition that we wouldn't talk about *it*. We went to Hilton Head and back before I made him take me home. The whole thing had turned into a shouting match—about *it*—that neither of us had a chance of winning.

That was why on Friday, the night we should have been celebrating our rehearsal dinner at the Harper Fowlkes House, I drove instead in the slapping rain to the townhouse and banged on the door. I still had a key but I didn't want to walk in on something.

Seth answered immediately wearing the sweats I'd seen hanging over the desk chair and a *Choose Life!* T-shirt with a glob of turquoise toothpaste stuck to it. His face didn't light up when he saw mine. He seemed to have stopped hoping. Maybe that would make this easier.

As he let me in he gave my head a dry touch. "Hey," he said.

"Hey," I said.

"I was just about to make some eggs."

"I'm not staying." I rewrapped my sweater and tried to remember what I'd rehearsed on the way over.

"You don't want to try out the new couch?"

For the first time I realized the living room was full of the furniture we'd picked out as we giggled and dreamed and tried out every chair in Georgia Furniture and Interiors. I had spent hours after that envisioning what the designer called casual elegance—a subtle palette of cream and blues, mixed with chrome and bright overstuffed pillows—and imagining us with our feet up on striped cube ottomans, snuggling on the rounded couch that pushed us together. Seth had arranged it just the way we planned; even the throw pillows were set at perfect angles. But it looked so cold and impersonal it might as well still be in the showroom.

"I can't," I said.

Seth dragged both of his hands through his hair. "What does that mean?"

"It means . . . until you get help, I just can't see you. That's what it means."

His face blanched. "I need *your* help, Tar. I can't do this without you beside me."

"I would walk beside you if you were going anywhere. But what are you doing? Just saying you're going to stop? Trying to will yourself to do it? That obviously doesn't work."

"I'm looking for help." Seth parked his hands on his hips and stared at the ceiling as if the crown molding could be the source of aid. "I've been going to the church every morning before work and every night after, and just sitting there begging God to take this away. I go to sleep praying. I wake up praying."

His voice caught, and something in me sagged and softened.

"Is it helping?" I said.

"Have I stopped having urges, you mean?"

"I guess that's what I mean. I don't even know how to think about this."

He shook his head. "I just keep coming back around to the same thing. If I had you, right here with me all the time, I wouldn't need—"

"You can't put this all on me, Seth! We were twenty days away from that and you couldn't wait. What makes you think my living here is going to make any difference?"

"Because then I'll know you aren't going to leave me. Then I'll have a reason to keep fighting. Please, Tar. I know you said you'd wait, but if I can't even see you, I don't know if I can believe that."

The air itself became heavy with the words that pressed on my head. *I need YOUR help. If I had YOU with me all the time. If YOU gave me a reason.*

You, Tara. All you.

But that wasn't what I came to hear, and agreeing to it wasn't what I came to say.

"I can't," I said. "It has to be you first. You have to show me you'd do it whether I was here or not. Until then, I can't see you anymore."

"Tar—"

"I can't look at you and want you and get pulled back into what we hoped our life was going to be. I can't—and that isn't just for me, Seth. That's for you."

I turned to go. He groped for me and found the tail of my sweater, and he used it to pull me against him until our lips were close.

"If you leave me alone with this I'll fail. I know I'll fail."

I shook my head. "If I stay, you'll never even try."

Why he still attempted to press his mouth against mine, I didn't know, but it was the final thing that made me wrench away. Because never before had he tried to manipulate me with a kiss. And it was so wrong. So very wrong.

"Don't," I said, and once more yanked myself from him. I caught my foot on the leg of the chair that was never there before and stumbled toward the door in a headlong rush to be gone—before I could change my mind.

Only Seth's voice crying, *"Tara!"* tried to pull me back. I slammed the door on it and ran, down the sideways steps I loved so much and across the bumpy brick sidewalk to my Mini Cooper. If I had locked it I might still be standing there, trying to find the button on the key amid the tears and the rain and the blacked-out vision that was never going to come again. As it was, I pulled the car door open too hard and slipped back almost to the ground on the slick leaves. By the time I got into the driver's seat and closed myself in, I was crying so hard I had to sit there until I was sure my heart was still beating.

Seth didn't come out after me. That was the only thing that finally allowed me to turn the key and pull away from the curb at Jones Street.

Where I was going from there I had no idea. Everything I thought of—*Just drive around the squares* or *Cruise down Bull Street* or even *Go to Lexi's apartment*—only taunted me with the memory of where I was supposed to be going tonight and who I should be seeing and what I should be doing. No. No more visions. No more dreams. No more memories.

I put on the brakes so hard at Liberty and Montgomery, the tires grabbed and I lurched forward and back. If I didn't have any of that, what did I have? What else was there to live on?

All I could think to do was get away from it, and as fast as possible. Go someplace else, out of Savannah, where there were no jeering reminders.

꧁꧂

Fritzie didn't come to mind until I was ten miles south of town, headed inland, where the Georgia pines mixed in with the nearly leafless oaks and the deep forests on either side of Interstate 95 seemed shriveled and forlorn, just like me. A green sign indicated that Jesup was fifty-six miles. That was the town where our sometime-nanny lived.

I hadn't seen Fritzie since my wedding shower. She'd texted me several times after Mama told her the wedding was postponed until further notice, but I hadn't answered. My phone was so full of unreturned messages it would take me days to go through them. If I wanted to.

Now, though, wouldn't Fritzie be the one to go to? Not to tell her everything but just to be in her raspy-voiced, Bohemian presence and chill? That was what she used to tell Kellen and Seth and little Evvy and me when she was hanging with us for a weekend while the parents went off to a church conference or some business thing.

"We've been doing stuff all day," she would announce after a full morning and afternoon of Burger King and Baskin-Robbins and the roller rink and all the other things said parents never took us to (even then I couldn't imagine my mother at the roller-skating rink in an Ann Taylor ensemble). "So now we're going to chill."

That meant a movie marathon—always something very boyish and noisy and full of cartoon punching and explosions—and her homemade pizza—and me falling asleep with my head in her lap, which always smelled like patchouli. Every time I'd gotten a whiff of that passing someone's dorm room in college, I'd felt a wave of homesickness for Fritzie.

Yeah. I should go to Jesup and curl up on her ancient yard-sale couch and let her brew me some kind of tea she'd made up from the things growing on her windowsills. She wouldn't try to get me to dish, or tell me I needed to reveal "whatever it is" to some neutral party, or attempt to convince me that the problems were all mine. She wouldn't tell me I was better off without Seth. She would just let me chill.

I drove as far as the Georgetown exit before it occurred to me that I should call her before I just showed up at her door. It was Friday night. She could have a date.

Okay, that wasn't entirely plausible. Fritzie was into the second half of her thirties now, and her prospects for getting married and having her own kids seemed to grow thinner every time I saw her. She wasn't the lean, raven-haired hippie who looked great without makeup anymore. The years had added pounds to her waist and an early cragginess to her face and a sardonic outlook to her whole being. At my shower she'd said to me, "Better you than me, honey, but I wish you all the best." I'd thought at the time that was kind of an inappropriate thing to say, but none of the appropriate things were working now, were they?

I got off on the Richmond Hill exit and pulled into the parking lot of a convenience store to call her on her cell. I almost gave up after three rings but on the fourth she answered with a breathless, "Hey, girlfriend!"

At the sound of her cigarette alto I sank into the seat. "Hey, Fritz."

"I've texted you, like, twelve times. How you doin', girl?"

"Not good," I said. "I thought I'd come see you."

"Awesome. No, I want them fried. Who eats calamari that's not fried?"

I held the phone out and blinked until I realized she was talking to someone else. Country music blared behind her voice.

"Sorry," she said. "When are you coming?"

"Um . . . now? I'm on my way."

"Now's not gonna work, babe. I'm in Panama City Beach."

"Oh."

"I took time off for your wedding, so I thought as long as I was on vacation I oughta get away."

"Sure," I said.

"Sounds like you need to get away too. Listen, do you just want to go to my place? The key's under the mat. I don't *think* there's anybody sleeping there tonight." She laughed—something akin to sandpaper rubbing on a two-by-four—but I got the feeling she was serious.

"That's okay," I said. "I'll do it another time."

"I'm planning on coming up for Christmas Day," she said. "Madeline said I should still come."

"Good," I said. "That's—that'll be good."

"Hey—are you okay?" The sandpaper softened to a finer grade.

"Not really," I said. "I did get a job."

"I need another one of these. His is on me too. Sorry, Tara—what?"

"No worries," I said. "I'll see you Christmas Day."

"You sure you're okay?"

Did I not just say I wasn't? This was a mistake. But then, actually, maybe everything I did was a mistake.

"Yes," I said. "Have a good time."

I ended the call and dropped my phone into my bag. Then I drove south some more and turned around at the next exit and went back to Savannah. The rain stopped, but the kind of drizzle that makes you adjust your wipers over and over continued to dot the windshield. Between that and turning the defroster on and off, I could see, then I couldn't see, then I could see again. By the time the pines gave way to the live oaks again, I wanted to scream. Maybe I would have if the phone hadn't jarred with jazz piano.

Seth.

What was it about "I can't see you; I can't talk to you" that he didn't understand?

I let it stop ringing, but I pulled into the parking lot of the bank next to the Distillery and waited for the voice mail. When it came, I didn't listen to it. I just called him back. Maybe it *was* time to scream.

"Tara," he said. His voice was faint. "I took too many."

The scream died in my throat. "Too many what? What are you talking about, Seth?"

"I took too many pills. I can't do this—but I wanted to say good-bye and tell you I love you."

"Where are you? Are you home?"

"I'm at our home," he said.

The call didn't end—I could hear rustling and thumping—but he didn't say any more, even when I cried into the phone, "Seth! Seth, answer me!"

There was nothing.

~*ℓℓℓ*~

What I did and how I did it, I'm not sure. Whatever it was, it brought my father and a screaming ambulance and several flashing police cars to the townhouse moments after I got there and found Seth half on, half off the couch. His eyes were almost closed and his chest rose and fell so slowly I expected his next breath to be his last. Sweat gleamed on his forehead and his upper lip—everywhere his pale skin was visible. When I leaned over him, a strong odor of urine filled my nose.

Faceless voices asked me questions. *How long since you talked to him? How did he sound? How many pills did he take? What did he take?*

I wasn't even sure I answered, or how Daddy and I got to the hospital, or when Mama arrived. I sat pressed in my father's arms on the edge of a bench outside the ER watching the thick double doors that stood like sentinels between Seth and me, waiting for him to walk through them smiling and whole and no longer sweaty and pale. I wasn't even aware of Randi Grissom until I looked up and found her scalding me with her eyes.

"Are you satisfied now?" she said.

Daddy pushed me onto Mama, who was on the other side of me, and stood up. He looked past Randi at Paul.

"She needs to back off," he said—to the man he played golf with and went to men's retreats with and opened his Bible with every Sunday morning. "We're not going to do this."

Randi sidestepped Daddy and leaned down into my face. "Do you see what you've done? If he dies, Tara, it's on you."

"He's not gonna die! He won't die!"

"Paul," Daddy said.

Paul put an arm across Randi's chest from behind and pulled her back. That didn't stop her from spitting words at me.

"You crushed his whole world."

"Enough!" Daddy said. "Madeline, take Tara out of here."

Mama pulled me off the bench and walked with her arms around me through the automatic outer doors and into the glass foyer.

"Is she right?" I sobbed into her shoulder. "Is it my fault?"

"No, sweet darlin'. She's wrong. She's so wrong."

But was she? Didn't I leave him crying out my name? Didn't he tell me before I left the townhouse that I was the only way out for him?

"How are we doing?"

Daddy's voice pulled me out of Mama's arms and into his.

"Randi is out of her mind right now," he said into my hair. "But you listen to me. This is not your fault. A man makes a decision like that on his own. Nobody else is responsible."

"I shouldn't have told him I couldn't see him any more until he got it fixed."

Daddy took my face in his hands and searched my eyes. "Got what fixed, Tara?"

The doors sighed open behind us. "The doctor's coming out to talk to the family," said a woman in scrubs.

I broke away from Daddy and followed her back into the hallway where Randi and Paul stood staring at the double doors the same way I had. They opened just as we arrived and a small man in a white coat with glasses too large for his face came through. He wasn't Seth. I wanted him to be Seth.

Randi wasn't the only one out of her mind.

"You're Seth Grissom's family?" he said.

We gave him a chorus of yeses. Randi turned to me, eyes still searing, but Paul squeezed her shoulders and she looked away. I didn't care what she did. I was staying.

"I'm Dr. O'Brien," he said. "Seth's stable, okay? You got to him soon enough. This was a benzodiazepene overdose, but we've prevented it from going into his blood."

"So we can see him." Randi was already pulling away from Paul and moving toward the doors.

"He's still groggy. Pretty confused. We'll keep him on the Flumazenil IV until he comes around completely."

"We'll be able to take him home then," Paul said.

Dr. O'Brien looked slightly patronizing. "He'll be in ICU with one-to-one precautions for a bit and then we'll admit him to the psych ward for at least seventy-two hours."

"He doesn't need a psych ward," Randi said, more to me than to the doctor.

"Your son—he's your son?"

"Yes—"

"Your son tried to commit suicide, okay? We can't let him go home until we can be relatively certain he's not going to do it again, which means follow-up psychiatric treatment." He nodded as if we were all agreeing with him. "I think the fact that he called—one of you—before he lost consciousness is an indication that he didn't actually want to die. That's a hopeful sign. A psychiatrist will give you a better picture of his prognosis—"

"My son does not need a psychiatrist either—"

"This is the law, Ms. Grissom, okay? Our hands are tied."

"They should be."

"Randi."

Paul seldom used a tone that could even cut warm butter, but the one he took now would have sliced *me* open. It didn't have that effect on Randi, but she did turn away from the doctor and yank her cell phone out of her purse. She poked numbers as she stomped out of our earshot.

"Who is she calling at two o'clock in the morning?" Mama murmured to me.

"It's two a.m.?" I said.

"Past that," Daddy said.

"Wow," I said. "It's my wedding day."

E L E V E N

I wasn't allowed to see Seth. Randi refused to put me on his limited visitors list, and I knew if he asked for me, she wouldn't tell me.

As the wee hours crept their small way toward the light, I sat on the window seat in my room, clutching the tea Mama made me that had long since gone cold, and tried to form scenes in my head. But no scenario I could twist and mold and shape into something acceptable would come to me.

So I spent Saturday under the covers in my bed, drifting in and out of sleep. It was the only way to keep the spines of anxiety from stabbing through my chest and into all the other parts of me. Mama brought more tea and, later, cinnamon toast. Daddy came once and sat on the edge of the bed. Kellen didn't, and I didn't ask anyone why.

Sunday I climbed out at about ten a.m. I had to be at work at two, and although my first three shifts hadn't brought me much closer to the efficient employee Wendy told me Ike wanted, I was eager to get to the Piebald and push the pain way back someplace where it couldn't spear into me every time I opened my eyes.

I was so eager, in fact, that I got there at twelve and sat at the small bar whose stools were within a few feet of the food counter. From there I could watch the morning shift people take orders and serve pastries and talk to the customers. I absorbed a whole lot more than when I was in the middle of it trying to catch up with myself.

Every time the image of Seth's eyes half-open and his hand dangling over the empty Xanax container tried to form in my mind, I smacked it out of the way and focused on how Zoo-Loo brewed a cup of Darjeeling or Ike coaxed a couple into adding two cranberry-walnut muffins to their coffee order. Smooth and cool and intentional. That was the way to be.

It was almost time for my shift when Ms. Helen appeared at the counter. She was the one with the salt-and-pepper bob and the round red-framed glasses whose sandwich order I'd botched. I hesitated on my way to grab my apron and watched her laugh with Ike as if she were delighted by his every word. And not just as if. I had only seen her twice, but I couldn't imagine her doing anything that wasn't genuine.

As she turned to take a steaming mug to a table, she caught me watching her and her hazel eyes brightened.

"How is it going, honey?" she said.

"I don't know," I said. "You'll have to ask Ike."

Ms. Helen looked straight at him, and the pause made me sorry I'd asked. Ike didn't do anything that wasn't genuine either.

"I think she's gonna be all right, Ms. Helen," he said. "We're starting her on coffee drinks today."

"She'll just be smashing," she said.

Ike grinned at me when she'd gone down the ramp to her table. "Did she just use the word *smashing*?"

"She totally did."

"I love that woman."

I didn't see how anybody wouldn't.

Wendy was off that day and we weren't slammed, so Ike took

every spare moment to teach me how to make lattes—so *that* was how they did it—and cappuccinos and mochas. The instructions were posted above the steamers and espresso makers, but I set a goal of not having to look at them by two days from then. I kept telling myself it was helping me forget.

"Take a break," Ike told me around four thirty. "The dinner crowd will be here in about thirty minutes, so now's your chance. Although"—he did the one-finger thing to push back his fedora—"the Sunday before Christmas? I'm not sure it'll actually be a crowd. You have big plans for the holidays?"

The shift was so subtle I almost didn't catch it. When I did, I fumbled all over myself. Fortunately I wasn't attempting to make a caffè americano at the time.

"No. I mean, I did, but then . . . it's just going to be family."

"No boyfriend?" he said.

"Not anymore."

For the love of the land, why did I *say* that?

Ike pressed his lips into a line and then said, "Sorry to hear that."

"Me too. But it's okay . . . you know . . . I'll be fine . . ."

"Yeah, but that's tough at Christmastime."

Something dinged. Literally saved by the bell, I pretty much ran to the toaster oven and pulled out the pear and Brie.

"That's for Ms. Helen," Ike said.

"I'll take it to her," I said.

"We don't usually do table service, but in this case, yeah, that would be nice."

When I delivered sandwich, chips, and napkin to Ms. Helen at the rickety-looking table in the corner next to the Christmas tree, she seemed to think it was more than nice.

"Well, bless your heart," she said. "Aren't you just the sweetest thing?"

"I'm not supposed to make a habit of it," I said. "But I wanted to thank you."

"I can't imagine what for." She patted the seat of the chair next to her. "Can you sit for a minute?"

"I'm on break," I said. "I guess it's okay. I don't even know all the rules yet."

"I think it's fine. You might want to take off your apron. They usually do."

I wasn't sure who *they* were, but I pulled it off and slipped into the chair. It rocked unevenly on the floor.

"Now, I just can't stand that," Ms. Helen said. "Let me fix it."

I sat there, eyes popping, as she reached into a rather large red-print quilted bag, pulled out a slim wooden wedge, and slid it under one leg of the chair.

"How's that?" she said.

"Perfect," I said. "You actually carry a shim in your purse?"

"Several of them. I love the Piebald, but honey, there isn't an even-legged chair or table in the place and that is a fact."

I really wanted to know what else was in that bag.

"Now, what did you want to thank me for?"

"Oh. You've just been so encouraging since I started working here." I glanced over my shoulder, but no one was sitting closer than three tables away. "I'm still a mess back there—"

"No, you are not. I've been watching you. You're lovely with the customers."

"Even when I give them the wrong sandwich?"

"Who could ever be upset with *you*? You're just as darlin' as you can be."

The tears were in my eyes before I could stop them, and they threatened to brim over onto my face. Ms. Helen reached into the bag, pulled out a Kleenex, and tucked it into my hand.

"This time of year can be so hard," she said, gazing briefly at the Christmas tree hung with art student ornaments. "That's one of the reasons I moved here after my husband died. I spent the first year still in Charleston trying to keep up with all our traditions, and it just broke my heart. I decided in January I wasn't doing that again, so in February I came here and just started over." She folded sweatered arms lightly on the tabletop. "My friends told me I'd be home in six months, but, honey, I think this is home now. Savannah wraps its arms around you and says, 'Why don't you stay? You know you want to.'"

"I guess it does," I said. "It's always been home to me."

I closed my eyes, but a few drops still escaped. The rest were caught in my throat.

"I'm so sorry," Ms. Helen said. "I'm so sorry."

There was no invitation to share more. We just sat in silence. A silence I could have bundled up in like a big quilt. Made by Ms. Helen.

That night I fell into a real sleep that didn't take me into dreams as dark and twisted as a Hieronymus Bosch painting. I was so sleep deprived it was going to take several more nights like that for me to feel human again, but that one was enough to get me out of bed and off to work, again two hours early. Any downtime just brought back images of Seth hanging off the couch or Seth begging me to help him. Or me refusing.

So that was my rhythm for the next few days, Monday the twenty-second and Tuesday the twenty-third. I went to the coffee shop at noon and watched the morning shift, which was helping my performance tremendously according to Wendy, and worked my own shift and then stayed a little after to chat with Ms. Helen. Actually she did most of the chatting while I listened to her life story, in complete gratitude that she didn't ask me any questions. It was nothing, really, and yet it felt like something.

I planned to do almost the same thing on Wednesday, Christmas Eve, but Mama put the kibosh on that.

"Okay," I said to her deflated face. "We're closing at five. I'll be home in time for dinner and the service and everything."

"Please do," she said. Tears were about to splash into the piecrust she was crimping. "Or Daddy will be so disappointed."

I knew Daddy wasn't the only one who was feeling the stinginess of this Christmas. GrandMary didn't come back after all. All the relatives who had planned to stay in town after the wedding had made other plans, probably to avoid the awkwardness that had become our life. It would just be the four of us, and it probably hadn't escaped my parents that Kellen wasn't talking to me.

"We'll make it wonderful," I said.

And then I sobbed all the way to the Piebald.

The snot-producing crying necessitated a trip to the bathroom to put myself back together. When I came out, Ike was standing there as if he'd been waiting for me. He was wearing a tie with a rather skinny Rudolph the Red-Nosed Reindeer cascading down it, and he had a sprig of holly in the band of his fedora. I hadn't even thought about wearing anything festive.

"Can you start now?" he said. "One of my people didn't show up."

"Sure," I said.

"I'll pay you time and a half."

"You don't have to."

Ike looked at me curiously. "Have you ever actually *had* a job before, Tara?"

"Yes," I said. "Kind of."

"Okay, rule number one for being an employee: never turn down extra money."

"Got it," I said. And felt like I was five years old.

I tied on my apron and got to the counter just as a woman rushed up the ramp with her red-haired ponytail swinging and her startling brown eyes already pointed at the pastry case.

"Is that all you have left?" she said. Her voice was gravelly but not in a way that grated on me. It actually made me want to laugh.

I turned to let Ike handle it but he wasn't there.

"Really—are those all the baked goods you have left?" she said.

I looked into the case at two lonely scones, three muffins, and a dozen Christmas tree cookies.

"Let me check," I said. "Can you just wait right here?"

"Where else am I going to go? I've been to every bakery and coffee shop that's open and you've got more than any of them. Why does everybody stop baking at nine o'clock in the morning?"

I listened to all of that, nodding for no apparent reason, until she looked pointedly toward the kitchen.

"Oh, right," I said. "Let me just go see."

I turned around, took two steps, and ran into Ike.

"Do we have any more baked goods in the back?" I whispered.

"Yes," he whispered back. "We have another batch of cookies that'll be ready in about ten minutes."

"Good. This lady wants them."

"Okay. Tara."

"What?"

"Why are we whispering?"

I let out a guffaw, and Ike grinned at me.

"You're killin' me, girl," he said. "You're killin' me."

I delivered the good news to the red-haired woman, who looked as if I'd told her that her German shepherd didn't have to be put down after all. Surely she had a German shepherd. Maybe two.

"Can I get you something to drink while you wait?" I said. "I can make you a mean latte."

"Make me a *nice* black coffee and you're on," she said.

As I poured her a cup of the Piebald House Blend I considered her voice some more. She had the Savannah dropping of *g*'s and elongating of vowels going on, but the accent sounded a little faded, as if some Yankee influence had come in and tried to steal it away. Something edged on aggressive about her. Assertive—that's what she was.

I needed to get me some of that.

"Here you go," I said. "Ike's boxing up your goodies and you can pay him at the register."

"You just saved my life," she said. "If I showed up at my mother's empty-handed I'd be in even worse with her than I am already."

The woman had to be thirty-five. But then, your mother is your mother, no matter how old you are.

"I hear that," I said.

She stuck her hand out across the counter. "Gray Murphy," she said.

"Tara Faulkner," I said.

"Any relation to William?"

"I hope not."

"Girl after my own heart. What's with the sentences that go on for three pages?"

"I know, right? You can never find the end of them and when you do, you forget what was at the beginning."

"Thank you. People think he's the father of Southern literature. Right. The *alcoholic* father."

"Oh, yeah," I said. "He was invited to speak to a group of aspiring authors at Harvard one time and he got there drunk, staggered out on the stage, and said—I guess slurred—'You people want to write?' They were all, 'Yes!' And he said, 'Then go home and write.' And then he, like, stumbled off the stage."

Gray gave me a long, sober look. "Oh. My. Gosh. I love that so much. Love. It. Where did you hear that?"

"Grad school," I said.

"Here you go," Ike said behind me. "Tara, you want to ring this up?"

"Glad to," I said.

"Listen," Gray said, "I'm leaving you a good tip. This is the first decent conversation I've had since I came back here." She tapped the counter with her wallet. "I like you."

I wanted to hug her.

~ 𝓵𝓵𝓮 ~

Christmas was another montage, a series of scenes I acted my way through with a less than stellar performance while Elvis sang "Blue Christmas." Our traditional Christmas Eve shrimp and crusty bread supper in front of the fireplace. Our family walk to the church on Johnson Square—one of Georgia's white-pillared mother churches that had tried to die in the 1970s and had been resurrected by a young Paul Grissom a little over thirty years ago. The candlelight service blossoming with carols and poinsettias and scripture I could have recited right along with Daddy as he stood at the lectern and read the nativity story in his sonorous baritone. The return home to open one gift before we toppled into bed. The Christmas morning of torn paper and tearful thank-yous and a warm loaf of Mama's banana bread.

We reenacted those scenes every year, yet this time each one was missing a piece and demanded a retake.

Kellen remained peevish over the Christmas Eve supper. When

one out of four people around a coffee table isn't talking, the conversation of the remaining three tends to be fairly stilted. I ate two shrimp.

En route to the church, when we usually followed Mama and Daddy and reminisced about Christmases past, Kellen did speak to me. He said, "I don't blame you for Seth trying to take himself out. But you could've helped him. I told you he needed you to help him." I stared at him in the light of the tree in the square just to make sure it was still my brother I was walking with. I didn't respond.

None of the Grissoms were in church except, of course, Paul. Seth was supposed to get out of the hospital Tuesday. This was Wednesday. Randi must be afraid to leave him alone. Seth had never missed a Christmas Eve service, even the year he had strep throat and couldn't croak out "Silent Night."

Back home, sitting at the foot of the family room Christmas tree—one of three in the house—the gift I opened was from Mama. It was a white flannel nightgown. Perfect for a winter honeymoon in Ireland.

I didn't crawl happily into bed and squeeze my eyes shut so I could fall asleep and make morning come fast. This was supposed to be my first Christmas married to Seth. I should be spooned against him under the snowy comforter and turning to him to make love. I didn't want to close my eyes. I knew I would only see flashes of things that weren't lovemaking at all.

I wondered what Seth saw now when he closed his eyes. It was a tormenting thought that kept me awake until Christmas morning dawned blue and clear and scoffing in its beauty.

We all tried—even Kellen—to salvage some joy as we opened our presents, but nobody's acting skills were up to the challenge. Finally, midway through the pile that Mama had added to for a week, perhaps in the hope of filling in the gaping hole in the festivities, I broke down.

"I'm so sorry," I told them. "I've ruined everything and I'm sorry."

Heads shook, except for Kellen's, and there were murmurs of "no" and "stop" and "we'll be okay."

"There's always next year, sugar," Daddy said. "And who knows what will happen between now and then?"

"Good things," Mama said. "All good things."

Those could start anytime they wanted to.

Fritzie's arrival around noon improved the atmosphere. She joined Mama and me in the kitchen, arms full of containers of her usual odd cookie concoctions and homemade salsa that was probably hotter than the surface of the sun and a black-bean-and-rice casserole flecked with red pepper. She always brought something that clashed with Mama's Christmas dinner menu, but my mother was too gracious to tell her. We would all "bless her heart" over it when she was gone.

Well, maybe not all of us. If Kellen was giving *me* the cold shoulder, the one he turned to Fritzie was of glacial proportions. He barely looked at her when he passed through the kitchen to refill a bowl of Chex Mix for him and Daddy.

"Merry Christmas to you too, buddy," Fritzie said when he'd gone back to the family room. "What's his damage?"

"We're all a little on edge this year." Mama's teetering voice offered proof.

"I'm here to fix that. What we need is some eggnog." Fritzie wiggled the eyebrows she'd stopped plucking several years ago and which reached toward each other over her nose like baby spiders.

"I didn't pick up any," Mama said. "I don't think there are any stores open today, do you?"

"Mama Faulkner, this is me you're talking to," Fritzie said. "I brought the fixin's. This is going to be the real deal."

She proceeded to unload a gallon of milk, a dozen eggs, and enough whipping cream to top half the pies in the historic district. While Mama and I tried to mash potatoes and make gravy and squeeze the green-bean casserole into the oven next to Fritzie's beans and rice, she took up one whole counter with her mixer and a bowl the size of a washing machine. I'd never seen someone whip for that long.

"When are we drinking this, Fritzie?" Mama said, eyeing the growing tub of foam.

Daddy was carving the turkey and simultaneously batting away droplets of nog that spattered his way. Kellen and I were ferrying dishes to the table in the dining room. Fritzie was still whipping with no sign of stopping.

"Anytime we want," she said.

And then as we all stared she unscrewed the cap from a fifth of Jim Beam and poured the entire thing into the mix.

"This," she said, "is exactly what this family needs."

The look on Daddy's face brought a chortle out of me that quickly morphed into uncontrollable laughter. If his eyebrows had gone up any farther they would have met in the back of his head. Mama tried to smother a giggle but was unsuccessful. Even Kellen gave up a grin.

"What?" Fritzie said, eyes wide.

"I'm getting a buzz just looking at it," Daddy said. "Let's eat."

Nobody drank any eggnog with dinner, but the conversation sounded like we'd all put our entire heads into the bowl and come out snockered. Mama couldn't put two words together and giggled at every outrageous thing Fritzie said, and since Fritzie pretty much didn't stop talking through the entire meal, Mama's husky laughter was constant from the lobster bisque to the coffee and mints. Daddy egged Fritzie on—pardon the pun—to recount her escapades with the families she'd nannied. I spewed cranberry sauce or gravy more than once when she delivered a punch line, and although Kellen didn't actually join in, he at least didn't leave the table until Fritzie finally leaned back in her chair and groaned and said, "Why did y'all make me eat so much? You're cruel."

She did, however, pour herself a tumbler of the nog while Mama, Daddy, and Kellen cleared the table. Then she dragged me by the sleeve out to the sunroom and plopped herself down onto the bright green canvas cushion on one of the curved-cane chairs, splashing the white stuff onto one hand even as she motioned for me to sit with the other one. I feared for the table tree with its plaid ribbons and antique Santas.

"All right, child," she said. "Let's talk about Seth."

"Do we have to?" I said. "I was actually having a good time."

"We don't have to . . ." Fritzie poked a finger into the glass and pulled out a dollop of foam that she deposited into her mouth.

The pause to savor, eyes closed, gave me a chance to line up how I was going to handle this. Of all the people I'd grown up with, Fritzie was the one most likely to pry me open and coax out the truth. She was the one who got me to confess my suspicions about Santa at age five. At age six, she was the only one I told that I wasn't sure Jesus loved me because I sometimes picked my nose in private. At eight I sobbed when she left us to go to Jesup and take care of some other family's kids. And she was the first one I called and told that I was determined to marry Seth Grissom. I was fifteen, and she didn't laugh.

So, no, I didn't have to talk to her about him now. But if I did, if I told her the truth, I knew I could trust her.

"Do you want me to start?" she said.

"Okay," I said.

She took another long swallow from the nog and set it next to the Christmas tree. "You found out about him, didn't you?"

I was glad I wasn't drinking or I would have choked.

Fritzie nodded knowingly. "I know good guys are hard to find, but . . . and this could just be me . . . he's just a little too squeaky clean. Bordering on puritanical."

All right, so she obviously didn't know about the porn. Only because this was a new take on the situation did I not stop her.

Fritzie flipped her mass of greying, drying, fading hair over her shoulder. "Don't get me wrong. I know you're pure as the driven snow, whatever that actually means, but you still have some sensuality to you."

"Thanks?" I said.

"I don't know, though . . . Seth seems sort of asexual to me. Not that I have any evidence."

"For what?"

"For him being all hung up about sex."

I stopped breathing. If I didn't end this conversation right now, I might never start again.

"I changed my mind," I said. "I don't want to talk about Seth."

Fritzie deflated. "I'm sorry, sweet thing," she said. "I think I've been around the block one too many times. I've gotten bitter about men." She picked up the almost-empty tumbler and stared down into the dissolving foam. "I loved all you kids. You know that."

"I do."

"But you . . . you were always my favorite. You were the reason I stayed even after the boys got to be teenagers and your parents didn't really need me that much anymore."

She breathed in sharply through her nose. Fritzie the Jaded was turning back into Fritzie the Vulnerable, and I watched her struggle to turn that around.

"I know you still love me," I said.

"I do, and that's why I can't keep my mouth shut about this."

But please do, I wanted to say . . . so desperately I almost did.

"I don't know what went down between you two and you're obviously not going to tell me . . ."

"Please don't be hurt, Fritz," I said. "I'm not telling anybody."

Pain did pinch at her face, but she nodded. "I have to say this, though. You might have dodged a bullet."

I opened my mouth, but she put up a many-ringed hand. "You are a woman of passion. Untapped, maybe, but it's in there. And I don't think you'll find it with Seth. Just sayin'. That's all . . . I'm just sayin'."

"Okay," I said. And yet it wasn't. At all.

~~*♃*~~

Whatever Christmas cheer we'd managed to stir up settled back down to the bottom after that, and Fritzie left not much later. It was back to the four of us, and we gathered somewhat listlessly in the breakfast nook where Mama served us pie.

"I still get a kick out of her," Daddy said. "But she pushes the envelope, doesn't she?"

Mama squirted a ribbon of whipped cream from the can onto the rim of his wedge of mincemeat. "I think she's just lonely."

"There's a really good reason for that," Kellen said. "Like nobody can stand to be around her."

"Kellen!" Mama said.

Daddy chewed thoughtfully. "You kids used to love her."

"I still do," I said. "But she's definitely changed."

Kellen grunted. "Not that much."

I suspected there was an explanation behind that, but he wasn't giving it. Mama sat down with her pie and picked up her fork.

"I have one question," she said.

Daddy smiled at her. "What's that, darlin'?"

"What on earth are we going to do with all that eggnog?"

I could almost hear Kellen's face crack into a smile. I thought we'd saved a smidgeon of Christmas, until my cell phone rang and I looked at the screen.

"It's Paul Grissom," I said.

"You don't have to take that," Mama said.

"Don't," Daddy said.

"I'll talk to him," Kellen said.

I shook my head at all of them and answered.

"Tara?" Paul's voice was grim. "You need to come over."

"Now?" I said.

"If you can. Yes, now."

"Okay," I said. I ended the call and looked at my family, who had all pushed their pie away and with it the last hope that we could save a slice of Christmas Day.

"I've been summoned," I said.

⸙

They all offered to go with me—Mama with less enthusiasm than Daddy or Kellen—but I went alone so I could rehearse all the way across Whitaker Street.

TARA: If you're going to tell me again that Seth's suicide attempt was my fault, I have nothing to say that will make you change your minds.

RANDI: You got that right.

PAUL: Come on, now, let's reason together.

SETH: . . .

I couldn't fill in for Seth anymore. I wasn't sure he would even be there. No one had told me if he'd come home, and he hadn't tried to contact me. I'd made it pretty clear to him before the suicide attempt that I didn't want to talk, but couldn't somebody at least have told me if he was okay?

Paul jerked open the heavy front door with its beveled-glass window and set the lush evergreen wreath swinging on its hook. Even in the half-light of the foyer his face was pasty-white and his eyes were shot with red. He looked even worse than he did the night at the hospital.

"Thanks for coming over," he said as he led me down the long entryway toward the great room, as they called it.

Randi's Fiest ancestors glared at me from their overbearing ornate frames as I passed, as if to say that *they* certainly hadn't invited me. Seth and Kellen had given them names as kids, all along the lines of Pickle Face and Bulldog. And those were for the women. I avoided their eyes because at the moment they all reminded me of Randi, accusing me with every glance.

They made me say to Paul, "I don't know what else I can tell you."

He stopped just before the wide great room doorway and looked sadly down at me. "In a way, I hope you can't," he said.

The spiny ball of anxiety came back to life in my gut. The sight of Randi Grissom curled up in the oversized chair by the fireplace did nothing to lessen that. She was, of course, dressed in black ankle pants and a slim-fitting red tunic and her hair had been freshly highlighted and was brushed back severely from her face. That was all the same as always. But in twenty-five years I had never seen Seth's mother cry.

I looked around the room but Seth wasn't there. Evelyn was, however. She stood behind her mother, arms folded, looking strangely smug. I couldn't have dreamed this up if I was Steven Spielberg.

"You want to sit down, Tara?" Paul said.

Evelyn didn't give me a chance to. "I'll start," she said. "Did you know Seth was seeing prostitutes?"

All feeling left my body.

Despite her gasping sobs Randi was still able to get out, "Your claim is unsubstantiated, Evelyn. You don't *know* that."

I tried to look at Evelyn but even my gaze was paralyzed.

"The night after you and I talked," she said to me, "I waited outside the townhouse, and when he came out, around ten o'clock, I followed him. Right down to Montgomery Street." She glared at the top of her mother's head. "I *saw* him meet up with a hooker and go with her—"

"You have no way of knowing she was a hooker," Randi said.

"Mother. Really? Skirt up to her butt. Shirt down to her navel. Nosebleed heels. Hand inside his shirt before they exchanged hellos. Do you want me to go on?"

"No, we don't," Paul said.

"Merry Christmas, Mother," Randi said.

I could almost taste her bitterness. I would have agreed with her that Evelyn's timing was cruel, but the gloat disappeared from Evelyn's eyes as she looked at me again.

"I only told them tonight because yet *again* the conversation had turned to how *you* were responsible for the breakup and it was *your* fault Seth tried to off himself. I'm sick of it. You've always been decent to me—you're practically the only one who has—and I can't stand around listening to that anymore." Her face stiffened. "It's not like *I* ruined Christmas. Seth pretty much took care of that when he swallowed a bottle of downers."

"Shut up, Evelyn," Randi said. "Just shut. Up."

Evelyn flopped onto the love seat on the other side of the room next to the Christmas tree, pristine with white angels and silver stars and twinkling lights that tried their tiny hardest to enchant the room. They failed.

Paul nodded at the chair across from Randi and I took it. He sat on the arm of hers.

"Did you know this?" Randi's eyes, bloated though they were, could still bore into me. "Did you ever have any indication that something like this might be going on?"

Something like this? No. A wild-maned woman on a screen was one thing. This? No. No, Evelyn had to be wrong.

"What does not answering mean?" Randi said.

I shook my head. "I never suspected this, no." But why not? Was it such a leap from cybersex? Wasn't this just acting out what he couldn't do on the Internet? How long could that be satisfying?

If I'd been home, I would have thrown up.

"Evelyn, get Tara a glass of water," Paul said.

"You get it." Evelyn was halfway to the door, and she stopped to fry her mother with her eyes. "You wouldn't believe me if I had video to prove it. You think I'm making this up because I despise my brother. But I don't hate Tara. I'm doing this for her sake. Except . . . why did I even bother? You're not going to take my word for it."

The old house shivered as she stomped down the hall and slammed out the front door. I was doing a fair amount of shivering myself, and it wasn't all from the draft that settled over the room.

"I don't know if she's telling the truth or not," Paul said.

Randi slapped the other arm of the chair. "Of course she isn't. When have we ever been able to trust her?"

"Maybe you can," I said. And I only spoke my next words because I couldn't stand the injustice playing out in front of me. "It isn't out of the realm of possibility that Seth went to a prostitute."

Randi came up sharply in the chair. "Why would you even say that?"

"Because your son is addicted to pornography. I've seen him."

I watched two strong, in-control people shrivel before my eyes. Paul sagged on the arm of the chair until his chin grazed the front of his sweater. Randi's hands went to her face. The Grissoms were a portrait of crushing disappointment, and for a fleeting moment I was sorry I'd told them.

But only for a moment. Before an apology could even reach my lips, Paul got up and rubbed the back of his head.

"All right," he said. "I've talked to men about this. Just because someone looks at porn doesn't make him an addict. We overuse that word."

"He's an addict," I said.

"*If* he is, then he'll have to deal with it. We'll get him help."

"Stop." Randi's hands were now pressed to her temples as she bored in on me. "When did you see this?"

"I walked in on him," I said. "He was sitting in front of a computer watching a woman on top of some guy and he was masturbating. I saw it. I heard it. He admitted it. Or don't you believe me either?"

Paul was motionless. Randi's always-in-control face blanched as if she were about to be sick right there on the Persian rug. She'd demanded it of me, and I gave it to her.

But I felt cruel.

"I can't make any decisions about this right now," she said finally. "I'm too—I'm too stunned."

"You're right," Paul said.

Once again my sympathy for them evaporated. *They* were making the decision? What about Seth? Why wasn't he here in this room having this conversation with us?

"Where is Seth?" I said.

"He's still in the hospital," Paul said. "He's not doing as well as they'd hoped—"

"He's doing as well as can be expected." Randi was throwing darts at me again and, like Evelyn, I was sick of it.

"Can't you see now why I couldn't marry him?" I said. "But I didn't out him, did I? I haven't told a single person because I knew what it would do to him." Randi's mouth slit open but I plowed on. "And you want to know why I didn't help him? He won't help himself. Every suggestion is, 'No, that won't work,' and 'No, I can't do that.' So enough with the blaming me, Randi. This is Seth's responsibility and nobody else's."

Paul put his hand on Randi's shoulder. Thirty-five years of marriage must equip you with the signals that your spouse is about to project herself at somebody. "Okay, we're all upset. I think we need to postpone this discussion until we've had a chance to calm down."

I looked straight at him. "I may never calm down again. Just so you know."

"I understand where you're coming from." Paul pressed his palms together. "But until we can figure this out, can we count on you to continue to keep this to yourself?"

I wasn't sure about that. At all.

"I know you must have been about to break. That's a heavy burden to carry alone." He was in pastor mode. "Now that I know, you can come to me if you need to talk—"

"Fine," I said, because if he'd gone any further I might have snatched the nutcracker off the mantel and hurled it at him. "I won't tell anyone. But I still want to see him."

"When he comes home," Randi said. "The doctor says the visitors there are distracting him."

"What visitors?" I said.

"Just us," Paul said. "And Kellen."

I clamped my teeth together and stood up.

"This has been hard for you I know," Paul said. "We appreciate that you've kept quiet about this. That shows that you still love Seth."

"Yes, I do," I said.

And as I stomped just as hard to the front door as Evelyn had, I wondered if *they* did.

T W E L V E

I was grateful to go back to work the next day, Friday, and not only to avoid my parents' questions so I didn't have to lie. I had yet another memory I wanted to get away from.

The day after Christmas, it was tradition for the Faulkners and the Grissoms to have lunch together at Mrs. Wilkes' Dining Room on Jones and Whitaker. They served the best real Southern cuisine in Savannah—fried chicken, Brunswick stew, Tybee shrimp, pecan pie, and, of course, the "house wine": sweet tea. It was put on the table family style, and every December twenty-sixth for twenty years we had eaten there as one.

Until today.

So I was extra chatty with the customers at the Piebald that day, asking the residents what they did and whether they liked their work, and the visitors what they were loving about their stay in Savannah. I could spot the upscale tourists, women with white bobs and carefully tied scarves, their husbands, thin and tanned in loose sweaters, looking mildly disinterested. Only once did I think of Seth, to wonder if that was what we had been destined for.

"You're acing the friendliness," Ike told me when there was a break, "but could you work a little faster when we have a line down the ramp? You get through Christmas okay?"

I was once again caught off guard by the shift. "Yeah," I said. "And sorry about being slow. I'll try to pick it up."

"Attagirl." Ike pulled down the brim of the fedora and went off to the kitchen calling, "I need a refill on that broccoli cheese."

Wendy grabbed a rag and made circles on the counter. "If you say you're sorry one more time, I really am going to empty a dishpan over your head."

I picked up the tip box so she could wipe under it. "What do you *want* me to say when I make a mistake?"

"Nothing. Just fix it and move on. That's just, like, life." Wendy tossed the rag in the bucket under the sink and dried her hands on her apron. "Or haven't you made any mistakes yet?"

There was a hint of disdain in those violet eyes. Alyssa would have told her where to go, in detail. Jacqueline would have had a decent comeback. Lexi would have cried. Three weeks ago, I probably would have enumerated all of my wrongdoings and still said I was sorry. But I wasn't any of my friends. I wasn't even sure I was me.

"I'm just messing with you," Wendy said. "I didn't mean to hurt your feelings."

"You didn't," I said. "I've made my share of mistakes."

Wendy's eyes rolled. "Probably nothing like *my* grand faux pas. That's how you say it, right?"

I laughed. "Yeah. But how could you even be old enough to do anything that bad?"

"How old are you?"

"Twenty-five."

"Me too. And I bet I've made twice the mistakes you have in the same amount of time. And bigger ones."

"Are we having a contest?" I said.

I thought I saw a flicker of respect go through her eyes. "All I'm saying is that I don't waste a lot of time saying I'm sorry. I'm working my butt off with two jobs—and I'm trying to pay off a bunch of debt so I can phase out of one of them. And in the meantime, I'm fixing my stuff instead of just apologizing for it."

I nodded. This girl with the slightly top-heavy hourglass body and the National Velvet gaze wasn't a ditz queen by any means. I couldn't imagine her ever getting herself into the situation I was in.

"And one more thing," she said. "I am *so* not waiting for some guy to come rescue me."

I didn't think she needed to be rescued. Any man who tried was probably going to get knocked off his horse, armor and all.

Wendy was staring at me. "Why did I just tell you all that?"

"Um—"

"You're a really good listener."

I didn't have to respond, because a bald guy and his plump wife stepped up to the counter, heads tilted back so they could look at the chalkboard.

"You're looking for a nice bowl of soup, aren't you?" I said.

"You read my mind," the woman said.

⁓

I was happy to see both Ms. Helen and Gray, the ponytail lady who was in need of emergency baked goods on Christmas Eve, come in about an hour before my shift was over. What surprised me was that they sat together. What surprised me even more: when I hung up my apron they both beckoned for me to join them.

"It's a watch of women," Ms. Helen said when I slid into a chair at her usual table. The shim was in place again.

"A watch?" Gray said. "Is that like we're a group of security guards?" She arched a brow at Ms. Helen. "No offense, but I don't think you'd be that effective. Not unless you're packin' in your bag there."

"Oh, honey, no," Ms. Helen said, patting Gray's hand. Who patted people's hands anymore? I loved it. "Watch is the name for a group of nightingales."

"That's me all over."

"Would you rather I called us a drove?"

"I'm afraid to ask."

"That's a gathering of pigs."

"You're scarin' me, Ms. Helen." Gray looked at me. "Do you need a watch of women?"

Something echoed from a not-so-long-ago conversation—faint but sure. I couldn't grasp it but I said, "If it means do I need somebody to keep me from putting my cell phone in the freezer or something, probably so."

Gray grinned a wonderful grin that made her look like nothing if not a hobbit. "You've done that too? For me it's either that or I drop it down the toilet." The grin widened. "All right, the Watch it is. Although I'm still not clear on why we actually *need* a name—"

Ms. Helen patted *my* hand this time. "Have you eaten anything today, honey? You look like you'd drop over if I blew on you."

"I'm good," I said.

"Well, I beg to differ. Now, I got you this sandwich and I want you to eat at least half of it." She wrinkled her nose in a smile. "It's ham and Swiss. And I brought you some good mustard from home." She reached into her quilted bag and pulled out not a handgun but a jar. "I already spread some on there."

I smiled back and broke off a piece of the sandwich, which meant having to catch a warm string of cheese before it stretched across the table. Ms. Helen's eyes stayed on my every move. I was going to have to eat the thing.

"Now, Gray," she said. "Is that a family name?"

"No," Gray said. "I substituted it for Grainne, which nobody can pronounce. My mother read too much Gaelic fiction."

"I like it," I said, mouth full.

"Call me that at your peril. Seriously, do I look like a pagan princess to you?"

Since my only idea of what one looked like came from some TV miniseries, I shook my head.

"Are you from here?" Ms. Helen said to her.

"Originally. Then I went away and now I'm back."

I was right about the accent.

"Where'd you go?" Ms. Helen said, and to me she added, "Keep eating."

Gray tightened her ponytail. "You really want to hear this?"

"I wouldn't have asked if I didn't."

I believed that about Ms. Helen.

"I got married young—really young—like parents-having-to-sign-for-you young—and went away with the 'love of my life'"—she pinched quotations marks into the air—"to Montana."

"Oh, honey, now it's *cold* up there, isn't it?"

"You have to keep your mouth closed when you go out in the winter or your spit freezes." Gray grinned again. "Obviously I didn't do too well in that climate."

"Is that why you've come home?" I said. "Too cold?"

"Too cold outside and too cold inside. My husband turned out to be the most unfeeling human being on the planet. But what do you expect? He's an equine dentist."

"A what?" Ms. Helen said.

I pulled the last of the half sandwich away from my mouth. "He works on horses' teeth?"

"Yeah, there's not much need for empathy or chitchat in his line of work, and he brought that same attitude home with him. Only took me eighteen years to figure out he would rather look at a mare's molars than talk to me. I'm a slow learner."

"Well, now, we all want to make a marriage work," Ms. Helen said. "You can't beat yourself up for trying."

Gray looked at her soberly. "Then I will absolutely stop. Right now."

I couldn't tell if she was kidding or not. It didn't seem to matter to Ms. Helen. And it sure didn't matter to me. I was laughing. Really laughing.

I knew my parents, especially Mama, would like to see me come home still yukking it up, but my gaiety didn't last a block after I left the Piebald, and besides that, I was headed for the Mellow Mushroom, where Evelyn worked. If I could catch her on break, I had some things to say to her.

The Mellow Mushroom was across from the Soho South where Mama and I'd had lunch, and although it was hippie inspired it was more a roosting place for hipsters. They offered gourmet pizza, calzones, hoagies. Since Evelyn wasn't on break yet when I got there, I thought I should order something. I asked for an "Enlightened Spinach Salad" and motioned for Evelyn to meet me when she had a chance.

I sat in a booth under a mural depicting, of course, mushrooms and, inexplicably, a large cow and a steer that looked like they'd been painted by someone who *did* some serious 'shrooms in the sixties. For the holidays, LED stars were strung over the area where the pizzas were made, and on the counter was a small Christmas tree topped with a black top hat. The wreath behind the bar had a sparkly peace sign on it among the bows and berries. Jamaican music played and my server—who had multiple, painful-looking piercings and wore the hipster habit of vintage clothes that looked like they'd been slept in—swayed to it as she deftly maneuvered around a tall mushroom sculpture in the middle of the dining room.

"Here's your salad," she said. "Anything else?"

It was a good thing I didn't have anything in mind because she danced off before I had a chance to answer. I was okay with that. I picked at the spinach and watched Evelyn dodge the dough-tossers in the pizza area. She was in her element here.

Not so much anywhere else. She'd always been kind of an odd little girl, although at about age twelve, when I was seventeen, she started looking up to me. I'd stopped being girly at that point, though I was still a romantic in a literary sense, and she related to that some-how. She always wanted to know what I was reading, and I'd tell her and within two days I'd see her reading it too. She had *Wuthering Heights*, *Jane Eyre*, and most of Jane Austen's novels under her belt before she was halfway through middle school.

I remembered the day when I'd come home from Duke on spring break to meet up with Seth and go off to the Gulf with him. Evelyn was eighteen then, and she came to me as I was hoisting a suitcase onto the roof of the Audi and told me—how did she put it?—she respected me as an intellectual. She said she saw both her-self and me as being "individuals" and in her mind that bonded us. Then she said, "Okay, tell me—I've been dying—what are you doing your thesis on?"

"Flannery O'Connor and Robert Lowell," I said. "I'm delving into how their relationship might have influenced their respective work."

"You are a goddess," she said. "I love Flannery O'Connor. I think I *am* her."

I only barely succeeded in not laughing. "Then we totally need to talk," I told her.

"Please," she said.

We never got to, at least not about Flannery and Robert. Evelyn started college that summer at Stetson University, down in Florida, and I thought she would probably be head of the English department before September. But she came home in December and announced she wasn't going back. That was two years ago now, and she was showing no signs of ever doing anything but waiting tables at the Mellow Mushroom. And raising her parents' blood pressure.

Interesting. She was always the problem child. Not Seth.

"Where the heck are you?"

I shook myself out of my reverie as Evelyn inserted herself into the booth across from me. She was wearing a lumberjack-plaid shirt over a faded green T, a grubby long denim skirt Mama wouldn't have allowed in her kitchen, and clunky boots. Like everybody else who worked in there, she adhered to the bathe-once-a-week philosophy and wore a knit cap over the rope of hair that was washed even less frequently.

"I'm glad you came in," she said. "I'm sure nobody's told you Seth got out of the hospital this morning."

I shook my head.

"I heard my dad tell him not to contact you because you're overreacting."

My teeth came together so hard I felt my jaw muscles seize.

"Why aren't you, like, totally swearing your head off?" Evelyn said. "Oh, wait, that would be me."

"So they still don't believe you," I said.

"No. But whatever *you* told them, they believed that, even if you did overreact. There have been long, clandestine meetings. First with Mother. Then with Father."

Her sarcasm went past ironic, straight to caustic.

"I, of course, have been completely excluded from all of that, even though I'm the one who told them what was going on. If it wasn't for me, they'd still think he was the golden child. But like I told them, I did it for you."

"And that's why I came," I said. "I wanted to thank you."

"I told you my brother isn't what he pretends to be. And now you don't have to be the bad guy anymore."

"I appreciate it—"

"I know what it feels like," she said. "And it bites."

Her voice threatened tears. She tapped the table and escaped from the booth. Before I knew it, she was dodging pizza dough again.

—◌◌◌—

I was off Saturday but I got up early after another restless night, the skin under my eyes beginning to resemble elephant hide. I showered immediately and while I was in there I scripted how I was going to get past Randi and Paul to see Seth. I should have saved myself the effort because before I was even dried off I heard my cell tell me I had a text message.

It was Randi with another subpoena. *Come over ASAP.*

I might have flushed the phone down the toilet if I hadn't been so anxious to see Seth, to find out if Evelyn was right . . . to make sure he was still in there someplace even if she was.

—◌◌◌—

The wreath was already off the front door when I arrived—my hair still wet, no makeup—and this time it was Randi who greeted me.

She didn't say hello and neither did I. What I did say was, "I want to see Seth."

"He's in the great room. But Tara . . ."

She grabbed my forearm with fingers hardened by years of holding a tennis racket. I stared at them until she removed them.

"Don't upset him," she said. "He's still vulnerable."

I got around her and made my way past the disapproving ancestors. Paul and Seth sat in two of the three Queen Anne chairs by the fireplace, both of them with their hands hanging between their knees as they sat forward. I was clearly interrupting a deep conversation, and I would have backed out of the room . . . except *they* had summoned *me*. It was as if every effort were being made to assure that I would feel like the outsider in whatever was to follow.

Seth looked up and at first he didn't move, which gave me a chance to take him in. The last week had left him thin and removed some of the tone from his muscles, making him seem like a miniature version of himself. I could see the tendons in his face and the tremor in the hand that went to his knee and the fingernails bitten to the quick. What I didn't see was the trace of a twinkle in his eyes. They were glassy, as if he were medicated to just this side of consciousness.

Well, yeah. He probably was.

He stood up and his arms fell awkwardly to his sides. I'd never seen him do that before. In fact, I'd never seen him exhibit any body language that wasn't completely confident and coordinated. He looked like an ungainly adolescent who hadn't yet grown into his skin.

I couldn't let him stand there feeling as undefended as I did. I rounded the small table that had been placed between them, cluttered with coffee mugs, and cupped my hand to his cheek.

"Are you okay?" I said.

His face collapsed on itself and he broke into soundless tears.

"Didn't I tell you not to upset him?" Randi's heels tapped the hardwood and then muffled on the rug. "I'm not going to let you do this."

Seth's hand slid down my arm and closed on my hand and squeezed. "I'm okay now," he said in a voice thin as tissue paper. "Just because you asked me that, I'm okay."

I didn't know what was happening physically and verbally behind me, but by the time Seth got control of the tears and I turned around, another chair had been pulled up to the table, making four, and Randi was sitting in one of them, staring as straight-lipped as one of her great-grandmothers at the coffee mugs. When I sat down, nobody offered to fill one for me.

"I want to talk to Seth alone," I said.

Paul put a hand on Randi's arm and nodded at me. "That's up to Seth, but he wanted you here when he told us what he's decided to do."

I sagged a little with relief. At least *Seth* was the one who'd done the deciding. I cast a sidelong glance at Randi. With a mouth as hardened as that? She wasn't happy about the reins being in Seth's hands.

"When I was in the hospital," Seth said, "and by the way, that was probably the best thing that could have happened." He stopped Randi with a tearful look. "I know I freaked everyone out and I'm sorry. I really am. But while I was in there I talked to some people and got information about some programs. Really good programs." He looked at me. "Better than any of the ones you and I talked about."

I nodded him on.

"I signed up for one this morning after I talked to the director on the phone. It's a six-week intensive that helps Christian guys who struggle with sexual addiction."

"I still have trouble with you calling it an addiction," Paul said, looking at me as if I had personally coined the term. "Just because—"

"Dad, I can't sleep without watching porn before I go to bed. I need more and more all the time. I started doing things I don't even want to tell you about because you'd throw me out of the house."

Randi trained her eyes on me, her thoughts coming at me like bullets: nobody had told him about Evelyn's evidence and nobody had better do it now. No wonder Evelyn hadn't been included in this meeting.

"I leave Monday," Seth said.

"Leave?" Randi said. "For where?"

"Colorado."

"What about your job, son?" Paul said.

"They're giving me a leave of absence. Without pay. But at least they're holding my position for me."

"What reason did you give them?"

I was surprised Paul would ask that. What else could Seth tell them but the truth?

"I told them I needed to go into rehab." Seth looked down at his ravaged fingernails. "I didn't say what kind and they didn't ask. They were incredibly supportive."

"You didn't have to lie, then," Randi said. "Good. That may come in handy later on if there are any issues."

I stared from one of them to the other, until I realized I'd been doing the same thing for twenty-eight days: telling half-truths because apparently being addicted to illegal drugs or alcohol or prescription medications warranted support, but pornography, maybe not, so why take a chance? It was deceitful rather than discreet.

Paul looked around at each of us. "Then we still agree—"

"I'm not going to say anything to anyone," I said.

"That includes your parents," Randi said.

"Now, honey—"

"It's okay, Dad. I don't want Madeline and Dennis to know." Seth looked at me, his former pleading back in his eyes. "If—although I'm counting on when—we do get married, I don't want this to be a thing with them. For you or for me. Okay?"

So let me get this straight. Seth gets to come clean with his parents and relieve that pressure. Seth gets to go off for six weeks and put his life on hold while he gets help twenty-four/seven. Randi and Paul get to discuss it with each other and continue to come to the conclusion that I am somehow to blame for this. But I . . . I have to continue to keep my mouth shut and essentially pretend it never happened while Seth gets himself fixed.

My mind almost blew.

"I want to talk to you alone," I said to him.

"That okay with you, Seth?" Paul said.

Dear God, please don't let me slap this man.

I realized with a physical jerk that I'd just spoken to God. My arms felt strangely heavy. I couldn't have smacked Paul if I'd tried.

"I want to talk to her too," Seth said. "I'll be fine."

Randi telegraphed *Do NOT upset him* to me with her face but I returned that with a blank stare. No matter how this all turned out in the end, I might never be able to mend the rip that had gone down the middle of my relationship with Randi Grissom.

"We're around if you need us," Paul said and ushered Randi out of the room.

When the door clicked shut behind them, the great room was thick with silence, interrupted only by the soft, measured ticking of the grandfather clock in the far corner. Seth and Kellen used to tell me when I was little that it was alive. That was intended to scare me out of the room, but I was fascinated by the concept. The man in there became magical to me. Too bad I didn't believe in magic anymore.

I turned quickly back to Seth. "Kellen came to see you in the hospital," I said.

"He did."

"Does he know?"

"About the—about my addiction?" Seth said.

He seemed comfortable with that word now, as if it was easier to say than pornography.

"No, he doesn't know. I told him the same thing I'm telling everyone else. I need to go to rehab and get some things sorted out."

"Is that what I'm supposed to tell people now?" I said. "Or do I have to keep saying the whole cancellation of the wedding was because I had second thoughts?"

Seth looked as if I'd given in to my urge and slapped *him*. "Cancellation? Not postponement?"

"That isn't the point!" I closed my eyes and waited for Randi to fling the doors open.

"It'll make a difference in my treatment if I know whether there's a chance for an us when I come home. That's what the director told me this morning on the phone."

To my own utter astonishment, it was my turn to burst into tears. I buried my face in my hands and sobbed wretched, painful sobs. I felt Seth's hand on my head and I shook it away.

Dear God, please don't let me scream at him. Please.

Actually there was little chance of that. My throat closed on itself and the sobs wracked my chest until they gave up. When I stopped, Seth had moved to the chair beside me. He tucked a Kleenex into my hand.

"You're probably right to let people think you're an alcoholic or a drug addict," I said.

"Well, yeah, Tar. If we're going to have any kind of future at all, I need to have a job to come back to—"

"That's not the reason. People get that. They forgive that. They don't have images in their heads that they can't erase. They don't close their eyes and see a Seth who would—I can't even say it."

Seth's eyes brimmed. "Are you talking about people? Or are you talking about you?"

"I was so scared when I thought you were going to die," I said, sobbing again. "I want you to get better. And I want to trust you again and believe in you again."

"I want that too. That's *all* I want."

"But can I unsee what I've seen? Can I unknow what I know? Can I get past that?"

He pulled back from me. His face paled and the very skin of his lips shivered, and I knew I'd pushed him too far.

But I was wrong. His voice when he spoke was like a flat piece of steel.

"I don't know, Tara," he said. "And I can't do anything about that. I can't erase your memory. All I can do is work on myself. You . . ."

He didn't finish. He just looked down at his hands again. But the rest of it was there in the air.

You have to work that out yourself.

It was the first thing he'd said in twenty-eight days that I believed.

"So," he said. "Cancellation? Or postponement?"

The old grandfather ticked in the corner, and I wanted to go to him and imagine as I had twenty years ago that he was indeed a grey-bearded wizard who had all the answers. All the answers was what I needed. And not for Seth, but for me. In the meantime, there was only one I could give to him.

"I don't know," I said. Seth was visibly encouraged by that, as if my not saying cancellation was all he needed to hear. I didn't ask. I just bolted out the front door even as Paul was saying, "I think we should all pray together."

I holed up in my room for the rest of Saturday, and even when I went to work Sunday and Monday, my efforts to forget by throwing myself into customer service were in vain. I was barely holding back tears the entire time.

"I don't know what's going on with you," Wendy said to me Monday at a point when things slacked off, "but you can't bring it to work. You have to be about the people who come in here for peace and quiet with their caffeine."

If that was supposed to keep me from crying, it wasn't working. I blinked like a person with an eyelash under her contact lens.

Wendy's violet glare softened. "Look, I think of it this way. No matter how I'm feeling, if I can get *that* woman to smile, that's the best part of my job."

I followed her nod to the woman coming up the ramp. It was Gray.

"I have to find the connection or it's just coffee," Wendy said.

"Okay," I said. "Thanks for that."

"You're welcome." The softness in her eyes faded, and I was once more at arm's length from this enigma of a girl.

But then, I was at arm's length from everyone. As for Seth, there were now several thousand miles between us. He was in Colorado, trying to change. I was in Savannah, staying the same.

And I just couldn't let that be. How I was going to even begin, I had no idea. But I couldn't stay the same.

THIRTEEN

Toward the end of my shift, Helen joined Gray at the now-usual table in the window. Outside, the light was dwindling and the streetlamps' winking-on made stars on the glass. When Ike turned me loose I joined . . . what did they call themselves? The Watch?

"Start eating," Ms. Helen said as I literally dropped into a ladder-back chair. She pushed a grilled chicken salad my way.

My stomach turned inside out but I picked up the plastic fork.

"No," she said, and pulled a metal one out of her bag. I didn't realize it was sterling silver until it landed, cool and heavy, in my palm.

"Who let *that* woman off the set of *Project Runway*?" Gray said.

I followed her point to the front door and let the fork go. It missed the table and clattered to the floor.

"Does the five-second rule apply here?" Gray said.

While she was retrieving the cutlery, Ms. Helen put her hand on my arm. "You okay, honey?"

I shook my head because the *Project Runway* escapee was Calla Albrecht, filmy sweater trailing out behind her like a royal train, hands flying as she talked to the African American woman who followed her. I knew if I looked away she might not notice me, but it was an inevitable train wreck. It was going to happen and I couldn't stop watching and waiting for us to collide.

Sure enough, Calla's ash-blonde head swung toward me and her gaze crashed into mine. Without missing a beat she headed straight for me, crossing the Piebald as she would her own boutique, as if anything and everything would make way for her. I actually glanced around for a table to duck under.

"Well, Tara. Sweetie," she said when she reached me. Her voice was as syrupy smooth and thick as always despite the laser beams she was now using for eyes.

I felt both Ms. Helen and Gray stiffen and with good reason. Calla was hostile in a way only we Southern women can be. You can't quite pinpoint the rudeness, but it is clearly there beneath the sweet-ies and the smiles as plastic as our American Express cards.

So much for being her favorite bride.

Her eye-shadowed look down at me was expectant.

"I should have come by and talked to you myself," I said. "I know my mother did, but I should have. I'm sorry."

"Tara sweetie," she said. "I knew something wasn't right the last time you were in, but I thought it was just the last-minute jitters. If you had said something then . . ."

The pause was once again expectant. What did she want me to say now? *I am a complete loser and I shouldn't even be showing my face in the city of Savannah?*

"Your mama hasn't told me what to do with the gown. Since it was custom made—"

"We'll pay for it."

Calla's face clearly went into shock. Rule number one for being rich in this town: you didn't talk about money and certainly not in public, among the commoners.

Her voice fell to an attempted *sotto voce* that wasn't all that *sotto*. "That has been taken care of. I just wonder what I'm to do with the dress." She tapped a french-manicured nail on the table. "But we don't need to discuss that here."

"Then why did you bring it up here?"

Calla looked at Gray. Actually, we all did, with varying expressions startled onto our features. Calla was clearly appalled. I knew I was gape-mouthed. Ms. Helen was barely concealing an I-wish-I'd-said-that smirk. Only the woman with Calla registered embarrassment.

"Calla," she said. "Did you want to go ahead and get coffee?"

"Yes, Betsy," Calla said, eyes still on me. "I'll have a latte, two shots."

The woman didn't move. Calla raised her brows at her. I think Ms. Helen did smirk.

"I guess I'll get it, then," Calla said, and swished away with a flat-eyed glare at Betsy over her shoulder.

"Right behind you," Betsy said. But she turned to me.

She was a beautiful woman. Tastefully voluptuous, stylish without being trendy. Skin the exact color of a caffè mocha with eyes to match. Her lips were rose-colored and full and they spoke to me, low and rich.

"I apologize for her," she said.

"There's no need," I said.

"The heck there isn't." Gray then peered at the tines of the fork she'd rescued. "Sorry. None of my business."

That was actually true, but neither she nor Ms. Helen took their eyes off of this woman and I was in no hurry for them to. I felt somehow vindicated with all of them there. Maybe Watch *was* the word.

"I'm not really apologizing for her," the woman said. "More for Calla's Bridal."

"You work for her?" Gray said.

She gave an obviously reluctant nod.

"Too bad."

The woman smiled. "It is, really." She put out a creamy-palmed hand to me. "Betsy Turpin," she said.

"You're Betsy," I said. "I heard Calla say something about you last time I was in there."

"I'm sure you did."

She glanced covertly toward the counter. Calla was gesturing at the chalkboard, no doubt telling Ike he needed to add canapés to the menu. Betsy turned back to me.

"Don't think for a minute your cancellation set her back financially. What she charges for one wedding keeps that place in operation for a year." She blinked her wonderful mocha-brown eyes. "Well, I'm gon' have to quit now, aren't I? I can't be bad-mouthing my employer and live with myself."

"I think I like you," Gray said, straight-faced.

Ms. Helen lifted her chin. "You're being paged, Betsy."

Something hiss-like exuded from the direction of the counter. I didn't look this time.

"You all right?" Betsy said.

"With this?" I said. "Yes. Thank you."

"Okay, then."

Betsy gave us a smile that stayed there even after she left the table. My gaze dropped to my wilting salad. No one asked me anything—there was no anticipation in the silence—but I still said, "I guess you gathered I canceled my wedding. Postponed it indefinitely, actually. To Calla it's the same thing."

Gray gave a soft grunt. "It was a little hard not to pick up on that."

"But we're not going to pry further," Ms. Helen said.

"Really?" Gray said. "Maybe you're not, but I am. I mean, you know, if you feel like talking."

"I might," I said. "Sometime."

Neither Ms. Helen nor Gray came in Tuesday or Wednesday, which may have accounted for some of my downhill slide that started on Thursday, January first. The Piebald was closed, and I stayed in bed until almost noon trying to forget how the Grissoms and the Faulkners always spent New Year's Day together. Randi and Mama alternated years putting on the feast, which was, hands down, a bigger deal than Christmas dinner. This year it was supposed to be our turn, but of course no one showed up for the traditional three-hour meal of ham and turkey and oysters, yams, peas, fruit, rice, and biscuits.

I couldn't begin to eat any of it. The centerpiece of apples and greens in a Christmas tree shape with a pineapple on top hearkened back to colonial days, which normally made me feel one with the Faulkners who had helped settle Georgia. That day it seemed to leer at me as if to say I wasn't one with anyone. I left the table before the nuts and sugar-frosted fruitcake appeared and ran to the fourth floor and covered my head with a pillow. But I could still hear my mother's quiet crying.

When I woke up before dawn on Friday, it hit me full in the face as if the sun were glaring into my room: that was the day Seth and I were supposed to leave for our honeymoon at the Abbeyglen Castle in Ireland. How many times had I envisioned us making love there, in every detail I could pull from my innocent reservoir?

I buried my face again until I couldn't breathe, but the image wouldn't leave me. It just became entangled with the ones on Seth's computer screen and the picture Evelyn had painted of him on the sidewalk on Montgomery Street with one of the women the Bridesmaids and I had probably scoffed about after we passed them at some point. And somewhere within that snarled, knotted mess I saw me—standing outside it all in the white lace nightgown I'd picked out for our first night in Ireland, looking scrawny and flat-chested and unlovely.

Was I not sexy to Seth? Did I turn him off—even though he said he loved me? Was I just the "right wife" but not the "wanted wife"? Was that part of the thing that had such a hold on him?

Was it?

I shook off the covers and went for the window, but I still felt like I was shrouded in something, something that clung to me like Shelob's web. It wasn't until I sank into the cushions and let it pull me into its trap that I knew: its name was shame.

~ᘓᘓᘓᘓᘓᘓᘓ~

Somehow I managed to get through my shift that day. Maybe because that strangling sense of inadequacy had choked off all my tears. Or maybe because Gray and Helen showed up a full hour before I was off and sat with their heads bent together at our table. Or because fifteen minutes before I took off my apron at the end of my shift, Betsy joined them.

"Your fan club is waiting for you," Ike said when I was finishing my side work.

"Is that okay?" I said.

He lowered his chin. "Why wouldn't it be?"

"I don't know," I said.

Because I didn't know anything.

When I sat down with them, Ms. Helen moved a bowl of chicken noodle soup in front of me, steam still curling from it. Her red nails, painted perhaps to match her checked scarf, tapped the plate beneath it as if she were giving me Morse code for "Eat this. Now."

"Hey, we were talking," Gray said. She leaned back and stuffed both hands into the pockets of her jean vest. It would have been an awkward position for anybody else, but it seemed as natural for her as the grin that twitched at the corners of her mouth. "The Watch has every angle of marriage covered here."

"Oh?" I said. My most unfavorite subject. I didn't have the energy to change it so I took the Reed & Barton spoon Ms. Helen produced from her bag and rearranged the noodles.

"Ms. Helen's a widow. I'm divorced. Betsy's happily married. And you . . . I take it the jury's still out?"

I nodded. Under Ms. Helen's hazel-eyed look I slurped some broth.

"Now, you say happily married." Betsy took a long sip of the iced tea, which I didn't see how she could drink on such a cloudy, sullen-skied day. "Let me qualify that. Leon and I have had our share of unhappy times."

Gray grinned. "How much do I love that your husband's name is Leon?"

"As much as I love that yours is Grainne and I don't care what you say, I'm calling you that."

Right then she could have called *me* anything she wanted and I wouldn't have argued with her. Her very presence at the table was like a mother's hand on a feverish forehead.

I moved away from that image. I was avoiding my mother so I wouldn't blurt out the truth to her, and I hated myself for the hurt that left all over her face.

Gray nudged me with her elbow. "You don't have to tell us, but I have to ask. That's just me. Why did you break off your engagement?"

"How do you know I was the one who broke it off?" I said.

"I would just assume that no man in his right mind would call off a marriage to you," Ms. Helen said.

"Maybe he's not in his right mind." Gray nudged me again. "Am I close?"

Betsy didn't say anything to get me off this hook. Why I wanted to tell them *something*, I didn't know. Was it the soup? The silverware? The questions that weren't asked with the licking of chops? The watching eyes that clearly didn't hope for answers they could savor like a forbidden piece of cheesecake? Was it some of that? All of it?

"Let's just say my vision of marriage to Seth was shattered," I said into the soup.

They fell silent, the way people do when a kid has said something naively adorable and nobody wants to laugh at her.

"Vision," Gray said. "I had one of those once. You, Ms. Helen?"

"Oh, honey, yes. Until the first time I found lipstick on one of my Douglas's handkerchiefs and it wasn't my shade."

"Ooooh," Betsy said. Or rather sang. Like some kind of exotic brown bird.

"I was afraid to confront him at first and then I did and he said he'd loaned it to a woman at a meeting because she was crying."

"What did you say to him?" Betsy said.

"I said the least she could have done was launder it and iron it before she gave it back to him."

Gray actually snorted. "That was the shattering of your vision?"

"I just knew I better not have a vision of perfection because anything *could* happen, and I needed to take off those rose-colored glasses, now, and start getting real."

"Oh, I know that thing." Betsy shook her head of closely cropped fuzz. "The first time Leon pushed himself back from the table and said my ham salad wasn't as good as his mama's, you *know* I was not happy. And when he suggested I might be fillin' out my jeans just a little too much. And when he started callin' me Mama just like the children did. Don't you know I gave him the silent treatment for *days*."

"And you're still married to the man?" Gray said and then shook her own head, setting the ponytail swaying from side to side like an indignant pendulum. "Actually I get that. I put up with so much stuff before I finally left. Serious stuff. I'm not talking about the whiskers in the sink and the horse poop on the rug and the jeans he wore until they stood up in the corner of the laundry room by themselves. All I had to do was whistle to them and they'd run to the washer. That's how much bacteria was on those things. And then I'd have to empty the pockets. You have no idea what you can find in a horse dentist's pockets. I actually found an incisor in there one time. Huge thing."

"Girl, you need to stop!" Betsy said.

She and Ms. Helen were both laughing to the point of tears. So was I. Except I passed the tears and went straight to hysteria. Cries I'd never let out beyond the vault of my own bedroom broke from my gut and wouldn't stop, not even when heads lifted from laptops and awkward silences fell over conversations like nets.

Fairly certain that would *not* be okay with Ike, I grabbed my purse and thanked the Watch of women and ran, through the misty, chilling night, all the way home. I ran and wailed because I might never get to check anyone's pocket or forgive him for dissing my ham salad. Just because of that.

~ ☙ ~

I begged off dinner and went straight to bed, but sleep wouldn't come. It wasn't just that I lay awake, frustrated by insomnia. I was plagued with racing, invasive thoughts that brought me straight up off the mattress in a clammy sweat.

The same thing happened the next two nights. No matter how hard I worked at the Piebald, no matter how much energy I expended keeping up a brave front for Mama and Daddy and putting on a failing façade of okay-ness with the Watch, even the fatigue that brought on wasn't enough to put me to sleep. By Monday, the fifth of January, I knew I couldn't face another night of wakefulness woven with heinous half-dreams.

And so at midnight, I put on the black North Face jacket I'd worn in the colder North Carolina winters of grad school, turned off the house alarm, and crept out to walk the streets of the historic district. If I was in any danger I didn't care, because the night mist and the directionless putting of one foot in front of the other made me numb. Numb was what I wanted.

The district's live oak trees, some of them two hundred, two hundred fifty years old, cut off the just-blocks-away highway noise and insulated me as I crossed from street to stony street, taking no notice of the sleeping old houses or the brooding statues in the squares or the fountains now silent in the night.

Occasionally I crossed someone else's path, usually a guy with a Yorkie or a Great Dane on a leash, but they never seemed to wonder what I was doing out there, hands parked in my pockets, gaze averted, clearly going nowhere but down.

As the night grew deeper and the dogs and their masters all went home, I was surprised at how many lights remained on in the row houses as I passed them. Each time I saw one gleaming in an upstairs room or caught the blue flicker of a computer screen, my mind snagged.

Was there some man up there looking at porn while his wife slept, ignorant of the box of pain she would open if she woke up and found him there? What atrocities were unraveling behind the haint-blue plantation shutters and the red doors, all painted to keep out the evil spirits?

The longer I walked—down Charlton, up Taylor, across Monterey and Madison and Chippewa Squares—the deeper my beautiful, romantic Savannah sank until she seemed nothing more than a sham.

The churches were perhaps the worst perpetrators. The twin spires of Wesley Monumental spiked in silhouette like a pair of horns. The stained glass of Lutheran of the Ascension was dark and leaden as lies. First Baptist's white pillars faded into the shadows as if they held up nothing.

I did the same thing the next night, crawling into bed exhausted at four a.m. and waking up at noon in time to get to the Piebald. There was no comfort in the walking, really. It just kept me from going mad.

Although, that may have only been my assessment of my mental state. Wendy took one look at me Tuesday and said, "When was the last time you ate something?"

"Yesterday," I said. Ms. Helen had coaxed me to eat half a croissant.

"Uh-huh." Wendy pressed a cup of tomato basil soup into my palm and waited for me to wrap my fingers around it. "On your worst day you look better than the rest of us do when we've spent six hours in front of the mirror. But anorexia isn't a good look for anybody, so don't even think about working until you drink that. All of it."

"You always look good," I said. "I wish I had your—"

"Don't go there. Drink."

She waited, arms folded, until I drained the cup.

"Thanks, boss," I said.

As Wendy took the mug from me she rolled her eyes. "I wish. I want to be a shift manager so bad I can taste it."

"You'd be great."

"I know I would. Somebody ought to tell Ike that."

"I will," I said.

Wendy looked abruptly stricken. "No. Don't," she said. "I want him to get it himself."

She was straight-arming me again as she took the mug and headed for the sink. Still, I couldn't help envying her. She knew where she wanted to go.

It wasn't that I didn't work hard when I was at the Piebald. I did. I refused to be like Zoo-Loo and the other SCAD students on my shift, who took every break in the action as permission to sketch on a napkin or stick their earbuds in each other's ears and go, "You gotta hear this. It's stupid good." But maybe my always looking for something to wipe up or reorganize or tidy was a substitute for a lack of passion. And not just the kind Fritzie talked about. Passion for anything. And that made me strangely angry.

On my walk Wednesday night, that anger rose to a peak as I stood in front of the brick Cathedral of Saint John the Baptist and watched the moonlight gleam on the bronze-colored iron columns and thought of my Seth, who had once seemed as holy and magnificent to me as those spires and arches. Why? I mean, really—*why?* Wasn't anything real? Wasn't anything what it seemed to be? Was there anything to trust? Anything?

I clutched both fists to my chest. "I need somebody to hear how awful I feel!" I cried out to the brick-silent church before me. "But who won't be hurt? Who won't try to make it okay? I want to be heard! Do *you* hear me?"

I couldn't contain that kind of fury, and its roar petered out and down into a sadness I couldn't hold either. So the anxiety came, spearing me with its needle-spikes, and all I could do was flee from it.

Letting my jacket flap out behind me, I ran, down Harris and across Madison Square. I wasn't aware until then that a chill rain was coming down almost sideways, soaking the already slippery street and the walkways I careened across as I fled blindly from my fear.

I was almost to the west side of the square when my sole caught a flattened assemblage of slick oak leaves and flew out from under me. I was already in full forward motion, and I landed on the arms I outstretched to break my fall, skidding all the way to the curb. Tires grabbed at wet pavement, and I waited for them to roll over me. In that instant I knew why Seth took those pills—and then called for help. The hope for final peace succumbed to the will to live.

Nothing happened as I lay still with my face hanging over the gutter. A car door slammed and hurried footsteps approached. When I lifted my shoulders I saw a pair of Nikes near my head.

"Are you all right?" a male voice said.

"Yes," I said, although I had no idea whether I was or not. My hands burned from their scrape across the bricks, and my insides felt as if they'd been ripped out and reassembled.

I started to get up and the man stopped me without touching me. His voice was enough—low and calm and Yankee tight. If I'd heard a Southern accent I might have become hysterical again.

"You may want to wait a minute," he said. "You fell pretty hard."

"Can I at least roll over?" I said. "I'll feel better if I don't have my face in the gutter."

I thought I heard him chuckle as I maneuvered myself around and looked up into the face of a guy around Ike's age, maybe a little younger, with brown-rimmed glasses and loose-curled hair that was starting to drip. I couldn't see much more even in the wet glare of the streetlamp, but he didn't look like a mugger, so I stayed there. Of course, my concept of people-to-be-afraid-of was limited to James Bond and *Mission Impossible* movies, so I said, "I don't have any money on me."

"I wasn't looking for any," he said. "You want to try to sit up?"

I nodded and got myself to a sitting position.

"Everything feel okay?" he said.

I nodded because it did, surprisingly. All except my pride, but then, there wasn't much of that left to begin with.

"I can stand up," I said.

He straightened and let me struggle to my feet. I was fine then, too, except for the fact that even my waterproof coat was soaked all the way through to my clothes. I immediately started to shake.

"Do you live around here?" the man said.

"Yeah, just over on Gaston." I knew immediately that I shouldn't have told this stranger that, so when he said, "May I drive you home?" I shook my head, splattering us both with droplets that mixed in with the still slanting rain.

It wasn't only that I shouldn't trust him. I couldn't go home. It wasn't time yet.

"Do you want to come inside and get dried out?"

I felt my eyes widen, but he was pointing to St. John's Church, waiting quietly on the other side of the street. Unlike the other churches in the historic district, it was quaint and unassuming and was bordered on one side by a cloister right out of medieval England.

"Inside there?" I said.

"Right."

It was that or go home or continue to wander around with my coat stuck to my body like a sopping sock. So I nodded and followed him across the small street and up to the arched red door, which he opened with a key.

I stepped inside and felt warmth start at once to do its work on my wet face.

"You probably want to take that off," he said, nodding at my coat.

I peeled it away while he removed his hooded windbreaker. He hung them both on hooks just inside the door and said, "Why don't you sit down for a minute?"

Okay, he had a key to the church, he hadn't tried to touch me one time, and he wasn't looking at me like I was a lunatic escaped from Silver Hill. And in the dim gold light of the church foyer, I could see that his brown eyes were kind, even more so when he took off his now foggy glasses and wiped them on a handkerchief. Besides, who but an old-school kind of guy carried a hanky—Ms. Helen's Douglas notwithstanding.

"My name's Ned," he said. "Ned Kregg."

"Like Daniel Craig," I said, stupidly.

"Different spelling. Mine's K-r-e-g-g." He gave me a soft smile. "And nobody would ever think I was related to James Bond."

"I don't know," I said. "You rescued me."

I hoped it didn't sound like I was flirting. Stuff was just coming out of my mouth so I wouldn't cry.

"I'm going to get you a towel," he said.

"No, really, I'm okay."

He smiled again. "You're not okay to get in my car. You really need to let me drive you home. It's not getting any better out there."

I agreed and he went off to get a towel, and I sat there with my arms wrapped around my damp self and wondered how in the world I got here and whether it really mattered. Just beyond the bench where I waited, a sign on a stand, penned in calligraphy, listed the worship service times. Seven a.m. every weekday? These people must be die-hard Christians.

I hadn't been to church since Christmas Eve—for three reasons. One, I couldn't look at Paul Grissom without seeing his face the day he asked Seth what half-truth he'd told his employer. Two, I couldn't bear the memories of Seth and me growing up together in those pews and the never-realized image of us standing together in front of the altar. Three, I had only spoken to God twice in my recent history. Make that three times, if you counted tonight's tirade in front of the Catholic cathedral.

Was I talking to God then?

"I brought two."

I jumped.

"Sorry, I didn't mean to startle you." Ned Kregg handed me a pair of scratchy navy-blue towels, obviously laundered by someone who didn't know about fabric softener. Who kept bath towels in a church?

I wanted to wrap one around my head but I felt a little awkward doing it in front of him. I threw one around my shoulders and wiped my face. That, combined with the cozy air, stopped the shivering.

"Am I dry enough to get in your car?" I said.

"You ready to go home?" he said.

No. But, really, I had no place else to go.

"Put this on," he said, and handed me a dry jacket, a brown windbreaker with a small white logo above the front pocket. "Otherwise you'll be right back where you started."

"I'll give it back when we get to my place," I said.

Except for telling him where to turn, we didn't speak on the five-block drive in his Jeep Liberty until we pulled up in front of the house. The rain was coming down in slanted sheets.

"I'm Tara, by the way," I said. "Tara Faulkner."

He nodded. "Good to meet you, Tara. I have an umbrella. I'll walk you up."

I didn't protest. I was so weary I didn't want steps like drying myself again to come between me and bed.

We hurried up the steep slate steps and I fumbled for my keys in the pocket of my own jacket, which was hanging like wet laundry over my arm. Both of us jerked back when the front door opened and Daddy appeared in the vestibule. It had to be one a.m., but he was dressed in his tan trench coat and he had his own keys in his hand.

This had to look awesome: me straggling up the steps in the dead of night with a strange guy who appeared to have pulled me out of a ditch because, well, he kind of had. I couldn't even start explaining because, as Daddy reached for me, I saw something hurry from his face, something that didn't belong there in the first place. It was fear, and Daddy was never afraid.

"You okay, sugar?" he said into my soaked hair.

"Yeah," I lied.

"Thank you," he said.

I didn't realize until I pulled away and turned around that he was thanking Ned and that Ned was already down the steps. Daddy pushed the door closed and looked me up and down like he was still certain I'd lost an arm or an eye out there. It was now time for an explanation.

"I was out for a walk and I slipped and fell and that guy—Ned— let me go into his church and dry off. I'm fine, really."

"You were out for a *walk*?" Daddy said, and then he simultaneously closed his eyes and shook his head. "We don't have to talk about this now. You need a hot shower. You want a hot—something to drink?"

I shook my head and started for the stairs.

"Tara," he said.

I didn't turn around.

"Sugar, is there *anything* I can do to help you?"

Please, God, don't let me look at him or I'll tell him and I can't.

"Not right now, Daddy," I said.

And maybe not ever.

F O U R T E E N

I slept an exhausted sleep but woke up to my alarm at six and took the shower I was too tired for the night before and hurried through a crisp but clear morning to St. John's Church with the windbreaker over my arm. If the service started at seven there would surely be someone there fifteen minutes early I could hand this to.

I hadn't looked at the jacket until I was putting my own on, and then I'd leaned over the bed to examine the logo. *Sewanee University of the South School of Theology* it said in clean white letters. Next to it was a white Celtic cross on a small field of autumnal gold. Yeah, it definitely had to belong to somebody there, if not Ned himself.

The red doors were open when I arrived, but nobody seemed to be around. I peeked through the narthex I'd huddled in the night before and into the sanctuary where two long rows of polished pews faced steps and a choir section, all under open arches and lined by bright stained-glass windows.

Even though the altar seemed miles away, I could see a flame wavering from each of the two candles in their brass holders. Somebody *had* been there and would surely return so I slipped into the back pew and waited. I could have just hung the jacket on one of the hooks, but it had occurred to me on the walk over that I hadn't even said thank you to Ned. I might be losing my mind, but I wasn't losing my manners.

Movement brought my eyes to the front again. A tall figure in a black frock reminiscent of the cover of *The Vicar of Wakefield* padded silently in through a side door near the altar and went straight to a kneeler/shallow table combination and knelt at it. The loose-curled head went down and Ned Kregg moved his lips without sound.

Okay. He was—a deacon? A pastor? I sure didn't have him for a minister, although now I couldn't see why not. He looked completely natural up there in the attitude of prayer. Some small part of me wanted to know what he was saying to God.

Several other people came in, most of them women of Ms. Helen's age, and took their places in pews up front. They, too, knelt and bowed their heads, and when I looked at my feet I realized there were kneeling things that pulled down on hinges. I could kneel too. If I wanted to.

Then everyone stood and Ned said, "From the rising of the sun even unto the going down of the same my name shall be great among the Gentiles . . ."

Unless my Veritas Academy education had been a complete waste, he was reading from the King James Version of the Bible. I didn't know anybody used that anymore.

". . . for my name shall be great among the heathen, saith the Lord of hosts."

The heathen. That could be me. Time to make my exit.

I crept from the pew and tiptoed back to the vestibule where I hung the brown windbreaker on a hook. I hesitated for a moment, thinking maybe I should leave a note. But the church was so quiet, except for Ned's low, calm, Yankee-tight voice saying, "Dearly beloved brethren . . . ," any rustling around I did to find pencil and paper would disturb this sacred place more than I already had. I left the jacket and opened the heavy door only wide enough to let myself out.

Yet something about that place stayed with me. And the words Ned read to the tiny knot of people: "My name shall be great among the heathen." It made me want to say God's name, just to see if it would still come out of my estranged mouth. I even opened my lips a few times but one question always froze them in place: How could I turn to a holy God with something so disgusting?

I may have actually been mulling that over for about the fiftieth time that afternoon when I looked up from the register to greet the next customer and saw that it was Lexi.

"Lex!" I said. "Hi!"

I was genuinely glad to see her, which you would have thought would make her glad too. Instead, her eyes spilled over. She pulled at them with the heels of her hands.

"I'm sorry," she said. "Just give me a minute."

"Okay," I said. "Can I get you something? You want a vanilla latte. I know you do."

"That's okay. I really just came to see you. I miss you."

I glanced nervously down the counter at Wendy, who was momentarily preoccupied with the timer on the toaster oven.

"Go sit and I'll bring your latte to you," I said. "It's on me."

Steaming the milk gave me time to tuck my own tears away. I didn't realize how lonely I was until I saw her, my tiny, intelligent, creative friend who cried over everything and yet didn't let anything stand between her and what she knew was right for her.

I tried to form a leaf in the foam and made an even worse botch of it than usual. I was never the artist she was. Every time we came home on breaks from our respective colleges, I'd listen to her with my skin nearly turning green as she talked about Vanderbilt, and then

I would assure myself Daddy was right to steer me into academia. I would never make it in the tough filmmaking world Lexi and I had romanticized after we watched *The Making of the Lord of the Rings* for the fourth time.

Something grabbed at me internally and I nearly dumped the mug. Seth wasn't the only dream I'd gotten wrong.

"I'm going on break, Wendy," I said.

"It's about time. Here, take this with you and drink it yourself. Do *not* give it to your friend."

She put a cup of broccoli cheese soup into my other hand and brushed me off with her eyes as if I were an extreme annoyance. I would never understand her.

Lexi murmured thanks for the latte but she didn't take a sip even after I sat down across from her in a lumpy chair at a less-than-sturdy coffee table. Where was Ms. Helen with her shims when I needed her?

"I don't want to make you cry again," I said. "But I miss you too. I'm sorry I haven't called or anything."

"It's okay. I've been busy. Classes started again."

"Ya think? Except for right this minute, we've been slammed in here since y'all came back." That wasn't surprising; the SCAD students added ten thousand people to the town's population, scattered in their countless buildings around the city.

Lexi pushed an index card across the table. "I brought you my schedule so in case you want to get together you'll know when I'm free. And don't worry, I'm not going to ask you anything."

"It's not that I don't *want* to talk about—"

"It's okay. Only, I wouldn't contact Alyssa or Jacqueline if I were you. They can't *wait* to find out what's going on. They just want an invitation."

"Thanks for the heads-up." I nodded at the cup. "You should taste the latte. I made it myself. I need to know if I'm any good at it."

Lexi took a sip and nodded more enthusiastically than she had to, bouncing the beaded earrings I knew she'd designed herself. I was also sure she'd put together the matching string she'd somehow woven into her hair.

"Remember what romantics we used to be, Lex?" I said.

"Used to be?" she said, laughing softly. "I think we still are, aren't we?"

I felt my expression darken. "That's all gone. I look back at how naïve I used to be and it's almost embarrassing."

"I'm not embarrassed."

Lexi looked past me and bit her lip. She was once again the seventh-grader who had been informed by some little *nouveau riche* snot that only babies still wore ruffles. I was the one who had defended her then, the one who told that mascara-wearing twelve-year-old that she didn't know what she was talking about. And now, I was the bully.

"I'm sorry, Lex," I said. "I didn't mean to sound so bitter."

"You probably have a right to. That's what I'm going to go with."

She stared into the latte. I stood up.

"I'm glad you came by. I really am," I said. "I'm just bad company right now. I love you, okay?"

"Love you too," she said.

When she didn't say anything else, I headed back to the counter. On the way I dumped the soup into the trash can.

⁓

Saturday was Wendy's day off, so it was mostly Ike and me working together. The afternoon was a steady stream of students, sometimes more a typhoon than a stream, and we didn't get a break until after six. Ike turned the counter over to one of the less spacy SCAD guys and invited me to have coffee with him in his office.

I offered to make it but he insisted I go on in and sit down and he'd bring me something. I sagged wearily into a leather chair that had obviously sat several generations of buns and played with a slit in the fabric as I looked around.

The office was a lot like Ike himself: relatively neat but with the occasional surprising touch. A bust of Edgar Allan Poe. A pipe like the one I'd seen in photographs of J. R. R. Tolkien. A huge conch shell with the smell of sand still stuck to it. The only photo was of Ike and a black Labrador retriever that smiled bigger than he did. Although—Ike didn't actually do a lot of smiling.

He came in then, closed the door, and handed me a mug with *Flannery O'Connor Childhood Home* printed on the side. "I'm not going to tell you what this is until after you taste it."

"Should I be afraid?" I said.

"Watch it now, it's hot. But don't let it cool off too much. It has to be just before scalding to be appreciated."

"You're the only person I know who practically requires a master's degree to drink a cup of coffee."

I blew into the brew with its lovely coffee shop crème look on the surface and watched Ike ease himself into a faded tweed club chair of about the same vintage as the one I was sitting in. Out in the shop he didn't look as big as he did now, shoulders passing the sides by several inches. He pushed the fedora to the back of his head.

"That should be just about right now."

I took a cautious sip. My eyes closed of their own volition.

"You like."

"I love. What is it?"

"A blend I'm working on. Keep sipping. Now, about that master's degree."

It was another one of those shifts. I was getting used to them.

"What master's degree?" I said.

"Yours."

"How did you know I had a master's degree?"

"Wild guess. What's it in?"

I felt my cheeks warm and not from the coffee. "Literary criticism—a completely worthless degree at this point in my life."

"I don't know." Ike folded his hands comfortably on his chest. "You obviously learned something useful. You're doing great here."

I had to laugh. "If I am, that's because of Wendy and you. I didn't pick up any of these skills at Duke, trust me."

"I gotta admit, I had my doubts at first but you caught right on. I've even seen you make some improvements out there. That's good."

"I can sure straighten those napkins." I took a gulp. If I didn't I'd start babbling.

"I'm not going to ask what a class act like you is doing working here. That's your business. And you're welcome to stay on as long as you want to." Ike leaned forward. "But it is my business to ask how long you think that's going to be."

"Honestly?" I said.

"No, I want you to lie."

"Right. I don't know. At *least* six weeks. At the very minimum."

"Not what I wanted to hear." Ike sank back again. "Here's what I'm thinking: I want to consider you for managerial work in the future, starting with an easy shift and taking it from there. I'm a little tired of being here from open until close seven days a week, but I haven't found anybody I can trust to turn it over to for even one day at a time."

I took another swallow so I wouldn't say what was screaming in my head: *No! Wendy wants that! Give it to her!* If she hadn't told me not to, I would have.

And maybe I would've broken that promise if he hadn't gone on. "I'd like to get a life, you know. This place was my dream, still is, and there's a lot more I want to do with it. But I'm thirty-five. Someday I want to get married, have a family."

My throat thickened. Was that going to happen now every single time somebody talked about the happy life they had planned for themselves? Was I always going to want to say, *Don't count on it?*

"But it's hard to find that right woman when I'm here all the time." Ike gave a short laugh. "Unless she just walks in through those doors."

"Maybe she will." My voice sounded middle-school shrill. "You're surrounded by some good-looking women out there." I almost added, *What about Wendy?*

Ike shook his head. "I've dated a couple of SCAD students. Didn't work out. They all want to be unique. There's unique, and then there's just flat-out weird."

He sounded so much like GrandMary I laughed.

"Now there's a sound we don't hear around here a lot."

"What?" I said.

"You laughing. You should do it more. So—what's the grade on that coffee?"

Another shift, back to Piebald World. I was grateful.

"A-plus," I said.

"Schmoozer," he said.

I realized as I followed Ike back out to the front that I'd just had a conversation about something besides my broken heart. It made me miss Seth more than ever.

─◦◦◦◦─

One thing did pull my thoughts away from my own quagmire. Sunday afternoon, my day off, Mama came to my room with tea and blueberry muffins and bad news. The bad news trumped the tea and muffins.

"GrandMary finally told me what's going on with her," she said after she'd poured and sugared and otherwise skirted the issue for ten minutes.

"You mean, why she had to go home and see her doctors?" I felt a deep stab of guilt. I'd barely thought about it since she left, when there was a time that would have been *all* I could think about. Who was I turning into?

"Yes," Mama said. I watched her swallow.

"It's bad, isn't it?"

"It could be. She found a knot on her hip and they've done a lot of tests—including a biopsy, which I didn't even know about or I would have been up there."

"And?"

"They know she has some kind of lesion on the muscle—which is a strange place for a tumor and that's why they ran so many tests."

"But it is a tumor."

"That's what the biopsy shows. She's having surgery on Tuesday."

"Tuesday! She couldn't have given us a little more notice?"

"I know, honey, but that's your grandmother. She plays everything right close to the vest." Mama's eyes leveled at me in a way I wasn't sure they'd ever done before. "I think it must be genetic."

"So are we going?" I said. "I can tell Ike I need the time off and I'm sure he'll—"

"I'm going. GrandMary says she doesn't want an entourage."

"You and I are hardly an entourage."

"I was hard-pressed enough to get her to let *me* come. As if I wouldn't anyway, but it's so much easier when you have her blessing." Mama squeezed my foot. "I need you to stay here and look after Daddy."

"I totally will," I said.

"And maybe." I saw her swallow hard again. "Maybe you two can have some good talks while I'm gone."

"Sure," I said.

The guilt knife went in even deeper.

So Mama left the next morning. I drove her to the airport and sobbed all the way back. It was impossible not to believe that GrandMary specifically didn't want me there because I'd be bringing my baggage with me. Who needed that when you had your own trunk full of cancer?

That one more layer of pain and darkness and self-recrimination kept me awake Monday night, until I finally got up and put on my shoes and jacket and headed for the back door. Daddy met me there as if he'd foreseen my escape attempt and had been waiting for me. He actually stood against the door, hands on his hips, face grim as a security guard. I would have laughed if I hadn't been halfway to fury.

"You planning to go someplace, sugar?"

"I need to walk," I said.

"I just don't think that's a good idea."

"Daddy, it's fine. The only reason I had issues the other night was because I was running in the rain, which was stupid."

"And you're lucky somebody with a conscience was the one to find you and pull you out of a puddle. I'm not going to let you do this. I'm sorry."

"You're not going to let me?" somebody who couldn't be me said to my father. "I'm twenty-five years old. If I want to go out for a walk I'll go out for a walk."

Pain shot across his face, but he still said, "My house. My rules. You've been through enough, Tara, and I'm sure I don't even know the half of it. In fact, I think your mother and I have been pretty respectful of you in not insisting you tell us why you broke it off with

Seth and why he's left town and why his father can't even look me in the eye." His voice was starting to falter. "I don't think it's asking too much for you to respect me and my need to keep you from having anything *else* happen to you."

I expected to cry, but it was as if I had no tears left. My anger gave way to despair.

"It's not asking too much," I said. "I'm sorry I was like that. I'm just—I'm sorry."

"It's okay, sugar. I don't want you to feel like you're in prison . . ."

I shook my head and kissed his smooth forehead and went back upstairs. I was in prison, but he wasn't the one who put me there.

The question now was what to do with the endless hours of the night when I couldn't sleep and couldn't turn off the thinking and the feeling and couldn't stand to have them turned on anymore. The fact that it took me until two in the morning to figure it out was a testament to how far I'd wandered from myself. Of course. I could watch movies.

Heaven knows I had the perfect setup.

The largest room on the third floor was a library for Kellen and me when we were growing up. With big comfy chairs and signed-by-the-author posters of children's books on the ceilings—because the walls were lined with bookshelves—and a long table for doing homework and working on computers, it was more conducive to learning than the classrooms in the private schools we went to. When I was in high school, after Kellen and Seth went off to college, my friends came over for group projects and forays into the collection of books that rivaled our academy library.

It was also the site of the conversation I had with Daddy about where I was going to college. Now that I thought about it, that was the only other discussion with him that had gone down the way tonight's almost-argument had.

From the time Lexi's parents took us to see *Finding Neverland* and we had that scintillating conversation at the Waffle House, I knew I wanted to study film. Lexi and I had researched every college that offered a film arts degree, and both of us were set on going to Vanderbilt. It had never occurred to me that Daddy wouldn't let me go to whatever university I wanted to and be anything I wanted to be.

The acceptance letter had come that day and I left it on the desk in his study. When I heard him coming down the hall toward the library at ten o'clock that night, when I was still up working on a paper, I squeezed my eyes shut and waited for the scene I'd rehearsed in my mind. The one where he would come in all shiny-faced and I would jump into his arms and he would say, "I am so proud of you, sugar."

The problem was, I hadn't given him the script. He didn't know the lines. He only knew his motivation.

Why hadn't I discussed college choices with him, he wanted to know. Did I not realize what the competition was like in the film industry? Didn't I think, with my gentle temperament, that I was better suited for a more academic career? Didn't I love English? Didn't I excel at that? How did I even know I would be good at film?

The whole time he was laying those questions on me like layers of baklava, the only thing I could think was that I had it all *planned* in my mind. How, then, could it not come true?

When he was through he asked me what I thought. I didn't think at all then. I only felt. And I said the one thing that, in his mind, proved the very point he was making: "But Lexi and I are doing this together. We're going to be roommates."

Daddy had nothing against Lexi. He liked her better than either Alyssa or Jacqueline, I was sure. But he shook his head at me and said, "Doing it just because Lexi is doing it isn't a good reason when it comes to your education, Tara. You'll find other friends."

I didn't, really—not like Lexi. Not anyone who shared the passion I watched melt away as she went off to Vanderbilt and I went off to the University of North Carolina in Chapel Hill.

I didn't push it. I didn't know what would have happened if I had, but Daddy knew I was disappointed. He still thought he was right, of course, but I was his sugar. When I came home for Christmas break my freshman year, the library had been converted into a state-of-the-art home theater with a Blockbuster Video store–size collection of DVDs and—to Kellen's delight—a popcorn machine. I loved it, of course, but I didn't have the heart to tell Daddy I wanted to make movies, not just watch them.

And then there was the summer I came home from school, at age almost twenty-two, when Seth Grissom finally looked at me and realized that I wasn't just Kellen's kid sister. That was the summer he fell in love with the girl who had been in love with *him* since she was fifteen. After that, it didn't seem to matter what I studied in school. I knew I was going to be Seth's wife, and that was all I wanted to be.

Since I'd come home from Duke in May and we'd all been so focused on the wedding, I hadn't been in the Faulkner Cinema, as Lexi named it, more than two or three times. It had sort of a musty smell when I entered that night, so I was pretty sure nobody else had used it either. I went to one of the cabinets in the back and pulled out a DVD and stuck it in the machine. A few remote clicks later and I had sunk into a film. I didn't even know what it was. It just let me not think and let me not feel.

I woke up there at ten o'clock the next morning.

FIFTEEN

I wasn't crying anymore.

Mama called me late Tuesday afternoon to tell me GrandMary's surgery had gone well and the tumor was contained. The pathologist's report would take a few days, but GrandMary was optimistic and, of course, adamant that she was leaving the hospital before then. I had no tears of gratitude to share with Mama's shaky relief.

Tuesday and Wednesday Wendy and Ms. Helen continued to feed me, and the kindness should have reduced me to sobs. But I sipped butternut squash soup and nibbled at the edges of a Brie and pear without so much as a whimper.

Ms. Helen and Gray and Betsy and I discussed a potpourri of topics—from the failure of the *Hobbit* movies to elicit the emotion of the Lord of the Rings series, to the amount of time Facebook, Instagram, Pinterest, and Candy Crush sucked from people's lives. But even when Ms. Helen admitted that she followed Pat Sajack on Twitter, no tears accompanied my forced laughter.

Lexi walking into Faulkner Cinema Wednesday night and sitting in the recliner next to mine and just saying, "Hey. Want some company?" had the potential to make me weep. But I merely said, "Yes," and made us popcorn. It was, however, the first night in three when I became aware of what movie I was watching. It was *The Great Gatsby* with Leonardo Dicaprio. Always before I'd identified with Nick, who observed the meaningless lives of the rich and learned about himself. This time I could only empathize with Gatsby, who had pinned all his dreams on one person and when she was gone he had no life. But still, I didn't cry.

When you don't feel, you *can't* cry. Or truly laugh. Or rouse yourself to anger. Or become vulnerable to love. But to me, then, a dull, numb state beat the constant throbbing pain and the relentless stinging of anxiety.

But it wasn't to last.

Thursday—it was the fifteenth of January—I was sitting with the Watch, drifting at the edge of a conversation about Betsy's departure from Calla's Bridal—Gray shamelessly pumping her for every delicious detail of Calla's thinly veiled rage—when a group of guys parked themselves at the table that had been moved close to ours after Ike took down the Christmas tree. It was obvious right off they weren't SCAD students. Too freshly shaven. Too studiedly casual in their attire. Too clipped and cocky and condescending to be artists.

Young businessmen, maybe. Perhaps from out of town, in Savannah for a meeting. But not classy the way my father and his contemporaries were. That wasn't even what they appeared to be going for as they plunked a bottle of wine on the table and critiqued the cheeseboard for its lack of manchego and sat with their spines halfway down to the seats of their chairs and their elbows leaning on whatever they hit.

I made a vague mental comment about the odd juxtaposition of them next to us and was about to return to our conversation when theirs started.

"So—man," the health-club blond said. "Did you score or what?"

The dark-haired one with the sinewy runner look leaned back and basically leered. "What do you think?"

The third, a ruddy redhead with an early paunch, said, "You played her like a freakin' Stradivarius."

"I did," Sinewy Runner said. "I know it's bad, but I did."

Blondie smiled without parting his lips. "It was bad, but was it good?"

I turned my body away and plastered my hands over my ears. My three women stopped, their own discussion still on their lips, and went on immediate alert.

"Tara, what the heck?" Gray said.

"It's like women are a sport!" I said, though how they heard me I still don't know because my teeth were soldered together. "We're a video game and they have to score! I can't stand it! I can't!"

Gray looked past me, over my shoulder, and let her scowl fall on the next table. There was a scraping of chairs as her eyes followed the three guys across the dining room to a spot . . . somewhere else.

"All right, honey," Ms. Helen said to me. "The coast is clear."

Betsy nodded. "Start talkin', girl."

I did. Three males I had never seen before and probably never would again had knocked open the gate I'd kept closed for forty-seven days, shutting out every person I cared about including myself. What I'd held there flooded out and drowned the promise I'd made to Seth and to Randi and to Paul. To Gray and Betsy and Ms. Helen I told my story, and even without names or graphic details it was a tawdry tale, one not fit for a Thursday afternoon at a sweet window table at Piebald Espresso.

But no one balked. No one drew back from me in horror. No one, not even Ms. Helen, looked at me as if I were the fool I was convinced I was. And when Ms. Helen said, "I am appalled," I knew the words weren't directed at me. Not with those hazel eyes bathing me in compassion.

"And you haven't told anyone else this entire time?" Gray said.

"I promised I wouldn't."

"So—no support?" Ms. Helen said.

"I've had some—"

"But nobody can hold you up if they don't know what's pushin' you down." Betsy put her ever-warm brown hand on mine, which quivered like a claw on the table. "You know why you feel ashamed?"

"Because this is awful!"

She shook her head. "What this man did was awful. You only feel ashamed because you're keeping *his* awful secret."

"Amen to that," Ms. Helen said. "You haven't done anything to be ashamed of—not that shame ever did *anybody* any good, but that's an entirely different subject." She prayed her hands under her tissuey chin. "You've had something stolen from you. You feel violated."

"And well you should." Gray tightened her ponytail. "I'm not going to go into what I think about Mr. Fiancé because that's not my call."

"Good on ya, Grainne," Betsy said.

"But I'm telling you, this is his fault, not yours."

"Then why . . ." I looked over their heads and swallowed. "Why do I feel so horrible? It's like guilt is prickling inside me all the time and unless I keep myself perfectly numb, I can't stand it. I can't eat. I can't sleep. I can hardly focus on anything when I'm not working here."

They were all nodding like I was currently getting everything right on an oral exam.

"Without a doubt," Betsy said, wonderful full lips working as if *she*, too, had to get this right, "you're suffering from post-traumatic stress. It's like you've been in a serious car accident or someone you love has died."

"Right," Gray said. "It's a normal reaction to an abnormal situation."

"You're depressed, honey," Ms. Helen said. "And there is no fault in that. But I don't want you to stay there. That's a hopeless place."

"I don't think I'll ever be able to get out of it," I said. "I can't see how it's going to get any better than it is right now."

"Wrong." Gray scooted her chair closer to mine so she could quite literally get in my face. "You start accepting what you feel and—how was it that one woman put it to me when I was going through my divorce? Okay, it's like you're drowning in a bowl of linguine."

I nodded vaguely.

"Okay, and every strand of that linguine is something you're feeling—anger, sorrow, resentment—"

"Bitterness," I said. "Guilt. Shame. Stupidity."

"Stupidity?" Betsy said. Her hands went up. "Girl, you are the exact opposite of stupid."

"What smart girl doesn't see what's going on with her guy? Why didn't I know something was wrong?"

Gray's face went blank. "Oh, I don't know—because you aren't clairvoyant?"

"Because you aren't God?"

Ms. Helen's voice was soft, but it slammed into my mind so I couldn't move.

"Back to the pasta," Betsy said. "I want to know where you're taking that, Grainne."

Gray gave me another long look before she went on, as if she were waiting for me to make a break for it. But where was I going to go? Back to the vault?

"Go ahead," I said.

"So all those feelings are strands of linguine," Gray said. "You have to follow each one and see where it comes from. Once you do, you realize it can't take you under."

I clutched my head with both hands. "I don't know if I can do that."

"You absolutely can't if you try to do it by yourself." That was Ms. Helen again, soft, firm, like a hand that doesn't let go of yours no matter how hard you pull away.

"If you want my help, I'm all in," Gray said. "If anybody knows how to start over, it's me, and one way or the other, my friend, you're starting over."

"You can count on me too," Betsy said. "I've had depression before. I know what it's like, but I also know how to see the light at the other end of the tunnel, and girl, it is *not* a train coming at you." She squeezed my hand. "I'll come in the tunnel and show you the way out."

Ms. Helen was quiet, and my heart, which had begun to lift, sank again. If she wasn't in, I didn't know if I could even start. What if she didn't believe I could get out of this? She was the wisest of us—

"I'll be here every evenin' you work, at six p.m.," she said finally. "But I'm bringing someone with me."

I looked up, panic clear in my eyes I was sure. Sharing with this . . . Watch . . . was one thing. Anyone else might push me back into that place that felt safe but wasn't.

But Ms. Helen leaned on that gorgeous tissue-paper chin and said, "I'm bringing God. When two or more are gathered together, if we let him in on the conversation, he'll take it where it needs to go."

She looked around the table as if to ask for objections. There were none. Gray shrugged like, *Of course. Why are we even talking about this?* Betsy closed her eyes and smiled, and no doubt she was already praying.

Me? If I wasn't a complete lunatic to think so, in the last few weeks I'd had God stop me from slapping Paul Grissom, keep me from screaming at Seth—and, I realized in that instant—he'd brought Ned Kregg to my rescue after I screamed for help in front of the Cathedral of St. John the Baptist in the middle of the night. Why wouldn't I expect God to show up here, among these godly women? It made more sense than a single thought that had come to me since my life turned in on itself and made me doubt everything.

"Yes, ma'am," I said. "Please."

"Well, then, ladies," Ms. Helen said, sitting tall. "I think we can predict that Tara will be healed."

"Amen," Gray said.

I sat back in my chair and felt its slight un-shimmed rock. Healed. *I* would be healed.

That had never occurred to me. I wanted Seth to be healed. I wanted GrandMary to be healed. But me? Was that what I was supposed to focus on? Not whether to marry Seth, but on me being somehow restored? So I wouldn't stay the same?

I didn't have Gray or Betsy or Ms. Helen's faith that it would without a doubt happen. But I had them, and maybe enough of my own faith curling through me like a wisp of incense.

"All right," I said to them. "All right."

⁓ℐℰ⁓

Lexi came over that night and we watched the entire first season of *Downton Abbey* and I cried myself to sleep. Friday I awoke at noon with a silky thread of hope dangling over me. I wrapped my fingers around it and, like Ms. Helen, I didn't let go.

Wendy didn't make that easy. When I arrived just in time for my shift, she was cool to me, barely acknowledging my presence and not making eye contact even when she called out orders for coffee and sandwiches. We were far from being BFFs, but she was usually at least civil if not friendly in that sarcastic you're-a-complete-klutz-but-I-respect-you-anyhow sort of way. That day she showed me all the warmth of an ice cube. There was no soup in a mug for me.

I, of course, went down several mental roads with that. Were the jeans I had on too pricey? Had Ike told her he was considering me for a management position? Had she heard my conversation with the Watch and was now completely disgusted with me?

That last possibility—remote as it was—became the topic as soon as I sat down at the table with the women that night.

"I know you said I wasn't stupid not to see that Se—that my fiancé was hooked on porn," I said, as Ms. Helen tossed a salad with small tongs she'd pulled from her bag and pushed it toward me. "But, really, did I miss red flags that maybe somebody not so naïve would have seen?"

"Really?" Gray said. "Why would you even be thinking about the possibility of porn? You weren't looking at *Playgirl*, right?"

"No."

"Then why would it even enter your mind?"

Ms. Helen poured a container of balsamic vinaigrette on my salad. "And don't even think about beating yourself up for being naïve. That's a rare and beautiful quality these days."

Too bad I'd lost it.

"Tara," Betsy said.

I tried to focus on her.

"As women, our sexuality is relationally based. Wouldn't y'all agree?"

"Definitely," Gray said.

Ms. Helen nodded, and my cheeks warmed. This was like talking about sex with GrandMary . . . except I *had* talked about sex with GrandMary. So, okay.

"I agree too," I said. "Which is why I don't understand what he was getting from cybersex. He doesn't even know those women."

Evelyn's story of the prostitute flickered through my mind but I let it go. I hadn't told the Watch that part.

"That's because you're looking at male sexuality through the eyes of a female," Betsy said. "It's different for them—not all the time, but we don't have to get into that. Just let me ask you this, if I may."

"Do it," I said.

"Did you see any flaws in the relationship itself, apart from all this?"

I didn't hesitate. "We were perfectly happy before I found out. At least I was. We never really even came close to having a fight until that night, when he was acting strange, I mean for him."

"Then I rest my case," Gray said, "because there was no way you could know. He deliberately kept it a secret—partly *by* being perfect." She tightened her ponytail. "You know, if everything else about him was above reproach, that one thing couldn't be that bad. Make sense?"

Going there meant I had to see Seth in a different light. A bare lightbulb light. I couldn't turn that on right now, but I nodded at Gray.

"And that's when the shame comes in," Ms. Helen said, "when someone is doing something so bad he can't let anyone know."

"Don't make his shame your shame," Betsy said. "You're not gon' get healed that way."

"We've been so much a part of each other for so long," I said, "separating me from him is like splitting myself in half. It *hurts*."

I got three versions of "I know." It was enough to get me through most of the salad and out of the chair that ten minutes before I thought I might just stay stuck in forever. It was the closest thing I'd felt to a start.

When we noticed Ike turning off the lights in the kitchen and clearing his throat, Betsy walked me partway down Bull Street.

"One more thing about shame," she said when we reached the

corner at Harris. "Shame never comes from God. So whenever you're feeling ashamed or foolish about this, that's not God talking to you."

I didn't have a clear conviction that God was talking to me at all. But at least now I knew when he wasn't.

Maybe that should have been my impetus for going back to church Sunday morning, especially since Daddy would be going alone and we hadn't seen much of each other since Mama left. But I still couldn't do it. God would be there, but so would Paul and the memories. I whispered, "I'm sorry, God." It was the best I could do.

SIXTEEN

I got to work early Monday so Wendy would have no reason to be annoyed with me. Her focus wasn't in my direction, though; that was obvious. When I arrived, she and Ike were having an intense conversation behind the loose tea display. I couldn't see them as I started in cleaning the toaster oven someone had burned cheese in during the previous shift and hadn't bothered to wipe out before it hardened into a weld. But I could hear the tautness in their voices. Neither one of them was doing an effective job of keeping the discussion to a whisper, so I decided I wasn't *really* eavesdropping.

"No, you can't change shifts," Ike said. "We've got a good team here in the afternoon."

"I'll switch with Zoo-Loo. He'll do fine with Tara."

"Zoo-Loo isn't long for this world, so no."

Wendy's sigh filtered straight through the tins of Earl Grey and Darjeeling.

"Okay." Ike's voice was a trifle less bullet-like. "If you can give me a solid reason why you want to change, I'll consider it."

I considered moving out of earshot. I didn't want to hear that Wendy could no longer stand working with me. But I was afraid if I moved now they'd know I was there, lurking.

"My schedule for my other job has changed," she said.

"Are you going to get fired from your other job if you keep your same schedule here?"

"No, but it would be easier—"

"Look, I'm not trying to be a jerk, but when I hired you we agreed that *this* was your real job and your other job, whatever it is . . ."

He seemed to be waiting for her to fill in a blank but she didn't. I could almost hear her eyes rolling.

"We said it would be secondary. Are we still there?"

"It's not like I want to work two jobs. I just need the money."

Do it, Ike! I wanted to shout at him. *Give her the management position! She can so handle it.*

Instead I heard Ike take a step back, imagined him adjusting the fedora with his index finger. "I can maybe pay you fifty cents more an hour, if that'll help."

"It will," Wendy said. "But not enough."

"So where does that leave us?"

I held my breath so I wouldn't whisper, *Wendy, don't quit. Don't leave me.*

"I'm staying," she said.

The conversation was clearly over. I virtually ran to the sink, ostensibly for some steel wool, and almost knocked Wendy over in the process. Our eyes met and she knew that I knew it hadn't gone well. Why she didn't just ask Ike for the management position, I still couldn't figure out. But who was I to give employment advice?

I had no idea what it was that yanked me out of a hard sleep at six fifteen Tuesday morning. Lexi and I had been up until one watching the Ethan Hawke production of *Hamlet*. The house was quiet, with Daddy probably off to work already and Mama still away. I knew it was the too-quiet that pulled me out of bed, but what possessed me to get dressed and walk to St. John's Church, that had to be the Watch, telling me that if we invited God in I could heal.

With the pain strumming inside me like a constant sad guitar, that healing was, as Hamlet would say, a "consummation devoutly to be wished." Otherwise I might go as nutty as Ophelia.

The Savannah January day was soggy and foggy and pocked with puddles, but I picked my way through it and slid into the back pew of the church just as Ned Kregg stood up to say those words again: "From the rising of the sun even unto the going down of the same . . ."

The thin gathering of people seemed to be following in a book of some kind, and there were two different ones in the rack on the back of the pew in front of me, but I didn't even attempt to figure out which one, much less find the page. I just watched Ned as he proclaimed more than read through the part about the name of God being great among the heathen and on into words that startled me.

"Awake, awake; put on thy strength, O Zion; put on thy beautiful garments, O Jerusalem."

He went on to lead the tiny congregation to "humbly confess" their sins unto Almighty God, which they did in unison. I sat on the edge of the pew, held there by the fact that I was in front of God with my terrifying inner life. I had no idea what was going on as Ned gently delivered an absolution and began the Lord's Prayer. I didn't even join in. I simply sat there, breathing hard, as if I had narrowly escaped the grasp of something horrible and had found refuge in this strange, confusing place.

The service continued up there, far from me, and I stayed until the people were invited to come to the altar for communion. I left then, not because I didn't feel like I could go up and figure out what I was supposed to do. I was just full. Any more and I would have overflowed and lost it all down the drain that always seemed to be open and waiting. That's how it felt.

I spent the rest of the morning walking, skirting puddles and sidestepping innocent-looking flats of slick leaves, and thinking. *Wake up, Tara,* the clearing morning said to me. *Wake up and put on your strength.*

If I was going to see myself as someone apart from Seth, I was going to need it.

~ · ~

And I wasn't the only one. At work that day, Wendy seemed more upset than yesterday's conversation with Ike warranted as far as I was concerned. I knew about trembling hands and chins, and brief lapses while you stared into space and tried to remember who you were.

She didn't bring me soup again that day, so I fixed her a mug of cream of asparagus and took it to her.

"Drink this," I said. "It's comfort food."

"Do I need comforting?" she said.

"Who doesn't?" I said.

And I left it at that.

~ · ~

The next day, Wednesday, I went to St. John's again, and sat about halfway up in the sanctuary and discovered which book to use. *The Book of Common Prayer* was its title. My lit crit training kicked in and I peeked at the publishing information. Its original copyright date was 1928. No wonder the language sounded as if King James himself had penned it.

When they got to the confession of sin, I didn't join in the unison reading, but I tried to take in the words—which were daunting. Evidently we had all erred and strayed from God's ways like lost sheep and "followed too much the devices and desires of our own hearts." All of us—the pronoun consistently being plural—had done things we shouldn't have done and not done things we should have. Fortunately God was asked to spare us and restore us. And in his solemn absolution, Ned declared that was a done deal. God forgave and was there to make "the rest of our life hereafter" pure and holy.

Everyone else went into the Lord's Prayer. I sat for the remainder of the service, realizing that I wanted that. In spite of the Watch telling me I had no reason to feel ashamed, I wanted that purging and that absolution. Or I might fester forever.

I stayed for the whole thing, even though I didn't take communion, and when it was over I waited until the gracious women and gentlemanly patriarchs—who all seemed to have floated in from a time long past—had said their good-byes to Ned before I approached him. If the light in his soft brown eyes was an indication, he was pleased to see me.

"I'm glad you came back," he said.

"Did you find your jacket?" I said. "I left it on the hook."

"I did, thank you—"

"I want to make a confession."

His only indication that I had just committed a complete non sequitur was a slight turning of his head, as if he were suddenly listening with a different ear.

"Do you do that?" I said. "I mean, do you have some kind of booth thingie or something? I know this isn't a Catholic church, but . . ."

Convinced I sounded like a moron, I stopped. But Ned just nodded.

"We don't have a confessional, per se, but I'd be glad to sit down with you and hear anything you want to tell me. When would you like to do that?"

"Now?" I said. I didn't add, *before I wimp out.*

He seemed to get that, though, because he said, "We can go over to the parish house. Nobody's there this early."

Having lived in downtown Savannah my entire life, I didn't know how I'd missed the fact that the Green-Meldrim House, next door to St. John's Church, was also its parish house. I'd been inside once, on the obligatory field trip back in elementary school, so I knew the story about how General Sherman—the "evil" leader of the Yankee army in the "War of Northern Aggression" as some of my older teachers had still referred to it—had stayed there with his officers during the occupation of Savannah. The tale went that the hospitality was so gracious, he decided not to burn Savannah as he had Atlanta and instead gave our city to President Lincoln as a Christmas gift. Then he promptly went off to Columbia, South Carolina, and burned it to the ground.

The other thing that stuck in my mind, naturally, was that the house had been used in Robert Redford's production of *The Conspirator.* The long rug we walked over was a gift from him; he'd used it in the movie to protect the original English tile floors.

Ned led me into a large room in the front where the sun was beginning to stream through the narrow doors that opened out onto the first-floor balcony, which was almost level with the lane it faced. The ceilings were fifteen feet high, but the arrangement of the furniture in conversational groups made it somehow cozy. When Ned motioned for me to sit on a vintage brocade divan, I hesitated.

"Should we?" I said. "It's an antique, right?"

"We use everything in the house," he said. "Including the period silver tea service, every Sunday morning for coffee hour."

"Do you live here?" I said. Could I sound any more like a fifth-grader on the aforementioned field trip?

"My apartment is in what used to be the servants' quarters, attached to the house."

"You are not serious," I said. "I love that."

"So do I," Ned said. And then he folded his hands softly in his lap and said, "How can I help you, Tara?"

"You remembered my name."

"I'll forget it if you want me to."

I was about to laugh but he seemed serious.

"You can say anything you want and I will keep it in strict confidence. As far as the rest of the world is concerned, we never had this conversation, unless you want to tell someone."

"Okay."

"But let's pray first."

I expected him to pull one of the books of Common Prayer out of his jacket pocket, but he simply bowed his head and murmured about God being there as a third party to our conversation, to free my mind and heart and tongue and to give him—Ned—ears to hear my heart.

He didn't say amen. He just whispered, "You can start anytime you want."

I thought the floodgates had come all the way open when I spilled my story out to the Watch. But that day, sitting on a sofa where perhaps other women since the Civil War had poured out their anguish to a priest, I emptied myself of everything.

The graphic specifics of what I saw, both times, on the computer screen and in Seth.

Our attempt to reconcile.

Seth's almost-suicide.

Evelyn's report about the prostitute.

Paul and Randi's reactions and my angry retorts to them.

My neglect of GrandMary.

My argument with my father.

My failure to have enough compassion for Seth that he could go to his healing with a fearless heart.

My conviction that I would never see the world as a loving place again.

And my refusal to completely believe that God was really in this and that I could be healed because I hadn't given God even as much attention as I gave . . . anything. I finished with, "I'm that heathen you always read about at the beginning of the service."

Ned looked puzzled.

"'For my name shall be great among the heathen, saith the Lord of hosts,'" I said.

One eyebrow went up. "I'm impressed. I bet I could ask every person who comes for the service *daily* what I said at the beginning and none of them could quote it."

"I guess it just struck a nerve."

"Undeservedly. If you were a heathen you wouldn't be here. We have plenty of heathens in Savannah, and you definitely aren't one of them."

"So," I said, "am I absolved?"

"I would be happy to give you an absolution," Ned said. "We could all use one about fifty times a day."

"I hear a but," I said. "Is this too bad for that?"

Ned actually looked dumbfounded. "Okay, it's obvious you've had some kind of religious upbringing."

"I was raised a Christian," I said. "I graduated from Veritas Academy."

"Then I'm curious . . . Where did you come up with the theology that there is some sin that can't be forgiven?"

I blinked. "I don't know. This just seems way too ugly."

"You don't think Seth can be forgiven?"

"Um, yes?"

"Because . . ."

"It says so in the Bible?"

"Is that a question?"

"No. It does say that."

"It does. I'm more concerned about what you think *you've* done wrong."

He was starting to sound like Betsy and Ms. Helen and Gray, and instead of being reassuring, that made me uneasy.

"I feel as if I should have more empathy for Seth," I said. "He's begging me to be supportive, to give him a reason to work at getting this thing fixed, but I can't totally. And that makes me feel so . . . un-Christian. I want to be all compassionate and forgiving and say, 'I'll stand by you through anything' . . ." I let the hands I was using to say it all drop to my lap. "I just can't."

"Well, no," Ned said.

For the first time I realized he did most of *his* talking with his eyes. The rest of his face was serene, almost unmoving, but his eyes seemed to hold all the emotion. They shone and softened and sparked. They even seemed to sigh.

"Just because you're a Christian doesn't mean you should deaden the pain you have every right to feel. You have to deal with that first before you can even decide whether to help Seth."

"That's not selfish?"

"No. That's loving yourself so you can love your neighbor."

"I don't have to feel guilty?"

"Even if you'd actually done something wrong you wouldn't have to walk around feeling guilty. That's what the confession of sin and the absolution is about. It's not just a ritual."

I sighed. It sounded as if it came from the pit of my soul.

"How do you feel?" he said.

"Drained?" I said. "Yeah, I feel drained."

"I think that's good." His eyes did a little dance. "I guess the absolution worked, huh?"

I smiled, faintly I was sure. Ned rubbed his hands together. "I have to go to a breakfast meeting, but if you want to talk again, any other morning this week, I'm free after the service. We can always come here."

I was almost too emptied-out to answer, but I managed to say, "I'll think about it."

And, in fact, I thought about almost nothing else for the rest of the day.

Until the call came from Seth that night.

SEVENTEEN

Seth had been gone for over three weeks and I hadn't heard anything from him or about him. I didn't expect Randi and Paul to keep me apprised, though Evelyn would have if she knew anything, and there was zero chance of that.

So I wasn't thinking about talking to him as I sat in the window seat watching for Lexi, who was bringing a selection of comedies for that night's marathon. I was musing over the fact that it was the day Seth and I were supposed to return from Ireland and start our new life on Jones Street for real. So when the phone rang I was grateful for the interruption and answered it without looking to see who it was.

"Hey, Tar," Seth said. "Do you have a few minutes?"

His voice was strong, but slightly hesitant, as if he were dipping his toe into my waters. I suddenly, inexplicaby, didn't want him to find them cold.

"Of course I do," I said. "How *are* you? Really?"

"Miserable," he said, as if that were the new fine. "But that's good. I mean, it's bad, but it's good."

"Okay," I said. Oddly enough, I understood.

"So," we both said at the same time.

"Go ahead," I said.

"I want to hear about you too," he said. "But I do have some things I want to tell you. That I have to tell you."

It took every amount of strength I had not to end the call. I wasn't sure I could hear any more of the sordid story that came out every time we talked. And yet, hadn't my own confession left me drained of the ugliness?

"Okay," I said, and hugged my knees in.

"This is going to be kind of random because I haven't connected all the dots yet," he said, "but it's what makes sense so far."

"Okay," I said again.

"We decided not to have sex before we got married because that's the Christian thing to do. Right?"

"Right."

"And it was hard. But harder for you than for me—and don't take that the wrong way."

I wasn't sure there was any other way to take it, but I bit my lip and let him continue.

"The reason for that was that I *couldn't* have sex with you. Because of the porn, sex wasn't a sign of love for me anymore. It was a sign of abuse. And I didn't want to abuse you."

The image of the video I'd discovered that day at the townhouse slammed into view. I shuddered. I couldn't even allow myself to replace the woman I saw there with a picture of myself. All I could manage to say now was yet another default, "Okay."

"What I'm trying to tell you," Seth said, "is that my addiction isn't about sex at all, so it definitely isn't about me not wanting you or you not being everything *any* guy would want. Some of the guys here have shared with me that their wives felt totally . . . undesirable when they found out, and it was a huge thing to have to overcome. So don't go there, Tar, all right?"

That ship had sailed but I didn't say so.

"Can I go on?" he said.

"Please," I said.

"Here's another thing you have to know: I never enjoyed porn, not really. It wasn't about pleasure for me. It was about releasing pain. But the more I did it, the worse the pain got because the secret was killing me from the inside out."

"I get that part." I sat up straighter on the window seat. "But what pain, Seth? I don't understand that."

For the first time in the conversation he paused, and I could almost see him measuring out his words into spoonfuls. That made me want to stop him again—to keep him from saying things that couldn't be unsaid.

And then he went on.

"I've had anxiety since I was ten. Bad. Like I thought I was going crazy sometimes. We haven't totally uncovered what that was about here and we will. But I'll tell you what I know."

Again he seemed to regroup. I nodded to nobody.

"The summer I went up to my cousin's in Maine—I was thirteen—they had that old beach house and my cousin was all *about* the *Playboys* and *Hustlers* the guy who lived there before left in the basement. I knew it was wrong to look at them; I just did it because he dared me. And then I found out it . . ." He sighed into the phone. "I don't know; it soothed me, I guess you could say? I could look at it at night and . . . do whatever . . . and I could really sleep for the first time in about three years."

I was doing fine until then. But the thought of my Seth at thirteen, using a centerfold and his barely pubescent body like a drug—it *was* another image I'd never be able to erase.

"Is that helping you?" I said. "Going back and knowing all this?"

"It is."

"Then I'm glad. But some of it I can't—"

"Does it make me seem dirty to you?"

It was more an accusation than a question. If it hadn't been partially true, I would have bristled more than I did. As it was, I still had to breathe before I spoke again.

"It's sad," I said.

"I don't want you to feel sorry for me."

"Then what *do* you want?"

"I just want you to understand."

"I'm trying. I am."

"But you don't want the nasty details."

"Do I *need* the nasty details?"

In the silence that followed I wasn't even sure what Seth would be doing, what body language to imagine. He was looking into a past I thought I knew everything about and obviously didn't, and it made me wonder in that chilling moment if I had ever really known him at all. Who was it, then, that I loved?

"I'm just scared," I said.

"I'm sorry," Seth said. "Maybe talking about it isn't the best way. Maybe I need to get my thoughts down on paper, you know? They encourage us to journal. That's helping."

"Good," I said. "Really, I'm glad, Seth."

"I love you," he said.

It was the first hint of desperation I heard, and I couldn't let that be the note we ended on. So I said, "I love you too."

But as we said our good-byes, I wasn't sure. For the first time since I was fifteen years old, I wasn't sure. And that was huge.

There was no doubt in my mind after the service the next morning that I needed to talk to Ned Kregg some more.

We went back to the room in the parish house and, sitting on the same salmon-colored brocade sofa, I told him about the phone call with Seth.

"I tried to be compassionate this time," I said. "But is it wrong of me not to want to listen to stuff that I can't get out of my mind?"

"No. Knowing the details isn't necessarily going to make you empathetic."

"It's going to make me throw up."

Ned's eyes smiled, and then they grew wise. "What you do need to know is that Seth's addiction to porn is only one manifestation of something more pervasive that's going on."

"That anxiety he was talking about—that I never even saw. Where *was* I?"

"You really are the self-flagellation queen," Ned said. "You didn't see because, one, he didn't want you to see it and, two, the porn was relieving it enough that he didn't feel it, until he needed another fix."

"So it really is like a drug."

"And it sounds like they're helping him get to the source of the anxiety itself. That's a good program he's in."

"He got really defensive when I said I didn't want the details. Then he didn't want me to feel sorry for him." I gave the shrug of all shrugs. "I don't even know how to talk to him anymore."

"He doesn't know how he needs to be talked to. The phone call was probably not the wisest thing at this point." Ned studied his hands, which were small for a tall guy, and uncalloused. There was a faint ink stain on his middle finger. "I don't know Seth so I can't say this with certainty, but I'm going to guess that he's more damaged than it even looks like right now. Something may have happened to him that he hasn't dug up yet and, again, I can't be sure about that." He turned his head slightly. "Does Seth seem to fear intimacy?"

I thought about it. Fear wouldn't be the word I'd use for the night in the kitchen when he nearly shoved me against the dishwasher because I vaguely hinted that I wanted to go further than a kiss twenty days before our wedding—even though I didn't mean head for the bedroom. But it had been something strong.

"He didn't *want* intimacy with me," I said finally. "But he said—"

I told him what Seth told me about abuse and the whole thing not being about sex.

"I think that's the truth," Ned said. "And that had to come from somewhere. When you're in pain you don't see a reason for . . . Let me see if I can help you understand that . . . if you want."

"I do," I said.

Ned studied his hands again. "What have you been doing since Seth left and you don't want all the thoughts and memories and images crashing in on you?"

"Walking. Watching movies."

"Let's take the movies. You've been using those as a distraction to kind of muffle the screams of your own pain. Does that ring true?"

"Like a bell," I said.

"*Seth's* distraction has been pornography. And once that got started, it was almost impossible for him to stop." Ned's gaze deepened. "He wasn't lying to you when he said he wanted to. Deep down, he does. But some excellent studies have been done, and they're discovering that the brain chemistry in a porn addict changes, just like it does in a drug addict or an alcoholic. But—this is the good news—the brain can be rewired."

"And that's what they're trying to do in Colorado."

"Right. Seth and his counselors and God."

I fingered the brocade and watched it blur as my eyes filmed. "He wants me to be part of that team. Why can't I just do that?"

"Because we're not there yet."

"We?" I said.

"I use that in a corporate sense. You, your team, whoever they are, and God."

I let the tears go, and I said, "Will you be on my team?"

"I'd be honored," he said.

⁓⟀⟀⁓

So I saw Ned Friday morning and we talked some more. I talked to my women too. I gave soup to Wendy and didn't talk, which was probably just as well. I even talked to God, haltingly, like a person learning a new language. It was maybe helping. I wasn't doubled over by spikes of anxiety in the core of me, so maybe.

Still, when Lexi called late Friday to tell me she couldn't make it for movie night—one of her siblings had an issue—I almost panicked.

Ned seemed to think it was okay for me to distract myself sometimes, so I was plugging in *The Princess Bride*, which was the furthest thing from real life I could come up with, when Kellen came in. I almost dropped the DVD.

"What are you watching?" he said. Nonchalantly. As if he *hadn't* been avoiding me for however long. I could play that game.

"Nothing yet," I said.

He nodded as if I'd given him a definitive answer. Then he ran his hand over his shaved head. Then he cracked his knuckles. Just as I was about to scream, "For Pete's sake, what *is* it?" he said, "Were you gonna make popcorn?"

"I can," I said.

"Look, Tar—I'm sorry."

I went still.

"I should've been there for you through this whole thing and I wasn't. I've been a jerk."

"I'll give you that," I said.

"I was seeing it through the guy lens."

"And what did that tell you?"

Kellen half-grinned. "You're not going to make this easy on me, are you?"

"Nothing about this *is* easy," I said. "Brushing my *teeth* is hard."

He cracked his knuckles again, something I hadn't seen him do since he was sixteen. "All I saw was you breaking Seth's heart. I didn't see what he could have done to tick you off that much, that couldn't be worked out, until he told me he was going to rehab."

"Did he tell you what he was going to rehab *for*?"

I immediately chewed at my lip.

His eyes squinted. "He said he couldn't talk about it because of his job. I assumed it was prescription drugs. I knew he took Xanax. That's what he used to try to . . . kill himself, right?"

"Yeah," I said. "I'll make us some popcorn—"

Kellen grabbed my sleeve. "That's not it, is it?"

"I can't say any more than he can."

"Is it porn?"

I did drop the DVD then.

Kellen swiped his hand across his shaved head.

"I thought he quit."

"You *knew*?" I said.

"I knew about it five years ago. He came to me, told me what was going on, wanted me to be his accountability partner."

"You *knew*?"

"I stood there in his room while he deleted everything off his hard drives. I took the DVDs to the dump. I walked him through it for six months, and he swore to me he was clean. I wouldn't let him start dating you until I knew he was done with it."

"But why didn't you tell me?" I clutched at my hair. "You didn't think that was something I should know?"

"No, Tar, I didn't." Kellen licked his lips as if his mouth were the Sahara. "I believed him. You were happy. Why would I throw that in there when there was no reason to?"

"Not even when I broke off the engagement? It didn't occur to you then that that might be the reason?"

"No. It didn't. I asked Seth why you did it and he told me you just weren't sure." His blue eyes squinted. "Looking back on it now, even if I had thought of it, I would have also thought you'd say something to us—you know, your *family*."

"He asked me not to."

"Why did you agree to that?"

"Because I didn't want his whole life to be destroyed!"

"No," Kellen said. "Just yours."

I was in my big brother's arms before I could think about resisting. I sobbed into his chest, and I could feel him weeping as well. It occurred to me that as close as we'd been, we had never cried together, not both of us at the same time.

"This started way before you, Tar," he said when he could speak.

I pulled away and looked at him. "You have snot everywhere," I said. "I'm getting you a Kleenex."

"Did he tell you about his cousin in Maine?"

"Yeah. Here." I handed him the entire box of tissues Lexi and I kept between us for tearjerkers.

Kellen blew his nose as only a young male can do. It was like listening to the call of a bull moose. I had missed him so much.

I picked up the wastebasket and let him drop the snot rag into it.

"He told me about that back when I was helping him," Kellen said.

"He said it started then. The weird thing is, I was supposed to go on that trip with him and at the last minute Dad said I couldn't. He said he had a bad feeling about Randi or Paul not being there with us. We had just about the only fight we ever had over that." Kellen shrugged. "Anyway, Seth said, five years ago when we were working on this, that he was glad I didn't go or I might be in the same position he was."

"I don't think so," I said. "Even Paul says not everybody who looks at porn is an addict."

"Yeah, well, just for the record, I never did."

I pulled out another Kleenex for him.

"So Randi and Paul obviously know about this," he said after another moose-like blow.

"Oh yeah."

"I still don't get why you couldn't have told us. Okay, maybe not me. I've been a jerk. And not Mama." Kellen visibly shuddered. "I hope she never finds out. But Daddy—"

"I told you. It was bad enough without everybody knowing. Like, right now, if Seth *is* healed, how would he come back here and face everyone if they all knew about it?"

"Yeah, but it left you tearing yourself up."

"I'm getting help. From people who don't know him. Or us."

Kellen pulled me against him again and let his hand go into my hair. "We've protected him too much, Tar," he said. "Maybe we enabled him."

I pulled away. "Maybe. But there's nothing we can do about that now. Besides, you and I can talk since you're not acting like Heathcliff anymore—but let me tell Mama and Daddy when I feel like it's time, okay? Please?"

"Yeah. So are you gonna make popcorn or what?"

"Do you have a broken arm?" I said.

EIGHTEEN

I was barely out of bed Saturday morning when I got a text from Randi Grissom, asking me to meet her at the Sentient Bean at ten. At least it was more like asking than *usual*, since there was actually a question mark at the end of it. That was the only reason I answered that I would.

The Bean was all the way at the other end of Forsyth Park, and as I walked the pathways under a seamless January sky, I was pretty sure Randi didn't frequent the place. It was too on-the-border with Ardsley Park, where the rich scarcely trod. My guess was she didn't want us to run into anybody we knew, and she, too, had gotten a call from Seth, so she wanted to review my commitment not to tell anyone. I sure wasn't going to confess that Kellen had guessed. I was pretty much over her.

She wasn't there yet when I arrived—probably a technique to set me off balance—so I resolved to stay calm. I sat at a table in front and listened to the conversation at the next one over.

The Sentient Bean was a cavernous place with a counter too small for it. People shopping at the Brighter Day health food place next door dropped in for coffee, but the hang-out clientele seemed to be mostly men who had nothing to do but play backgammon and tell lies. The group next to me was a case in point.

One guy, who sounded like he was probably from Philadelphia, was dropping a name a minute while he watched two others play. In the time I sat there waiting for Randi, he claimed that he knew everyone in the film industry from Daniel Day-Lewis to "Bob" De Niro. Not only that but his mother hung out with Eleanor Roosevelt and his uncle was Eleanor's plumber at Hyde Park. It made me wonder if anybody was real.

I shook my head at my own self. Of course there were real people. Good people. Honest people. Like my Watch, who I wished were going to join me instead of the straight-haired woman in too-expensive sunglasses and teetery ankle boots who approached me from the door.

"Thanks for coming," Randi said. "Can we move to a table further back?"

Only because Mr. Name Dropper was launching into how he was going to revamp the entire film arts program at SCAD did I agree.

"Do you want coffee?" Randi said when she'd selected the table in the most remote corner of the place.

"No," I said.

"I do," she said, "but it can wait." She tossed back her hair. Thin as it was, it fell right back against her face. "Paul wasn't sure you needed to know this, but I think legally it's best."

I felt my own face drain of color.

"Seth is not as financially stable as he led us to believe. He left me in charge of paying his bills while he's gone, and I don't know how he thought I wasn't going to discover this but he has spent thousands, and I do mean thousands, of dollars on"—she forced her voice down to a hoarse whisper—"pornography, including paying for the ultrahigh-speed Internet he needed for those big sites."

Randi was rattling off the information as if she were talking about one of her clients. I expected her to whip out a file any minute and check to see if she had the name right.

"The upshot is: He has missed his last two mortgage payments on the townhouse. I've paid them so he's now current, but that can't continue. Contrary to popular belief, we are not made of money."

That was entirely untrue. I had never seen a woman more made of money in my life, and I'd known some very rich people.

"So why tell me?" I said.

"Because Seth still believes you're going to marry him when he gets past this, and I think you should have all the information before you make that commitment."

Suspicion nearly made my hair stand up on end. She was suddenly concerned about my welfare? Even as I watched her turn her gaze from me in a rare moment of self-consciousness, I knew. She wasn't.

"No," I said. "You're telling me because you want me to have every reason *not* to marry Seth."

Randi's head came up. "Why on earth would I do that? I want my son happy."

"You want your son protected—no, your family. Your name. And as long as I know, the threat of other people finding out will always be there. If *I* am the one who decides not to be his wife, why would I ever out him? Only a woman scorned would do that."

"You always were a dreamer," she said.

"For once, Randi," I said, "I'm not dreaming. But from now on, if there is anything I need to know about Seth, let Seth tell me."

⁓℧℧⁓

I ran all the way to the other end of the park before I stopped to breathe and massage the stitch digging into my side. Was there ever going to be a bottom to the layers that had to be ripped off? Was there always going to be one more thing that had to be exposed?

As I limped across Gaston to the house, I knew one thing for sure: this didn't feel like healing.

The postal guy was at our box as I approached the wrought-iron fence. I wasn't usually the one who brought in the mail, but I retrieved it and took it inside. Daddy would want to see it and I needed to see *him*. We'd barely spent ten minutes together since Mama left for Virginia.

I was surprised to find him in the kitchen, whisking eggs in a bowl.

"Look at you," I said.

"Fixing myself an omelet," he said. "You want one?"

"No, thanks." The thought made me turn green from the inside out.

"It has feta cheese in it."

"Really, Daddy—I'm good."

"You don't *look* good." He tapped the whisk on the edge of the bowl and frowned at me. "Do you need to see the doctor?"

"Okay," I said, "I'll have an omelet. Just no garlic."

"What? That's the best part."

"I brought the mail in," I said.

"Give me the bad news. Where does your mother keep the garlic anyway?"

"I'm not telling." I hiked myself up onto one of the stools and flipped through the stack. "Okay, Bell South . . . American Express, that one's kind of thick . . . AARP—"

"Pitch that one. It makes me feel old. Ah, garlic salt. That'll work."

"*Business Weekly* and . . ." I stopped because I was staring at a vanilla-colored envelope with a Denver postmark. The return address said, simply, *Seth Grissom*.

"You okay, sugar?" Daddy said.

"Y'know what?" I said. "I'm going to pass on the omelet after all. Maybe tomorrow?"

He just looked at me—sadly—and nodded. I retreated to the fourth floor with the letter pressed against my chest.

But when I hit the window seat, I couldn't open it. What had Seth said on the phone? *Maybe talking about it isn't the best way. Maybe I need to get my thoughts down on paper.*

Was that what this was? More thoughts? More layers? One more thing to rip off the places that were just beginning to scab over?

I closed my eyes against the sun slanting in through the slats of the shutters and striping the room in light. This was difficult enough when I knew almost *nothing* about porn and addiction and Seth's raw past. *Seeing* it was too much. It was too hard.

The sun lightened the space behind my eyelids anyway. I opened my eyes and watched the dust dance in its shafts.

Nothing about this is *easy*, I'd told Kellen.

I pulled the envelope from my chest and ran my thumb over Seth's perfect printing. I had to read it. I hated it, but I had to know that one more thing. And I would.

But not now. Not alone.

I tucked it under the cushion of the window seat.

Betsy wasn't at the Piebald Sunday; according to Gray she had a "church thing." When I told Gray and Ms. Helen about the letter, neither of them asked me why I hadn't opened it. They seemed to know . . . more than I did.

"So," Gray said, poking the wooden stir stick up and down into her latte. "You're afraid to."

"Yes," I said. "Coward that I am, yes, I'm afraid."

"All right, let's get something straight."

We both looked at Ms. Helen, who had her hands on the hips of her pale purple slacks.

"Uh-oh," Gray said.

"I do not want to hear you calling yourself any more names, Tara," Ms. Helen said.

Speaking of name-calling, when she stopped calling me honey and started calling me Tara, I knew she was not to be argued with.

"Did I call myself a name?" I said.

"You haven't stopped. We've heard coward, stupid—"

"Heathen," I added. "But somebody else put the kibosh on that one."

"Whatever you call yourself you're eventually going to believe. And why would you want to believe things that aren't true?"

"Did you ever get bullied when you were a kid?" Gray said, and immediately shook her head. "No, you probably didn't. I did—I got Gray Beard, Lard Butt, oh, and my personal favorite, Thunder Thighs. I bought all of it, which made it very easy for me to believe my husband's lack of interest in me was all *my* fault."

Ms. Helen tapped the table with a nail—taupe today. "The point is, honey, just because you're afraid doesn't make you a coward. I'd be afraid too."

"But you'd open it," I said.

"Eventually."

"I think we ought to look at exactly what you're afraid *of*," Gray said. "Besides TMI from Mr. Fiancé."

"I don't know what else there would be."

"You mind if I take a guess?"

"Okay."

"What if he does reveal something, I don't know, icky."

I had to laugh. "Icky would be euphemistic, but okay."

"Did you actually use the word *euphemistic*? My gosh, I like you. Okay . . . what if it's awful? What do you think you're going to do?"

"Explode," I said, without hesitation.

Gray leaned in, ponytail flopping to the right. "And that scares you to death."

I nodded. "I've never been so all-over-the-place with my emotions. It's like the thing with calling myself names. I never did that. I've always had pretty solid self-esteem. And now . . ."

"This whole thing has sucked that right out of you."

Ms. Helen pushed her hand across the table until it reached mine. "But, honey, you have the power to take that back."

"It's hard when everything has fallen apart."

"Except you." Gray's already pink face deepened to a rose, born of suddenly feeling pretty good about her sweet self, I was sure.

"What?" I said.

"Just remember—you are gonna love this—this is about *self*-esteem, not *Seth*-esteem."

"Oh, honey," Ms. Helen said. "That is so bad it's good."

"Really," I said.

Gray nudged my arm. "You get it, though, don't you?"

"Yeah," I said. "I get it."

<hr />

Fear of breaking apart into confetti still kept me from opening the letter by myself. But it didn't keep me from taking it with me when I talked to Ned after the service on Monday. Winter had taken a rare bite out of Savannah during the night, and I could see wisps of my breath as we walked together across the cloistered lane and into the Green-Meldrim House. Even after we settled onto our couch in the corner I still couldn't get warm. I must have looked pathetic because Ned took off his light leather jacket and tossed it over my lap. I buried my hands under it until my fingers could open the envelope.

"Do you want to read it out loud?" Ned said.

"Oh," I said. "I think I do. Maybe if I hear it, it'll make more sense . . . I don't know."

"Give it a go. If it's too hard, you can stop. It'll still be here tomorrow."

I nodded and unfolded a sheet of plain vanilla paper covered in single-spaced type. We were going to *need* until tomorrow. The sheer length of it made me shiver.

"*Dear Tara,*" I read. I skipped the paragraph about how good it was to hear my voice and how he knew this was hard for me and went to paragraph two. The one that started with,

I need to tell you what happened when I came back from Maine.

I looked up at Ned, who had his eyes closed. "Do you remember that part?"

"Beach house. Cousin. *Hustlers* and *Playboys*. Seth found comfort."

"Right." I located my place again and read,

I went into withdrawal when I came back. My anxiety was worse than ever and I was sleeping maybe three hours a night. It was getting to be time to go back to school and I was starting eighth grade. I was freaking out because I just knew I was going to flunk out.

I looked up again. "Seth was a straight-A student. That was a huge deal for him."

I read on.

There was this kid at church—he was a freshman then and he was only there for a year or two—but I went to his house

235

one time with Dad when they first moved to Savannah and this kid had a computer in his bedroom. He was actually the first kid I ever knew who had his own and he started showing me all this cool stuff on the Internet. And then it was like he read my mind, and he said, 'I want to show you the coolest thing yet, but you have to swear you'll never tell anybody. Especially your dad.' He opened up this porn site and I just got a rush, better than anything I ever got from a magazine.

I stopped. "Why would this kid take that chance with the pastor's kid?"

Ned gave a small shrug. "My gut response is that he sensed something in Seth. He even says it was like the kid read his mind."

"You mean, like, one addict being able to recognize another?"

"Something like that."

It was my turn to close my eyes. "This is so freaky, Ned. It's like he was a part of a whole other world I never knew about, and I thought I knew everything about him."

"That's painful," Ned said.

You might not remember this,

I read on,

but my relationship with that kid—I think his name was Micah—caused kind of a rift between Kellen and me because I was spending more time with Micah than him. I know Kellen wondered why I didn't include him, but I didn't want him to know. That might have ruined our friendship totally if I hadn't gotten a laptop for Christmas that year. Then I didn't need to go to Micah's. I had access to porn in my own bedroom. And I was never without it again.

"Does that surprise you?" Ned said when I paused. "That his Internet usage was unsupervised?"

"Not really. Why wouldn't Randi and Paul trust him? He was such a nice kid. He was the Good Kid, especially compared to Evelyn, who was already giving them fits, and she was only three." I found myself warming to the subject. "This was the kid who always knew he wanted to work with some kind of ministry. Of the three of us—Seth, Kellen, and me—he was the most Christian. And it wasn't just because his dad was the pastor. There was just something in him that we didn't have." I let my gaze flow down the page, picking up a word here and there. The next sentence was,

There's more.

My throat closed.

"Can you read the rest to me?" I said. "Would that be okay?"

"If that's what you want." Ned took the letter and adjusted his glasses before he looked at me. "I'll stop anytime you say."

"Okay," I said, but I knew if we didn't get straight through this I might never come back to it again. I buried my hands under the jacket once more and nodded for Ned to begin.

Two words in and I almost regretted that choice. Hearing it spoken by a male voice close to Seth's age made it more real somehow. More like the truth.

Since I talked to you, I've uncovered some memories I'd buried.

Ned read.

They weren't very far down, but it was still hard to dig them up. It was like they were embedded in rock. Here's basically what happened: When I was ten, maybe a little before, I was molested by someone I trusted. Numerous times.

Ned's voice slowed.

And sworn to secrecy and threatened if I told. I know you don't want to hear the details, so I'm going to spare you those. I hope it's enough for you to know that I'm getting to what's caused my pain and anxiety all these years and doing that is making me less dependent on porn already. Will you trust that I'm being healed? I love you, Tar. Seth.

I had to swallow twice before I could speak. "Is he saying he was sexually abused?"

Ned looked grim as he folded the letter. "I was afraid of that. It's not uncommon for sex addicts to have that in their past."

"So that's the pain he was talking about? That was the reason for all the anxiety?"

"The pain is from being abused. The anxiety is from having to keep it a secret."

I felt like a piece of wood, except for one small flash of realization. "You know what's weird?"

Ned shook his head.

"This is like the first time I actually know how he felt. I mean, just a little, you know."

"The anxiety of keeping something locked up?"

I put my hand against my solar plexus. "It's like this big ball of spines and it shoots out everywhere. Sometimes I can't stand it."

"Neither can he."

My hands balled into fists. "That part—being abused—that wasn't his fault."

"And can you imagine what that's like at ten, when you don't have the resources yet to realize you didn't do anything wrong?"

"It's hard enough at twenty-five." I let my head fall back on the sofa. "Now I totally feel like a heel, not helping him."

Ned's eyes grew firm. "You really want to go there, Tara? Look, you didn't know where this all came from. He didn't even know. And while that explains a lot, it doesn't excuse anything. He hurt the person he loves most in the world, and it's going to take time for you to heal."

"Every time I think, okay, I know it all, now I can move forward, there's one more thing and it's worse than the thing before it."

"It does seem that way."

I brought my head back up. "For instance, who *was* this person he trusted? Is that going to be another big ol' steel pole hitting me in the head?"

Ned gestured with the letter he still had in his hand. "Seth seems to sense that you wouldn't want to know."

"I feel so horrible for him. Oh my gosh, how could someone—he was just a little boy—I don't even know how to think about this." I plastered my hand to my mouth and spoke through my fingers. "Ned," I said, "I'm going to be sick."

I made it to the kitchen. Ned waited discreetly in the hall and handed me a wet washcloth when I came out.

"You really are the full-service priest, aren't you?" I said. My voice trembled like a candle flame.

"I'm not going to ask you if you're okay. Nothing about this is okay." His eyes went from concerned to very sure about something. "Except one thing."

I pulled the washcloth from my mouth. "Please tell me what's okay. Please."

"God is in this, somehow, some way—God's slogging through this with us. Do you want to keep going?"

"I don't know what to *do* next," I said.

"Let's pray," he said.

NINETEEN

I walked until nine thirty, although where I went I couldn't say. At least physically. Where I went mentally? I went to Seth at ten, into his bedroom, and saw him smiling up at some person he trusted, maybe loved, his big brown eyes wide and innocent . . . saw them widen in disbelief and fear—

I couldn't go there. I turned another corner and found myself face-to-face with his eleven-year-old self, lying in the dark with his black hair sticking out in anxious, hand-raked spikes against the pillow, rocking himself in his bed to try to get to sleep and escape from—

Not a route I could take either. Nor could I watch him slide a *Playboy* under his T-shirt, sick with guilt, and lock his beach house bedroom door. Or take all the back alleys to some kid named Micah's house, looking over his shoulder, terrified that his best friend might be following him. Or log onto the Internet that Christmas night in the very room where his innocence had been torn from him and spiral down to a place he would be trapped in for years.

I stopped on Harris Street and leaned against the front window of E. Shaver Bookseller. Behind me in the showcase, dancing cupids and lacy hearts and a selection of romances reminded us that Valentine's Day approached and we would need Danielle Steel to show us what perfect endings never looked like.

If I couldn't go to any of those dark, wretched places where Seth had lived, alone and frightened and seething with self-loathing—if I couldn't . . . how could he?

I closed my eyes and waited to fly apart into the dreaded red-and-pink confetti. It didn't happen. I only felt one break, one final, painful rent—right down the middle of my heart.

Once again with no place to go, I headed for the Piebald. Ike would be facing the midmorning rush. Maybe he'd need some help. Maybe I could just distract myself until six o'clock when my women would be there to help me put the two pieces back together.

I was right that Ike could use some assistance. The line was all the way down the ramp when I got there, and some of the tables hadn't been cleared. People were supposed to bus their own dishes, but there were always those few who left the detritus of their break-fast while they rushed off to important places, cell phone pressed to ear.

I hung my jacket on a hook by the door and, with my purse still over my shoulder, attacked the first table. The *Savannah Morning News* was scattered on the tabletop and chairs, as if the reader thought covering his crumby plate and half-empty cup would make it okay. Unlike most of the rest of my life, this I could clean up.

I picked up the front section and folded it into a tidy rectangle and tossed it to the seat of the one chair that wasn't littered. Before I could turn to the rest of the mess, the headline grabbed me and turned my head as if it were a hand on my chin.

CFO OF GREAT COMMISSION MINISTRY
OUTED AS SEX ADDICT

Before I could stop them my eyes went down the column.

Seth Grissom, son of prominent Savannah attorney Randi Grissom and popular Christian pastor and author Paul—

—source who prefers to remain anonymous reports excessive use of pornography—

—currently undergoing treatment—

No. Nonononononono—*no!* This didn't happen. This. Did. Not. Happen.

"Tara."

Ike was at my side. The air in the Piebald was dead. The line of people down the ramp were all pulling their gawking gazes from me as if *I* was now the train wreck.

Because I was. Because I could feel the strain in my throat from screaming all of it—from wailing again and again, "No. This can't happen! It can't happen!"

"Come on, hon."

Ike already had his arm around me, and he half-carried me until I found myself in his office. He deposited me in the leather chair and squatted in front of me. I plucked at the newspaper and shook. Now I *was* coming apart. Soon, very soon, there would be nothing left of me at all.

"What's going on, hon?" Ike said.

"This." I waved the paper up and down but I couldn't let go of it.

"You talking about the story? The sex addict story?"

"It's not a story," I said. "It's true."

"Do you know this guy?"

I gasped. Oh no. I wasn't supposed to tell anyone. I couldn't—

And then the full impact of what I held in my hands hit me in the face like the flat of a powerful hand. It didn't matter who I told now. Because now . . . everyone knew.

"Tara?" Ike said.

"Yeah, I know him," I said. "He's my fiancé."

Ike sat back on his heels and his face worked. Hard. As if he were trying to get control for both of us.

"Did you know about this?" he said.

I nodded.

"Holy *crud*, Tara, how were you even functioning?" He put his beefy hand on my arm. "Never mind. Just let me take you home."

"No, please. Can't I just stay here until I can get myself together?"

"You can stay as long as you want, but I really think—"

"Please?"

He nodded reluctantly and stood up. "Can I at least call some-body for you?"

"No."

"Then you call *me* if you need something." He started to the door and turned back. "I just don't want to leave you alone like this. Let me at least call Ms. Helen. Can I do that?"

"She'll be here soon," I said. Crazily. Like someone who was los-ing her mind.

"Sit right here," Ike said. "I'll be back."

The minute the door closed behind him I panicked. He was right. I couldn't be alone. What if I came all the way apart? Who would stick the pieces back together?

I looked down at my hands, which still gripped the sides of the folded newspaper, so tight my fingers were smeared with newsprint, so hard the paper was beginning to dissolve. Maybe if I could make it go away, no one would know. No one would know about Seth.

My breath was coming out in shreds. I inhaled, long and full, and then again. I couldn't lose it now. Everyone was going to know—and everyone couldn't find me in a pile of rubble when they got to me. Everyone—

I stood straight up, shoving the chair back behind me. Daddy was going to see this. No. Nononononono—I had to get to him first.

Still clinging to the paper that was now no more than a rag in my hands, I bolted from Ike's office and somehow made my way outside without smashing into any of the people who stood between me and the corner door. I paused, anxiety shooting needles, and tried to think. It would be faster to run home, get my car, and drive to Daddy's office than to run straight there. Yes.

I took off, coatless, the purse that was still on my shoulder flailing out behind me. Twice I barely avoided colliding with a car at a corner. Miraculously it wasn't more than that because, as I tore insanely toward Gaston Street, all I could think of was getting to my father before he saw.

The fact that I ever imagined that as a possibility was proof of how much of myself had broken off from me already. It was ten a.m. Dennis Faulkner had probably read the *Morning News*, the *Wall Street Journal*, and the *New York Times* by then. I lost all hope when I opened the back door and the alarm was off. Daddy was standing in the kitchen, leaning on the counter with the front page spread out in front of him.

Somehow, that made it real. It could happen. And it had.

"Daddy?" I said.

The eyes that met mine were livid.

"Please don't be mad at me. I couldn't tell you."

He was on me so quickly and so firmly I stopped breathing. His hands gripped my shoulders and he pulled me close to his face.

"Sugar, *why*—"

"Because I promised I wouldn't tell *anyone*!"

"No. Listen to me. Why would you ever think I would be mad at *you*?" He shoved me into his chest and then pulled me out again to search my face. He might not be mad at me, but the anger in his eyes still raged. "You knew, then."

"I did. I'm sorry."

"Stop! Just stop that right now. There's no sorry—unless it comes from *him*." He let go of me and smacked the paper with the back of his hand. "Have you read it? Is it all true?"

"Yes, sir."

Daddy spaded one hand into his pocket and used the other to massage his forehead as he paced the kitchen. "This explains a lot— but dear Lord in heaven, I thought this kid had at least the sense of a *stump*." He stopped in front of the sink and stalked back to me and tilted my chin up with his fingers. "Are you all right? I mean, do we need a doctor? This has to be tearing you up. I wish your mother were here."

I gasped, for the second time that day. At once we both said, "No."

"Can we please not tell her while she's up there with GrandMary?" I said.

"I wish we didn't have to tell her at all. All right, you and I can handle this, Tara. What can I do for you? Besides go out to Wyoming or wherever he is—"

"Colorado—"

"And beat the—"

"Daddy."

"What do you need, sugar?" His face edged toward collapse. "What do you need?"

"I just need you," I said.

246

His arms came around me, and all the pieces of me cried. He put me back together.

~ℐℓℓ~

Daddy convinced me to lie down around one o'clock and I feigned sleep on the family room couch, just so for a while I wouldn't have to watch the pain and the anger volley back and forth in him. I heard him slip out the back door and opened my eyes to peek at my cell phone: one thirty. I sat up and found a note on the ottoman.

> Going to the *Morning News* to put a muzzle on this thing.
> We'll have dinner together. Rest.
> Daddy.
> P.S. I stand behind you.

I scribbled a note of my own on the back, promising to be home by six thirty, and did some damage control on my face and hair. Giving that up as hopeless, I headed back to the Piebald.

I knew Ike wouldn't be expecting me, but it was the only thing I could think of to do. He watched me walk up the ramp and shook his head. "Not happenin', Tara."

"I have to—"

"Go sit at your table. Do it, or you're fired."

I did. Within moments, Ms. Helen was there.

"Betsy and Gray will be here as soon as they can get off work," she said. "Now, have you eaten anything?" She waved me off at once. "That is a ridiculous question. Let me get you—"

"Done."

I looked up at Ike, who was putting a bowl of something warm and lumpy and creamy in front of me.

247

"Make her eat the whole thing, Ms. Helen."

"That was my plan."

"I'll be there as soon as I'm done," I said.

"What part of 'you aren't working today' don't you understand? When you're done, you're going home."

He walked away muttering something about me being a hardhead.

"So," Ms. Helen said, once I'd taken several spoonfuls of what turned out to be potato leek, although it could have been wallpaper paste for all I knew. "Which linguine noodle are we working on right now?"

I let the spoon splash into the soup and said what I didn't know until that moment. "I am so *angry*, Ms. Helen."

"And who are we angry with?"

"Whoever that anonymous source was. I just want to find him . . . or her . . . and scream in their face. Who would *do* this?"

"Aw, man, I was hoping you'd know so we could all hunt the coward down." Gray slipped into the chair next to me, face flushed and hands hot as they grabbed mine. "Don't you have any blood? You need a mug of something." She peered into the soup. "Something stronger than this."

"I don't know who did it," I said. "Who would hurt Seth like that?"

"And you," Ms. Helen said.

"Somebody who knew, obviously," Gray said. "Think about it while I get you a tea."

"Only five people knew besides me," I told Ms. Helen. "And you three, and I didn't tell you his name or anything . . . not that I think you would." I pulled my hair back until I felt my eyes slant. "I don't know what I think."

"Then I'll tell you what I think."

She didn't have a chance. A warm presence was suddenly there, and a pair of wonderful lips pressed my forehead.

"I am so sorry, sweet thing," Betsy said. "How you holding up?"

"Better, now that I'm with y'all," I said. "I just wish I knew who did this."

Betsy sat across from me and folded her brown hands neatly on the table. "And what will you do if you find this person?"

"Vent?" I said. "I'm so angry I could spit. Maybe I'll spit at them."

"I got a life-sized picture of that happening." Gray set a steaming cup in front of me. "Chamomile," she said. "I had to tell that Wendy child three times to heat up the milk. She's out there someplace."

Ms. Helen turned to me. "What this person did is unconscionable, yes, ma'am. But isn't the one you're really angry at . . . Seth? That's his name?"

"I can't scream at Seth," I said. "He has more to deal with than I knew about until I read his letter this morning. I haven't had a chance to tell you about that."

Gray put the cup of tea into my hand and all but wrapped my fingers around it. They all waited while I sipped. A telepathic conversation seemed to go on between them.

"What?" I said.

"You have every right to be angry," Ms. Helen said.

"And it might help you to be able to go off on whoever exposed this whole thing to the press," Gray said. "Okay, it would feel *great*."

"But . . ." Betsy reached across the table and curled her warmth around my wrist. "Just make sure you don't use finding this person to distract you from what you're feeling."

"I'm tired of feeling," I said. "I'm just so tired."

~oÕℓ~

Daddy came home with takeout from Zunzi's and a promise from the *Morning News* that no further stories would be released about Seth.

"How did you pull that off?" I said.

"I called in some favors," he said.

He didn't leave me alone for the rest of the evening, which I was grateful for. Alone was the most frightening thing I could think of, and for an introvert like me, admitting it was scary in itself. I woke up at six a.m. with my head in his lap. How I got there, I couldn't remember and Daddy didn't explain. He just kissed the back of my hand and told me to go crawl into bed.

I didn't, of course. I went to St. John's and sat in the back again and sobbed through the entire service. Ned didn't even ask me if I wanted to talk. He just led me silently to our place on the salmon sofa and handed me a hanky. The man must have an endless supply.

"I need to make another confession," I said. "A real one this time."

"Fire away."

"I want to claw the skin of the person who outed Seth in the paper yesterday."

"Is that all? You don't want to punch him—or her—in the face? Strip their skin off?"

I giggled, which came out as more of a most attractive snort. "This from a priest?"

"I was thinking for you. Me? I'd go more along the lines of an AK-47."

My eyes widened. "For real?"

"No, just in my prayers."

"Your *prayers*?"

"Have you ever read the Psalms?"

"Sort of. The twenty-third, for sure."

"Let me draw your attention to Psalm 109."

He stood up and pulled a book from the case behind us. I was surprised to see that it was a copy of *The Message*.

"Not the King James?" I said.

"That works, too, but for this situation, I'm thinking Eugene Peterson's our guy." He flipped some pages and came to rest on one. "I want you to repeat after me."

"O-kay."

"My God." He looked up.

"My God," I said.

"Their lying tongues are like a pack of dogs out to get me."

I repeated it.

"Good, now with feeling. 'Barking their hate, nipping my heels—and for no reason!'"

"'Barking their hate—'"

"That's all you got?"

"You want me to yell?" I looked up at the ornate molding. "In here?"

"I'd have you do it in the church if they weren't cleaning in there. Come on, work with me. 'Barking their hate . . .'"

I yelled it. That line, and the next ones he fed me. *Give him a short life. Give his job to somebody else. Turn his children into begging street urchins.*

By the time we had the bank foreclosing and his family tree chopped down and the curses raining down on him, I was almost hoarse. It was exhausting but I wanted to keep going.

And then we got to the next part. The part where my anger dissolved into something else. Something pulled out by *I'm at the end of my rope, my life in ruins. I'm fading away to nothing, passing away, my youth gone, old before my time.*

I swayed as I cried out to God that I was weak from hunger and could hardly stand up, my body a rack of skin and bones. When Ned's voice became a whisper, so did mine. *Help me, oh, help me, God, my God. Then they'll know that your hand is in this. You* do *the blessing . . .*

my mouth's full of great praise for God [who rescues] a life from the unjust judge.

We were quiet as Ned closed the book and I stared down at my hands.

"I thought I'd done all my crying," I said.

"Me too," Ned said.

I looked up to see unashamed tears running down his face.

T W E N T Y

Through my whole shift even the guys in the kitchen gave me pity-ing looks. Ike finally had to tell them to leave me alone and get back to work. The only person who wouldn't look at me at all was Wendy, and for some reason that brought the anger that had been simmering in me since yesterday to a boil.

I waited to approach her until our shift was almost over and she was squatted down rearranging mugs on the shelves behind the counter.

I squatted next to her. "I don't know if you overheard my con-versation with Ms. Helen and everybody, but I know you've seen the paper or heard people talking and so you know what's going on."

She still didn't look at me but she did nod.

"And I know you think I'm an idiot to have ever ended up in this situation, so why won't you just say it—because, really? The iceberg thing isn't working back here."

Needless to say I'd worked out all the possible responses from Wendy:

You're right. I do think you're an idiot.

I don't just think you're an idiot; I know *you are.*

What are you talking about? I don't even think about you.

Which raises the question, why did I bother to bring it up? Maybe because I just wanted to have an excuse to yell at somebody—because I couldn't yell at the anonymous source and I couldn't yell at Cousin Whoever up in Maine and I couldn't yell at the person who abused my Seth when he was only ten years old.

But apparently I was losing my scripting touch. Wendy's violet eyes nearly burst from her face, and then she ran for the bathroom. When she didn't come out for ten minutes, I slunk away.

I really was an idiot.

※

That was one of the reasons I almost didn't answer the text I got from Alyssa the next morning, Wednesday. I overslept and missed church and was making myself a cup of coffee in the kitchen when it came, and I sat on a stool at the snack bar and read the words at least five times: *NOW you can talk. Come to the Mansion.*

I had already driven poor Wendy to tears because I wanted to blow at somebody. Alyssa was one of my oldest friends . . . although I didn't have to read between the text-lines too much to know *she* was ready to blow at *me.* I didn't need that either.

But as I ran my finger around the rim of my coffee mug and read the text again, it hit me. Now I *could* talk. And maybe it was time to start putting some of those broken-off pieces back together. Everybody was telling me I needed to be getting myself healed while Seth was off doing the same. Everybody, including Seth himself.

I got dressed and walked down to the hotel.

※

I'd never visited Alyssa when she was on the job as a concierge at the Mansion on Forsyth Park, but I wasn't surprised to see how vivacious she was with the middle-aged couple she was advising when I walked across the art gallery of a lobby. She was drawing happy purple circles around things on a Savannah street map with so much spontaneous energy, you would never have known she'd done it at least five hundred times before—and complained about it to her friends every chance she got.

Her blonde hair was up in a neat bun and shiny silver droplets dangled from her earlobes. She was striking, really, and so self-assured. She and Wendy and Jacqueline were finding a confident place in the world.

I waited until the couple was cheerfully on their way before I went any closer to the gold-trimmed concierge desk. I got about three steps when Alyssa saw me, whipped out a sign that said *Back in Five Minutes*, and came out with a sleek black sweater around her shoulders.

"Hey," I said.

"Across the street."

"Look," I said as she took off ahead of me across the lobby, "I know you still don't get—"

She put a hand up behind her and pushed through the Victorian Romanesque doors. I shut up until we got across Drayton Street and sat on either end of a bench on the west side of the park. That gave me enough time to work up a head of steam.

"I didn't meet you so you could yell at me," I said. "I know you're mad because I didn't talk to you but I couldn't and that's the way it was. I'm sorry."

Alyssa stopped with only one arm in the sleeve of the sweater. "What makes you think I'm going to yell at you?"

How about everything you're doing right now?

"I just need to tell you something," she said, and slid the other arm into a sleeve.

My heart took a dive straight down. Did she see Seth with a prostitute too? Didn't I have enough "evidence" already?

Alyssa put her arm on the back of the bench and leaned toward me. Whispering wasn't her strong suit but she gave it a try. "I don't know how much you know about what Seth was doing."

"Enough," I said. "I've seen some of what he was watching. I caught him at it."

She closed her eyes and talked with them shut. "So you've seen, what, five minutes?"

"Less than that. I don't need to see any—"

"No, you don't." Alyssa glanced over her shoulder as if the porn police were walking their beat. "But I have. Prepare to be disgusted."

"I don't want to be disgusted anymore," I said. "Really—"

"I'm not going to give you graphic details, but you need to know this." She stopped and looked over my head and for the first time I saw in her eyes how hard this was for her. Pain tightened her pretty mouth.

"Okay," I said.

"I've dated two different guys who asked me to watch porn with them. It was more like they said, 'Let's watch a movie,' and it turned out to be *Las Vegas Vixens* or something." She closed her eyes again, almost as if she didn't want to see me watching her. "I know. I should have just left, but these were great guys before that. When the video started talking about these not-all-that-attractive women being dogs and whales and pigs, the first guy turned it off. But I still never went out with him again."

I was almost too dumbfounded to nod, but I did.

"The second guy . . . I'm not even sure why I said I'd date him except he was cute and I was alone and he seemed decent, you know?" She blinked rapidly, but I knew we weren't talking eyelash in the contact. "I went to his place to pick him up because he said his car wasn't running and I'm thinking we're going out the door and he turns on this . . . awful video and he starts . . ."

"You don't have to tell me." Please, *don't* tell me.

"He starts acting it out with me." Alyssa looked straight at me, face writhing. "Tara, I went and threw up and I haven't been out with anybody since. It's like, is there a guy out there who can enjoy sex if it doesn't involve props?"

"I'm so sorry," I said.

"So, you're not going to marry Seth now, are you? The paper said he was getting treatment, but I just think you should run and not look back." She grabbed my hands. Hers were cold and clammy. "I work in probably the classiest hotel in this town, and guys come to the concierge desk *all* the time asking me to come up and watch a movie with them . . . like I'm some call girl or something. It just makes me feel so dirty."

"But you're not!"

"You know how it feels, though, right?"

"Yeah," I said, because I did.

"I'm looking for another job, something where I don't even have to come in contact with men. Maybe I'll go back to school and become an elementary school teacher."

I couldn't picture that—even with *my* imagination—but I kept saying yeah. Until she said, "Promise me you're not ever going to marry him, Tara. Swear to me."

I pulled my hands away. "I can't."

"Tell me you aren't going to try to save him."

"No!" I said. "But there's more to it than just Seth being a jerk. Not that he is."

I paused and looked back across the street at the hotel's cupolas. That was the first time I was the one to say this wasn't all Seth's fault. And it might be the first time I believed it.

"Okay," Alyssa said. Her arms were folded.

"Okay what?" I said.

"If you marry him, don't count on me to be a bridesmaid because I won't have any part in it. Matter of fact, I already sold my dress."

I stared at her. "So you're saying we can't be friends if I even consider marrying Seth?"

"I love you, Tara," she said, "but I can't, like, hang out with you and listen to you talk about helping him and go, 'Yay, girl.' I might not be as deep as you, okay, but I won't be a hypocrite."

She stood up and did everything a person does to keep from weeping—swallowing, blinking, chomping down on the lower lip. Finally she just walked across the street and disappeared inside the Mansion. I watched until I could no longer see her beyond the windows.

That was one friendship out of three basically gone. Didn't I predict to myself that day when Mama and I had lunch at Soho South that friendships would unravel over this? I couldn't just sit here and let all the threads come loose. I called Jacqueline.

⁓

We met an hour later during her lunch break in Oglethorpe Square. I could tell from the way she walked toward me, her longer-in-the-back-than-the-front skirt dancing flirtatiously in the breeze, that she wasn't angry with me. That wasn't her. What I saw on her face when she joined me at a live oak facing the Owens-Thomas House with a smoothie in each hand was something more akin to fear. A straight vertical line cut between her eyes that couldn't quite seem to settle.

"Thanks," I said as she handed me one of the cups.

"You look like you could use it. How much weight have you lost?"

"I don't know," I said.

"You're not okay, are you?" she said.

"No. But it'll get better."

"Yeah?"

"Look, I want you to know I'm sorry I couldn't talk to you about this—"

"No, no, I totally get it now. That must have been so hard for you."

I felt a little guilty that I was surprised by Jacqueline's empathy, but, really, she was the practical one, the one to give advice for moving forward instead of compassion to let you rest where you were for a while.

She leaned against the great tree, carefully positioning her feet in the leaves so she wouldn't slide. "So what are you going to do?" she said.

Ah, there it was.

"I don't know yet," I said. "I'm trying to heal and Seth's trying to heal and then I guess we'll see."

"Don't wait."

I quit pumping my straw and sighed hard enough to stop her. "I already heard this from Alyssa."

Jacqueline tucked her chin. "I know you didn't hear *this* from Alyssa. I'm sure she told you to cut and run."

"She did."

"She's wrong . . . in my opinion." Jacqueline set her cup on the ground and all but wrung her hands. "I'm sure she told you all about the guys asking her to watch porn with them."

"She did," I said again. I was gladder than ever that I'd not told Alyssa before. The girl couldn't keep her mouth shut even about her *own* secrets.

"I never had anybody do that, but I had a lot of guy friends at Auburn, and Oliver told me about some too . . . You can hardly find a guy who doesn't struggle with porn, Tara. Oliver said he didn't—and I guess I believe that—but it's, like, an epidemic. Even with Christian guys."

"Why did I never know that about men?"

She did the chin tuck again. "Really? Who's going to tell *you* that? You're so sweet and innocent and perfect."

"Stop!"

"I'm serious. But it's true, all of it." She pulled away from the tree. "The thing about Seth is, he's willing to get help, and that's so hard, especially now that somebody's blabbed it to the newspaper. Do you know who—"

"No."

She seemed to shake that off. "It's huge that he admits he has a problem and he's doing something about it. Whoever you marry is going to have issues." Jacqueline's eyes filled. "I've been through a breakup with the guy I thought was the one, and if he'd take me back I'd go in a heartbeat. I don't know if I'll ever love anybody again."

I scanned the balustrade on the house without seeing it. "Neither do I."

"Then don't lose him."

There was no point telling her it wasn't that easy, just as it had been senseless to argue with Alyssa. Maybe unless you've been there, you just shouldn't say anything at all.

Jacqueline pulled her arms around her middle and looked down at me, mascara puddling under her eyes. "Well, just so you know, I still have the dress."

"Duly noted," I said.

"If you need anything, call me, okay?"

"Okay," I said.

But as her heels clicked down the brick pathway, I knew I never would.

⁓℘℘⁓

That left Lexi. She hadn't been over to watch movies for a while because she said she was working on a project she had to do at night. I knew Lex. I knew the bond between us. But with so many pieces scattered on the ground around me, it was almost impossible not to think she didn't want to be around me now that she knew.

"It's ridiculous. I know," I said to the Watch after my shift that night. "But it's like I'm not sure I know anybody anymore."

"Let me ask you this," Gray said. She had her hair down and she looked somehow wiser without the ponytail. "Is it good that you found out what you did about—what are their names?"

"Alyssa and Jacqueline," Ms. Helen said. I had to wonder if she took notes.

"Is it a good thing that you know what you know? Not, 'Is it easy?' Is it good?"

"It kind of is," I said. "It's clear to me now that I don't want to dump Seth right now, but I can't just marry him and hope for the best either." I drew my shoulders up to my earlobes. "I guess I knew that before, but saying it to them made it more like the truth."

"Then that's a good thing," Betsy said.

"So?" Gray wiggled her hand. "Maybe talking to Lacy? Lindy?"

"Lexi," Ms. Helen said. "Gray, honey, honestly."

"Maybe talking to her will show you something else you need to know."

"What if I don't want to know?" I said.

"Oh, darlin'," Betsy said, warm hand on mine. "Wantin' isn't the same as needin'. Never has been."

"I hate that," I said.

"Uh-huh," Betsy said.

"I guess I'm calling Lexi."

Gray pushed my phone toward me.

Lexi's voice was quiet during the call, as usual, so I couldn't really read anything, but she said my timing was perfect and invited me to her apartment.

Oddly, I'd never been there before. She'd only been in it since just before Thanksgiving—she lived with her parents out in Ardsley Park after undergrad until she could save enough money for her own place—and with all the wedding plans, there hadn't been time to go see her new digs.

As I walked the three long blocks to Montgomery Street, which included making my way around the monstrous civic center, I tried not to feel guilty about that. She'd never actually asked me over. In fact, throughout our whole friendship she'd always spent more time where I lived than vice versa. I didn't have four younger siblings in a three-bedroom house with one bathroom and a kitchen that could have fit in my mother's walk-in closet. It wasn't that Lexi was ever ashamed of her home. Mine was just quieter.

Most of the streets of Savannah weren't bustling on a Wednesday night in late January, but that end of Montgomery was a different matter. I never spent much time there, not being a fan of pizza joints that made the Mellow Mushroom look like a Ruth's Chris Steak House and dark-windowed bars that brought Jason Statham movies to mind, but whenever I did go there late in the evening like this, it felt like a neon noon. My father would be having a fit if he knew I was down there.

I shoved my hands in my jean jacket pockets and tried to look like I belonged, which probably made me look even less like I did, and hurried up the outside steps Lexi had described to me on the phone. They led to a door with a smeared glass window, which in turn led to a narrow hallway with dark green carpet that had obviously been laid two decades ago. That many years' worth of drinks had been spilled on it and left to soak in.

Oh my gosh, Lexi.

She answered before I knocked and pulled me into her place, and there all resemblance to the rest of the complex ended. It. Was. Precious.

We're talking one room with a kitchenette and a bathroom no bigger than one you'd find in a motor home, but what she'd done with it was nothing short of amazing. The walls were the color of real butter and textured in a way that was vintage Lexi. I remembered her saying the landlord had given her permission to paint as long as she didn't do anything weird.

A few nice pieces of her own art hung on those walls, bordered above with lengths of fabric that found their way around the windows like magic wings. The rug I recognized from her room at home—a woven affair she'd saved up her money to buy in Charleston at a street market when she was seventeen. A futon in a frame that converted into a bed, a trunk for a coffee table, and two blue director's chairs were all the furniture she had, but she'd grouped it cozily and punctuated it with pillows I knew she'd beaded and embroidered herself. A selection of pots and small sculptures she'd made over the years completed the look. There was never a place that more clearly announced who lived in it.

"Lex, this is awesome!" I said.

"You think?"

"Yes! I love it."

"I fixed us some food."

I resisted saying, *You didn't have to,* because I knew she loved doing it. I'd learned to cook only because I was getting married. Lexi learned it because it was yet another art to master.

"You still like quesadillas, right?" she said.

"Do I live?"

She laughed her soft laugh and produced two folded tortillas bubbling with cheese and smelling of chicken and cilantro. It was the first thing I'd had put in front of me in weeks that I actually wanted to eat. I had half of it down before she could get the lemonade on the table-trunk. That was, of course, homemade too.

When she sat down, I said, "So what have you done with *your* bridesmaid's dress?"

"I'm sorry?" she said.

I wiped my mouth with the bandana she'd rolled up by the plate as a napkin. "Alyssa sold hers because she thinks I should flush Seth and our whole relationship down the john. Jacqueline's keeping hers because she thinks I should marry Seth immediately—and would probably think that even if he were a serial killer. So—you?"

Lexi just shook her head at me and said, "What dress?"

And then she burst into tears. I let the quesadilla drop to the plate.

"Lex," I said. "I'm sorry."

"No—don't be sorry. I'm just so relieved."

"Okay, you're gonna explain that to me, right?" I handed her the bandana.

"Now we can talk," she said. "Or not talk, but now we know what we're not talking about."

"You know what's scary about that?"

She shook her head.

"I actually know what you mean."

A laugh bubbled from her nose, along with a glob of something that *really* needed the bandana. "Why do women always look so beautiful when they cry in movies?" she said.

"Except Vanessa Redgrave in that old version of *Camelot*, remember? She looked so miserable."

"Do I?" Lexi said.

"No," I said. "You look beautiful."

TWENTY-ONE

I wasn't the only one making phone calls. I got two myself in the next few days, calls that kept the spin going.

The first came right after I met with Ned Friday. It was Fritzie. When I answered she said, "Holy frijoles, Batman."

"Hi, Fritz," I said.

"You poor kid."

"I'm okay."

"Right. This is me you're talking to." Her raspy voice went lower. "Look, I only have a couple of minutes. I'm starting a new gig today and this mother is expecting me to be Mary Poppins so I need to— well, what I need to do is get out of the nannying business but I love the kids so much. It's the parents I can't—anyway, yada yada yada—I just want to say this one thing to you."

I was sure there would be more than one thing so I sat on a bench in Madison Square.

"I know what I'm talking about when I tell you this," she said. "My father was an alcoholic. My brother was a drug addict. All the addictions have stuff in common."

"Their brain chemistry changes."

She gave a soft grunt. "I hadn't heard that one. Here's what I do know. The people who run these programs are all into addicts figuring out what happened in their pasts that made them susceptible to getting hooked on whatever. That's all fine and good, but when you get right down to it, they either stop what they're doing or they don't."

"I'm not exactly following you," I said.

"Don't let Seth spend years digging into his childhood. Okay, so he had a mother who wasn't warm and fuzzy and a father who couldn't teach him to kick a soccer ball. Wah-wah, you know? I practically raised Seth Grissom and I know he never suffered any kind of psychic pain. If he wants to think that and it helps him sleep at night, fine, but Tara, don't let him wallow in 'poor me' while he keeps looking at porn sites. See what I'm saying?"

If she'd asked me if I *agreed* with it, that would have been a whole other thing. I didn't, not entirely, but I could still say, "Yeah. I see."

"Good. Okay, I gotta go find an umbrella that will float me into this woman's living room. I sure wish I could get a gig like I had with y'all when you were growing up. And here's the thing—and the whole reason I called." There was a funny silence that made me think I'd lost the call, but she continued. "I loved all four of you, but Tara . . ." Fritzie's throat clogged. "I told you this before: you were the special one, and I just want you to have the happiest life you can have. You deserve it, okay?"

"Okay, Fritz," I said.

"I gotta go. Kiss Madeline for me."

ℐℓℯ

I processed that with the Watch later and we sorted it out into two piles: find the reasons you're an addict and stop indulging your addiction.

"What do you see when you look at that?" Betsy said.

"I think it feels contrived," I said.

Gray looked at Ms. Helen. "Do you love her vocabulary or what?"

"I do," Ms. Helen said. "What do you mean, honey?"

"I don't think you can totally separate one from the other. And besides, Seth *said* in his letter that he was molested and Fritzie doesn't know everything about our families. I know more than she does, and even I didn't know that."

"So what's your plan?" Gray said.

"Nothing different from what I'm already doing," I said. "Except, I think I'll stop listening to everybody else's advice. Except y'all's."

Ms. Helen gave me a blank look. "I don't recall us giving much advice. Except eat and pray."

"I think we're just askin' the questions," Betsy said.

"Then please keep doing it," I said. "Oh, and can I ask you one?"

"Do it," Gray said.

I suddenly felt middle-school shy. "Would it be okay if I brought Lexi to meet with us sometime?"

"I would love to meet this sweet thing," Ms. Helen said.

Gray grinned. "Pretty soon Ike's going to start charging us rent on this table."

"No," Ike called from the counter. "Just keep ordering; that's all."

The man had the hearing of a bat.

⁂

My second phone call came Saturday morning. Daddy had gone to the airport to pick up Mama. GrandMary wasn't going to start radiation for another two weeks and she insisted Mama come home and tend to us and then go back if GrandMary really needed her. I still hadn't talked to GrandMary myself and I was glad. Mama didn't know about the pornography and I was afraid I'd let something slip. Daddy's plan was to tell her on the way home from the airport, and then we'd sit down over breakfast and talk about how we were going to deal with it as a family. I was looking forward to that in a guarded sort of way.

So I was setting the table in the small dining room when my phone rang, and it was Evelyn.

"Evvy!" I said.

"Did you hear?"

"Did I hear what?"

"You probably didn't. I only heard it being whispered behind closed doors. I'm turning into a better spy than Jason Bourne—"

"Evvy, *what?*"

"Seth got fired."

I dropped an entire handful of silverware on the table.

"I guess I should have asked if you were sitting down," Evelyn said. "Sorry."

But she didn't sound sorry at all. There was a hint of triumph in her voice that made the hair on my arms stand up.

"Was it because of the newspaper article?" I said.

"They found *out* from the article but they fired him because he's a fraud. Did I not tell you that?"

I might have asked Evelyn right then if she was glad about this, but in the first place it was obvious she was. And in the second place, I also probably would have blurted out my sudden insight: *You're the one who went to the press, aren't you?*

In the third place, I heard the garage door open, meaning Mama and Daddy were home, and in the fourth, the doorbell rang.

"I have to go, Ev," I said. "I'll call you later."

"Do. I'm working today but come by the 'Shroom."

I hung up on the way to the front door and called over my shoulder, "I'll be right there, Mama." I wanted to get rid of whoever this was so I could go to her. She was probably a mess by now. This shouldn't be hard since nobody we knew ever came to the front—

I pulled it open to find Paul and Randi standing there.

If it isn't the Brothers Grimm, I wanted to say.

"We need to talk to you," Randi said.

"Now's not a good time," I said. "Mama just got home."

"Good. She needs to hear this."

In her usual brazen fashion Randi pushed past me and tilted her head as if she were listening for people who might be in hiding. There was no need. Daddy, Mama, and Kellen's voices were all chiming from the kitchen like the come-and-get-it dinner bell. Randi charged toward them with Paul and me behind her. Fortunately she was quick on her feet because if I caught her, I would have done her bodily harm. Look out, Psalm 109.

When we got to the kitchen Daddy's arms were loaded with Mama's bags, Kellen was already grinding beans for coffee, and Mama herself looked like she was trying to remember where she was. And why wouldn't she? Moments ago she'd learned what the rest of us already knew and none of us could believe.

All three of them stopped and stared as we invaded the kitchen with Randi in the lead. The first thing I saw was Kellen's entire face darkening like a thunderhead.

"I'm glad you're all here," Randi said. "I—"

"Paul, for Pete's sake," Daddy said. "Madeline just got home. Her mother's ill—"

Paul immediately shmushed his face into pastor mode. "I had no idea." He gave Mama a pitying look. "Is it serious?"

"She's holding her own," Daddy said.

"I'm sorry," Randi said, eyes closed as if that was the only way she could tolerate this. "I really am, Maddie. You know I love your mother."

Mama still hadn't spoken a word. She just gave Randi an infinitesimal nod.

"If you need to go lie down, regroup, whatever, do. But I think the rest of you need to hear this."

Mama and Daddy exchanged glances and apparently came to the consensus that Mama was staying. At that point we were still standing between the sink and the snack bar with Randi in the middle in full command. Bless my father. He apparently sized that up in short order and pretty much herded us to the breakfast nook, where, still, nobody sat down, but at least I didn't feel like Randi was halfway down my throat. Not physically anyway.

"So what's this about?" Daddy said.

"I just want to let you all know that I plan to have a private investigator look into who went to the newspaper." Randi breathed in sharply through her nose. "When he finds out, and he will, I'm filing a defamation of character suit."

"Really," Daddy said. "Is it still defamation if it's the truth?"

Nothing about Daddy changed when he said that except the skin around his eyes, which tightened until I thought it might snap.

Randi wheeled on him. "I didn't intend for this to turn ugly, Dennis. I came as a courtesy to Tara."

I knew I looked vacant. "I don't care if you hire an investigator. I want to know who did it too."

"That's not what I mean, Tara." Could she be a little more condescending?

Kellen groaned from the snack bar. "Geez, just say it, Randi."

"Fine." Randi pointed her courtroom eyes at me. "I'm giving you an opportunity to admit that it was you."

My whole being seized.

"Do that and we'll settle this quietly. I think we've all had enough scandal and notoriety."

"You. Are. Not. Serious." Whether she heard that coming through my welded-together teeth I couldn't tell, but she did see me lunge at her because she backed into Mama. *Startled* didn't begin to describe the look that sprang to her face. Kellen grabbed me from behind by both arms and held me against him while I breathed like a freight train.

"Why would I *do* that?" I said. "I *love* Seth!"

"But you didn't love him enough to marry him." I looked aghast at Paul. "If you had stood behind him from the beginning, this wouldn't have happened."

"And then it would all be behind closed doors for Tara to handle by herself."

I'm not sure anyone even had a pulse as we all turned to my mother. Chin tilted, she looked up at Paul with a blue blaze. I knew she'd actually said it because it was still etched around her mouth.

"I think you folks need to leave," Daddy said.

"My offer is good for twenty-four hours," Randi said. "If I don't hear from you with a confession, the PI goes to work."

Daddy bore down on her with his eyes. "First, shut it, Randi. *Then* leave. And do not make personal contact with my daughter again." His head thrust forward. "Are we clear?"

"Very." Randi glowered at me. "I don't want to have my face clawed."

We Faulkners stood like a statue garden until the front door slammed on the Grissoms. Kellen was the first to move. He paced around the kitchen for about fifteen seconds and then did his own slam out the back door. I went to Mama and put my arms around her.

"I can't stand that you have to go through this."

She kept her face buried in my neck, but her words were clear—the words I had never given her credit for being able to say. "*We* are going through this," she said, breath soft against my skin. She pulled away just far enough to look deep into me. "I meant what I said. You shouldn't handle this alone."

I curled the corduroy sleeve of her jacket into my fingers. She felt solid enough for me to cling to her and not fall.

Daddy rubbed his hand against her back. "And can I just say I'm glad you're on our side, darlin'. You flat took Paul Grissom out at the knees."

Mama gave us a damp smile. "I did, didn't I?" she said.

~ॐ~

She and I spent the day together since I was off work. Talk and tea and tears were woven with regret on my part. I'd underestimated my parents. Or was it just the pull Seth had on me to protect him from the shame that stalked him?

Or the shame that followed me?

It had caught us, hadn't it? But I didn't have to let it shred me with its claws, because it wasn't just me facing it now. And it had never had to be.

That was why when Mama and Daddy retired around nine, I told them I had to see a friend and made tracks for the Mellow Mushroom. It was time to clear the air with Evelyn.

I guess I looked like I was spoiling for a fight because when Evelyn saw me she came straight to the door and pushed me outside with a bony hand. The night was on the edge of chilly, but that didn't seem to faze her, even in a tank top and a skirt that looked like it was made out of first aid gauze.

"You're going to deck Randi, aren't you?" she said. "Finally." She leaned against the window. "I'd have popped her weeks ago, but that's just me. I still might."

I hadn't rehearsed this on my way over, so I had to plunge in with improv.

"She thinks I told the press about Seth," I said.

I watched her olive eyes.

"You? Why would you do it?"

"Exactly."

"She's certifiable."

"Maybe she's going down the list of people who knew," I said. "I was at the top."

"Who's gonna be next? Me?"

I tried, so hard, not to flinch, but Evelyn must have caught— what?—an intake of breath? My heart rate picking up? My complete inability to pull off a poker face?

"You think *I* did it?"

"I didn't say that."

"You didn't have to." Evelyn pulled herself from the window and darted her eyes in seven different directions before she homed back in on me. "Look, I can't stand my brother and I think he deserves to be exposed for the tawdry fraud he is." She shook her head, hard. "But I would never do that to you. How many times do I have to tell you people that?"

"Why do you hate him so much, Evvy?"

She stopped flailing. "Where's that coming from?"

"I don't know." And I didn't. But somehow I had to know.

"Okay." Evelyn's face set as if I'd just challenged her to a dare. "I don't think you'll get it since you have a brother who protected you from the time you were an infant, if family legend is to be believed."

"It's true," I said.

"Mine never did."

"Yeah, but Evvy, who among us really needed protecting? We were more sheltered than Chelsea Clinton."

"You don't know."

Her voice went so low and flat with fear, I had to peer closely to make sure she'd actually said it. I realized she wasn't seeing me anymore. Her mind had taken her sight with it to whatever memory she was suddenly trapped in.

"It was bad," she said. "It was something bad and he didn't keep it from happening. I shouldn't have been there."

"What happened?" I whispered.

"I can't remember. It was just something bad."

The fear left her eyes and anger replaced it, and then the feigned apathy that had lived there for almost as long as I could remember.

"So no, I didn't out my brother to the press," she said. "I gotta get back inside."

"Ev, I'm sorry," I said.

"Whatever," she said.

When she was gone, it was my turn to lean on the window, while a deep sadness weighed my shoulders down. That was relationship number three gone, and in spite of Evelyn's prickliness I felt the worst about this one. There was something else, too, something dark and haunting. Evelyn was telling the truth. She always told the truth. That was why she was so hard to be around.

The door opened and I decided it was time to move on before I was picked up for loitering, but Evelyn's voice stopped me. Only her head was visible.

"I forgive you for thinking that," she said. "You're the only one I do forgive. And Tara?"

"Yeah?"

"Run away from my family—as fast and as far as you can."

TWENTY-TWO

Nobody in the Faulkner house went to church Sunday, and I knew how hard that was for my parents. We were private with each other about our faith. I'd never discussed how I prayed or didn't with my mother or what I believed with my father or how it played out with my brother. We could go for months without ever mentioning God's name in our house except to say a blessing at the table, but somehow I just always figured we all believed. Church, though, that was always central to who we were as a family. It was probably part of the reason I went to St. John's every day, just for a taste of church. Now Mama and Daddy didn't even have that much, which made the loss of Seth-and-me wider and deeper.

Maybe that was why on Monday I followed the rest of the small gathering up to the altar for communion. When Ned tucked a flat white wafer, thin as Mama's pastry, into my hand, his fingers lingered as he said, "The Body of our Lord Jesus Christ, which was given for thee, preserve thy body and soul unto everlasting life."

"Body *and* soul," I said to Ned later on the salmon sofa. "Why did that stick with me?"

"Maybe because it feels like both of those have been betrayed?" he said.

"Is that a question?"

"It is."

"I'd rather have an answer."

"You're finding it," he said.

I traced a pinkish paisley with my fingernail. "Am I?" I said.

"I think so."

"How do you know?" My hand flew to my throat. "I'm sorry—
that was rude."

Ned's eyes smiled. "It's a valid question."

"I'm not challenging your instincts or anything. It's just that I'm
not sure I'm getting any closer to a decision. You know, about Seth."

"Is that the goal?"

"What else would it be?" Again, I fumbled at my neck. When did
I turn into a blurter? Out of sheer desperation, maybe, but still . . .

Ned didn't look insulted, though. He was, in fact, rubbing his
hands together between his knees, sending the signal: *Now we're getting somewhere.*

"I can only speak into you from two places," he said. "The gospel
and my own experience on my journey with God."

"Speak *into* me," I said. "What does that mean?"

"It means you're open to take it in. Otherwise I'd just be speaking
at you."

I didn't ask how he knew that about me. I did have an empty
space inside. It was between the two pieces of my broken heart.

"Speak," I said. "Please."

Ned gave me a long, soft look and I caught my breath. He wasn't
just speaking into me. He was seeing into me. It was panic-worthy.
I even dug my nails into the brocade. But did I have a better choice?
What else was I going to do with that painful void but let him tell me
what he saw there?

"Really," I said. "I want to know."

He turned his head in that one-degree way he had, as if he were listening to a voice I couldn't hear. "This is more about you than it is about Seth," he said finally. "You can't decide about him until you know you." The smile almost reached his lips. "You're finding the right thing to do by finding the self God made you to be."

I had no clue what to do with that. From the way Ned eased back into the sofa, I knew I wasn't supposed to, not right then.

"Are you saying I have to sort of live into it?" I said.

"That's exactly what I'm saying."

I released the brocade and made sure I hadn't worn through the antique threads. "So which of the two sources did that come from?" I said. "Gospel or experience?"

"Both."

The catch in his voice made me look up quickly, in time to see something flee from his eyes. Something he wasn't telling me.

I didn't ask what it was.

~ 🌿 ~

"Did the groundhog see his shadow today?" Ms. Helen said at the table that evening.

"How could he miss it?" Gray said. "I was out mulching azaleas and sweating like a pig."

"I thought you lived in an apartment?" Betsy said.

"I do. But I'm a landscaper." Gray half-smiled. "I never mentioned that before?"

"No," I said, "because we're always talking about me." I turned to Lexi who was sitting shyly beside me. "Just so you know, they *will* get inside you and it'll happen before you realize it."

Gray nudged me. "Are you complaining?"

"Absolutely not," I said.

Gray's even gaze shifted to Lexi. "So you're an artist. What medium?"

"All of them, but I'm focusing on photography and film."

Before ten minutes had passed, the Watch knew as much about Lexi's art as I did, and then some, including the project that was keeping her out at night.

"I'm doing a series of sketches of women in the darker occupations, trying to get at who they are under the—well, I guess you could call it a façade."

"Forevermore," Ms. Helen said. "Where do you find them?"

Lexi gave them her soft laugh. "I live down on Montgomery Street, so I'm pretty much surrounded."

"Bless your heart," Betsy said.

"That answers my question." Gray repositioned herself in the chair. Her brown eyes were alive. "I'm thinking, what does she do, stop hookers on the street and say, stand here while I draw your picture?"

"I try to be discreet," Lexi said.

"You girls amaze me," Ms. Helen said. "You face the underbelly of life head-on, don't you?"

"I'm just trying to understand it." Lexi looked at me. "I guess we both are."

"Let's drink to understanding," Gray said, lifting her tea mug. "Everybody have a beverage?"

"If you don't it's too late now," Betsy said. "It looks like Ike is getting ready to close."

True. Wendy was currently headed for the front door, a stuffed canvas bag big enough for Lexi to fit into hanging from her shoulder. She looked so separate, compared to those of us who crowded around our table. That had to be why I called out to her, "Wendy? You want to join us?"

She stopped with her hand on the doorknob and turned only her head to us. The violet eyes seemed to have to catch up, as if her mind was already halfway to wherever she was going with that bag. She looked tired and surprised. And beautiful in that moment of an expression she didn't manufacture.

It didn't last long. Her brows came down in a V, the international signal for *You're not serious.*

"Can't," she said. "But thanks."

Pain shot through the moment. I couldn't tell if it was Wendy's or mine.

"Doesn't she have the prettiest eyes?" Ms. Helen said when she was gone.

"Does she wear contacts to get them that color, do you think?" Gray said.

Lexi tugged gently at my sleeve. "I do need some more tea. Go up with me?"

"Ike doesn't bite," I said, but I scraped back my chair and followed her up the ramp. She stopped me halfway to the counter.

"Is that girl a friend of yours?" she said, voice low.

"I have no idea. I thought we were getting there and then she just shut me out. I get the feeling she thinks I'm a rich girl who got what she deserved. Something like that."

"Huh."

"Why?"

"Do you care about her?"

"Of course I care about her."

Lexi still just stood there, rubbing her hand up and down on the wrought-iron rail.

"What?" I said.

"She's a stripper."

"Excuse me?"

"I guess I should say exotic dancer. She works at a club in my neighborhood. She's one of the girls I've been sketching."

"Seriously?"

"I've taken a bunch of pictures of her and then I go back and sketch them for a storyboard. I want to do a film at some point."

Even though my mouth was going numb I managed to say, "This is the project you were talking about."

"The project's almost done but now it's, like, personal. That's why I wanted to know if you care about her."

"Because you do."

"You ladies want something?" Ike called from the counter.

I looked at Lexi and she shook her head.

"I'm going to go ahead and shut everything down then. Last call, Tara."

"I'm good too," I said.

But I was far from it.

When Betsy, Gray, and Ms. Helen left, Lexi and I wandered toward my house. We didn't talk at first, and I knew Lexi was waiting for me to start. I didn't know where to so I just grabbed onto the next thought.

"Wendy doesn't want that life, Lex," I said. "Back when she was still talking to me, she told me about twenty times that she had almost enough money to quit her second job and get on with what she really wanted to do."

"What does she want to do?"

"Be a manager for Ike. It's not like she wants to be a surgeon or something, but now it makes sense. She just wants a clean life." I stopped on the walkway leading into Madison Square and pressed my fingers to my temples.

"What?" Lexi said.

"I accused her of thinking I was an idiot for being involved with a porn addict. Why didn't I just slap her in the face?"

"You didn't know."

"I have to apologize to her."

Lexi grabbed my wrist. "You can't tell her how you know."

Her face was all concern, eyes wide, mouth vulnerable. She was all things compassionate without even having to think about it.

"I won't," I said.

"Maybe you shouldn't even tell her that you *do* know. I mean, she's trying to get out. Why make her feel ashamed in front of you?"

We started to walk again, once more in silence. Above us the moon fuzzed through a circle of high fog and cast the dark, wet branches of the live oaks in silhouette.

"You know what's really strange?" I said.

"Everything?" Lexi said.

"I know, right? But if you'd told me this before I knew about Seth, I would have judged her. I probably *did* judge her if I ever saw her down on Montgomery—"

"She's not a prostitute," Lexi said. "I'm pretty sure of that."

"Still . . . now I feel bad for her, like there has to be a reason she got into that. You know, like if there's a reason Seth turned to porn, there's a reason she's doing what she's doing. Don't you think?"

"I do." Lexi walked a few steps, short legs trying to keep up with my long ones, before she looked up at me. "But you're not mad at her the way you were at Seth when you first found out."

"Well, no."

"Why? I mean, she's not close to you like he was, but what's the difference?"

I stopped and looked at Lexi in the light from the corner streetlamp. Her face was so earnest, as if these questions and their answers would teach her something she couldn't live without. Like there could be real meaning in what we determined here.

"You're such a better person than I am, Lexi," I said.

"No," she said. "I am not."

"Just don't think I'm a selfish wench when I say this."

"I'm not even going there. Just say it, will ya?"

I tilted my face toward the foggy moon. "The reason I'm not angry with Wendy is because she isn't doing this to *me*. I told you it was selfish."

"It doesn't sound selfish," Lexi said. "It just sounds real."

ℓℓₑ

I didn't talk to Wendy after all, except for a brief exchange when we were cleaning the steamers and I said, "I'm sorry I went off on you the other day. I was projecting my stuff onto you." Her answer: "I don't even know what that means." It was all I could do not to hug her neck and say, *I want to rescue you!*

I told Ned that the next morning. We didn't have much time because he had his Wednesday breakfast meeting to go to, but I wanted his take on it.

"My dad gave Lexi a loan to go to SCAD," I told him. "Which she insists on paying back even though my father probably won't accept a dime from her. We could do the same for Wendy, help get her out of that life."

We were still standing in the church vestibule. Ned removed the stole from his neck and looped it around his hand. It was the first time he ever seemed to want to avoid my eyes. The silence got thick.

"Did I say something wrong?" I said.

"Not wrong," he said. "But maybe untimely." He set the rolled stole on the arm of the carved bench I'd sat on in my wretched wetness that night about a hundred years ago. "I did that—tried to reach out before my arms were strong enough."

Experience. That came to me in a sliver of realization I didn't have time to examine.

"It didn't work out. I got my hand bitten, actually. But it did teach me what I was talking about yesterday: that I had to find out what was true about me before I could help anybody else find out what was true about them." His head turned a notch. "It's what I was trying to say to you—I think you're finding that out, about yourself, I mean. I think communion is helping. I think your—what do you call them?—your Watch is helping. I think being able to talk to your family is helping."

"And you. You're helping more than you even know."

His eyes smiled almost shyly. "I just wouldn't want to see you go off track. Having compassion, praying, that's one thing."

"Then I shouldn't try to adopt Wendy," I said. My own laugh surprised me.

"Just ask yourself what's true about you. When's Seth coming back?"

"Next week sometime, I think."

"That's something you'll want to at least begin to know before you see him again."

He said it with more confidence than almost anything else he'd ever said to me. I was hit with a longing to sit with him all day and ask how and why and did I get this right? But he had a meeting. And I was pretty sure he wouldn't answer those questions anyway.

⁓ℐℓ⁓

Where were the answers, then? Where was I going to find out what was true about me? I couldn't just sit around thinking about that, so I did what I did best. I walked.

In other places they called this time of year the last six weeks of winter. In Savannah we knew it as the early days of spring. The azaleas bloomed with the glorious antebellum profusion of the opening scene of *Gone with the Wind* in pink and white and coral puffs of blossom that lined the yards and gardens of the historic district. The magnolia leaves grew shiny again and began the gestation of what would be their giant summer blooms. The camellias and flowering quince heralded the embarrassment of floral riches that was to come.

The very elderly tourists poured in, confident in the winter warmth and wary of the blistering months of summer that would be on us all too soon. I loved their slow creep around the city, their stops to read every plaque and monument. I loved it, so I did it too.

I also paused in front of the churches that seemed on my midnight haunts to have given up hope. Now . . . I knew prayer still happened inside them, whether out of books or out of hearts. People brought their doubts there as well as their faith. Inside those walls people got on their knees and drank from the cup and yearned and longed and praised. So maybe . . . maybe God was still in Savannah.

He was definitely at St. John's every weekday morning when I knelt—yes, knelt—in the pew behind the almost-fossilized lady whose hands shook when she held the prayer book, and watched what page she was on so I could find the response to Ned's "Glory be to the Father, and to the Son, and to the Holy Ghost." I could say with her, "As it was in the beginning is now and ever shall be, world without end. Amen." I learned to stand for the gospel and bow in respect for the sacrament and savor Ned's blessing: "The peace of God which passeth all understanding, keep your hearts and minds in the knowledge and love of God and of his Son, Jesus Christ . . ." And I could join my amen with her crackled one.

On Friday I waited until she wobbled from her pew and held out my hand. "I'm Tara Faulkner," I said.

"The peace of the Lord, Tara," she said. "I'm Mary Louise Anderson Bales."

Of course you are, I wanted to say. *You are Savannah personified and I love you.*

Whether I was finding what was true about me, I didn't know. But I was finding my city again. At least I knew I could still fall in love with something.

TWENTY-THREE

When I got to work Monday afternoon, the ninth of February, I didn't have a chance to get my apron from the hook before Ike was beside me, jerking his head toward the aisle by the loose teas. Evidently that was the place for all clandestine conversations. My mouth was dry before we even got there.

"Did I do something wrong?" I whispered.

"You are *killin'* me, girl," he whispered back and then raised his voice to a low hum. "No, you didn't do something wrong. I just want to check this out with you because I'm a little uneasy about it."

He found out about Wendy. That had to be it. Or he was offering me a management position. Even worse.

"A guy came in here looking for you. I didn't like the looks of him, so I didn't commit one way or the other to whether you worked here. He's out there waiting for you."

"Where?" I said.

Ike took me by the shoulders and turned me around so I could peek through the display of tea cozies and loose tea balls, but there was no need. I knew before I saw the figure in the window that it was going to be Seth. It was *sometime next week*, and he was home.

"You know him?" Ike said.

"I used to," I said.

"That your ex-fiancé?"

"Yes.

"You want me to get rid of him?"

"No. But I might be five minutes late for my shift? Is that okay?"

"Take all the time you need." Ike looked down at me, mouth firm. "You just shout if you need me."

I wanted to whimper for help right there and let Ike usher Seth out onto Bull Street and then—do what? Keep finding ways to avoid facing the inevitable?

Besides, as I went down the ramp and wove my way among the mismatched furniture to the window, something soft wound its way through me, some inkling of the way I used to feel when Seth came home from college, or we met at the beach when I was in grad school—something at first timid, something tender and expectant. Because his profile cut into the light from the window and it was still classic and handsome. It was still familiar.

But when he turned to me, I saw little that I knew.

He stood up from the table—our table, the Watch—and watched me come closer. With every step I was more aware of the drastic change that had come over him in six weeks.

His dark hair was longer and, though it was combed, various parts of it didn't seem to know which way they were supposed to go. His clothes were obviously clean but rumpled and mismatched and they hung on him as if they belonged to someone who pumped twice the iron he did. The muscles were still there yet they seemed long and stretched. He even appeared to be shorter, although when I got to him and he placed a tentative kiss on my forehead, he was still the same eight inches taller than me.

It was his face, though, that made me keep searching it to

make sure this wasn't someone impersonating Seth. He was trying to hide behind the once well-kept beard that now took over his jaw like a garden gone to seed. I was sure if he could have grown it around his eyes he would have, but they were very much uncovered. I could see the deep half-moons of sleeplessness and the sagging skin left behind by sobbing and the weary look that could only be brought on by ceaseless searching. I knew that look. I'd seen it in the mirror.

"We can sit," I said.

"Do you have time?"

"I do."

I sank into a chair and folded my arms on the table. Without Ms. Helen's shim it rocked.

"I'm sorry you're having to work here," Seth said.

I felt my eyebrows rise. "I'm not. I'm enjoying it. When did you get back?"

"A couple of hours ago. I just stopped by my folks' house long enough to drop off my stuff."

"You haven't seen them, then."

"No. I saw Evelyn."

"How did that go?"

"It didn't." Seth shrugged. "I don't have much hope for that relationship. She hated me before and she has even more reason to now."

My last conversation with Evelyn flashed through my mind but I tucked it away. Maybe another time. Right now, something was making me uneasy. Something was missing that was there the last time I talked to Seth. Something that was there in his letter and wasn't here now.

"Are you okay?" I said. "I mean, I don't know, I guess I expected you to be—more healed? Does that sound right?"

"I'm getting healed," he said. His voice was wooden. "I've been clean for forty-two days. And not because I've been on lockdown. I haven't been. I just don't want it anymore."

"That's good, right?" I knew I was bordering on forced-perky, but Seth seemed to be sinking right in front of me. Old habits like the Coax die hard.

"They say I'll have urges, go through cycles. Right now I just feel like nothing matters."

So not what I was expecting. At all.

"I really thought I could come home and get my life back," he said. "Or maybe even a life I never had. And then some . . ." He stopped and inhaled. "Somebody had to plaster this thing all over the news. Now I don't have a job. I'm broke. Just walking from our place to here, three people did double takes when they saw me and then they looked away like I was some kind of pervert."

Seth stared at his hands on the tabletop, folded close to mine. I could see that he'd gone from nail biting to cuticle shredding. Had I not noticed it earlier, or was he just now short of breath?

"Do you want some water?" I said.

"No."

"Coffee?"

"I have a headache."

That didn't make any sense to me but I let it go. It apparently made less sense to him. He leaned back in the chair and scratched at his arms.

"I can't even imagine what it's been like for you since it came out," he said.

"People have pretty much left me alone," I said. "But you need to know that I kept it a secret until the article."

"It didn't do us a lot of good, did it?"

"Maybe it did for a while." I spread my fingers. "Look, Seth, people will forget—"

"Will you?" His eyes flared, and just as quickly the fire in them died. "I'm sorry. I've been up since three."

"You should go home and get some sleep. We can talk later."

"I can't sleep. That's the worst part. I was doing better with that until—that stupid article just turned everything to—"

"Seth," I said.

My tone brought his face up from its slow sink to his belly button.

"It's done, okay? I don't know who did it, and if I ever find out I *will* bring my full wrath down upon them. I'll beat your mother to it."

"You talking about her threatening to hire a PI?"

I pulled in my chin. "Threatening? I thought she did it."

"She was just trying to scare you. I told her to back off."

"Okay, so I don't get revenge," I said. "Maybe that's better for everybody."

I tried to smile at him. He didn't smile back.

"But you can't give up just because people know."

"I thought I could do it, you know, keep doing the inner work, keep fighting, even without the twenty-four-hour support I've been getting. But now?"

He put his hands back up on the table and grabbed mine. His were cold and sweaty and desperate.

"There is only one way I can do this and that's if you trust that I can."

"What about God?" I said.

"That's a given, isn't it?"

"Is it? Because it sounds like you're saying God is all well and good but if you don't have my trust, forget about it." I shook my head. "I told you before—this can't be on me."

His head dropped. "It's not, okay? It's not. I'm sorry. But it would help, Tar, you know? If I know you trust me to keep fighting, I'll know you love me."

I untangled my hands from his and squeezed them between my knees. "I never said I didn't love you. But I don't think love and trust automatically go together. Just because the thought of living without you still breaks my heart, that doesn't mean I know you're going to stay on this even when the whole world has just crashed down around you."

"Then you don't believe in me."

"I don't believe in the fake Seth," I said, though where that came from I had no clue. "You were a fake self before because you were hiding all your pain and doing stuff that wasn't you."

He was breathing even harder now, and I recognized it as the kind that holds back tears.

"I have to get to work," I said.

"What's it going to take for you to believe in me again?" he said.

I stood and waited until he looked up at me with tortured eyes.

"When you find out what's true about you," I said. "And it isn't what was in that article."

I hurried up the ramp. When I turned to look, the corner doors were closing behind him, and my own breath turned ragged. Was I too hard on him? He was going home alone. Surely nobody would have left medication available. Should I call Paul?

I might have, if I hadn't heard Ned's voice echoing through the vestibule of my mind: *I did that—tried to reach out before my arms were strong enough.*

I continued my plod up the ramp, although what was true about me in that moment I couldn't have said.

There was no time to ponder that because when I reached for my apron the second time that afternoon, Ike came to me, face beet-colored, nostrils in dragonlike flares. He looked for all the world like Smaug.

"I'm sorry I took so long," I said.

"Wendy just left," he said. "No explanation, nothing. She just ran out of here like something was chasing her." Ike hooked his hand on the back of his head. I expected to hear a sizzle. "I give you people time off whenever you need it. If an emergency comes up I cover for you, no problem. All I ask is for a little information, you know?"

"I do," I said.

"I was considering her for a management shift too. But I don't know if she can handle it." It was the first time I ever saw someone gnash his teeth. "It's that other job. It's like she's got a loan shark after her or something."

He looked at me so hard I wanted to back myself into the wall.

"I don't want to ask you to betray a confidence, but do you have any idea why she would just leave without saying anything?"

"No," I said. "We're not that close."

"She doesn't let anybody get close. She's like a feral cat." Ike shook his head. "Thanks for letting me vent. I'd like to help the kid, but I have to know what's going on or I can't."

"I'll cover her work this shift," I said.

His face finally softened, as soft as Ike's face ever got. "I know. I can always count on you."

He gave my arm a squeeze and went into the kitchen, already barking for more sandwiches. I stood there for a minute and closed my eyes tight. At first it was to shut out the automatic scenarios of me going after Wendy and pulling her out of the club on Montgomery and taking her home with me.

And then it turned into a prayer. A spontaneous mixture of King James and Psalm 109 and Ned's third-party conversations that somehow ended up sounding like a me I hadn't heard before. A me crying into an empty space.

I didn't sleep much that night, for the first time in a while. Several times I went to the window seat and opened the shutters far enough to see if the light was on in Seth's room. It never was, at least the times I looked, but the light in Paul's study was on all night. Each of us was dealing with this in our own dim isolation. And now that seemed so wrong.

Which was why I sat down with Ned the next morning after the service and told him about my conversation with Seth.

"I know you want me to figure this out for myself," I said, "but can you just tell me if I handled it okay?"

I asked it even though I expected him to turn that into another question for me.

What I didn't expect was for him to go to the long window and stand with his back to me. His voice, when it came, had a faraway sound.

"You said all the right things. I wish my wife had said that to me."

The salmon sofa began to swallow me.

"Do you know how I have so much knowledge about porn addiction?"

No, and please don't tell me. Please don't.

Ned turned to me, though I could see in the set of his face that it was because he knew he should face me. Not because he wanted to. Still, inside I pleaded, *Please don't tell me.*

"I've been there. From age fifteen to twenty-five. Your age. Ten years of absolute misery."

I sank further.

"That misery didn't stop for three years after I got clean. Those were the years I spent mopping up the mess I made."

I floundered, flailed for someplace safe. "You were married," I said.

"Got married when I was twenty-one, right in the thick of it."

Ned returned to the sofa, but he seemed to think better of

it and positioned himself on the edge of a high-backed sea-green chair opposite me. The divan stopped trying to swallow me, and I didn't know which was worse—the threat to take me away or the lack of it.

"I was a lot like Seth," Ned went on. "I thought it would all be gone once I had her with me all the time. Truth be told, it got worse." His gaze drifted to the bookcases behind me. "Hiding it from her was harder. I hurt her as much before she knew as I did after. I finally went to her and confessed it and told her I wanted to get help, but she just couldn't get past it, and I didn't blame her." His brown-eyed gaze returned to me. "Never blamed her for a minute."

I tried to swallow and found out I couldn't. My hand went to my throat before I could stop it.

"I'm sorry, Tara," Ned said. "I didn't think we should go any further with this unless I told you."

That made sense. It did. I still couldn't swallow.

Ned rubbed both hands on his thighs. "I say I wish she'd told me she still loved me. I actually don't know if that would have helped." His head pulled forward, and his eyes deepened. "I had to take a chance revealing this to you because it's why I know what you said to Seth is what he has to hear."

I found my voice and whispered, "Do you think so?"

"He needs all the help he can get and that *will* get him through at times, but he won't be healed unless he knows God is the only one he can absolutely trust to stick it out with him."

"Your wife left you, then?"

"She did. I've never heard from her again."

"I'm sorry," I said.

"I deserved it. And it might have been the best thing because I had to heal for me and for God. And, it turns out, for a lot of other people." He tilted his head at me. "I'm not saying I had to go through that to end up being a priest, but God used it. That I know."

"You think God will ever use Seth?" I said.

"Is that the point here?"

"Again with the questions."

"Do you have an answer?"

"You're saying the point is whether God will use me."

"It is if you want to keep coming to me and talking."

He waited, his eyes giving me no indication which way he wanted me to go. But I already knew. I really did.

"Then that is the point," I said.

I heard the soft catch in his breath.

"But can I ask you something else?"

"You can ask me anything," he said.

"Is there hope for Seth? Really?"

Ned didn't hesitate. "Yes. But you need to understand that even with a deep faith and a lot of support, it may be a year before he starts to heal into someone you recognize. Or into the real Seth." He nodded, as if to himself. "Maybe that's a better way to put it. And some of that is neurological, just like it is for an alcoholic or a drug addict. He has to detox his mind and allow his neurology to settle down. And deal with that abuse issue. That alone is huge."

"Okay," I said. "I think I get that."

"And probably—and this is just what I know from working with a lot of guys and talking to other pastors that run programs—it will be two to five years before he's ready for a relationship, judging from how far into it he was. Even if you were already married and decided to stay married, those years would be very fragile."

Ned stopped and I let that soak into me.

"So I'm not lessening his chances by not marrying him," I said.

He was slower to answer this time. "No," he said. "You're not. But, Tara, that decision has as much to do with you as it does with him."

"I have to know what's true about me," I said.

And since that wasn't a question, he didn't give me an answer. I knew it anyway.

TWENTY-FOUR

I barely got across the square after talking to Ned when my phone rang. The screen read Spencer, Groate, and Grissom.

Daddy had made it clear Randi wasn't to contact me, but this wasn't her personal number. So . . . what? She'd decided to press charges for defamation of Seth's character after all? Poor Randi. I tried to laugh up at Sergeant Jasper. She really was losing it.

The phone went into its second ring, and what I'd just thought nudged me like Gray's elbow. *Poor Randi.* She actually was suffering, and really, weren't we all? Didn't Paul sit up all night in his study? Didn't Seth look one bath short of a homeless person? Wasn't Evelyn going to crack right down the middle if she had to spend one more day pretending not to care? Not just poor Randi. Poor all of us.

The phone rang a fourth time. "This is Tara Faulkner," I said into it.

"Oh. Sorry." I could hear some fumbling and bumping as if whoever answered had dropped the receiver in the process of retrieving it from its trip back onto the cradle.

"Hello?" I said.

"Yes. Hello." The voice was high-pitched and young and definitely not Randi's. "This is Ms. Grissom's assistant—Randi Grissom—the attorney?"

First day on the job? I wanted to ask. Instead I said, "Yes?"

"Um—"

Speaking of poor somebody. "Did Ms. Grissom want to speak to me?" I said.

"No. I mean, not about this."

"I'm sorry?"

"She might want to speak to you. She didn't say she didn't. But about this, no."

Okay, enough with trying to make things easier for this child.

"Do you have a message for me?" I said.

"Yes. I do."

"And it is . . . ?"

"Yeah. So, Ms. Faulkner?"

"Ye-e-s?"

"You need to get your personal belongings out of the residence at 3 West Jones Street and then return the key to this office because that property is being sold."

There. She'd said it.

I sank to the base of the monument.

"Do you need for me to repeat any of that, ma'am?"

"No," I said. "Is that all?"

"That's all she said."

The pause that ensued must have been interminable to her, but I was beyond caring if she got through this conversation without getting fired. They were selling the townhouse. Even if Seth healed into some real self I could fall in love with again, we would have to start all over someplace else. I closed my eyes and saw only stark white.

"Ma'am?"

"Yes."

"So, yeah . . . if you'll just do that . . . When do you think you will . . . do that?"

I stiffened a little. "Did Ms. Grissom give me a deadline?"

"I don't think so . . . let me see . . . no, no deadline."

"Then I'll just do it as soon as I can."

"Okay, so what shall I tell her?"

I let my shoulders relax. "Sweetie," I said, "tell Ms. Grissom whatever is going to make her yell at you the least."

I hung up and started my march for home and pondered the fact that I had just called a secretary sweetie.

～ℭℓℓ～

Mama was in the kitchen when I completed my march through the back door. By then I was losing the battle to maintain my poor-Randi attitude. Mama pointed to a stool and I sat, and while she wiped the already spotless countertop, I vented. Ike had nothing on me.

I finished with, "I guess it doesn't matter how she does it; it's still going to tick me off."

"And it's still going to hurt," Mama said. "You had so many dreams about that place."

"About our whole life," I said. I shoved my hair out of my face and reached for a pad and pen on the snack bar. "I need to make a list—I don't have that much stuff over there, but I need to know when I can use your car—if that's okay—"

"Why don't we go right now?"

I looked up at my mother. Her face was smooth, her eyes bright as if she were suggesting we take an impromptu shopping trip.

"You're serious?" I said.

"Why wait? Do you have more than we can fit in the SUV?"

"We filled it up last time we went to Pottery Barn. But I'm not sure I want all of it. I picked it out for Seth and me, and now . . ."

"I'll get the keys." Mama took off across the kitchen, still talking over her shoulder. "You don't even have to stay. Just tell me what you want and I'll put it in a pile and Kellen can come by after work and load it up. How does that sound?"

It sounded awesome. Awesome and supportive and sad.

ॐ

I had only been to the place on Jones once since the Monday I was waiting for the furniture. The day I found out Seth was still using porn. The day I completely flipped out on the corner of Whitaker and Gaston. I expected to be sickened or angry or even hysterical again when we walked in the front door, but at first I didn't feel anything.

Even when I saw that the furniture was all gone, every end table and floor lamp and striped ottoman, I didn't feel any emptier than I did before. Everything had been spilled, poured, or dumped out already. There was an end to done after all.

"Let's not linger, Tara, you think?" Mama said behind me.

"No. Let's not." I headed for the kitchen. "Most of what you and I bought is in here, I think."

"I'll check upstairs just to make sure," she said and headed for the steps.

I stopped at the granite counter and started to cave. I had loved that countertop. Somehow it had held so much of the promise—of rolling out dough for piecrust to take to Gaston Street for Thanksgiving and slicing tomatoes from Fritzie's August garden and leaning across to get a kiss from Seth when he came home from work with his eyes twinkling.

I spread my hands on the vanilla cream and cranberry and gold and tried to disappear into it. It was the last thing I'd stopped to savor before we had the spat that started the slow unspooling of barbed wire. What if we hadn't had that argument? Would I be married to Seth now? What would I know? What would be left to be discovered in years to come?

I knew only one thing as I surfaced from the depths of my beloved countertop. I knew that Mama was right. I would have been left behind closed doors to handle it alone.

"I tell you what." Mama somehow appeared on the other side of the counter with a box, her tidy body in full efficiency mode. "I found a few things I think might be yours. Why don't you go through this box and toss what you don't want. I'll take care of the kitchen. This all goes?"

I let my gaze sort of glaze over the pottery jar full of wooden spoons that had never been used and the smoky grey teapot on the stovetop.

"Yes, ma'am," I said. "But I don't know what I'm going to do with it."

"Oh, Tara." Mama's eyes shone. "I know this feels like the end, but I have a feeling it's just a beginning for you. Go on now—here."

I took the box and sat with it in the middle of the living room floor and pulled out a few random items. A pair of pink socks. A to-go cup sleeve Fritzie had knitted for me at some point. A silver hoop earring (so *that* was where it was). And my *Finding Neverland* DVD.

I couldn't remember having any of the other stuff here, but the night I'd brought *Neverland* was digitalized in my memory.

ME: (*snuggling in next to Seth on floor cushions and pressing Play on the remote*) This is my all-time favorite movie.

SETH: (*grinning and tugging my hair*) Does it have a car chase?

ME: No.

SETH: Gun battle?

ME: No-o.

SETH: Not even a fistfight?

ME: This from the paragon of Christian virtue? No!

SETH: (*tugging my hair again*) So it's a chick flick.

I gave him the you-are-made-of-slime sigh and homed in on Johnny Depp. Five minutes later Seth was asleep with his warm head in my lap. He never was as into movies as I was.

The irony of that cut straight through me.

As I tossed everything back into the box, it occurred to me that most of what was true about me wasn't necessarily true about Seth, and vice versa. I was movies; he was music. I was casual elegance; he was starched and tailored. I was dreams; he was plans. It had seemed like a perfect balance. It had all seemed perfect.

That should have been my first clue, shouldn't it—that everything before that night in the kitchen was perfect? If any one of the movies in my collection had featured a perfect couple, Lexi and I would have ripped it apart for lack of realism.

We'd have been right.

I closed the box and pushed it against the empty wall. Knowing that it had never been completely real—that helped somehow. Maybe a vision was easier to let go. Maybe now we really could heal, both of us. Maybe now I could find what was true.

~✦~

If I could have measured feeling better by inches, I would have given myself at least three by that afternoon when I got to the Piebald. Not so Ike. He was simmering because Wendy didn't show up again, and she wasn't answering his calls or texts. The only thing that gave him even a half inch was the fact that I did both our jobs and didn't give anybody the wrong sandwich or put ketchup in somebody's cappuccino.

"I'm telling you—you're management material," he told me as I was leaving to join the Watch. "Think about it."

I didn't. I didn't even stay with my Betsy and Gray and Ms. Helen very long, except to tell them about the townhouse being for sale.

"You okay with that?" Betsy said, reaching for my hands across the table.

"I am," I said. "I know I'm going to have my tough times, but it seems like the worst is over now."

If anybody disagreed with that, they didn't say.

~~oee~~

I actually wanted time by myself so I could go back in my mind to my meeting with Ned, and I couldn't process that with anybody. It looked like I had the perfect setup when I got home. Kellen's car was gone and Mama and Daddy were off at a dinner, so I fixed myself a helping of Mama's homemade macaroni and cheese. She'd left me a note about it with a *P.S. I dropped off the key at Randi's office. New beginnings.* I was headed for the sunroom with a steaming micro-waved plate when someone knocked on the back door.

Dang it.

"Yeah?" I said.

"It's me," a thready voice said. "Evvy."

I was less in the mood for an anti-Seth tirade than I was for a root canal, but I set the plate on the counter and let her in. She looked like an alley cat that hadn't had a handout in days.

"Are you okay?" I said.

"No," she said. "I can't be in that house right now. Can I just hang out here for an hour or so until Paul and Randi retire for the evening?"

I didn't point out to her that the house was so big you could be in it for a week and not run into the other people who lived there.

"Sure," I said.

"You don't even have to talk to me. I'll just sit in a corner or something."

"Don't be a martyr, Evvy. I'm fixing you a plate of mac and cheese."

"No—"

"Hush up. You're eating with me. It'll take me two minutes."

That two minutes stretched into an eternity as Evelyn paced the kitchen, pulling knives out of the holder and examining them and putting them back. I had to find something to occupy her or she was going to plan a homicide. Lizzie Borden came to mind.

The microwave dinged and I had a stroke of genius.

"Let's take our plates up to the theater," I said. "We can watch a movie. Sound good?"

"Yeah," Evvy said. "I want something really depressing so I'll feel better about my life."

When we got to the theater, I discovered the box from the townhouse. Kellen must have brought it up.

"There's one in here," I said, tapping the box with my toe. "I haven't seen it in a while." I felt a surge of sisterliness. "Watch it with me."

Evelyn set her plate on a table by one of the recliners and opened the box. "*Finding Neverland.*" She almost smiled at the case. "This has Johnny Depp. He rocks."

"Because . . ."

"He gets to be whatever he wants, and there's nothing he *can't* be."

"I thought you wanted something depressing."

"I changed my mind." She barely looked up from the box. "It's impossible to be depressed around you."

I sat in one of the other recliners and watched her as she threw her hair impatiently back over her shoulder and headed for the DVD player.

"You are going to love this. I know you are," I said. "This is the movie that started me wanting to be a filmmaker."

Evelyn sat on the floor with the remote in her hand. "What happened to that?"

"Life, I think."

She shrugged. "You've got nothing stopping you now."

I nodded at the remote. She pushed the button.

On the first chord of music I knew the wrong DVD was in that case. Instead of the strains of "Where Is Mr. Barrie?" there was silence, followed by breathing that was sickeningly, horribly familiar. The camera pulled out to reveal a mop of thick black hair hanging over a woman's face.

"Stop it, Evvy," I said.

"What is this?"

"Just turn it off!"

She went for the remote but it bounced off the table and onto the floor. As she scrambled for it I couldn't pull my eyes from the screen. The hair parted and a face came into view, with perfect teeth and a pair of eyes like National Velvet.

"That's her!"

I jerked to look at Evelyn. She was pointing frantically at the screen. "That's the prostitute I saw with Seth. I swear it is."

The camera zoomed in until only the lips were visible. Wendy's pretty lips in a pant that was anything but.

Evelyn fumbled with the remote and fast-forwarded until we could see her face again, which was hard because her face wasn't what the camera was interested in.

"That is totally her," Evelyn said.

"She's not a prostitute." My voice was so thin it was all but not there.

"What do you call that?"

"Turn it off, Evvy. Give me the thing."

Evelyn threw the remote in my direction and I had to lunge for it. An entire lifetime passed before I could snap the image from the screen.

"Now do you believe me?" Evelyn said. "My brother is a gross, disgusting phony . . ."

I didn't hear the rest. Because it wasn't Seth I was thinking about.

TWENTY-FIVE

It was never going to be over. Ever. The pain would just go on and on and on because there would always be one more thing to tear open the healed places. One more thing to make the next wound deeper and bloodier and more debilitating than the one before.

I sat curled into a tight ball in the window seat after Evelyn left and tried to keep that last thing from digging into me, but I couldn't stop it. And as it opened me up again, I felt all of the things.

My first glimpse of the black-maned woman on Seth's computer screen and the sound of his moans.

The promise shattered by my next look, the abusive horror I found on the new, supposedly innocent hard drive.

The lonely shame of keeping the secret. Randi's accusations. Paul's insinuations. Evelyn's revelation.

My brother's withdrawal.

And then Seth's suicide attempt and more secrets and the life-ripping newspaper article by someone who hated him.

Seth was abused. Seth was fired. Seth was broke. Seth was broken. My poor Seth.

That Seth I could understand and forgive and love and maybe trust again when he found his true self.

But now? Now with this new, heinous, too-real vision of him in my head, watching a girl he *knew*, if Evelyn was to be believed. Wendy—the girl I admired and respected and learned from—who took care of me and . . .

Who had suddenly pulled herself away from me.

I raised my head and stared out at the park without seeing it. In my own reflection in the window I could almost find Wendy beside me.

"When did it start?" I whispered to her.

When you overheard me tell the Watch about my porn-addicted fiancé?

Surely when you heard about the article in the paper. Yes, then.

But why did you run away from the Piebald? Why did you start believing you couldn't come back?

I put my fist to my mouth and closed my eyes. I knew. I knew it was just yesterday, when she came to work and saw me there with Seth.

Bile rose in my throat. *It doesn't mean anything*, he'd said to me, again and again. *Wendy isn't doing it to me*, I told Lexi.

I couldn't sit there any longer. I paced the room, kicking shoes and pillows and discarded clothes out of my way as I tried to clear some kind of path in my mind. But every one led to a dead end.

Could I ever, ever have a new vision with Seth after this?

Ever have a vision with anyone? After I'd experienced thrusts that cut so deep I couldn't breathe?

Ever take a step without falling over someone dragging this heinous thing behind them? Alyssa. Jacqueline. Wendy. Seth. *Ned*.

I collapsed onto the floor next to my bed and rocked. Screams died in my throat as desperate croaks. "Oh, *God*! Help me! Help *us*!"

I couldn't remember the rest of the psalm and I wanted to. I reached for it in my soul where I'd tucked it away with Ned's voice.

Ned's voice. *Find out what's true about you. Then you can reach out—*

I pulled myself abruptly from the floor and paced again. This—this *thing* was not what was true about me. It was a sick thing that had gotten stuck to me when I was busy trying to build a life. Same for Seth. Same for all of us.

Including Wendy.

I tore across the room and snatched my cell phone from my dresser. My hand might get bitten, but I couldn't just stay here and let this agony go on. My hands shook as I poked at the screen. Lexi answered right away, but her voice was thick with sleep.

"Tara?" she said. "What's wrong?"

"Where does Wendy come out of the club when she gets off work?"

"There's a door on the side that opens out to the alley. Why?"

"What time?"

"Huh?"

"What *time?*"

"About one thirty, usually. Tara, what is going on?"

I pulled the phone out to look at the time. One ten. I could get there.

"Lex, can I come to your place, say, before two o'clock?"

"Yeah, but—"

"I'll see you then."

I hung up while she was still asking questions.

None of my midnight promenades in the historic district could compare in darkness and desolation to the trek I took down Montgomery Street at 1:25 a.m. The sidewalks were empty, except for the one couple who spewed from the door of a bar on the corner as if they'd been hurled through a Roman vomitorium.

All the noise and fear came from inside the handful of clubs I passed, which vibrated with music like gangsta cars. Their doors were mostly open but I tried not to look in. The smell of liquor and sweat and sex painted all the picture I could handle.

I was close to vomiting myself as I took a deep breath and turned into the brick-paved alley that ran beside the club where Wendy worked. Garbage cans overflowing with empty beer cases and reeking like retch lined the outside wall until the side entrance interrupted them. Three cement steps led sideways to a thick metal door marked *Personnel Only.*

I had no intention of disobeying that edict. I wrapped my jean jacket tighter, even though the February night was humid and almost warm, and prayed for Wendy to come out alone. And soon. I didn't let myself even think about what my father would say about this. If he said I was stupid, he'd be right. I probably should have told somebody besides Lexi. But who?

The door opened and I took a step out of the shadow of the nearest trash can. A man stepped out, dressed in a sheened jacket with the collar up to his ears.

I turned away and pressed my cell phone to my ear. "You'd *better* be here in fifteen seconds!" I said, so loudly only an imbecile would have believed I was actually talking to someone.

I kept my head down and pretended to be listening intently. The man's footsteps echoed in the alley as he came lightly down the steps. They paused near me. I died several deaths. When he moved on, I waited until his footfalls faded onto Montgomery Street before I sagged against the garbage can. My insides were the exact consistency of one of my mother's congealed salads.

Knowing I wouldn't be able to pull that off again—as if I'd actually pulled it off *then*—I stuffed my phone in my jacket pocket and went up the steps. My hand was poised to bang on the metal door when it opened, nearly knocking me back into the railing. Wendy came out.

If I hadn't seen her in the video, I might not have recognized her at first. The violet eyes wore so many layers of smoky shadow she seemed barely able to operate her lids, and the perfect white teeth were whiter yet against the thick lacquer of red lipstick. Her hair fell over her shoulders and sparkled with glitter that was more menacing than pretty. But one thing I did recognize because I had seen it in the mirror too. The moment she registered that it was me, her face was shrouded in shame.

She tried to recover and head for the steps, but I stood in front of her.

"Don't run away from me, Wendy. I know everything and I just need to talk to you. That's all."

The words came out in a rush because I knew I only had as long as it would take for that to sink in before she bolted. I grabbed her arm and pulled her with me down the steps and up the alley.

"Tara—what are you doing? Let *go!*"

She tried to wrench away and I held on, but I knew she was ultimately stronger than me. I got us as far as Montgomery Street and then I released her and put my arm around her shoulders and headed toward Lexi's apartment building.

"Walk with me, please," I said.

"Where are we going? Tara, stop!"

She tried to dig her heels in and I let her, but I got myself in front of her again.

"You can run away if you want to," I said. "But it's going to follow you unless you give me a chance. Just give me a chance, and then if you still want to go you can."

"Yo! Gio!"

I peered past her shoulder. It was Mr. Stand-Up Collar. When I looked back at Wendy, her eyes were wild.

"Come on," I said.

I gripped her with my arm around her shoulders again and ran with her tripping against me into the narrow passageway beside the apartment building and up the stairs and through the smeared-window door.

"Lexi!" I screamed as we made our way down the green den of a hallway.

Lexi's door opened and I threw Wendy inside and dove in after her. I stood against it, holding my breath. The outside door creaked open. Footsteps fell and then stopped and retreated. The door closed.

"I think he's gone," I whispered.

"Who?" Lexi's eyes were the size of dessert plates.

"My manager," Wendy said.

"Was he going to hurt you?" Lexi said.

"Not if I do what he says."

"And you just didn't, so now he *might* hurt you." I cringed. "I'm sorry."

Wendy, who was still leaning against Lexi's futon couch where she'd landed, lifted one shoulder. That seemed to be all the energy she had for a shrug. The rest, the vitality that always filled the Piebald, was gone.

"It doesn't really matter now," she said. "I'm busted."

"And you don't mean by what just happened, do you?" I said.

Lexi backed the two steps to the kitchen. "I'm gonna go ahead and make some tea. Wendy, you want to . . . sit down?"

"Come on," I said. "I just want to talk to you."

Wendy resigned herself onto the couch and clutched one of Lexi's throw pillows. I took a director's chair across from her, and I sat there, saying nothing, because I hadn't prepared a script. All I knew was that the secrets had to be over.

"I'm just going to put this out there," I said. "But Wendy, I'm not attacking you, okay? You have to believe that."

She didn't say anything. The confidence she always had behind the coffee shop counter seemed to have been smothered in makeup.

"Seth had a copy of the video you were in. And tonight, totally by accident, I saw some of it."

Wendy swore softly. It was a far more graceful piece of profanity than Evelyn's, or the string I spewed when I first knew. I had to give her that.

"Seth's sister was with me and she said she'd seen you with him on Montgomery Street."

"I'm not a hooker."

"That's not it. Before tonight I could still believe that Seth was one step removed from actual human beings, real women. But you . . . you're somebody's *daughter*."

Wendy gave a laugh hard as a fist. "I used to be. Look, I know what you want to ask me, so why don't I go ahead and tell you?"

She waited for my nod.

"He—what's his name, Seth?"

"Yes." She didn't know his *name*?

"He told me it was Johnny. Anyway, he used to come to the club to watch me dance. He tried to proposition me but I told him what I just told you: I'm not a prostitute." Her attempt to be cavalier was failing, but she still lifted her chin as she went on. "I sold him one of my movies, but we never actually . . . had sex."

She ended with a jerky shrug, but I knew that wasn't everything. It was my turn to wait. Finally she shook the thick, glittery hair as if she were jostling the subject back into place. "Here's what you want to know: I was nothing to him. Even after I told him no on sex, it was like he just wanted to talk. You know, about his past—"

She looked at me sharply. I guess it was my gasp that stopped her.

"Not about you," she said. "I never even knew he was engaged. He told me about his parents, who I gathered were a trip. Especially his mother. Mostly her. And the more I kind of got to know him, I started putting it together. All the working out and the muscle building—I've seen it before. It's about proving he's a real man. You know, has power. All that."

I didn't even pretend to know what she was talking about. Seth had to prove that he was a man? To whom?

"It's like you talk to these guys and you become sort of their therapist." Wendy licked her lips and shuddered. "Do you have any Kleenex?" she called to Lexi. "I have to get some of this makeup off. I feel like a harlot sitting here."

Lexi brought a box of tissues from the bathroom and I waited while Wendy smeared at her face. My heart felt too heavy to even beat. Seth had told her more than I knew about him, and the betrayal ached again.

"You want me to go on?" Wendy said. She looked years younger without the makeup, and a hundred times more real.

"No, I don't," I said. "But yes."

She gave me another eyebrows-raised chance to change my mind, and then she said, "I knew something was hurting underneath. I mean, this was no sleaze bag." She nodded, the way a therapist actually might. "A guy like that doesn't come on to . . . somebody in my line of work unless something's tearing him apart. He's sitting there in a club—not drinking, looking like a freakin' swan in a pack of hyenas—and it was like I had to know why."

I heard all of that, but a few words formed a separate stack. Proposition. Power. The past.

I grabbed the one on top.

"What else did he tell you about his past?"

"Only what I pried out of him." Wendy looked away. "I asked him who hurt him when he was a kid."

"Why would you ask him that?" I said.

"Because I knew he'd been abused." She forced her gaze back to me. "Why else does a guy like him turn to a girl like me?"

I couldn't answer that question. I wasn't sure I wanted to, but we were too far in to stop now.

"Go on," I said.

"He admitted he'd been molested, and then I said, 'Was it a guy?' because I knew it wasn't. I was just giving him a chance to say it him-self." She smiled ruefully. "He said it, all right. He went *off* on me."

"Went off how?"

"He was just, like, raging, and that was what I wanted. I wanted him to get it out." Wendy's voice slowed, and each time she came to the end of a sentence, it broke off as if pieces of the story were splintering away. "So I said, 'It was a woman, wasn't it? Somebody you trusted.' Then I *did* think he was going to hit me." She put up a hand to my gasp. "He pulled back. He's just not that kind of guy. But I decided it was time to stop."

I wanted to say she was lying, that Seth didn't have that in him. That he would never even think about hitting a woman. But the sick feeling in my throat said she was telling the truth. I had seen it flash through his eyes—when I caught him, when I pushed him to admit he lied to me. When I chipped at his perfect idea of purity.

Wendy watched me, waiting as if she knew the sound of every one of my thoughts.

"There's more, isn't there?" I said.

She didn't answer.

"Wendy, please—"

"I'm not sure you want to know this."

"I don't." I pressed my folded arms against my stomach. "But I need to."

She tapped her fingers on her lips with garish nails I'd never seen at the Piebald. "I was about to get up and leave and he covered his eyes with his hands—the way little kids do, like they think if they can't see you, you can't see them. And then he just blurted it out." Wendy's eyes saddened. "He said when he was ten and eleven and twelve years old . . . his babysitter molested him."

The whistle on the teakettle pierced the air and the shaking started someplace deep inside me.

Wendy's voice snapped off another brittle piece. "Then he uncovered his eyes and said something like, 'There, are you satisfied?' He looked so humiliated and I felt horrible. I tried to tell him that wasn't his fault and he didn't have anything to be ashamed of but he just got up and knocked the chair over and left." The look she gave me was broken. The violet eyes could no longer hold their focus. "I never saw him again until Monday when he came to the Piebald and you two were sitting there with all this history, like, right on the table between you. When I realized he was your ex-fiancé, I just couldn't face you." The final piece split off. "I can't even believe I'm facing you now."

As if to catch that last shard, Wendy smothered her face with her hands—maybe the way Seth had. There was still some voice left, though, and it wailed so long and so deep I was afraid she was dying.

In a way, maybe she was.

But I couldn't go to her. She had just jabbed another knife into the layer upon layer of pain that had become everything I was. She didn't even know how she'd done it, but I couldn't care.

I got up and motioned to Lexi who stood white faced between the kitchen and us with a rattling tray of teapot and mugs. "Can you—?" I said.

"Absolutely," she said.

She set the tray on the counter and went to Wendy and I let myself out the door. Outside in the dank green hallway I flattened myself against the wall.

His babysitter when he was ten and eleven and twelve years old.

He covered his eyes because he couldn't look at her when he told her that his female babysitter had abused his just awakening little male body.

Fritzie? Did she mean Fritzie?

Fritzie and Seth?

No. Just no. Nonononononono.

I slid down the wall toward the filthy carpet. Dear God, just let it be no. Because if it was yes, I couldn't—

The door opened at the end of the hall and I halted in midslide. As my calves burned a shadow fell across the rug. That stupid stand-up collar.

My first instinct was to duck back into Lexi's apartment, but then he would know where I'd taken Wendy.

I pulled away from the wall, turned all the way around, and walked as casually as my on-end nerves would let me until I reached the next door that led outside. I pushed through it as if I were going out for cigarettes—and then tore down the steps and off down the alley.

Garbage cans and trash bags and rancid odors flipped past me, but I didn't stop or breathe until I got to the edge of North Bull, and I only flung myself behind a Dumpster then so I could make sure he wasn't following me. The street was as quiet as it should be at close to three in the morning.

I couldn't run anymore but I walked fast and hard, cutting through the squares and across lawns until Gaston Street was finally in sight. All the lights in the main house were off but I wasn't headed there. I took the steps up to the carriage house apartment three at a time and banged on Kellen's door.

The heels of my hands were bruising by the time the curtains parted on his living room window and his swollen eyes looked out at me.

"Kellen!" I shouted at him. "Let me in!"

The door tried to come open but it caught on its chain. Mumbling the third set of curses I'd heard that night, Kellen fumbled with it and finally set it loose. The metal banged against the frame as he yanked the door open and stared at me in the yellow light that spilled out onto the landing.

"What the—"

"I need to talk to you."

He stepped back and let me blow past him. Scratching at the front of his T-shirt with one hand, he ran the other over the stubble on his head, as if he were making sure it was there and he was him. Who I was, he hadn't seemed to figure out yet. I tried to pull it together.

"I'm sorry I woke you up," I said.

"I'm sorry you did too." His upper lip curled. "You smell like a brewery. Are you drunk?"

"No! Kellen, listen to me."

He pulled a fingertip across my forehead. "You're sweating. What the—what's going on?"

"I just need to talk to you."

"In the middle of the night?"

"Yes."

Finally the angst in my voice seemed to find its way in. He sobered and gestured toward the couch.

"You want coffee or anything?"

"No." I sagged onto his sofa that smelled like dirty clothes and Mexican food and everything else boy. I could feel my perspiration seeping in where it would eventually add to the aroma. "I have to ask you something and I want you to be totally honest, okay? No matter how bad you think it'll sound—you have to tell me the truth."

Kellen's skin passed white and went straight to almost blue, and he lowered himself onto the early Attic coffee table with agonizing slowness.

"You're scarin' me," he said.

"It *is* scary. Oh, Kellen . . ." I breathed in. "Okay, I can't cry. I just have to say it."

"What?"

Both his face and his voice splintered at their edges. "Tara, come *on*."

"You remember Fritzie."

One furry eyebrow went up. "Do I remember Fritzie? Ya think? She's a crazy person. What about her?"

"She's worse than a crazy person. Do you know what I'm talking about?"

Kellen let out a long breath and tucked his hands under his thighs. I knew it was to keep them from shaking. "Maybe," he said. "Tell me."

I told him the whole thing, pieced together from every scrap I could remember from Wendy and from what Seth said in his letter. As I talked and Kellen watched me, the rosiness that was Kellen returned to his face. For him, maybe the knowing was better than the not knowing.

"Did you know about any of that?" I said.

"Sort of." Kellen scrubbed at the back of his neck, eyes closed. "Just this one time. We were maybe ten and she was with us for the weekend and Seth was over here. You were already in bed and she let us stay up to watch some old movie with her. I think it was *Top Gun*."

"*Top Gun*. You were ten."

"I know, right?" Kellen got up and relocated to the beanbag. His hands were steady again. "Seth and I were all into the whole fighter pilot thing so we thought it was cool, until we got to the sex scene." He folded his arms across his chest. "There we are, these little prepubescent virgins, and there's Tom Cruise and what's her face goin' at it."

"Fritzie didn't fast-forward it."

"Uh, no. She starts, like, trying to act it out with *us*." Kellen looked at me sideways. "You don't want the details, right?"

"No."

"Seth kind of froze but I was all, 'Gross! Knock it off!' so she backed off and I said, 'Come on, Seth, we're outta here.'" Kellen stared at the hairs on his arms. "The worst part of it for me was that we didn't get to see the end of the movie. I guess that wasn't the worst part for Seth."

"Obviously she pursued it with him later. A lot."

"You know what's weird?" Kellen said.

"This whole thing?"

"Yeah, but I'm talking about . . . I pretty much forgot about that incident until you just brought it up."

"Seth never told you about the rest of it?"

He gave me a deadpan look. "Guys don't talk about this kinda stuff. I mean, come on, that must have been humiliating for him."

"Especially since it obviously wasn't happening to you because you told Fritzie to knock it off and he couldn't."

"I don't get that. Why couldn't he do that?"

"I don't know," I said, and then I shook my head. "Maybe I do. Seth was always way more cooperative with adults than you were. He was the rule-follower. You were like the rule . . . questioner."

"Ironic, right?" Kellen's voice suddenly had a bite to it. "He becomes the poster kid for the Ten Commandments and gets hooked on porn."

"Yeah. It seems like both of those were reactions to the abuse. I mean, right? That has to be it, doesn't it?"

Kellen stood up and paced to the window and looked out between the curtains and slapped, barefoot, to the kitchen and leaned on the counter—until I finally said, "What are you *doing*?"

"I'm just trying to decide whether to say this or not."

"No more secrets. Say it."

"It's not a secret. Look—"

Kellen came back to the coffee table and sat on the edge of it again. He leaned his forearms on his thighs, so that I could see his eyes as he locked his blue gaze onto mine.

"Yeah, it stinks that Seth got abused by that witch. I even get how it messed him up and he turned to porn and all that. But, see—and this is where you're probably gonna get ticked off at me—but I don't see that as an excuse. He still screwed up. He still hurt you. He hurt our whole family, and I don't think we oughta let him off the hook because of something that happened to him when he was ten years old."

He held on to my eyes for another moment and then stood up again. "Now you're mad at me."

"No, I'm not. I go back and forth with that about fifty times a day." My breath caught. "Oh my gosh."

"What?"

I sat up on the couch and breathed into my hands.

"*What?* Are you hyperventilating? What?"

I dragged my hands through my hair. "Okay, just let me say this because I just now thought of it and I have to hear if it makes sense."

"You're already not making sense, but go for it."

I tried to set it up with my hands. "Okay, we can sit here and judge Seth and we'd be right. He messed up; he hurt people; I have scars I'll never get rid of, all that."

"Right."

"That's all about him." I looked from my hands to Seth. "But what about us?"

"What about us?"

"What does that say about us—okay, about *me* if I just keep coming back to how horrible that is. If I say, he suffered but look how he made *me* suffer, then I never get over it. I'm just bitter."

"You have a right to be."

"But I don't *want* to be, Kellen. I'm sick of it."

I started to cry—that wet, loose kind of crying that finally feels good. It apparently didn't feel good to Kellen.

"Aw, man, don't do that," he said. "I can't handle it when you do that. You need a Kleenex? How 'bout some toilet paper? I got toilet paper."

I cried free, soft tears until he brought me an entire roll of Cottonelle, and then I laughed.

"Make up your mind what you're gonna do," Kellen said. "If you're just gonna laugh, give me that. I can't be wasting my TP. That stuff's expensive."

I kept laughing, even as I let my head fall back and said to the ceiling, "God, please let this be the last of the secrets I have to uncover. I can't take any more discoveries like this."

Kellen was quiet. I blew my nose and handed the roll back to him.

"I love you," I said.

"I love you too."

I looked up only quickly enough to see a trace of pain go through his eyes.

Yeah. It was time for all of us to let it go.

TWENTY-SIX

I finally crawled into bed at four thirty a.m., but as down-to-the-marrow exhausted as I was, I couldn't sleep. I wrestled for two hours with varying opponents.

Seth, the one who tried to drag Wendy down into his mire.

Wendy, the one who gave him the chance to.

And Fritzie, who might be at the root of it. Fritzie who I loved and trusted and whose growing flaws I even forgave. Before I knew what they really were.

I beat myself up as hard and as brutally as I did them, until by six thirty I felt too battered to get out of bed.

But I did and I went to church anyway, and I said the confession loud enough to startle Mary Louise Anderson Bales, and I let the communion wine burn in my throat so I could hold on to the forgiveness. I had to . . . since I kept having to forgive over and over and over.

It was Wednesday and I knew Ned wouldn't have much time after the service, so I talked as we walked through the morning shadows of the cloister.

"I guess I had to find all this out," I said when I'd filled him in.

"That doesn't mean it doesn't hurt." Ned stopped at the door to the house. "Unfortunately, you can't skip the hurt. Fortunately, God's there."

He pushed the door open and let me pass him. The smell of the polished wood and the beeswax candles and the anguish and joy that had dwelt in those rooms for over 150 years came around me in a way it hadn't before, like arms that had been waiting for me.

"Yeah," I said. "God is."

"Okay. All better."

I looked back at Ned. His eyes were teasing.

"I wish," I said.

"Do you?"

He nodded me into "our" room, where I only perched on the edge of the sofa.

"I know you have to leave soon," I said. "We could talk about this tomorrow."

"Or we can talk about it right now." Ned settled into his corner of the couch and strung his arm along the back of it. "Things have reached a point of no return. I'm thinking you need to be prepared for what you're walking into today."

"I just have no idea what I'm supposed to do with all this now."

Ned's eyes grew firm. "You could start by removing the phrase 'supposed to' from your vocabulary."

"I'm sorry?"

"That and 'you have a right to.'"

"That's Kellen's phrase."

"And 'nobody would blame you if—'"

I actually laughed. "That's everybody's phrase."

"You're finding out what's true. I'm saying it again: that will show you what to do." Ned ran his finger along the copy of *The Message* on the shelf just behind us. "It's true that God's here so you'll get through the pain. But the operative word is *through*."

"I just want to know what through looks like."

"What does true look like?"

I scooted forward until I was almost off the couch. "You sure you don't have to go? I don't want to keep you—"

"Tara." Ned leaned toward me. "Nothing is more important than this right now."

"And that scares me. What if I get this wrong?"

"Then you'll do it until you get it right. Now, ask yourself, what does true for Tara look like, let's say, as you face Wendy again?"

"Okay."

"What does it look like with Seth, now that you know all this?"

"Okay."

"Not what no one would blame you for doing. Not what you have a right to do. Not what you're supposed to do. But what's true."

"I can't hold on to it anymore," I said. "That's what's true."

"Good."

"So I let go and see where that takes me."

For the first time since I'd known Ned, he smiled with more than just his eyes.

"The Lord be with you, my friend," he said.

"And also with you," I said.

"Let's pray."

⁓

Clouds had gathered to brood as I crossed Madison Square, but what I was going to do was absolutely clear to me. Not all of it, not everything. Just the next thing.

I went first to my house and packed some clothes and toiletries in a beach bag before I headed back to Montgomery Street. Neither it nor Lexi's apartment building felt as threatening in the daylight, although I looked over my shoulder more than once going up the stairs and down that hall that reminded me of the Haunted Woods in every fairy-tale movie I'd ever seen.

Evidently Wendy was looking over her shoulder, too, because I practically had to hold credentials up to the peephole before she would open the door.

"I'm glad you're still here," I said, as she bolted and chained everything behind me.

"I was scared to leave." Wendy's shrug was shy. "It was nice of Lexi to let me stay here when she doesn't even know me."

I didn't correct her. I was leaving that one up to Lexi.

"You want coffee? She made some before she went to class."

"No," I said, "because as soon as you take a shower and put some of these clothes on, we're going to the Piebald. They make great coffee there."

She wasn't amused. In fact, her eyes immediately widened with nothing short of alarm.

"I can't go back there," she said.

"What else are you going to do?"

"Ike is pi—furious with me, I know he is."

I took Wendy's hand and wrapped her fingers around the strap of the bag. "Mostly he's worried about you. Yeah, he'll read you the riot act—whatever that actually is—but once he finds out you're okay, he'll take you back."

"How do you know?"

"Because he's a decent guy. There *are* decent guys. We have to remember that."

Wendy blinked furiously, although as swollen as her eyes were I couldn't see how she could have any tears left. Or maybe I could.

"Why is it," she said, "that I say things to you I swore I would never say to anybody?"

"You're going to tell me where to go?"

"No. I do that all the time." I watched her swallow. "I'm going to ask you to stand there with me when I talk to him."

"Of course. I'll even hold your hand."

A trace of the sardonic wit I liked passed across her face. "No," she said. "You will not."

Yeah, well, she was the one who grabbed for *my* hand the minute we walked into the Piebald and Ike saw us. She didn't let go until we left his office, *after* she apologized for not calling him and asked him to let her stay on, and *after* I persuaded him not only to keep her on but to give her more hours and a chance at a manager's position so she could quit her other job. I skipped the part where she sort of already had.

Then I had to pry her fingers from mine because Ike asked me to stay behind while she went to the bathroom to finish sobbing.

"I can't tell you what happened," I said when she was gone.

"I'm not asking you to."

Ike picked up his pipe, looked at it, and put it back down. It didn't dawn on me until he did it again that he was nervous.

"I'm doing all of this for Wendy on your word," he said.

"She won't let you down. I was the reason she took off in the first place, but that's all worked out now."

"You're a good person."

I shrugged. "I do okay."

"Have dinner with me tonight?"

Only because he did that adjust-the-fedora-with-one-finger thing did I not say, *I'm sorry, but did you just ask me out?*

"Dinner," I said.

"You know, the meal after lunch."

"The one before breakfast."

"That's the one."

His eyebrows lifted and stayed there. My turn. Geez, a date? Now? When my entire life had been shaken like a snow globe and none of the flakes had settled yet?

But Ike wasn't a flake. He was the most solid thing I could think of in that moment.

"It's just dinner, Tara," he said.

"Yes," I said.

His face eased into a smile. I hadn't brought a look like that to anybody's face in so long I wanted to cry. Again.

"Sweet," he said. "After we close. Maybe I'll do it a little early."

"I'll want to get cleaned up," I said.

"I don't see how you could get any cleaner. Although, do me a favor."

"Yeah?"

"Both you and Wendy go home and get some sleep before your shift. If I didn't know better, I'd say you were both out on a bender last night."

Something like that, I wanted to say. Something like that.

$$\sim \!\!\mathcal{SQ}\!\!\sim$$

I took Wendy home with me so we could follow Ike's orders. I fell into an immediate coma, but I wasn't sure about her. She covered it well, but from the way she gazed up at the nine-foot ceilings and ran her hands over the furniture and seemed to count the lights in the chandeliers, I guessed she was a little overwhelmed by our house. Maybe our life. At one point, just before I drifted off, I heard her whisper, "So this is what it looks like to have."

Three and a half hours' sleep wasn't enough but we were both significantly more focused when we got back to the Piebald—Wendy more than me. While she went at her shift like she was upper management already, I could hardly make a cup of hot chocolate without having to read the same directions I knew by heart the day before. With Wendy back on track, and hopefully headed off the other one, my mind went straight to Seth. And Fritzie.

Do what's true, Ned had said to me. But he also said I had to go through the pain, and I realized I was now starting with another whole layer of it. Fritzie had set a rankling chain in motion—and not just any chain. A chain in a horror movie of the Vincent Price era. One thing I did know. I was tired of having it wrapped around my ankle.

Toward the end of our shift, Lexi came by to take Wendy home with her. Somewhere between the time I left them the night before and the time I'd returned for Wendy that morning, Lexi had gleaned the information that Wendy shared a place with three other dancers, but when she told her manager she was quitting—moments before I accosted her at the back door of the club—he'd threatened to hunt her down because she owed him. So no, she wasn't going back to the dancer house.

Ike let her go early, and he told me to go ahead and hang with my "ladies" while he finished up, and then we could leave for dinner.

I fully intended to talk to the Watch about my date with Ike and process just exactly why I'd accepted, which I hadn't had time to figure out. But as I headed toward them, the weight of the day sank down on me again. Without Wendy for the first time in twelve hours, I had no one else's stuff to carry but mine.

So I did what was true. Without mentioning Wendy's name I spilled everything about how I found out about the abuse and Fritzie, all to the beat of Betsy's warm hand squeezes and Gray's nodding ponytail and Ms. Helen's tapping spoon on the rim of my latte mug.

"I'm trying to let go of the anger so I don't get bitter," I said as I wound down. "Y'know, so I can see what to do next. But this . . . this cuts so deep."

Gray rubbed her hand up and down her arm, a rare conflicted look on her face. "Define 'let go of the anger,'" she said.

"That's just it. I wish I *could* define it."

Betsy raised a creamy palm. "Can I try?"

"Go for it," we said in unison.

I looked at Gray. "That was scary."

"You don't want to keep hating this Fritzie person, is that right?" Betsy said.

"Right."

Gray grunted. "You're a better woman than I am."

"But you can't just swat the anger away like you would a horsefly."

"No," I said. "I can't."

"But you have to find something to do with it."

"Something that isn't going to hurt any *more* people." I felt my throat tighten. "I'm so sick of pain."

"Honey, I know you are." Ms. Helen tapped my mug again. "You have to keep up your physical strength, though. You need to drink that. Have you eaten anything?"

"I'm actually going out to dinner," I said, and then for no apparent reason my face flushed like I was thirteen and had to pass my crush on my way into the bathroom.

"Ah," Gray said, eyes narrowing deliciously. "Do we have a date?"

"Now don't badger her," Betsy said, and then she leaned into the table. "Who with?"

"Honey, that is so easy," Ms. Helen said. "Y'all must be blind. You haven't seen ol' Ike looking over here and looking at the clock and looking over here?"

Gray broke into a grin. "You're going out with Ike?"

"Yes," I said. "But it's dinner, not—"

My phone rang and I snatched it up like it was a life preserver. God bless Lexi.

"What's up, Lex?" I said, as I escaped from the table and moved several feet away.

"She went to work."

I could have asked *Who? Wendy?* and said, *No, she's on her way* back *from work.* But I knew from the tremor and pitch of Lexi's voice exactly what she meant.

"At the club," she said. "She got a call and she took the phone in the bathroom. I heard her whispering in there and then she came out crying and said her manager talked her into dancing one more night—he said she owed him that and then he'd let her go." I could hear the tears in Lexi's voice. "She looked so scared, Tara. He's not gonna let her go."

"Okay," I said, "don't panic. I'll be right there and we'll figure out what to do."

As we hung up, someone said, "Tara?"

I jumped, dropping the phone on the table I was standing next to.

"You okay?" Ike said.

Even as I nodded I was headed for the door. "I'll call you," I said over my shoulder. "I have to take care of something. It won't take long."

I hoped.

I hoped that all the way up Bull Street as the safe arms of the historic district folded behind me and I half-ran back to Montgomery. I heard footsteps gaining on me and I quickened my own steps, until Gray called out to me, "Tara! Wait up!"

I faced her and kept walking, backwards. "I have to go help a friend," I said.

"Stop. You're going to—Tara, *stop!*"

I did, just as a black pickup rushed past me on Congress, so close I could feel its draft.

Gray reached me before I could start moving again.

"You aren't going to help Wendy by getting yourself run over by a truck. I'm surprised you've lived this long."

I glossed over the fact that she knew exactly who I was going after and said instead, "I really need to go."

"Fine," she said, "I'm going with you."

She fell into step beside me. I didn't try to argue and instead brought her up to speed on the remaining walk-run to Montgomery Street. There was no point in not telling her, and by the time we got to Lexi's building I was glad she was with me. Gray may have been brought up Savannah with as much class as my mama, but she had the aura of a woman who's been places a lot closer to hell and come back stronger for it.

Lexi looked beyond surprised when I showed up with Gray, but she didn't ask questions. She didn't have a chance.

"We need a plan, ladies," Gray said. "Do you mind if I—"

"Please," I said. "Coming down here was as far as my plan went."

Lexi just nodded.

"Okay, Lexi," Gray said, "you stay here and be ready to open this door when we come back with Wendy. Don't open it to anybody else."

"Ya think?" Lexi said.

"Tara, how much money do you have in the bank?"

I told her.

"That's not enough." She looked me over. "Do you even have your purse with you?"

"No."

"Don't either of you ever try to become undercover agents. We'll stop at the ATM—I saw one outside the club—and I'll get some cash out." She glanced at her watch. "I'll tell you the rest on the way."

"Be careful, y'all, please?" Lexi said.

"Put the teakettle on," Gray told her, and she and I stepped out into the hall.

By the time we got to the ATM, I knew what our plan was, and I was convinced beyond all doubt that I wasn't going to be able to pull it off.

"Pretend you're in a movie," Gray said. "Besides, you've got the easy part."

For somebody who had the hard part, Gray looked like she was actually enjoying herself as we sauntered—she had to show me how to saunter—into the club and she plunked about half of the cash into the outstretched hand of the guy inside the door.

"Cover charge," she muttered to me. "Here—you take the rest. And stop looking like you just walked into a haunted house."

Hadn't I?

The placed smelled worse than it did from the sidewalk. The air was clogged with the fumes of stale liquor and male sweat and suffocating perfume, and I could barely breathe. Even my gape at the almost-naked woman straddling a carousel horse two feet from me was choked off by the smog of ugliness. Seth had hung out here? Really?

Gray gave me the familiar elbow nudge. "Go behind that curtain," she said, pointing with her chin. "The dressing room is probably back there. I'll distract Mr. Man. Is that him?"

I followed her steel gaze to a guy standing at the end of the bar, looking over the crowd like he was deciding who to gun down. He wasn't wearing the jacket, but the collar of his black shirt stood at alert the same way. He was every lounge lizard in every cop movie made in the 1980s. And he was Wendy's bad guy.

"Yeah," I said. "He's evil, Gray. I don't know about this."

"Go," she said. "I've got it handled."

She gave me a push and I was gone, slithering through the press of men who fortunately only had eyes for the woman on the tiny stage who was . . . I didn't see what she was doing because I didn't look long enough. I didn't want to know if it was Wendy. I ducked behind the curtain that someone had obviously marinated in gin and squinted against the glare on the other side.

Once I could see, I realized I was in a room where at least six theatrical dressing tables bordered the walls, each with enough 100-watt bulbs around its mirror to light the Rockettes. It wasn't hard to find Wendy. She was the only one who resembled a real human being. The rest all looked like Stripper Barbie.

Nobody said anything to me as I maneuvered my way past a rack of sequined G-strings and stood behind her. When her eyes met mine in the mirror, they reflected momentary bewilderment back to me, followed by fury and then fear. They stopped at the one she least deserved to feel.

"Nuh-uh, Wendy," I said. "The shame stops here."

The girl at the next dressing table twisted in her seat, a thick false eyelash poised on the tip of her finger like a tarantula. "You want me to get Van, Gio?" she said.

"No," Wendy said. "It's okay."

She pushed back the metal folding chair and stood up and pulled me by the wrist to a space between the cement block wall and the costume rack. As if anything hanging there was big enough to conceal us or keep the entire room from hearing us. The place went eavesdropping-silent, which meant our conversation had to be an exchange of hisses.

"What are you *doing* here, Tara?"

"I came to get you out."

"I'm *getting* out. I have to do tonight so I can get out clean. I don't want to owe him anything."

"You really think he's going to let you go? Really?"

"You don't get it."

"That's just it. I *do* get it. As long as you do this on his terms you're just prolonging the shame. It has to end right now, for all of us."

I didn't know where the words were coming from and I didn't try to stop them. Wendy wasn't choking me with a thong, so I had to go with believing a space was opening up in there. I had to believe I could speak into her.

"You're in a mess," I said. "But it doesn't *define* you. It's not who you are. Those videos you make aren't you either."

"Maybe they are." Wendy tried to harden her face, unsuccessfully. "Look, I didn't grow up the way you did."

"And Seth didn't grow up the way *you* did. But that babysitter he told you about? She twisted him, and I know somebody twisted you." I picked up her hand and squeezed it. "But you and Seth, you can't let them win. *You* have to win. The true you."

For a second or two, I thought she was there, the way she sought my face for something more than I was saying. She pressed my hand.

And then she pulled away and yanked the shades down on the trust in her eyes. "You don't know what it's like," she said.

"Yeah," I said. "I do. I was twisting too. That's why I know I can *help* you."

"I don't see how you can." Her face wilted, but she lifted her chin, as if she were defying herself more than me. "No," she said. "I can do this on my own. All I need is tonight."

Perfect. Gray said she'd do this. She said this would be my chance, and my only chance, to get her out of here.

"How much are you going to make tonight?" I said. "What's Van paying you? That's his name, right?"

"Fifty dollars," she said.

"That's before tips," said a voice with a ripe Alabama accent.

Enough *shhhh*'s ensued to cover a librarian for a year, but the same voice said, "You do at least another hundred extra, Gio, and you know it."

Nobody bothered to hush her up that time. If I'd had enough

time I would have gone out there and hugged her. Instead I dug into the pocket of my jacket and pulled out the rest of Gray's cash.

"Here's two hundred," I said. "Now let's get out of here."

"I can't take this."

"Take it, Gio."

The rack rolled away and three women in various stages of undress stood in front of us. They didn't look so much like Barbie clones now. Although every one of them had on foundation they'd no doubt applied with a trowel and cleavage so deep you could hide a Chihuahua in it, each face wore a different expression of envy and urgency and dusty hope.

"Do it, Gio," Alabama said. "You know you want to."

She bobbed her head at the others, her face young and earnest under the hard mask. They joined her with, "Go . . . we'll cover for you . . . really, get out."

Alabama grabbed Wendy's gigantic canvas bag from the floor and shoved it into her arms. "Just stay as far away from here as you can."

I bit back all the rest of the things I wanted to say. It was up to Wendy now. I closed my eyes and tried to pray, but all that came to mind was, *God, step in.*

"Okay," Wendy said. "Y'all—"

"You don't have time for good-byes," Alabama said. "Go."

One of them had already opened the metal door that led to the alley. I pushed Wendy out ahead of me, and when I got to the threshold I turned back to Alabama.

"I hope you can all get out," I said.

"Shut that door!" someone hissed.

"Go!" Alabama gave me a shove and tried to pull the door shut but a harsh voice behind her stopped us both.

"Where's Gio? Get the—Move! Where is she?"

I didn't even have to see the obnoxious collar to know it was Van.

As the lacerating voice cut across my back, I knew why Wendy was giving him one more night.

And then there would be another, and another, until she was slashed to nothing.

I turned and stumbled out to the landing, screaming, "Run, Wendy! Go to Lexi's!" With another twirl I threw my side against the door as it swung toward closing and still I cried, "Don't stand there, Wendy! Go!"

But she didn't move from the bottom of the steps, and the door came open and slammed me against the railing. The face between the upturned collar came at me like a mask of raging no-color eyes and flaring nostrils and a cruel mouth that spit words between his too-white teeth.

He was so close I could see the blood vessels that mapped those eyes—those eyes that told me I was about to be bent backwards over the alley. Already my kidneys were crying out as my back pressed the bars.

"Where is Gio?" The heels of his hands hit my shoulders and I cried out and braced for the second blow. "Where the—"

The most profane word of the night was jolted out of him as hands yanked him back by that wretched collar, pulling half the shirt off with them. Gray's cheek pressed against his.

"Touch her again and you'll go right down those steps on your face." Gray bugged her eyes at me. "Tara—go!"

I tried. I even got to the first step. But the element of surprise Gray had on her side evaporated quickly and Van jerked from her grasp and came at me again. I tottered backward and felt myself falling with nothing to grab but air. I thought I screamed.

But the guttural cry came from Wendy. I never knew whether that was before or after I fell against her and drove both of us to the bricks. Everything happened in such a chaos of violence both verbal and visceral I was hard put to understand it even as it went down.

Wendy pushed me off of her, and from my paralyzed vantage

point on the ground I watched her fling herself straight at Van and dig her fingernails into his chest.

"Don't! You! Touch! Her!" she screamed into his face. "You want to hit somebody, you hit me."

The momentary shock left his eyes and he closed both of her hands into his fists. "Not a problem . . . I'll beat the . . ."

His face blackened as he disgorged curses like projectile vomit. He transferred Wendy's hands to one of his and lifted her from the ground. Dear God, he was going to *throw* her. I did scream then, and Van flicked his now maddened gaze at me. Gray reappeared behind him and tried to wrap her arms around his chest, but he pulled up his free elbow and brought it back straight into her belly. She moaned and fell to the bottom step. Wendy was able to wrench her hands from his and she tried to run to me, tried to reach down, but he got her by the back of the hair.

I somehow got to my feet screaming "No!" from a place in me I didn't know existed. I was within inches of his heinous face with my claws bared when I was shoved sideways and fell to the sidewalk again. Wendy came down beside me and she pawed at me and clung to my clothes like a drowning child.

Someone stepped over us—a figure wider and taller than Van. When I was able to pull away from Wendy, I saw that he had Van by both shoulders and in one muscular heave threw him into the wall and held him there with his forearm across Van's throat.

"You want to hit somebody, pal," Ike said, "you hit me. Go on." He pushed Van harder against the bricks. "What's wrong? You can only hit women?"

Van, of course, didn't answer because his air supply was being cut off.

"Tara," Ike said, not taking his eyes from the spluttering face in front of him, "get your cell phone out of my pocket and call 9-1-1."

"Done," Gray said from the bottom step. "Savannah's finest should be here any minute."

Wendy had by then turned to jelly in my lap, and I was not far from that myself. Until a pair of small arms came around us both and Lexi said, "I told y'all to be careful."

"Damage assessment," Ike said, still immobilizing Van. I was actually relieved to see that the man was breathing.

"Tara, you okay?" Ike said. "Physically, I mean?"

I was actually too shaken to know if I was or not, so I said, "Yeah, I'm fine."

"Wendy?"

She nodded against my chest.

"That's a yes," I said.

"Gray?"

"I think he probably broke a rib. Which is fine by me. That'll look good on his rap sheet."

A siren split the night and blue lights designed to blind perpetrators before they ever got to jail flashed all over the alley. Then it really did get confusing.

In the midst of strobe-lit images and rapid-fire questions and a stew of sweat and spit and tears, Van was handcuffed and we were interviewed and he was arrested for assault and Ike was cleared of any wrongdoing and Wendy, Gray, and I were pretty much ordered to go to the ER.

"You're going to need all the evidence you can get," one officer told us after his partner had deposited Van into the back of the cruiser. "This is simple assault. He'll be out on bail by morning, probably, and he won't get much jail time if he's convicted."

With a grimace he turned to go, but Wendy pulled her hand from mine, which she'd been wringing out for the last half hour, and said, "Wait."

He paused. "Was there something else?"

"Yes." Wendy pointed to the back door, which, now that I thought about it, had not opened since Gray came through. How scared *were* those poor women?

"There's a girl in there, one of the exotic dancers," Wendy said. "She's only sixteen."

"Are you serious?"

"She's a runaway and she goes by Arwen, but her real name's Taylor."

The officer nodded toward the cruiser where Van glared through the window, still cursing us all.

"He know how old she is?" the officer said.

"Oh yeah," Wendy said. "He knows."

"Okay." I heard a smattering of satisfaction in his voice. "Will you come by the station in the morning and make a statement?"

"No doubt," Wendy said.

We all watched in silence as the cruiser pulled away. It felt almost reverent, that silence, as if we were watching evil being driven into the darkness.

Ike was the first to break it. "I guess I need to escort you ladies to the ER. And then, for Pete's sake, can we eat?" He dropped a grin on us. "Nothing like a good fight to work up your appetite."

"You're an animal," Gray said.

But I found myself grinning back.

TWENTY-SEVEN

My dinner date with Ike turned out to be breakfast for all five of us at the Waffle House after the ER visit. Fortunately it was a slow night at the hospital, so it only took two hours to find out Wendy and I were going to be bruised and achy the next day and Gray had not one but two broken ribs. She seemed pretty proud of them.

By the time we finished doing a respectable job with a table full of waffles and potatoes done every way you could have them, it was two a.m. I was going on my third night without sleep, and I could hardly wipe the syrup off my mouth.

Ike narrowed his eyes first at Wendy and then at me. "I don't want to see either one of you in my coffee shop today. Are we clear?"

I nodded. Wendy stared into her lap.

"What's up?" Gray said to her.

Wendy shook her head, but I knew, and so did Lexi.

"You're coming to my place, right?" Lexi said.

Gray shook her ponytail. "Not without a police escort."

"I'll walk you in," Ike said. "But Gray has a point. Once Mr.— what the heck's his name anyway?"

"I forget," Wendy said.

I loved that.

"Once he's out on bail," Ike said, "it's not safe for either one of you to be there."

"Can we figure that out later?" Lexi said. "I'm brain-dead."

So we sorted it through that we would take Lexi and Wendy to Lexi's place while Gray went home, and then Ike would take me home. By the time it was just the two of us in his Tahoe, I should have been brain-dead, too, but my mind was still churning.

"Can I run something past you?" I said as he maneuvered the SUV around Monterey Square.

"Absolutely."

"When I was talking to Wendy in the dressing room—or undressing room, I guess you'd call it—"

"Good one."

"Stuff was coming out of my mouth that I didn't even know I thought. Have you ever had that happen?"

"Not sure. Like what?"

"I told her that the mistakes she made, having that job and . . . some other things. I said that didn't define her."

"Sounds right to me."

"So doesn't the same thing apply to Seth? I know what probably made him susceptible to porn now and, I mean, I don't *excuse* what he's done. But I understand it. I just don't think that's all he is."

Ike didn't answer. Maybe that was okay. Hearing it come out of my mouth again, I knew it was true.

When we pulled up to the curb on Gaston Street, he told me to wait until he opened the door for me and then he was going to walk me up to the house. I was pretty sure no one had ever done that for me. Except maybe Seth on prom night, because Paul told him he ought to. It was the downside of growing up together.

Ike still hadn't said anything else when we got to the porch.

"I don't even know how to start thanking you," I said. "I know it wasn't the evening you had in mind, but you probably saved Wendy's life."

He smiled faintly from under the brim of his hat. Then something dawned on me.

"How did you know how to find us?" I said.

"Because you left a trail of bread crumbs." He pulled my phone out of his pocket and handed it to me. "You left it on the table."

He frowned at me.

"I know," I said. "Stupid."

"So I looked up your last call and phoned it and—what's her name?"

"Lexi."

"She got me to the back door of the club. And there you were." Ike pushed back the fedora with the inevitable index finger. "You're killin' me, Tara. You're killin' me."

I leaned against the iron railing. "I don't think that kind of thing will be happening again. We'll figure out a way to get Wendy *and* Lexi out of that apartment, and I'll go with Wendy to the police station and then . . ." I let out a long sigh. "Then I think that's the last of the layers of this whole thing. No more secrets. No more shame. We're done."

Ike just looked at me. I couldn't read what was in his eyes.

"I'm sorry," I said. "That was kind of a rant."

Ike motioned for me to move over and leaned on the railing next to me, arms folded. "All right, I want to say a couple of things . . . if I get to have a turn."

"Stop it."

I felt him grin.

"One. I think you're right about one mistake or one issue not defining a person, although I still say you're too good for him."

He gave me a look from the corner of his eye.

"Two?" I said.

"Two, if it doesn't define Wendy and it doesn't define Seth, I gotta tell ya, from where I'm standing, it doesn't define you either."

I stared at the side of his face. He had a wise profile that made me want to believe him.

"Three . . . can you handle three?"

"I'm still working on two," I said. "But go on."

"Three," he said again.

He stared off in front of us, although at what I couldn't know. I got the sense he was looking more in than out.

"You were right about something else," he said finally.

"Okay," I said.

"When you said the woman I was waiting for just might walk through the doors of the Piebald, you were spot on. She did."

I held my breath. I didn't want to let any words slip out before I thought them through this time.

Ike pulled away from the railing and stood in front of me, hands in his pockets, head tilted. "You've been beaten up pretty good and I know you aren't ready for a relationship. But I don't see me looking at anybody else who comes through those doors, so if and when . . . I'll be here. Until then, no pressure." He lifted his chin at me. "We good?"

I knew how to answer that. "We're definitely good," I said.

He pulled the hat ever so slightly from his head and kissed my cheek. Fedora back in its place, he stepped back and waited while I punched in the code and let myself in.

"Thank you, Ike," I said without looking at him. "Thank you for everything."

I slipped inside and leaned the door shut and stayed there, eyes closed. Everything drained from me—the violence, the fear, the total bewilderment—all of it. It really was over. I knew everything and I could walk through it and I could leave even the pain of Fritzie behind me. No more secrets. No more shame. And maybe . . . someday . . . Ike.

I could go and sleep now.

But when I opened my eyes I nearly split out of my skin. My brother stood three feet from me in the foyer.

"You about scared the pee out of me, Kellen," I said. "What are you *doing*?"

"Waiting for you."

I gave a weak laugh, all wobbly with relief. "I get it: this is payback for me getting you out of bed at two in the morning, right?"

"I have to talk to you."

It took me that long to realize Kellen's voice was small and terrified. I switched on the lamp on the side table and looked at him. He was ash-grey and his lower lip trembled, and his hand clutched at the bottom of his shirt. Clutched and released and clutched.

"Kellen, what is it?" I said. "Is it GrandMary?"

"No."

"Mama? Daddy? What *is* it?"

"It's me."

"You. You what? You're freaking me out here."

"I did it, Tara," he said.

"Did . . ."

"I told the paper about Seth. You said no more secrets so I'm telling you. I outed my best friend."

His face collapsed on itself. Sobs came out of him like dry heaves. I stood there for a few seconds before I realized my hands were covering my mouth, as if they knew I shouldn't speak whether I knew what to say or not. And I didn't.

Kellen? *Kellen* told? Not only did I not know what to say, I didn't know what to feel. Even anger was shocked into silence.

Kellen, however, couldn't seem to *stop* freeing the agony that had apparently been imprisoning him for weeks. "I was trying to make it up to you, you know? For not protecting you from Seth when I knew about the porn five years ago." He swiped at his face. "When I went to see him in the hospital he was doing everything he could to make trying to off himself your fault. I wanted to off him myself." He gave his head a miserable shake. "I thought if it went public he'd be totally screwed and people would stop blaming you for messing up his life." He was crying so hard I could hardly understand his next words. "I'm sorry, Tara. I messed it up more and I'm so sorry."

The sobs were almost convulsive and whether I could grasp what I felt or not, I couldn't let him go there. I wrapped my arms around his shoulders.

"Stop," I said. "You have to stop. It's okay."

"No, it's not. Why don't you hate me?"

I stepped back, hands sliding to his biceps. This one thing I did know. "Hate you? Are you serious? None of this is worth hating over, Kellen."

"Why aren't you mad at me?"

"I don't know what I am! But Kellen . . . look at me."

He didn't.

"*Look* at me." I waited until he dragged his eyes level with mine. "I am so over this undoing everybody's world and tearing apart our relationships. You understand? Done. So, yes, I may want to smack you tomorrow and, yes, right now I think you're an idiot." My voice finally broke. "But I love you."

Why our parents didn't hear us crying in the foyer, sobs echoing up the stairs, I had no idea. Maybe they did. Maybe we all knew now that we could weather this thing without being blown away.

When Kellen pulled back and wiped his face—and nose—on his sleeve, he said, "Are you going to tell Seth?"

"Not my story to tell," I said. "Are you?"

Kellen gave his nose another smear. "You said no more secrets."

"I did." I moved to the opposite wall of the foyer and leaned against the full-length mirror. "Y'know, maybe there aren't any rules for this. But, okay, think of it this way." I peeled away from the mirror and shaped the words with my hands. "Did it do any good for you to tell Seth's secrets to the entire city?"

Kellen answered with a shudder.

"So think about what would be gained by adding to his pain by telling him." I shrugged. "I don't know. I don't have it all figured out. I'm still trying to just do the next true thing."

"I have to think about it," he said.

"That would be novel."

"Bite me."

Kellen put his arms around me again. "Thank you," he said.

"Yeah," I said. "But Kellen, whatever you decide, don't let it fester. Do it or don't do it and then let it go. That much I do know."

"Okay," he said. "Hey, who was that guy who brought you home? What's up with him?"

"You're killin' me," I said. "Just killin' me."

TWENTY-EIGHT

I woke up the next morning—well, afternoon—feeling just as the ER nurse predicted I would. Every part of me throbbed like I'd been beaten with a large stick, which basically I had, and I climbed out of bed the way Ms. Anderson Bales probably climbed out of hers. A full body inspection in the mirror revealed two large bruises surfacing on my back and assorted smaller ones dotting the rest of my body.

I was far more bummed about the fact that I missed church, and Ned, and, for that matter, lunch. Of course, I *had* eaten breakfast at two a.m. I was headed downstairs to the refrigerator when my cell phone rang. It was Lexi, and I answered with, "Oh my gosh, Lex, I slept through taking Wendy to the police station!"

"No worries," she said. "Ms. Helen and Betsy took her. And by the way, hi."

"I'm sorry . . . Ms. Helen and Betsy?"

"It's kind of a long story and I don't know the whole thing, but I guess Gray called them and they volunteered because they knew you'd be exhausted and I had to go to class."

"You went to *class*?"

348

"Yes, and now I'm going to bed."

I stopped on the second landing and pressed my free hand to my forehead. "Lex, wait. You're going to your apartment?"

"Ye-ah."

"It's not safe, though."

"We're okay for now. Wendy asked and they said What's-His-Nose is still locked up because nobody's bailed him out yet."

"I don't know which I love most," I said, "that or you calling him What's-His-Nose."

"I thought of other names but, y'know, I'm a good Christian girl and all that."

"You definitely are." I continued down the steps. "He's not going to be in jail forever, though. We need to come up with a plan for y'all."

"Ms. Helen's looking into apartments. I guess the man she's dating is a Realtor."

"The man she's *dating*?"

"I know, right?"

"I really have been talking about myself too much. I don't even *know* these women and they're like some of my best friends."

Lexi was quiet.

"You okay?" I said.

"Kind of." I heard her sigh. "I know whatever she finds that's decent is going to be more than we can afford."

I'd reached the kitchen by then. Mama was there, mixing something in a bowl. She smiled and pointed from me to the fridge. I nodded.

"We?" I said to Lexi. "You and Wendy are getting a place together?"

"Crazy, right? It makes sense, really."

"It does."

"But still—I just don't know if we can afford something nice, you know, in a safe part of town. Listen, I need to go to bed. I'm about to fall over. I'll call you tonight."

She ended the call, and I stood there looking at the phone.

"Good morning, sleepyhead," Mama said. "Everything okay? I've hardly seen you for days."

"How's GrandMary?" I said.

She looked a little surprised. "She's tired from the radiation but she's doing better than they expected. Of course. I'll warm up a bowl of chili for you. How would that be?"

"That would be great." I leaned against the counter. "You were surprised when I asked about her."

Mama opened her mouth but I put up my hand.

"You don't have to answer that. I just feel like I've been so far down in this . . . pit, I haven't been thinking about other people."

"Doesn't sound like it to me." Mama put a bowl in the microwave and nodded at my phone. "Was that Lexi?"

"Yeah. She and another friend of ours are looking for an apartment. Where Lexi is right now—she's, like, in danger of a home invasion every night."

"Shall I ask around?" Mama said.

"Sure. Mama."

She turned from poking at the microwave and smiled as only she could. As I hadn't seen her do in a while, all full of Mama-mirth. "Yes, darlin'?" she said.

"I think we all need to sit down tonight—you and Kellen and Daddy and me—and have a family meeting. There's a lot I need to tell you, and I need your help figuring some of it out."

"Is it about Seth?" she said.

"Partly. Mostly it's about me. Can we? Can we do that?"

"Oh, sweet darlin'," she said. "There is nothing we would rather do."

We made a date for seven p.m. At five I called Lexi, who answered, groggy but awake.

"Can you two meet me at the Piebald in ten?" I said.

"You and Wendy aren't supposed to go there today."

"Not to work. Just to talk."

There was some mumbling with, I assumed, Wendy, and Lexi came back with a yes.

Ten minutes later we were gathered at the Watch table, minus the three older members. Ike pretended to scowl at us from behind the counter, but before we even got settled he brought three mugs of hot chocolate and said, "On the house. But I'm not making a habit of it."

"You're a prince, Ike," Wendy said drily.

I grinned at her when Ike was gone. "You're feeling better."

"I should, seeing how I couldn't have felt any worse before. But, yeah, I'm better. Thanks to you." She looked at Lexi, who was blowing into her mug. "Now if we could find a place to live."

"Money's the issue," I said.

"Yes." She leveled the violet eyes at me. "And I am not taking any more money from you. Oh, and here's what you gave me last night."

She reached for her purse but I shook my head. "That's Gray's money so you'll have to *try* to give it back to her. Emphasis on the try."

"I'm not taking charity," she said.

"I'm not offering any," I said.

"Or a loan."

"Not offering that either. Just because my parents have money doesn't mean I do."

Lexi was watching me through the steam from her cup. "I know that look," she said. "You're dreaming up something."

I felt myself shiver. "Dreaming? No, not so much with the dreaming. But, okay, as we're sitting here trying to figure this out, I'm getting this idea and I'm just going to go ahead and say it because lately things I don't even *know* are coming out of my mouth and it's all been right—"

"Tara," Wendy said, her face deadpan. "I have never *known* anyone who can beat something to death trying to get it out. Say it already."

"Okay," I said. "Here it is."

"Thank the good Lord."

"What if we got a place big enough for all three of us and split the rent three ways? I do have enough money for first and last, and if you're uncomfortable with that you can pay the utilities for a couple of months until we're even. Do you think? That could work, right?"

Lexi was clearly about to sob. I was reading that as a yes.

Wendy I could never read. Especially not now as she looked at me completely without expression.

"You're almost a complete spaz," she said. "You're all up in other people's business. And you start every sentence three times before you even start to get it out. And you expect me to live with you?"

"Well," I said. "Yeah."

"Good," Wendy said. "Because I would love that. I would totally love it."

Lexi was full-out crying by then, and Wendy dug into her canvas bag and brought out a hunk of Kleenex.

"So you said Ms. Helen's boyfriend has some leads on some places?" I said.

Lexi stopped blowing her nose and nodded.

"But we're not going to be able to move in, like, tomorrow, right?"

"Not even," Wendy said.

"Which leaves probably a week with"—I grinned at Lexi—"What's-His-Nose on the loose, and by the way we *are* putting a security system in our apartment, just so you know."

Wendy frowned. "And who's paying for that? I should since—"

"Somebody probably owes my father a favor," I said. "He always has a guy. We'll work it out. That's a separate issue."

"From . . . ?" Wendy said.

"From where you two are going to stay between now and the time we move in. I have an idea." I gave Wendy my best don't-mess-with-me look. "And I want you to hush up until I say the whole thing."

Wendy looked at Lexi. "Let her in a nightclub one time and she thinks she's all tough."

Huh. I guess I was.

⁂

Wendy grudgingly agreed to my proposal—like she had any other options—and I took it to my family that night when we gathered in the small dining room with a veritable Italian feast on the table. Kellen ate like he hadn't in days, which I realized was probably true. Guilt consumes a person's appetite. Daddy was, of course, in his fatherly element, literally beaming at us and squeezing Mama's hand and saying things like, "Don't we have great kids?" At one point, about the time the tiramisu made its appearance, he grew somber and said, "You aren't kids anymore, either one of you. You're fine adults."

"You're not gonna cry, are you, Dad?" Kellen said.

"No," Daddy said. "Absolutely not."

Mischief danced in Mama's eyes. "Not right now, anyway. Check our wastebasket for Kleenex in the morning."

Nobody cried when Kellen and I told them about Fritzie. There was anger, yes, and I knew that would smolder for some time. My announcement that I was moving in with Lexi and Wendy received mixed reviews. That one would have to settle in. What lifted the collective mood again was my proposal: that Wendy and Lexi stay with us on Gaston Street until we could get into our apartment.

Daddy gave an unconvincing grin and said he was sure he would get no sleep with all the giggling going on. I didn't remind him that we weren't twelve.

Kellen wanted to know if we were going to watch anything but chick flicks. What that really meant was that I was bringing an unknown female into the house and he wanted a chance to check her out. Kellen and Wendy. Wouldn't *that* be amusing?

But Mama was the one who took the idea and ran with it like Usain Bolt. We could make it a spa week. She would treat us all to manis and pedis and put candles all around the hot tub and bring Greta, her massage therapist, in. Telling her we didn't need to be pampered would be like saying we didn't need to eat. Before we finished our coffee she had the week's menu planned.

Kellen got up to help Mama clear the table and I was about to when Daddy told me to sit down.

"I need to clarify a few things," he said.

The mood turned serious, but I was okay with that. No anxiety sent out its spikes from my midsection.

"You obviously have enough money to get into this place," he said first.

"Yes. I have it in savings. And we've made arrangements for Lex and Wendy to pay me back."

He nodded. I got the sense he must look this way when he was running a board meeting.

"And you can swing your share of the rent working at the Pie Face."

"Pie*bald*, Daddy. Yes. Ike wants to put me in a manager's position."

"Do you have any plans beyond that?" He put both palms up. "I know you've been through a lot and you haven't had a chance to look at the future." He reached across the table and covered my hand. "I think, though, that you've decided there *is* one."

"It was looking a little bleak for a while," I said. "But, yeah, I'm hopeful."

"So . . . you're going into food service?"

I shook my head at him. "Daddy, just say it: you don't want to see me working in a coffee shop forever."

"I don't want to see you working in a coffee shop forever."

"I'm not going to."

I looked into my own palms. This was another one of those moments when I was about to say something that must have been forming in my mind while I was busy doing what I thought I was supposed to be doing. I could hear Ned again, telling me, *Not what you're supposed to do. Just the next true thing.*

"I want to go to film school," I said. "Here. At SCAD. I'll have to apply and save for it. And maybe you would consider giving me a loan like you did Lexi."

He leaned back in the chair and toyed with the spoon parked on the saucer. Shades of that night in the Faulkner Cinema when he said no to this same idea. Fine. I could do it on my own. Wendy was doing it. Lexi had Daddy's help but she could make it, too, if she didn't. This wasn't dream stuff, not a gauzy vision with no idea what reality was like. I hadn't gone through the last two months without facing that—and finally staring it down.

"Two percent interest," Daddy said. "And I won't go any higher."

My breath caught. "Five," I said.

And then I hugged my daddy's neck the way any self-respecting Savannah daughter would do.

When Valentine's Day dawned, I tried not to notice. I had Wendy and Lexi arriving at noon and a meeting with Ike at one to discuss my future. That was enough to keep me from thinking about the last several February fourteenths with Seth. Year before last, showing up at Duke unannounced with a dozen roses and a pound of Ghirardelli chocolate, which we shared by moonlight in the Sarah Duke Gardens. Last year taking me to St. Augustine for the weekend and proposing to me again on a carriage ride along the waterfront. I managed to keep it all at bay until I answered the front door to a delivery guy from the florist who brought an almost embarrassing number of long-stemmed American Beauty roses for Mama.

A thirty-five-year marriage that still brought flowers to the door. It was hard not to wonder if I would ever have that.

"Let me get you some cash for a tip," I said to the guy, who looked barely old enough to drive.

"It's been taken care of," he said. "I got another thing in the van for ya."

I took Mama's arrangement to the formal dining room, because it was the only place big enough for it, and came back to find the kid with a pot of geraniums. The card said *Tara*.

I read the rest when he was gone.

I thought you could enjoy this in your NEW home. But remember, THIS home is always here for you.
Love,
Daddy

The realness of it trumped a box of chocolates and a carriage ride anytime.

As I set it on the windowsill in the breakfast nook for safe-keeping, I thought two things. One, I hoped it wouldn't die within the hour of coming into our apartment; I'd never tried to grow anything. And two, all the bitterness among no-boyfriend girls notwithstanding, Valentine's was supposed to be a day to show love. And it was time for me to show some.

ℐℓℓ

I didn't call first. I just showed up at the Grissoms' front door and waited while Randi peered through the glass for fifteen seconds before she deigned to open it. She wore workout clothes that fit her like they were painted on her and she was strapping some kind of device around her arm, the Randi signal for *I hope this isn't going to take long because I have things to do.*

The first, apparently, was to get right into my face as soon as she closed the door.

"I see you haven't wasted any time finding a new man," she said.

What was she even talking about?

"I'm actually glad you've moved on, but I don't understand why you're here."

"What new man?" I said.

"Please. The one you were kissing at your front door the other night. Or should I say morning."

Not that it was any of her business, but really. Poor Randi. I could throw her a bone.

"You mean the friend who kissed me on the cheek?" I said. "That guy?"

"He was clearly charmed by you." Randi pulled her hair into the thinnest of all ponytails and slipped the hair tie on it she'd been wearing on her wrist. "Like I said, I really am glad you've moved on, Tara. I am."

I bit back the sarcastic retort that was just begging me to let it

357

out. This was Randi Grissom. She wasn't going to say she forgave me for whatever wrong she thought I'd done. She wasn't going to treat me like a daughter anymore. But this was Randi for *I'll let it go if you will*.

"Thank you," I said. "But I haven't moved on, at least not that way. It'll be a long time before I get into a relationship again."

Randi planted her hands where most people have hips. "Then, again, I don't understand why you're here. If you don't want a relationship with Seth anymore, why come here and torture him?"

"Mom."

We both turned toward the stairs that curved into the hallway. Seth was on his way down, and even in the dim light I could see that he had shed the nearly homeless look since the day he came to the Piebald. His hair and beard had been trimmed, and although he was in light sweats, they fit and gave him a put-together look. He still seemed small, for Seth, and as he came nearer to us I felt a faint wisp of pain at the worry-weary expression that remained on his face.

He did, however, give me a smile. The almost-dimples almost appeared.

"You here to torture me, Tar?" he said.

"Uh, no," I said. "I'm here to talk to you."

"Okay, then."

"Seth, we need to get to the gym," Randi said. "I have to be back by twelve—"

"Go on ahead, then."

Seth waited. Randi gave me a warning look and stalked off toward the kitchen. He waited some more, until the door to the garage slammed.

"I think she's going without you," I said.

"Thank the Lord." Seth pushed up the sleeves of his sweat jacket.

"I know she's just trying to help, but she's driving me a little nuts. Dad too."

"I'm not here to drive you further," I said. "I just need to tell you one thing. Can we . . . ?"

I nodded toward the doorway to the family room but he shook his head.

"That's the interrogation room," he said. "Let's sit outside."

He let us out through the front door, but he didn't sit. He leaned against the porch railing, and I decided one of the wicker chairs was best for me. Give him the upper hand, as it were. This wasn't about me shutting him down anymore.

"You know I love you, right?" I said. "And I always will."

Seth closed his eyes. "You've already said 'I love you but' enough times, Tar. You love me but you can't marry me. I'm not dense. I get it."

"That isn't—"

"And 'I can't marry you *yet*' doesn't make it any better. It would never be the same and we both know it. I'm accepting that."

"I know," I said. "That's not what I came to talk about."

"Oh." He bounced a fist lightly on the rail. "What else is there to talk about?"

"I want to help you," I said. "I want to be there while you go through this." I moved to the edge of the chair. "Maybe this doesn't sound realistic. You know, maybe it's too much to ask of you, but I want to be your *friend*. I want to help you see that this stuff doesn't define you. And I want to do it without anything romantic between us. No wondering if maybe we'll get back together. You just said it— it'll never be the same. But it can be something different. Maybe something better."

I sat back and closed my eyes. I didn't want to watch whatever was going to pass over his face. I wanted him to let it all be true.

Beyond the porch, kid-laughter wafted up from Forsyth Park.

Adult voices called to each other: "Are you watching him?" "Did you see that? He rode six feet!" Tennis balls thudded into rackets. Lives were being lived there. Maybe a girl even sat on a bench twisting her hair and pretending to read *Jane Eyre* while she dreamed of a wedding cake like the Parisian fountain.

"I can't," Seth said.

I opened my eyes to a face fallen into sadness. My heart, my whole self, sank.

"I can't make a decision right now," he said. "I have to think about it. New concept for me, y'know, but I'm learning."

"You will, though? You'll think about it?"

I was trying not to beg, but it was all over my voice. Seth just nodded.

"Okay," I said. "Well, I'll leave you to it."

I stood up and headed for the steps.

"Tar?" he said. "Happy Valentine's Day."

I was near tears as I hurried back over to Gaston Street, so I wasn't in the mood for Evelyn, but she was suddenly there as if she'd been lurking in the bushes. I stopped at the corner and faced her.

She was in the usual hipster slash hippie habit, but rather than steeped in her just-as-usual ennui, she seemed genuinely tired. There was something else going on there, too, but I couldn't get it to come into focus. It was enough to make me push my impatience aside.

"What's up, Evvy?" I said.

"I just wanted to say good-bye."

My chin dropped. "You're leaving? Like, leaving Savannah?"

"I never loved it the way you do," she said. "I'm going to Oregon."

"Whoa."

"I've saved up enough money, and I want to get as far away from them as possible." A trace of the caustic Evelyn crept in, but there was still that something else in those olive eyes.

"I want to see something different, do something different." She looked just past me, as if she didn't want to say the next thing to my face. "Mostly I just want to get away from the hate. The more I'm around Seth the more I hate him, and now I'm starting to hate myself because I don't know why."

"I think I do," I said.

She darted her gaze back to me.

I put my hands on her shoulders and felt the vulnerable bones. "Go to Seth and ask him what happened that you saw when you were tiny."

She pulled away from me, gaze darkening.

"I know you think Seth didn't protect you from seeing it, but he's not the one who didn't protect you. It was someone else. Tell him that. If you can get him to talk about it, I know it'll make a difference."

"How do you know this?"

"Through a lot of different things that have happened. But this is between you and Seth." I took a step toward her so we were close again. "No more secrets, Evvy. And no more shame."

She didn't say anything, but I saw what it was in her eyes that I had never seen there before.

It was the faint gleam of olive-green hope.

TWENTY-NINE

Friday, February twentieth, Wendy, Lexi, and I moved into our two-bedrooms-and-a-loft apartment on Drayton Street. Ms. Helen's Carl, a man of the dying breed, the Southern gentleman, found that perfect place for us, and Mama talked the landlord down on the rent and insisted he put in a new refrigerator and paint the bathroom.

"You can't live with that dark green, girls," she said. "You just can't."

We didn't argue with her. It was the exact shade of the haunted woods hallway in Lexi's old building.

So the apartment smelled of fresh color and new appliances when we—with the help of Kellen and some buddy of his who couldn't take his eyes off Lexi—carried in Lexi's futon couch and director chairs and Wendy's coffeepot and my geranium, as well as enough furniture from my parents' attic to fill the two bedrooms, the loft I was using as a bedroom, the dining area, the living room, and the patio in the back. The three small desks, one for each of our rooms, were a gift from Mama and Daddy.

"It's a housewarming present," Daddy said to Wendy when she started to get her hackles up. "So get over it."

Each one of the six days Wendy and Lexi had stayed at the house on Gaston Street, Daddy had breakfast with them while I went to church. Of course he renewed his love for Lexi. As for Wendy, he sized her up in about fifteen minutes and was treating her like a feisty daughter in a half hour. He even told her she had a good head for business. I informed her later that was like being given the Pulitzer Prize.

And speaking of housewarming gifts, the Watch could not *stop* buying us towels, sheets, bedspreads. We called a limit to it after Ms. Helen showed up with full sets of dishes, flatware, and pots and pans she was supposedly going to get rid of anyway. The two things I didn't let anyone give us were a teakettle and a jar full of wooden spoons. I was finally going to get to use them.

With five women besides the three of us in there hanging curtains and unpacking mugs and stuffing the linen closet with enough towels for us to open a small hotel, the basics were done by six. Especially with GrandMary as the organizer.

She surprised me by showing up Thursday, the day before the move, looking somewhat worn from the radiation, but showing no other signs that she had just had a bout with cancer.

She did feel brittle to me when I hugged her and held on, but there was nothing fragile about her spirit. She sat me down in the sunroom that day—I didn't know where she dismissed Mama to—and served the tea from the same china set we'd used that Sunday morning in her bedroom upstairs. She looked into me with her clear eyes.

"I'm not going to ask you how you are," she said, "because it's obvious you're almost happy. Am I right about that?"

"I'm getting there," I said. "This feels like the next right thing to do—moving in with my friends, working, hopefully starting school. It's not what I thought was going to happen, but I think it's good."

"Well," GrandMary said. She poured herself a second cup, thin, blue-threaded hands aristocratic as they moved. "There's having a plan, and there's just dreaming. I'm seeing a plan here."

"As far ahead as I can see, yes."

GrandMary's face looked . . . how else to describe it . . . pleased.

"I like the way you're talking, baby girl. This is new, this one-step-at-a-time vocabulary."

"I did what you told me to," I said, although until that moment I hadn't quite put it together.

"And what was that?"

"I found someone to talk to, someone outside the family. Actually, four somebodies."

"They've obviously guided you well."

"They have." I set my cup and saucer on the table. "Do you want me to tell you what it was that split Seth and me up?"

"I know enough. There is talking things out so you can see what you know, and then there's rehashing until you can make nothing of it at all. You seem thoroughly talked out."

"How do you do that?" I said.

GrandMary blinked. "How do I do what?"

"See everything exactly the way it is and put it so it's just so clear."

"Do I?" She folded her hands under her chin. "Well, if I do, it's all God. All of it. I pray and I stay close and I guess it just comes to me." She smiled, almost to herself. "Sometimes it comes out of my mouth before I know I've thought it, and that's when I know it's God."

Oh.

Oh. My.

If my grandmother noticed that I was having an epiphany, she didn't say.

"I suppose under the circumstances you aren't attending the Reverend Paul's church right now."

"No," I said.

"Are you worshiping anywhere? I don't mean to sound like the Sunday school monitor, but I think it's important if you want to hear God."

"I've been going to St. John's."

Her eyebrows lifted.

"It's liturgical," I said. "But . . . it's like things got so dark I couldn't even pray, and having the prayers already written . . . that kept me going. And the sacredness of it, when it seemed like nothing was sacred anymore. And the communion, which . . . I don't know, I just couldn't seem to get enough of hearing and tasting Jesus."

"You don't have to sell it to me," GrandMary said. "I can see it means a great deal to you."

"And then there's this wonderful priest," I said. But I stopped there. I didn't want to try to put Ned into words. I knew, in that moment, that relationship was sacred too.

So GrandMary was there Friday when the apartment was put together except for Lexi's art and the other touches we wanted to put on it ourselves.

"This makes me want to get a couple of girlfriends to move in with me," Gray said. She looked around the room at us in our various states of moving day exhaustion. "But anybody I'd want to share a place with is right here."

"I'm just so happy for you girls," Ms. Helen said. "But, now, do you have enough food? That pantry doesn't look very full to me."

I loved that woman. I loved them all. I loved Betsy, who was still fussing with the curtains, and Mama, who had wiped the counters to within an inch of their Corian lives. Wendy with her bristly way and Lexi with her sweet one. And GrandMary who oversaw it all like the matriarch she was.

"I feel so rich right now," I told Wendy and Lexi when the women had finally left—probably to continue the party at the Piebald, from what I could gather.

"Now that's bizarre," Wendy said. "You just moved out of a

five-bedroom house into a thousand-square-foot apartment and *now* you feel rich."

"Yeah," I said. "I do."

"I'm too tired to feel anything," Lexi said. "I think I'll sleep right here on this couch tonight. I can't move."

"Not me," Wendy said. "I can't wait to sleep in my own room." She crossed her arms to their opposite shoulders, in as much of a hug as Wendy was going to give herself. "It's the first one I've ever had to myself."

Lexi lifted her head. "Your whole life?"

"My whole life. Good night, roomies."

Lexi's breathing became sleep-deep even before Wendy's door closed. I could go anywhere I wanted in *our* home and start to get to know it. Except that my phone rang.

It was Seth.

His first words when I answered were: "Is this a bad time?" His voice was thin. Not frightened or panicked. Just worn down.

"No," I said. "Are you okay?"

"Tar . . . I want to take you up on your offer. Will you help me?"

"Yes," I said. "Oh my gosh, Seth, I'm so glad."

"Can you help me right now?"

"Okay. Do you want to meet somewhere?"

"Can I pick you up? There's somewhere I need to go, and I need you to go with me."

"Okay," I said again. "But, Seth, where?"

"To Jesup," he said.

⁓⁓⁓

We didn't call Fritzie to tell her we were coming. We had no idea if she would even be home, but on the way down I-95, with Savannah slipping away behind us, we decided if she wasn't we would hang out on her doorstep until she showed up.

"The key's under the mat," I said. "We could just go in."

I felt more than saw Seth flinch.

"Or not," I said. "Have you thought through what you want to say to her?"

"Some of it. Mostly the legal issues."

"What legal issues?"

In the fleeting light of a convenience store sign I did see Seth almost dimple. "I finally found a way to get Mom off my back."

"You told her about Fritzie?"

"I guess a mean part of me wanted her to feel guilty about leaving us with her so much. But mostly I needed to know if I had a case."

"As in, a court case."

"Yeah. The statute of limitations has run out for me."

I grunted.

"What?" he said.

"Too bad there isn't a statute of limitations on pain."

He swallowed. It looked like it was hard to do. "But she's still working as a nanny, right?"

My mouth went dry as I nodded. "Why didn't I think about that?"

"I didn't either before—and this is weird . . ."

"What is?"

"Evelyn came to me and pretty much held me hostage until I told her everything. She said she saw . . . something. She told me she was terrified of . . . I can't even say her name anymore."

I felt Seth's face pinch in the darkness.

"I get that," I said.

"And since I didn't protect her the way Kellen always did you, she hated me."

I swiveled under the seat belt to face him. "You're not the reason she's so wrecked, Seth. You know that, right?"

"Yeah, I do. But that's why I have to try to stop this from going on. Before any more kids get messed up the way we did."

"What does Randi say about the legalities?"

"She's working on it." Seth did dimple this time. "She thinks if we can get the cooperation of more recent families we can nail this woman."

"Is that a direct quote?"

"Oh yeah."

The dimple disappeared and an anxious silence seemed to grip him again.

"That's not the part you're worried about," I said. "In facing Fritzie, I mean."

"No. It isn't." His fingers jittered on the wheel. "I probably should have figured out how to actually confront her. I guess I'm hoping it'll just come out."

"Huh."

"What?"

"I used to do that."

"Do what?"

"Make up possible scripts in my head for how a conversation was going to go." I tried on a laugh that didn't quite fit. "That probably came from watching so many movies . . . wanting to *make* movies."

Seth took his eyes off the road just long enough to glance at me, and then his profile returned, sharp and handsome as ever against the darkness.

"You wanted to make movies?" he said. "I never knew that."

That struck me like a chord I didn't really want to hear. There was a lot we never knew about each other. But I couldn't say that to him now, not with his hands gripping the steering wheel so tight his knuckles looked blue in the lights from the dash.

"Anyway," I said, "I just realized, I don't make up scripts in my head anymore."

"Why not?"

"Because. They never quite turn out the way I write them."

"Yeah," Seth said in an almost-whisper, "I bet they don't."

I rested my head back and closed my eyes and wondered how long it would be before everything stopped stirring up guilt in him like silt from the bottom of a pond.

Suddenly something occurred to me. I blurted it out before I could second-guess it.

"Have you prayed about this?"

The surprise that jumped to his face sent a pang through me.

"So you knew I wasn't the praying wife you pretended you were getting," I said. "I've learned since this all went down. I know it means everything."

"I was going to teach you," Seth said. "How twisted is that?"

We didn't say anything else until we got to Jesup.

Every light in Fritzie's bungalow was on when we pulled up to the curb across the street. It hadn't occurred to me that she might have company.

"If she's got people there, all bets are off," Seth said.

"Understood," I said.

We sat there for a minute, watching the house. No figures passed the windows. And come to think of it, no cars were parked on the street or in the driveway except Fritzie's rusting once-blue Nissan.

"I feel like we're on a stakeout," Seth said.

"I don't think there's anybody else there. I could go check it out and if she's alone I could signal you—"

"No. Let's just go." I watched his Adam's apple bob in his throat. Above his beard, his skin was porridge-colored. "I'm serious, Tar, if you leave me for a second I'm not sure I can do this."

369

"You could," I said. "This just makes it easier. You ready?"

"No."

Once more I turned sideways in the seat to face him. "If you're not, you shouldn't, Seth. You know Fritzie. She rolls right over people and you don't need that right now. So if you don't feel like you can stand up to her, we can do this another time."

"I thought I could, but Tar, there's so much . . . much stuff in this. She didn't just molest me, she humiliated me in ways you don't even want to know."

"That's it right there."

He looked at me miserably.

"I've been where you are," I said. "The one who's been hurt. The one who didn't do anything to deserve the horror that's become your life. *You* are the victim this time. *You* don't have anything to be afraid of because *you* haven't done anything wrong."

He was shrinking again. I wanted to grab him and hold on before he disappeared altogether.

"Look at me, Seth."

He didn't. I took his chin and turned his face toward me.

"I know what this feels like and the only way out of it is to do the next true thing. And this is it. I'm going to be there to protect you because nobody else ever did. Okay?"

He tried to pull away but I held on.

"Okay?"

"Okay," he said. "Okay."

─◦◦◦─

To say that Fritzie was surprised to see us at her door would be more than an understatement. It would be a flat-out lie. Her eyes shifted from one of us to the other, and her mouth fell open, quadrupling her already doubling chins. And that was all before she got it together enough to say to me, "Tell me you aren't getting back together with him."

"We need to talk to you," Seth said.

Fritzie recovered the bravado she always relied on. "Tara I have time for. You, not so much."

"Both of us," I said. "You need to hear this."

Seth glanced at me, and I didn't blame him for the questions in his eyes. But her standing there, already trying to villainize him . . . I knew exactly what my lines were going to be in this scene.

But first Seth needed to say his.

"So can we talk or not?" he said.

"Fine," she said. "But you're not coming in my house."

She grabbed a shawl that looked as if it should be used to scrub a floor and came out from behind the screen door. She passed between us and parked herself on the top step so that we had to practically climb over her to get to a place where we could face her. I sat on the bottom step. Seth stood with one foot on the second one.

"So," Fritzie said, "talk. No, wait."

She looked at Seth for the first time, with eyes so self-righteous I wanted to pluck them out. Or at the very least, chop down her family tree.

"I do have a few things to say to you."

She went into a tirade about the sins of pornography, punctuated with proclamations of her own disgust. This was exactly what I didn't want her to do to Seth, and I tried to stop her twice, but both times he shook his head at me. *Come on*, I wanted to cry to him. *You know all this. You don't deserve to hear it from her.*

And then she said the one thing I realized he'd been waiting for, the opening he needed.

"I practically raised you, Seth Grissom," she said. "And I can't believe you turned out this way."

"You can't?" His voice teetered toward its upper range but it was somehow still strong. "Why can't you believe it? You're the one who twisted me into the monster I am when I'm in front of that screen."

"*Excuse* me?" Fritzie's torso rose in indignation, but I could already see the oncoming panic in her eyes. "*I* twisted you?"

"When I was only ten years old. And it went on for two *years*. Two of the worst years of my life." Seth leaned over his thigh. His hands were talking with him, slicing the air. "You didn't raise me. You molested me. And now I'm paying the price."

"You're blaming *me* for what you are? I touched you before you even hit puberty and it's *my* fault you lost everything?"

"Hey, Seth," I said. "That sounds like an admission of guilt, doesn't it?"

"Sure does. But I don't care if she admits it or not, I know. I made my own choices after that and I take responsibility for them." He squinted at Fritzie. "But you? You're just sick."

Perfect segue, Seth. That was my cue to take my turn.

"While we're on the topic of responsibility," I said. "What you did to Seth was a crime. You're a sex offender."

The panic was full-blown all over Fritzie's face, but she still laughed as she shook her head, vehemently, about six times.

"You can't take me to court for this. There's a statute of limitations—"

"You're still working as a nanny, right?"

Seth sent me a thank-you with his eyes. His energy was spent for the moment.

"You've been doing that for, what?" I went on. "Eighteen more years since you left us. Is that about right?"

"Give it up, Tara," Fritzie said. She stood up, flapping her arms as if she were trying to take flight. "I haven't touched a kid since this one."

The lie was so obvious I almost screamed, but I kept my cool. For Seth.

"I hope not," I said. "But still, it seems like your current employer should know about your history. Don't you think, Seth?"

He had pulled himself out of his sag and his eyes were steely. "No question. And all the other families she's worked for. In case any of their kids are starting to act like—what did she call me? Monsters?" His voice was calm now, and it bit. He was, after all, Randi Grissom's son.

"Randi's already on it," I said.

"No," Fritzie said. "No Randi."

Neither of us said anything. We just watched her grope for the upper hand again.

"No, you know what?" she said, voice shrill. "Sic Randi on me. She'll never make this stick. Do you know how hard it is to convict somebody as a pedophile?"

"That's the word I was looking for," I said. And then all sarcasm, all of my own bravado fell away, and I looked Fritzie hard in the face, true me to whoever she was. "You have to take responsibility for your part in this. Just like the rest of us have."

She flattened her eyes at me, but her body shook. "What does that even mean?"

"It means you quit the nannying job you have right now," Seth said.

"The Mary Poppins gig," I put in.

"Then you get out of the business for good. And you apologize to every family whose kids you ever touched."

Go, Seth. I folded my arms and watched.

"That way the DA might go easier on you after I expose you and the families you've turned inside out decide to press charges. Either you tell them or I will." Seth leaned in. "But they *will* know."

Fritzie attempted a laugh that fell so hard I thought I heard it crack on the concrete. Still, the outright fear sharpened every part of her to a point. I knew the feeling. Only . . . this woman I'd loved and trusted and told my secrets to . . . she deserved it. Because she showed no remorse.

"What are you going to do, Seth?" she said. "Hire a private investigator to follow me around and make sure I do it?"

Seth's eyebrows came completely together. "Have you *met* my mother? And we're putting a time limit on it. You have one week."

"Don't do that, man," she said. "Don't even try it."

"Or . . . ?" Seth said.

Fritzie didn't answer. She struggled to get her cumbersome self off the step and turned with a frenzy of shawl and hair and terror and opened and slammed doors until she was inside her house. I heard the unmistakable sound of pottery hitting a wall.

I jerked my head toward the car. "Let's get out of here before she takes aim at us," I said.

⁓↺↻⁓

We were quiet half the way back to Savannah. As our mossy, shaded city drew nearer, the muscles in Seth's face softened and his death grip on the wheel loosened.

"How you doin'?" I said.

"Better than I thought I would."

"You were awesome."

"She really is sick, isn't she?"

"Beyond."

"I am too."

"It's a different kind of sick," I said.

"How?"

"You know you're sick and you're getting help. You don't want to live the way you were living anymore. That's right, isn't it?"

"Right" he said. His voice was thready.

We were entering the city limits and the live oaks seemed to be holding their arms out to us. I sighed at them.

"What?" he said.

"This is a healing place, y'know? We both got hurt here, but it's also the place to get better. Don't you think?"

Just when I thought he had used up all his words for the night—and I wouldn't have blamed him—he said, "I'm getting help."

"Good."

"I'm still working the Denver program. I'll go back in a couple of weeks for a check-in. And I found a guy here to talk to."

"A counselor?"

"No. He's a priest, actually, and, I guess I can tell you this . . . he's been through this stuff too. So it's not just 'pray and God will make you better.' If that were the case I would've recovered a long time ago. It's 'God's with you, but you have to do the work too. You have to find out what's true and be true *to* it.'"

"He sounds like the perfect guy, then." I turned my face to the side window so he wouldn't see the smile I had to smile.

Seth pulled up to the curb in front of the apartment. My new home. Not Gaston Street. Not the dream of Jones Street, but here. Everything had changed, and I had a moment of longing for what wasn't anymore and what could have been. But it passed into something I knew for the first time.

"What are you going to do now?" I said. "Besides work on recovery."

"I got a job at a bank in Brunswick. It's a little bit of a commute, but I couldn't get anything here. I'm persona non grata right now."

"That'll fade," I said.

"I hope. I'm moving into an apartment next week."

"In Brunswick?"

"No. Here in town. I want to be near Ne—the priest—and my parents. I think I can help them get what happened with Evelyn. I need to be in Savannah."

"And I want you to be. I meant what I said. If you want my help, I'm here. Especially when all this legal stuff starts happening."

"I do want your help. But we have to give that time." Seth looked at me and then turned his face away. "It's still hard for me to be with you and not think about what we could've had."

"Then maybe this will help," I said. It was a night for perfect segues. "There's this one last thing I want to tell you."

"I don't know if I can take it."

"No, this is totally about me." I picked the words with the tips of my fingers. "I know now that I wasn't ready for marriage. I was ready to *get* married. Nobody's wedding was ever better planned. But I wouldn't have been a good wife to you. I had no idea who I was. I did what I was supposed to do but not what my soul wanted to do." His eyes looked hurt but I shook my head. "I didn't think I was supposed to marry you. I wanted to with what I thought I knew about life. What I'm trying to say is, it isn't just because you're healing from an addiction that I won't marry you. It's because *I'm* healing."

"From me? From what I did to you?"

"From a whole life of not realizing I even had a self. I guess you could say I'm in recovery too."

Seth was quiet then, and I let him be.

"Do you think it was God?" he said finally.

"Do I think what was God?"

"That you walked in on me that night?"

"I don't know. Why would you think that?"

"Because that moment saved both our lives, Tar."

"Maybe so," I said.

The silence fell again. It was soft this time.

"I should go in," I said. "When you're ready?"

"I'll call you," he said. "When I'm ready."

I got out of the car and watched him drive off, a little too fast for a wet Savannah street, but I got that. He would probably go cry, and I got that too.

But as I went up the brick walkway to our haint-blue front door, I didn't feel like crying. That scene with Fritzie, that really was the last layer, the last thing to be opened and debrided and left to heal. The last thing to let go of.

I put my hand on the doorknob and pressed my forehead to the door.

And now it was time for the first things.

ACKNOWLEDGMENTS

We've been told by those we trust that some people actually do read the "who helped" section, and we hope you're among them. This book in particular could not have been written without some serious help from some generous people.

Special thanks from Rebecca to:

Amanda Bostic and the team at Thomas Nelson. Thank you for believing in the message of this book and in Nancy and me!

David Smallbone, **Jonas Applegate**, and **Amanda Jilek** at Smallbone Management, for your support of *One Last Thing* and also *Sarah's Choice* and *The Merciful Scar*! Dad, thanks for seeing this project before it was. You are a true visionary.

Andrea Heineke, for believing in me and for being such an incredible friend. So grateful for you!

Nancy . . . thank you for being a precious, kind, and incredibly talented partner! You are a joy, and I'm honored to call you friend and sister.

My husband, **Cubbie**, for your unconditional love for me, for being my best friend for life and also the most amazing husband and father! I praise God for the answer to prayer that you are!

My daughter, **Gemma**. You are a daily inspiration, little girl! Your smiles, laughter, and snuggles delight your mama's heart to no end! You are our treasure!

And to **Jesus**, our reason for writing and the inspiration behind the words. How we love You! May this book do Your work and fulfill Your purpose.

Special thanks from Nancy to:

The Reverend Craig O'Brien, St. John's Church, Savannah, Georgia. He *isn't* Ned Kregg, but he definitely inspired the character with his gentle interest and quiet twinkle.

Toby Aldrich, docent of the Flannery O'Connor Childhood Home, who gave me my first overview of Savannah.

Jennifer M. Silva, author of *Coming Up Short: Working-Class Adulthood In an Age of Uncertainty* (Oxford University Press, 2013), who helped me understand Wendy's world.

Michael John Cusick, author of *Surfing for God: Discovering the Divine Desire Beneath Sexual Struggle* (Thomas Nelson, 2012), and **Fred and Brenda Stoeker with Mike Yorkey**, authors of *Every Heart Restored: A Wife's Guide to Healing in the Wake of a Husband's Sexual Sin* (WaterBrook Press, 2010), whose works were invaluable in providing me with insights on why men seek pornography.

Julianne Cusick, **Shannon Ethridge**, and **Fred Stoeker**, who all gave up precious time to talk with me and answer questions about Tara and Seth and their tragedy.

Dr. Dale McElhinney, who walked me through all the hard scenes, just as he has so many, many times in my writing journey.

John Painter, N.P., who shared the necessary knowledge to take Seth's attempted suicide beyond what I might have seen on *House*.

The lovely people of Savannah, Georgia, who opened their doors and arms to me as they shared their beautiful city.

Our editors, **Amanda Bostic, Jamie Chavez**, and **Jodi Hughes**, without whom we'd pretty much look lame.

Our agents, **Andrea Heineke**, the late **Lee Hough**, and **Joel Kneedler**, who made the acquisition and the continuing of all three of our books not only possible but satisfying.

And the **members of The Café Nudge blog**, who gave their honest opinions as the very New Women we write for. You can join us at www.tweenyouandme.typepad.com/the_nudge.

REFLECTION QUESTIONS AND RESOURCES FOR *ONE LAST THING*

Although we want girls and women who have experience with loved ones addicted to pornography to find hope in Tara's story, we don't think you have to have been there personally to relate to her and find a door to healing for whatever it is you are dealing with—and everybody is dealing with something, right, especially when it comes to relationships and discovering who you are. As you consider our reflection questions, just apply them to your own situation and see what happens. We've got your back in prayer.

Blessings,

Rebecca and Nancy

Questions to ponder:

1. Just to get you focused on you, what part of Tara's story did you relate to the most? What made you go, "Oh, I hear *that*!"

She is certainly wealthier than most of us, but hopefully there were things in her life that resonated with you.

2. Right now are you living for dreams? Dreams that you haven't questioned or really looked at all the way through, the way Tara dreamed only of her wedding and not the marriage itself?

3. Seth wasn't the only dream Tara "got wrong" as she puts it. Her vision of becoming a film director got lost. Have any of your visions for your life been put aside or thwarted by someone else (even someone well-meaning, like Tara's dad)?

4. Tara's "Bridesmaids" were her friends from high school and they seemed to stay together more out of tradition than real connection. Take a look at the people you currently hang out with. Are they guys and girls who see and accept the real you? Have similar values? Are there any you don't fully appreciate, as with Tara and Lexy? Do you leave yourself open to unexpected friendships, like Tara and Wendy?

5. Tara's "Watch of Women" came together organically, a God-thing to be sure. Do you have mentors? Women older than you who have some life on them and serve as allies? If not, what relationship could you cultivate? How is this different from friendships with your peers?

6. Tara turns away from the church she grew up in and finds spiritual direction in Ned Kregg. Do you think she was right to do that? Is there anything about your current church situation (or lack of one!) that isn't serving your needs right now? Are you open to looking at other Christian resources, even if their practices aren't familiar to you?

7. Savannah is almost another character in the story because it figures so strongly not only into Tara's past but her healing. Do you have such a place? It doesn't have to be your entire town or even your own neighborhood. It might be a certain section

of town where you like to go for coffee and take your journal with you—your own Piebald. We all need a Third Place—not our home and not our workplace. What's yours?

8. Do you think Tara makes the right decision about Seth? Is there a relationship you need to look at in much the same way she did hers? Do you have her courage, her allies, her spiritual direction?

9. Our resources for this book have told us that even in a Christian college it's hard to find a guy who doesn't at least look at porn. It's out there in a pervasive way. Have you taken anything away from *One Last Thing* that may be helpful to you in dealing with this issue if/when it comes up for you or a friend?

10. Finally, the question we always ask: Picture a free, secure, whole life for yourself, the kind God intends for each of us. Write it down, maybe in a journal. Now consider: What keeps you from living in that place?

Resources for those who face pornography issues in a relationship or want to help someone who does. These are all from a Christian perspective:

- *Every Heart Restored* by Fred and Brenda Stoeker with Mike Yorkey (WaterBrook Press, 2010)
- Restoring the Soul program and website http://restoringthesoul .com
- *Somebody's Daughter,* a documentary film available on DVD through www.visionvideo.com
- *Surfing for God* by Michael John Cusick (Thomas Nelson, 2012)
- YouTube video with Michael John Cusick https://www.youtube .com/watch?v=CkJuvDArya0

The Merciful Scar

REBECCA ST. JAMES AND NANCY RUE

Part ONE

He . . . went a day's journey into the wilderness, and came and sat down under a solitary broom tree. He asked that he might die.

1 KINGS 19:4 (NRSV)

Chapter ONE

It was the only real fight Wes and I had ever had. Actually it was the only fight I'd ever had with anyone. That's probably why I wasn't very good at it.

Now *discussions* . . . We'd had those, and that's how it started out that night. Another conversation about Wes moving in with me.

I should have known that was where we were headed when he tugged at the back of my shirt and pulled me against his lean self and said, "You know what I love about your couch?"

"That you never have to get off of it from the minute you walk in the door?" I said.

He let his blue eyes droop at the corners until they teased at his cheekbones. That was Wes pretending to be hurt. "Are you saying I'm a couch potato?"

"I'm saying I wait on you like you're the couch prince." I leaned forward and picked up the all-but-licked-clean plate from my IKEA coffee table. "More quesadillas, your highness?"

Wes scooped me into him, plate and all. "It wouldn't be that way if I wasn't a guest, Kirsty."

Yeah, there it was. Again.

"First of all," I said, "you know I hate it when you call me that. It makes me feel like I'm on a Jenny Craig commercial."

"Huh?"

"Kirstie Alley. She was their poster girl before Valerie Bertinelli—"

"You're getting off topic."

"What topic?"

Wes scooted himself sideways so he could face me without letting go. He knew as well as I did that I was about to wriggle away and go do . . . something. Anything to not have this discussion for the ninety-sixth time.

"Come on, babe. You know what I'm talking about. It doesn't make any sense for me to get an apartment for the summer when you've got room here."

"I have one bedroom." Which, may I just add, was incredibly difficult to say with his long-fingered hands holding my face and his nose headed for mine for that irresistible pre-kiss thing he did. "And I need my other room for my studio—"

"I know."

"And you also know where I am on this."

"I do. You've been there for three years, six months, two weeks, four days, and . . ." He glanced at his watch. "Twenty-seven minutes."

He let his lips bounce off my nose and onto my mouth but I talked right through the kiss.

"It's going to be another however long," I said, "so get over it."

This was the part where he was supposed to say, *You're killin' me, Kirsten. Killin' me.* And then I would let him kiss me one time and then I'd get up and make another batch of quesadillas. That was how this déjà vu conversation was supposed to go.

But Wes stiffened all six foot two of himself and took me by both shoulders and set me away from him like he was stacking a folding chair. I watched him step over the coffee table and shove his hands into the pockets of his cargo shorts and pace to the back window where he stopped, rod-necked and tight-lipped, his blondness standing stiff on his head. It wasn't a pose I'd ever seen him take. That's when my skin started to burn.

"What does 'however long' mean, Kirsten?" he said.

Until we're married. That was the answer, stuck in my throat where it had been for three years, six months, two weeks, four days, and twenty-seven minutes. I just closed my eyes and crossed my arms so I could rub both shoulders. The burning kept on.

Wes faced me now, muscles working in his square jaw. "Do you know how hard it is to love you and not be able to . . . love you?"

I attempted a wry look. "Uh, yeah, I do."

"Then what the—" He crossed to the coffee table and sat on it. "Look, I think I've been way more patient than any other guy would be."

"Good thing I don't want any other guy," I said.

"Stop it, okay? Just stop it."

"Stop wh—"

"The cute remarks and the little dance you always do. I want to talk about this. Now."

I pressed myself into the couch. "We've talked about it a thousand times, Wes. We've worn it out."

"So you just want to keep on dating forever?"

I swallowed, hard. "Way back when we first started dating, we both agreed that neither one of us wanted to have sex outside of marriage."

Wes let his mouth soften and took both my hands. "How old were we then, babe? Eighteen? Nineteen? I think we were pretty naïve."

We'd never gotten this far into the discussion. If we had, I might have come up with a retort to get us out of it. Something along the lines of *No, naïve is when you think you can lose ten pounds before Christmas.* But here we were, and my determination that I wasn't going to be the first one to say it seethed under my skin.

"I thought we were being true to the faith that, if you'll recall, *you* introduced me to," I said.

"I'm not buying it," Wes said. "We haven't been to Faith House since you started grad school. What's that, nine months? When was the last time we went to church, either one of us?"

"That doesn't mean I don't still believe—"

"Nuh-uh." Wes let go of my hands and waved his palm like he was erasing my words. "That's not what this is about. You want me to marry you, don't you?"

My throat closed in on itself. At least once a day during those three years and twenty-seven minutes, or whatever it was, I had imagined Wes broaching the subject of marriage. The images went from Wes on one knee amid glimmering candlelight to a proposal tucked into a Big Mac. But none of them had included an accusation in those blue eyes or all my anxiety mobilizing under my flesh.

"That's it, isn't it?" he said. "Why didn't you just come out and say it?"

"Because I wanted you to say it first!"

The words sliced their way out of me before I could stop them, and they seemed to want to keep on slicing all on their own.

"I don't want us to be like everybody else—just having sex and living together and then someday deciding we might as well get married. Look at Caleb and Tess. They're like a pair of reclining chairs. I'm not doing that, Wes. I'm not."

He was staring at me as if I was a stranger suddenly intruding on the conversation that had long since stopped *being* a conversation.

"Y'know," he said, "I've been practically begging you for, like, forever to open up with me and tell me what's on your mind."

"I wanted it to be on yours." My words had lost their edge. Others spun in my head. *Clever, Kirsten, very clever. You picked a fine time to, I don't know,* grow a backbone.

Wes sagged onto the couch beside me. "Look, babe, I'm not in a good place for this. I didn't graduate—I have to make up the class this summer—I don't know what I'm gonna do after that."

"I know all that—"

"But you—you're set. You always are. That's why you're my rock. I just need you to be here for me just a little while longer. Can you do that?"

What does that even mean? I wanted to scream. But I'd done all the slicing I could do for one night. It was more slicing than I'd done my whole life. At least, that kind.

"Okay, look, I'm gonna go," Wes said.

"Now?"

Nice touch. Pathetic is always good.

"Now." Wes gave me half of his usual who-loves-ya-baby smile. "Before I get you drunk and take advantage of you."

My reply was automatic. "Like either one of *those* things is gonna happen."

Again, that was his cue to say, *You're killin' me, babe.* But what he said was, "Yeah." Just yeah.

He pulled me up from the couch and walked ahead of me to the door. Hand on the knob, he turned only slightly toward me. "A bunch of people from my class are hiking the M tomorrow."

I groaned silently. Hiking the M was a Montana State graduation tradition that entailed making one's way up a steep trail and a long ridgeline in the brutal Montana sun to get to a huge M made from white rocks, and then partying and turning around and coming back in the now even more brutal Montana sun to party some more. I'd skipped that when I graduated the year before; I would actually rather poke a fork in my eye than have that kind of fun. Since Wes had missed graduating by one class, he hadn't gotten to have that kind of fun either.

"I'm sorry," I said.

"No, they want me to go with. What's three credits? To them I'm there. I just didn't have to sit through a bunch of speeches in a bathrobe with a board on my head."

"I don't even know what to do with that," I said. "So what time?"

"We're leaving Caleb and Tess's at seven." Wes lifted a sandy eyebrow. "If I can get them out of their reclining chairs."

Ouch. Bet that gotcha right in the heart.

"You want me to pack a picnic?" I said.

Wes's gaze shifted away, and he ran a hand over his flattened blond spikes.

"Or we can grab something at the store in the morning," I said.

"Here's the deal . . . I think I just need to go single. Most of these people I'll never see again, which is weirder for me because I'm staying here. I don't know, it's just a thing."

Right in the heart fell far short. I was stung to the bone. I didn't want to go. I just wanted him to want me to go.

Beyond pathetic. We've moved into pitiful. I mean, way in.

"Okay, so . . . okay," I said.

"I knew you'd get it." Wes kissed my neck. "You always do."

The Nudnik voice didn't wait until Wes was out the door before she started in. I always thought of it as the Nudnik, which was what my kindergarten teacher used to call us kids when we pestered her to the brink. *Nicely done,* the Nudnik said now. *Ya made everything all right when it clearly isn't. Another layer of unadulterated bad stuff, right under your skin.*

Forget it. I'm not doing it. I haven't done it for—I don't know—a long time.

Not since Valentine's Day when yet again our sweet Wesley didn't come through with a ring. Or was it Easter? Yeah, you did it on Easter. But then, who's keeping track?

You are! I wanted to say out loud. But I always stopped short of audibly answering the Nudnik. If I did that, I really would have to admit I was crazy.

But she was right. I'd been holding back for six weeks, since the beginning of April. I promised myself that was the last time because I was so sure Wes would propose when he graduated. And then he didn't. He'd spent last Saturday hiding out here playing Scrabble with me instead of walking with his class to receive his diploma. It wasn't a good time for a proposal. Clearly there never was a good time.

The story continues in *The Merciful Scar* by
Rebecca St. James and Nancy Rue

ABOUT THE AUTHORS

Author photo by Allister Ann

Rebecca St. James is both a Grammy and multiple Dove Award recipient as well as a bestselling author whose books include *Wait for Me* and *What Is He Thinking??* Her leading role in the pro-life film *Sarah's Choice* won critical acclaim. A passionate spokesperson for Compassion International, Rebecca has provided sponsorship to more than 30,000 children through her worldwide concerts.

Author photo by Hatcher and Fell Photography

Nancy Rue is the bestselling author of more than 100 books for teens, tweens, and adults, two of which have won Christy Awards. Nancy is also a popular speaker and radio guest due to her expertise in tween and teen issues. She and her husband, Jim, have raised one daughter of their own and now share their Tennessee lake home with two yellow labs.